"I'm a kilt convert! After plunging into the rowdy world of *Some Like It Kilted*, I would follow Allie Mackay's hot Scot anywhere!"
—*New York Times* bestselling author
Vicki Lewis Thompson

**Praise for the Novels
of Allie Mackay**

Tall, Dark, and Kilted

"An engaging urban romantic fantasy with a touch of a mystery and a terrific twist.... The story line is brisk and breezy from the moment the ghost and the American meet and never slows down. With a strong cast, paranormal and human, fans will enjoy Cilla's Scottish adventure in love."   —Genre Go Round Reviews

Highlander in Her Dreams

"Scottish charm, humor, and ... hot romance."
—Night Owl Romance

"Sexy ... imaginative ... a fascinating mix of exciting action and passionate romance."
—Romance Reader at Heart

"Cleverly plotted and well written ... a fun, sexy story."
—*Romantic Times*

"[A] pleasing blend of wit, passion, and the paranormal ... a steamy romance that packs emotional punch."
—Romance Reviews Today

"A fabulous mixture of magic and romance. Allie Mackay has penned an enchanting romance of lovers from different times.... A captivating paranormal romance and a wonderful addition to a book lover's library."   —Fresh Fiction

continued ...

Highlander in Her Bed

"[A] randy paranormal romance. . . . The premise is charming and innovative. . . . This novel definitely delivers a blast of Scottish steam."　　*—Publishers Weekly*

"A yummy paranormal romp."
　　　　—USA Today bestselling author Angela Knight

"A delightful paranormal romance. The writing is poetic, compelling, and fun, and the story features an imaginative premise, crisp dialogue, and sexy characters whose narrative voices are both believable and memorable. HOT."　　　　　　　　　　　　*—Romantic Times*

"A superb paranormal romance."
　　　　　　　　　　—Midwest Book Review

"A sexy, humor-filled romance with delightfully amusing characters. Artfully blending past and present, *Highlander in Her Bed* is an entertaining read. Well written. Readers will enjoy this one!"　　　　*—Fresh Fiction*

"Appealing and amusing. Sizzles with passion."
　　　　　　　　　　—Romance Reviews Today

"A whimsical read that will have you panting from start to finish! Mackay knows what a Scottish romance novel needs and socks it to you! Red-hot, sizzling chemistry ignites from the moment Sir Alex materializes in front of feisty Mara. . . . A sure-bet bestseller."
　　　　　　　　　　—A Romance Review

ALSO BY ALLIE MACKAY

Tall, Dark, and Kilted
Highlander in Her Dreams
Highlander in Her Bed

Some Like It Kilted

Allie Mackay

A SIGNET ECLIPSE BOOK

PB
Mac

SIGNET ECLIPSE
Published by New American Library, a division of
Penguin Group (USA) Inc., 375 Hudson Street,
New York, New York 10014, USA
Penguin Group (Canada), 90 Eglinton Avenue East, Suite 700, Toronto,
Ontario M4P 2Y3, Canada (a division of Pearson Penguin Canada Inc.)
Penguin Books Ltd., 80 Strand, London WC2R 0RL, England
Penguin Ireland, 25 St. Stephen's Green, Dublin 2,
Ireland (a division of Penguin Books Ltd.)
Penguin Group (Australia), 250 Camberwell Road, Camberwell, Victoria 3124,
Australia (a division of Pearson Australia Group Pty. Ltd.)
Penguin Books India Pvt. Ltd., 11 Community Centre, Panchsheel Park,
New Delhi - 110 017, India
Penguin Group (NZ), 67 Apollo Drive, Rosedale, North Shore 0632,
New Zealand (a division of Pearson New Zealand Ltd.)
Penguin Books (South Africa) (Pty.) Ltd., 24 Sturdee Avenue,
Rosebank, Johannesburg 2196, South Africa

Penguin Books Ltd., Registered Offices:
80 Strand, London WC2R 0RL, England

First published by Signet Eclipse, an imprint of New American Library,
a division of Penguin Group (USA) Inc.

First Printing, February 2010
10 9 8 7 6 5 4 3 2 1

In loving memory of Lisa Trumbauer.

Dear friend, best-ever travel companion, and talented author, she was taken from this world much too soon.

Lisa loved animals, lived for soft misty days, and saw such wonder in woodland walks and the drift of cloud shadows across Highland hills. She loved Scotland passionately and when I'm there, I see her everywhere. She was the most *just-like-me* person I've ever known. I'm so grateful for the years we had, the great times in Scotland, and the privilege of being her friend.

I wish I could tell her one more time how much I loved her.

ACKNOWLEDGMENTS

Scotland is always my greatest inspiration and I feel blessed to have a career that allows me to spend my workdays revisiting my favorite places there. Although I love all of Scotland, my own ancestral ties bind me most strongly to the Hebrides. For that reason, I really enjoyed bringing Bran of Barra's world to life.

The Hebrides are known as "the Isles on the Edge of the Sea," and there are more than five hundred of them stretched along Scotland's west coast. Wild, magnificent, and almost too beautiful to describe, they fire the imagination of the poetic, fill the dreams of Diaspora Scots, and steal the heart of anyone who ever visits them.

Bran's Barra has held a special place in my heart for years. Actually a grouping of twenty small-to-teeny islands in the remote Outer Hebrides, Barra truly is remarkable. The spark of Bran's tale came to me on my first visit to Barra's Kisimul Castle, ancient seat of the Barra MacNeils. This impressive isle-girded stronghold became Bran's beloved tower.

My affection for Barra includes the Barrachs themselves, especially the Barra MacNeils. When I originally needed a bold, larger-than-life Hebridean chieftain, I looked no further than the MacNeils. I hope Bran of Barra does them proud. I certainly tried to give him their fierce love of Barra, their bighearted spirit and openhanded generosity, and their hallmark joy in life.

A proud and noble race, they also had a rollicking sense of humor. It's true that, in days of yore, one of the more colorful MacNeil chiefs sent a trumpeter to the battlements each night to blast a fanfare, announcing that the great MacNeil of Barra had dined and now that he'd done so, the rest of the world was then free to begin their own evening meal.

It's also true that after Kisimul Castle fell to ruin, the eventual restoration was undertaken entirely by the men of Barra. Funds for the project poured in from MacNeils around the world, proving their devotion to the clan's ancestral home.

I believe I chose well in letting the Barra MacNeils be the clan who changed Mindy's mind about Scotland. I knew she'd fall in love with the Hebrides. But I wanted her hero to be a very special Hebridean man. One she couldn't possibly resist. Only Bran of Barra would do!

A thousand thank-yous to Roberta Brown, the best agent in the world. She's my closest friend, my trusted confidante, and so much more. I couldn't do this without her. Special thanks to my fantastic editor, Kerry Donovan. I so appreciate her support and enthusiasm. And I'm especially grateful for her suggestion to include something magical to bind Bran and Mindy. Her comment about *something magical* became Bran's sword, the Heartbreaker.

Much appreciation to my very handsome husband, Manfred. He proves every day that real-life heroes exist. As always, my sweet little Jack Russell, Em, my constant companion and greatest love. His cuddles and tail wags mean more to me than all the world's gold. I only wish all dogs were as cherished.

Special thanks to my readers—you're fantastic! For those wishing to visit Bran's Barra, there is air service. The flights are unique, landing on a beach, the Traigh Mhor. But I prefer the ferry. Either way, I promise you'll love Barra!

"While I'll no' argue that a man in a kilt is greater than any other, I'm here to tell you that a kilted Highlander is more. He is a god."

—Saor MacSwain, Highland ghost, master of carouse, and kilt-wearer extraordinaire

Prologue

The Long Gallery at MacNeil's Folly
New Hope, Pennsylvania
In a dimension not our own ...

"Since when do MacNeils make war on women?"

Roderick MacNeil, proud fifteenth-century chieftain of his clan, hooked his thumbs in his sword belt and glared round at the other ghosts crowding the narrow, dark-paneled room they'd called their own for longer than was tolerable.

He also took immense pleasure in how his deep voice echoed from the rafters.

Unfortunately, the stubborn looks on his fellow ghosts' faces indicated they weren't paying him any heed.

"I say you, I'll no' be a part of it." He lowered his brows and scowled until even the misty haze in the room shimmied and drew back from his wrath.

"And I say we have no choice!" Silvanus, likewise a fifteenth-century MacNeil, and Roderick's cousin, waved his arms until the billowing mist drifted back in Roderick's direction. "If we let the lass escape us, the saints only know how many more centuries we'll be doomed to wallow here."

"Bah!" Roderick whipped out his sword and used it to cut the swirling mist. "There has to be another way."

"Nae, there isn't." Geordie, of the same blood, albeit of the sixteenth century, lifted his own voice. He stepped forward, the blues and greens of his kilt aglow against the room's haze. "I'm with Silvanus. We must act now, even if the by-doing leaves a dirty taste in our mouths."

"Hear, hear!" another kinsman agreed from the far end of the long gallery. "'Tis this *folly* that makes my bile rise, no' the means we need to make things right."

Roderick jammed his sword back into its sheath, then swung away to stomp the length of the room. He took pains to ignore his kinsmen and even more care not to glower at the rows of empty portraits lining the long gallery's walls.

Huge, gilt-framed, and just recently vacated, the portraits, which had once been the pride of each respective MacNeil chieftain, now bore the shame of trapping them in a world they despised.

MacNeil's Folly should still be MacNeil's Tower.

Strong, safe, and intact.

Above all, in its original location on the Hebridean isle of Barra, not perched atop some fool hill in New Hope, Pennsylvania, carted there stone by stone by a lackwit descendant who chose not only to emigrate to America but to take the MacNeil ancestral seat along with him.

It was scandalous.

An abomination beyond bearing.

And—he had to admit—blowing steam out his ears and clenching his teeth so fiercely that his jaw ached wasn't going to solve a thing.

His cousins had the right of it.

Mindy Menlove was their only hope.

Wheeling about, Roderick saw at once that his kinsmen recognized his capitulation. Silvanus didn't bother to hide how his chest swelled with satisfaction, and Geordie, e'er a thorn in his side, thumped his walking stick hard on the floor. Others exchanged triumphant glances, while one or two shuffled their feet or fussed with their plaids, clearly not at ease in stirring his spleen.

Only one proved oblivious.

Not that it was likely Bran of Barra even knew of their quandary. If he did, chances were he'd be displeased. The unavoidable disruptions might annoy him. Unlike the rest of them, the fourteenth-century MacNeil of MacNeil didn't haunt his portrait. He chose to remain in his chiefly hall, celebrating nightly revels with other like-minded spectral friends who appreciated his skill at maintaining MacNeil's Tower as it was in his day.

Bran of Barra's ghostly conjured tower, that was.

The true tower was *here*, across the great wastes of the Atlantic. Exactly where it shouldn't be. And whether Roderick liked it or not, it was up to him and his kinsmen to see every last stone returned to Barra.

Curling his hand around his sword hilt, he scowled at Bran's portrait, the burly chieftain's grin and his air of joviality deeply offending him.

He looked as if he were about to throw back his head and laugh.

Roderick felt his own face turn purple with fury. "You, Silvanus!" He flashed a look at his cousin. "I'd hear what you said earlier. Mayhap you were mistaken and the lass—"

"Och, I heard her right enough." Silvanus tossed back

his plaid with a flourish. "I might be on the wrong side o' the living, but there's naught amiss with my ears! She's bent on selling the castle, she is. Wants to hie herself to a place called Hawaii."

"Haw-wah-ee?" Roderick's brows shot upward.

Silvanus shrugged. "That's what it sounded like, aye. Said she's tired o' rain and dark woods and gloomy old piles and wants to go someplace where the sun shines and"—he raised a dramatic finger—"where she's sure she won't be meeting any MacNeils!"

"Pah-phooey!" Geordie made a dismissive gesture. "She just met the wrong MacNeil."

"Indeed!" Roderick jumped on his chance. "Which is why I'm no' for this fool plan! Scaring the wits out of her will only make her think less of us."

"Nae, it'll make her help us." Geordie wagged his walking stick for emphasis. "If we tell her we'll follow her to the ends o' the earth, haunting and pestering her all her days, she'll surely see reason and agree to have our castle sent back where it belongs."

"And if she refuses?" Roderick frowned at him. "Are you prepared to chase after her to some heathenish place with a name we can't even pronounce?"

Roderick shuddered.

MacNeil's Folly was shameful enough, but the thought of having to endure a place called *Haw-wah-ee* was even worse.

The very notion jellied his knees.

"Well?" he thundered, pinning his wrath on Geordie. "I'll ask you again. What say you if she refuses?"

"She won't." Geordie set down his walking stick with a *clack*. "She's already afraid of us. You can't deny how she hastens through here, always glancing over her shoulder as if she expects us to jump down out of our portraits and whisk her away to some harrowing fate."

"Geordie speaks true," rumbled a voice from the back corner. "She'll do anything rather than risk having us hovering around her."

"I ne'er thought of myself as a man to set women cringing." Roderick's pride bit deep. "If you'd know the way of it, the ladies were e'er fawning all o'er me. And I sure didn't mind their attention! Mindy Menlove is a fine lassie. She didn't deserve what was done to her and she doesn't need—"

" 'Tis the only way, Roderick." Silvanus clamped a hand on his shoulder. "If we lose her, it may be another hundred years before someone else as likely to help us comes along."

"You know it as well as the rest of us." Geordie spoke the inevitable. "We have to do it."

Roderick harrumphed and jerked free of his cousin's grasp.

Then he nodded.

He'd be damned if he'd voice his assent. A head bob would have to do.

Still fuming, he went to stand beneath his portrait frame. "When do you propose we confront her?"

"It must be soon." Silvanus looked at the others. "She's already speaking with estate agents."

The mist swirling around Roderick went cold and glittered darkly.

He folded his arms, ignoring the chill. "How soon?"

"I'd suggest tonight." Geordie glanced at the long gallery's tall, diamond-paned windows. "The full moon will lend a dash of eeriness to our appearance."

Roderick snorted.

Ignoring him, his kinsmen cheered as one, and then

the otherworldly haze in the room began to shimmy and swirl, individual wafts spinning back into the portrait frames whence they'd come.

Only Roderick waited, looking on in disgust as they assumed their usual poses, their faces once again turning as cold and silent as the oiled canvas that held them.

"So be it." Roderick spoke to the empty room. "I ken when I'm outnumbered."

Then he, too, slipped back into his heavy gilt frame.

And as he settled into place, he glared out into the quiet of the long gallery, absolutely refusing to think about what would happen when the moon rose.

He just knew it would be a disaster.

Chapter 1

MacNeil's Folly
New Hope, Pennsylvania
Definitely our dimension . . .

Mindy Menlove lived in a mausoleum.

A thick-walled medieval castle full of gloom and shadows with just the right dash of Tudor and Gothic to curdle the blood of anyone bold enough to pass through its massive iron-studded door.

Once within, the adventure continued with a maze of dark passageways and rooms crammed to bursting with rich tapestries and heavy, age-blackened furniture. Dust motes thrived, often spinning eerily in the light that spilled through tall, stone-mullioned windows. Some doors squeaked delightfully, and certain floorboards were known for giving the most delicious creaks. Huge carved-stone fireplaces still held lingering traces of the atmosphere-charged scent of peat-and-heather-tinged smoke. Or so it was claimed by visitors with noses sensitive to such things.

Few were the modern disfigurements.

Yet the castle did boast hot water, heat, and electricity. Not to mention cable TV and high-speed Internet. MacNeil's Folly was also within the delivery area of the nearest pizza shop. And the daily paper arrived without fail on the steps each morning.

These luxuries were made possible because the ancient pile no longer stood in its original location somewhere on a bleak and windswept Hebridean isle, but on the crest of a thickly wooded hill not far from the quaint and pleasant antiquing mecca of New Hope, Pennsylvania.

Even so, the castle was a haven for hermits.

A recluse's dream.

Only trouble was that Mindy had an entirely different idea of paradise.

White sand, palm trees, and sunshine came to mind. Soft fragrant breezes and—joy of joys—no need to ever dress warm again. A trace of cocoa butter tanning lotion and mai tais sipped at sunset.

A tropical sunset.

Almost there—in her mind, anyway—Mindy imagined the castle's drafty drawing room falling away from her. Bit by bit, everything receded. The plaid carpet and each piece of clunky, carved-oak furniture, and even the heavy, dark blue curtains.

She took a step closer to the window and drew a deep breath. Closing her eyes, she inhaled not the damp scent of cold Bucks County rain and wet, dripping pinewoods but the heady perfume of frangipani and orchids.

And, because it was her dream, a whiff of fresh-ground Kona coffee.

"You should never have dated a passenger."

"Agggh!" Mindy jumped, almost dropping the mint chocolate wafer she'd been about to pop into her mouth. She'd forgotten she wasn't alone.

All thoughts of Hawaii vanished like a pricked balloon.

Whirling around, she returned the wafer to a delicate bone china plate on a tea tray and sent a pointed look across the room at her sister, Margo, her elder by all of one year.

"What of your watercooler romance with Mr. Computer Geek last year?" Mindy wiped her fingers on a napkin and then frowned when she only smeared the melted chocolate, making an even greater mess. "If I recall, he left you after less than six weeks."

"We parted amicably." Margo peered at her from a high wingback chair near the hearth. "Nor was it a *watercooler affair*. He only came by when the computers at Ye Olde Pagan Times went on the blink. And"—she leaned forward, her eyes narrowing in a way Mindy knew to dread—"neither did I move in with him. I didn't even love him."

Mindy bit the inside of her cheek to keep from snorting.

It wouldn't do to remind her sister that she'd sung a different tune last summer. As she did with every new Romeo that crossed her path, whether he chanced into the New Age shop where Margo worked, or she just stumbled into him on the street.

Margo Menlove was walking flypaper and men were the flies.

They just couldn't resist her.

Not that Mindy minded.

Especially not when she was supposed to be mourning an unfaithful fiancé who'd choked to death on a fish bone during an intimate dinner with a Las Vegas showgirl.

A fiancé she now knew had had no intention of marrying her, had used her, and—much to her amazement—

had left her his family's displaced Scottish castle and a tidy sum of money to go along with it.

Generosity born of guilt, she was sure.

The naked pole dancer from Vegas hadn't been Hunter MacNeil's only mistress. Mindy had spotted at least three other possibles at the funeral.

They rose before her mind's eye, each one sleazier than the other. Frowning, Mindy tried to banish them by scrubbing harder at the chocolate smears on her fingers. But even though their faces faded, her every indrawn breath suddenly felt like jagged ice shards cutting into tender places she should never have exposed.

She shuddered.

Margo noticed. "Don't tell me you still care about the bastard?" She leaned forward, bristling. "He used you as a front! His lawyers all but told us he only needed you to meet the terms of his late parents' will. That they'd worried about his *excesses* and made arrangements for him to lose everything unless he became a bulwark of the community, supporting their charities and marrying a good, decent girl!"

"Margo—"

"Don't 'Margo' me. I was there and heard it all." Margo gripped the armrests of her chair until her knuckles whitened. "What I can't believe is that you didn't see through him in the first place."

Mindy gave up trying to get rid of the chocolate. "You'd have fallen for him, too," she snapped, scrunching the napkin in her hand. "If he'd—"

"What?" Margo shot to her feet. "If I were a flight attendant working first class and he'd sat in the last row—wearing a wink and a smile—and with his kilt oh-so-conveniently snagged in his seat belt?"

"It wasn't like that. . . ." Mindy let the words trail off.

It *had* been like that and she was the greatest fool in the world for not seeing through his ploy.

But his dimpled smile had charmed her and he'd blushed, actually *blushed*, when she'd bent down to help him with the seat belt buckle and her fingers accidentally brushed a very naked part of him.

When the buckle sprang free and his kilt flipped up, revealing that nakedness, he'd appeared so embarrassed that accepting his dinner invitation seemed the least she could do to make him feel better.

He'd also been incredibly good-looking and had a way with words, even if he hadn't had a Scottish burr. He could look at a woman and make her feel as if no other female in the world existed, and topping it all, he'd had a great sense of humor. And, besides, what girl with red blood in her veins could resist a man in a kilt?

What wasn't to love?

Everything, she knew now.

Furious at herself, Mindy slid a glance at the hearth fire. A portrait of one of his ancestors hung there, claiming pride of place above the black marble mantel. An early MacNeil chieftain, or so Hunter had claimed, calling the man *Bran of Barra*, his was the only ancestral portrait in the castle that didn't give Mindy the willies.

A big brawny man in full Highland regalia and with a shock of wild, auburn hair and a gorgeous red beard, he didn't have the fierce-eyed glower worn by the other clan chieftains whose portraits lined the castle's long gallery. His portrait—the very same one—hung there, too. It was his mirth-filled face that she always sought when she was convinced that the gazes of the other chieftains followed her every move.

Bran of Barra's twinkling blue gaze looked elsewhere,

somewhere inside his portrait that she couldn't see. Yet she'd always felt that whatever held his attention, if he'd been aware of her ill ease, he'd turn her way. His eyes would twinkle even more and he'd say something bold and outrageous, guaranteed to make her smile. He'd been that sort of man; she just knew it.

Mindy took a breath.

She couldn't help but compare Hunter with his rough-and-ready ancestor. Where Hunter would have chided her for her fears, Bran of Barra would've banished them.

Silly or not, he made her feel safe. Only by keeping her eyes on him could she flit through the endless, dark-paneled gallery without breaking out in goose bumps.

Sadly, his roguish smile now reminded her of Hunter's.

Scowling again, she turned away from the portrait and curled her hands into tight fists. How fitting that Hunter had also dashed her only means of reaching the upper floors of the castle without having a heebie-jeebies attack.

"You can get back at him, you know." Margo stepped in front of her, a conspiratorial glint in her eye. "Have you thought about turning the castle into an esoteric center? I know the customers at Ye Olde Pagan Times would love to hold sessions here. Fussy as Hunter always was about *image*, he'd turn in his grave."

Mindy stared at her. "Didn't you hear what I said earlier? I'm selling the castle. I want nothing more than to get as far away from here as—"

"But you can't!" Margo grabbed her arm, squeezing tight. "The castle's haunted. I told you, I got an orb on a photo I took in the long gallery yesterday. Three orbs if we count the two faint ones."

"Orbs are specks of dust." Mindy tried not to roll her eyes. "Everyone knows that."

Margo sniffed. "There are orbs and *orbs*. What I got on film was spirit energy. I'm telling you"—she let go of Mindy's arm and tossed back her chin-length blond hair, a style and color both sisters shared—"you can put this place on the paranormal map. People will come from all around the country to ghost hunt and—"

"Oh, no, they won't." Mindy flopped down on a chair, her head beginning to pound. "There aren't any ghosts here. Hunter was sure of that and so am I. And"—she aimed her best my-decision-is-final look at her sister— "the only place I'm putting this miserable old pile is on the market."

"But that's crazy." Margo sounded scandalized. "Owning a haunted castle is the chance of a lifetime."

"Yes, it is." Mindy sat back and folded her arms. "It's my chance to go back to the airlines and move to Hawaii. I can invest the money from the sale of the castle and what Hunter left me and live off my flight attendant salary. It'd be no trouble at all to commute from Oahu or even Maui. And best of all"—she felt wonderfully free at the thought—"I doubt there are many Scotsmen in Hawaii. They can't take the heat.

"The Scots thrive on cold and rain and mist." Mindy lifted her chin, well aware her words wouldn't sit well with her Scotophile sister. "You did know that the hottest-selling clothing article in Scotland is thermal underwear?"

"You're not thinking clearly." Margo picked up her purse and moved to the door. "I'll come back in the morning after you've had a good night's sleep. We'll talk then."

"Only if you're ready to help me find the right real

estate agent," Mindy called after her sister's retreating back. "I've already spoken with a few."

And each one had sounded more than eager to list MacNeil's Folly.

Mindy smiled and reached for the mint chocolate wafer she'd almost eaten earlier. Then she helped herself to another and another until the little bone china plate was empty. Chocolate was good for the soul.

And there weren't any ghostly *souls* spooking about the castle.

Not disguised as orbs or otherwise.

Her sister was crazy.

And *she* was going to Hawaii.

But first she needed some sleep. Margo was right about that. Regrettably, when she left the drawing room, she found the rest of the castle filled with a thin, drifting haze. Cold and silvery, thready wisps of it gathered in the corridors and snaked past the tall, Gothic window arches. An illusion that surely had everything to do with the night's full moon just breaking through the fast-moving rain clouds and nothing at all to do with the *orbs* that her sister claimed were darting around the long gallery.

Or so she thought until she neared that dreaded room and caught the unmistakable strains of a bagpipe. A haunting old Gaelic air that stopped the instant she neared the gallery's open door.

A door she always took care to keep closed.

Mindy's stomach dropped and her knees started to tremble. But when she heard footsteps on the long gallery's polished wood floorboards and the low murmur of many men's voices, she got mad and strode forward.

It wouldn't surprise her if Margo and her crazy New Age friends were playing a trick on her.

A notion she had to discard the minute she reached

the threshold and looked into the angry faces of Hunter's Highland chieftain ancestors. There could be no doubt that it was them because, with the exception of Bran of Barra's portrait at the far end of the long room, the ferocious-looking clansmen's large gold-gilt portrait frames were empty.

She also recognized them.

And this time they weren't just following her with their oil-on-canvas eyes.

They were in the room. And they were glaring at her.

Glaring, and *floating* her way.

Some even brandished swords.

"Oh my God!" Mindy's eyes rounded and she clapped a hand to her cheek.

Heart thundering, she tried to slam the door and run, but a handful of the scowling clansmen were quicker. Before she could blink, they surrounded her, their huge kilted bodies blocking her escape.

Kilted, plaid-draped bodies she could see through!

Mindy felt the floor dip beneath her feet as they swept closer, their frowns black as night and their eyes glinting furiously in the moonlight. Soon, she feared, she might be sick. She *wished* she could faint.

Her sister wasn't the crazy one.

She was.

Or else she was about to meet a gaggle of real live ghosts.

And since the latter seemed unlikely, she'd just lost her marbles. She took a deep breath and lifted her chin, peering back at them as if they weren't a pack of wild-eyed, see-through Highlanders.

Then she folded her arms and waited calmly. It was a trick she'd learned in airline training.

How to keep cool at all times.

She just hoped they couldn't tell she was faking.

She was sure she didn't want to know what would happen if they guessed.

About the same time, but across the dark and icy expanse of the North Atlantic, Bran of Barra grinned as he surveyed his crowded great hall. Never in seven hundred years had MacNeil's Tower looked so grand. But then, he'd used every one of those centuries to hone his skills in keeping his hall as it pleased him.

Loud, raucous, and filled with merrymaking.

Evenings were spent in the company of like-minded revelers who enjoyed their ghostdom as much as he relished his own. This night they'd come in astonishing number. High-spirited friends from every corner of the Highlands and Isles packed the trestle benches, each man—and not a few of the women—roaring with laughter and bursting with good cheer as they dined or danced, singing their host's praises all the while.

Deservedly so, for nowhere else could they be assured a warmer welcome. Hospitality as only an openhanded Hebridean chieftain knew how to give. With pride, Bran dazzled his guests with succulent roasted meats and the frothiest ales. Drinking horns rimmed in silver, the pointed tips winking with jewels. Each well-laden table dressed with sparkling white linen and illuminated by the glow of fine wax tapers, though—in truth—the many-armed candelabras gleamed bright enough to light the hall on their own.

Creamy custards and sugared almonds tempted the palate, while superb Rhenish wine impressed the discerning. If a savory was missing, Bran could provide it with a snap of his fingers. But mostly, he thought of everything. Such as the strutting piper who ensured lively music for reels and jigs. And the discreetly curtained alcoves in the shadows between torches that offered privacy to those so inclined.

After the feasting, fresh pallets and plaiding were available for all, with sumptuously appointed bedchambers kept ready for a favored few.

Life—or, rather, *un*-life—was good on the fair Isle of Barra.

No matter that Bran's Barra hovered in a dimension that defied time and place.

MacNeil's Tower was as real to him as the two feet he stood upon, and he'd challenge anyone who claimed otherwise. Just now, in celebration of the night's gaiety, he felt a need for another kind of contest.

One that would take the edge off the strange tension that had been riding him of late. Mostly nothing more than a prickling at his nape, but sometimes an odd humming in his veins that sent him up onto the battlements, where the crashing of the waves and the roar of the wind drowned out the rapid pounding of his heart.

He felt that peculiar quickening of his blood coming on now and meant to dash it before the chills started rippling up and down his spine.

"Friends!" He looked around, letting a broad grin split his face. "Who will pit their strength against me? Who"—he thrust a fist in the air, pumping his muscles—"would test their skill at arm wrestling? The winner—"

A blast of heat scorched his hip and he jumped and wheeled about, certain one of his more ale-headed friends had jabbed at him with a torch flame.

It would be like some of the loons to do so.

But no one stood within an arm's length.

And the nearest torches crackled innocently in their wall brackets, the smoking blazes an impossible source for whatever had burned him.

He rubbed his hip, his grin slipping.

At the high table, his good friend and fellow ghost-in-revel Saor MacSwain threw back his dark head and laughed. "Ho, Bran!" The Hebridean's deep voice boomed. "Be that a new dance or did a flea bite you?"

"Neither!" Bran scowled at him. "But you"—he warmed to the idea—"just became the man to prove your prowess, though you've forfeited a prize if you win!"

"I shall win!" Saor leapt to his feet, laughing still. "And I already have my prize for the e'en!" He flashed a wicked smile at the plump, scantily clad ghostess who'd been sharing his trencher. "Naught you could offer would satisfy me more."

"No doubt." Bran felt his good humor returning.

He even slung a comradely arm around his friend's shoulders. "Maili"—he flicked a glance at Saor's trencher mate, winking—"will please you well."

The glint in Saor's eye said he knew it.

Of Bran's own height and breadth, and with his bullish strength, Saor was also the only man in the hall who'd prove a worthy wrestling opponent. Even so, Bran would best him. The brute force he'd need in doing so would take his mind off the pestiferous chills nipping at him.

And—it must be said—with his other close friends having been lured away from ghostly realms in recent years, choosing instead to spend their days with *American* seductresses of the modern world, Saor was one of the few souls remaining whose company Bran truly enjoyed.

Saor, like Bran, held no aspirations to leave their

spectral paradise. Pleasing Bran even more, Saor gloried in the boisterous and colorful trappings of their own fourteenth century. He harbored no high-flung wishes to dally in worlds where he didn't belong.

For that, Bran was grateful.

Not that he'd admit any such softness.

But he had grown extremely tired of losing friends.

It did him good to know that Saor, with his laughing eyes and ready smile, would not be tempted elsewhere by an American female come to the Highlands for the sole purpose of claiming a kilted man.

A fool would know these women's fixation with plaid was all that drew them.

And, perhaps, an appreciation for bonny knees!

Bran drew an annoyed breath.

Releasing Saor, he flipped back his own plaid and blotted the brazen vixens from his mind. Experience had proven their persistence and—he shuddered— their penchant for finding fourteenth-century High-landers even more appealing than Scotsmen of their own time. It scarce mattered how many of them were blessed with long legs and bouncing, well-rounded bo-soms. They roamed Scotland's heathery hills like rav-enous, bloodthirsty predators and were to be avoided at all costs.

If a man wished to keep his wits.

And Bran did, so he flexed his shoulders and strode over to a trestle table against the dais wall. A flick of his fingers cast away the crisp linen draping and the spread of victuals arrayed down the board's length. A second finger click conjured two low and fat tallow candles, each one burning hotly on a flat iron pricket.

Pleased, he threw a look at Saor, eagerly awaiting his friend's reaction. "There you have it!" He indicated the candles. "First man to douse the flames with the other's arm is the winner, taking all!"

Saor arched a brow. "All of what?"

Bran thought a moment, then rocked back on his heels. "All the pleasure of chasing away any American lassies who might darken my door!"

Hoots of laughter greeted his outburst. Many merrymakers slapped their thighs or pounded on the trestle tables. Some gave mock gasps of horror.

All were amused.

Saor simply stared. "An American?"

"So I said." Bran nodded, not quite sure where the notion had come from. "Dinnae tell me you've ne'er heard of them. Everyone knows they enjoy poking about our glens and castles, searching for their roots, as it were!"

More sniggers and snorts answered him.

Bran marched across the dais to jam a finger into the plaid-draped chest of the man who'd laughed the loudest. "You'd sing another tune if one of the long-fingered lassies snatched you into their day!"

He leaned down, nose to nose with the other ghostie. "I've been to their America. Once, it was! A place called *Pen-seal*-somewhere. The memory jellies my knees and"—he straightened—"still has the power to tie my toes in knots. Trust me, you dinnae want to land in the clutches of an American, most especially the ones that call themselves Scotophiles. They're the worst o' the lot.

"And I'll no' have any here." Bran glared round, in warning. The idea of falling prey to such a female on Barra—or anywhere—made his insides quiver.

Blessedly, the possibility wasn't a likely danger. He rarely visited modern times and absolutely refused to sift himself to Barra of the current day.

But it wouldn't hurt to have a plan if the unthinkable ever happened.

Relieved that he did, he raised his arms above his head and cracked his knuckles, eager to arm-wrestle Saor and put American wenches from his mind. A wink and a smile were all he needed to find himself seated at the table he'd readied. Proud of his flourish, he shoved up his sleeve and planted his elbow firmly on the board, grinning.

Not to be outdone, Saor flicked his wrist to fetch a cup of ale from the air, downing the brew to its dregs in one long gulp. He laughed when the emptied cup vanished from his fingers, and quick as winking, he, too, had claimed his place across from Bran.

"So, my friend!" He plunked his own arm on the table and grabbed Bran's waiting hand. "Let us see who shall have the pleasure of chasing American lassies from this fine isle! But be warned." His deep voice held a note of amusement. "The ghosts one calls are e'er summoned!"

Chuckles and hoots rippled through the group of gathered onlookers. Several nudged one another or exchanged merry-eyed glances, though one or two tried to hide their laughs behind sudden bouts of coughing.

Bran ignored them all and concentrated on keeping his arm steady. At his elbow, the pricket flame leapt and danced. He could feel the candle's warmth licking him, waiting. Unconcerned, he let his lips twitch, sure of victory. His wrists were free of telltale burn scars and he wasn't about to put one there now.

So he kept his arm relaxed and let Saor do the straining. Already his friend's jaw was setting, his teeth gritted, and tiny beads of sweat began to dot his brow. No longer laughing, the crowd around the table drew near, some men leaning down to bang the table with their fists. Saor grimaced, pushing fiercely as the pounding beat became a rhythm.

Bran paid no heed, the roar of his own blood in his ears louder than his friends' thunderous encouragement. Saor was squeezing his hand now, the other man's grip almost bone crushing as he tried to push Bran's arm onto the candle.

"You cannae win." Bran ground out the words, his own brow growing damp. "Give and spare yourself a brand!"

Saor flashed a grin and strained harder. "You are the one about to be burned!"

Bran snorted.

In truth, he *was* burning.

The muscles in his neck and shoulders had suddenly caught fire, sending scorching heat shooting through his veins. But still he thrust Saor's arm closer to the flame, determined to triumph. Until the blood rushing in his ears became a shrill buzzing, and a scalding flash of white-hot pain exploded against his hip.

"Yee-owwww!" Lightning quick, he slammed Saor's arm against the candle, the hiss and stink of burnt flesh lost in the shouts of his men and the agony of the blinding heat stabbing into his side.

Saor blinked and sat back, his grin returning. "It would seem the American lassie shall be yours," he announced, shaking his singed wrist.

Around them, revelers whipped out swords and raised them high in tribute. Bran pushed slowly to his feet and left the table, scarce seeing or hearing the cheering throng for the raging blaze he couldn't ignore. No longer just at his hip, the heat raced through him, searing his very soul.

Every inch of his body burned.

His blood sizzled and each indrawn breath left a fiery trail that roasted his lungs.

It was a misery he finally recognized.

Though he'd rather cut himself than admit the flames came from the pommel stone of his sword.

His nape prickled at the possibility and icy chills sped down his spine. The Heartbreaker's crystal was said to be enchanted. Formed by the tears of a MacNeil ancestress who lost her love in an ancient battle, the gemstone was believed to heat and glow in times of grave danger to the clan.

Or so legend claimed.

Not wanting to think about the *other* claims, Bran lurched through the hall, sifting himself into the cold night air of the bailey only when he was sure none of his men was looking his way. Dark mist swirled across the cobbles and the wind was picking up, the air damp with the smell of rain. Beyond the curtain walls, he could hear the sea crashing against the rocks. MacNeil's Tower, after all, claimed its own wee isle, set just off the nearby coast of Barra. The keep was a nigh-impregnable stronghold and utterly defenseless against the dread churning inside him.

He stopped near the lee of a wall, letting its towering stones and the drifting mist shield him from prying eyes. If the Heartbreaker was branding him, he meant to keep his fate to himself.

Even so, it cost him greatly to toss back his plaid and clamp his hand around the sword's rounded pommel.

The heat was excruciating.

But it was the bright blue light seeping through his fingers that nearly stopped his heart.

Shimmering blue light that legend called *the truth of the sword* and that—for which he'd always been most grateful—had never deigned to show itself in all the long centuries he'd possessed the fabled blade.

It was truly magnificent—finely honed steel just as ghostly as himself. And—his gut clenched—still possessed of the powerful magic of the true Heartbreaker.

Bran shuddered.

The saints only knew where the earthly blade now rested.

Not that it mattered. His chiefly wits already told him that his beloved sword had determined to disrupt his eternal peace.

Now he looked on in horror as the light deepened in brilliance and began curling past his fingers to weave and dance before him. Eyes wide, he staggered backward, releasing the pommel. But if clutching the crystal had unleashed its magic, letting go didn't break the spell.

Far from it, the blue light began spinning into a long, glittery wand that bobbed and bounced in the air, slowly stretching itself into a glowing rectangle, bright against the cold gray of his castle walls.

He was cold, too.

Blistering heat no longer blasting him, a black chill now swept him. It was a terrible, icy grip on his gizzard that would have brought a lesser man to his knees.

Bran did his best not to flinch.

Such weakness was beneath his chiefly status.

Hebridean chieftains, in particular, were known for their stoutheartedness and valor. Frozen innards were nothing to men of his ilk.

Ghostly or otherwise.

But when a woman appeared inside the blue-edged shape hovering in front of him, his mouth went dry and he could feel his throat working.

The woman wasn't just any female.

She was a *modern woman*, he was sure.

Comely and fair, she stared right at him, her eyes wide with horror and every bit as blue as the shimmering light surrounding her. An unseen wind tossed her sun-bright hair about a face that—under different circumstances— would send lust thundering straight to his loins. But her mouth, sweet and lush as it was, had opened in a silent scream, the sight dashing any such urges before they could rise.

He did take a step closer, drawn like a moth to flame even though he knew he should flee.

But her lush curves beckoned and her urgent need . . .

Bran swore and reached out a hand, compelled to comfort her. As if she knew, her lovely eyes rounded with an even greater look of terror. Then she veered away, dashing deeper into the mist trapped inside the glowing blue frame.

She vanished almost as quickly as he'd seen her.

Sadly, not before he noted her clothing.

She was wearing breeks.

The heavy blue kind folk of her day called jeans.

Bran swallowed hard, his own horror mounting as the shimmering blue light contracted back into a single spinning beam. A brilliant wand of dazzling light that again bobbed and danced in the air before him. Until it suddenly stopped weaving and floated toward him, pointing straight at his heart before, with a crackling *hum*, the beam leapt back inside the Heartbreaker's crystal, leaving him alone with the icy-cold truth.

The bards hadn't lied about the mythic blade.

There were times when a woman's distress could summon the crystal's magic.

Women who carried MacNeil blood in their veins. Or females who—Bran couldn't deny it—were inextricably bound to a MacNeil male, usually a chieftain.

Either way, the *truth of the sword* unerringly revealed the MacNeil destined to champion the woman.

Such fates were etched in stone.

Bran shoved a hand through his hair, certain the cobbles beneath his feet had just opened up to swallow him. He felt decidedly ill. After seven hundred years of merry ghostdom, his own beloved sword had finally brought his world crashing down around him. There could be no escape.

Not from the Heartbreaker's prophecy. Nor from the American lass he knew would soon land on his doorstep. He should have listened to Saor's warning about calling ghosts.

Now he was doomed.

Though the Heartbreaker's crystal was quiet now, its glistening roundness cold and benign as the night's chill mist, Bran could still see the woman's startled blue eyes. They pierced him through dimensions and—he knew—across great distances.

Bran scowled. His chest tightened with fury.

As if the Heartbreaker meant to torment him even more, images flooded his mind. They were wanton, lascivious glimpses of tumbling the lass on a bed of turf and heather. That, he could well imagine.

More damning yet, he could feel the maid's presence. Taste her kiss on his tongue as if he'd already ravished her. Soon, he knew, she'd be here. Tempting him as only modern-day sirens could.

Bran groaned. Then he tipped back his head and stared at the moon, peeking out from behind a wisp of torn clouds. If only he could be somewhere as distant.

But MacNeil's Tower was his home and he wasn't leaving.

He'd deal with the American when she arrived. As long as she wasn't from *Pen-seal*-where'er, his chances of withstanding her were good.

It was just a matter of preparing.

Chapter 2

Mindy stood in the doorway to the long gallery, refusing to budge. Not that her legs would carry her anywhere even if she wished to flee. Her knees knocked furiously, her feet felt like lead, and a good dozen angry-looking MacNeil ghosts were blocking her way. Big, bad medieval *spooks* with bushy beards and flashing swords, and—she was sure—not a one of them stood under six feet four.

They were towering, plaid-draped hulks of menace.

In a word, they were terrifying.

Mindy swallowed. A chill of fear streaked down to her toes. If she'd thought Hunter's ancestors looked ferocious before—safely trapped within oiled canvas and heavy gold-gilt frames—now they'd give Attila the Hun a run for his money.

Their shouts alone turned her blood to water.

Even worse, escape meant darting through their glowing, translucent ranks.

It would also require an intimate brush with their steel. Swords that somehow managed to look much more substantial than the ghosties wielding them.

Clearly retreat wasn't an option.

As if they knew, the see-through Highlanders whooshed closer, their eyes glinting with malice.

A strange blue mist shimmered and billowed around them, filling the long gallery and casting its dark-paneled length in an eerie, otherworldly light. Icy tendrils of the mist slid through the open doorway to float in the corridor beyond, hovering as if in wait.

It was a no-win situation.

So she remained where she was, careful to keep her back straight and her expression unperturbed. The Highlanders' faces darkened, their scowls turning formidable. Those who weren't yet waving swords whipped out their blades now, brandishing them with flourish. A few snarled and growled. One waggled the scariest eyebrows Mindy had ever seen. She gulped and tried to pretend the ghosts were irate passengers, riled by overbooked flights and weather delays. A dreaded middle seat when, the passenger swore, he'd booked a window or aisle.

The list of upsets was long and Mindy had heard—and dealt with—them all.

Unfortunately, in all her ten years of flying, she'd never encountered sword-wielding complainers. Even the most unpleasant business travelers and VIPs hadn't packed anything more daunting than laptops and newspapers. Some did arm themselves with oversized hand luggage and could become threatening when faced with objections.

But not a one of them had been dead.

Dust and bone for centuries.

Mindy shivered.

Then she remembered the mint chocolate wafers she'd eaten, gobbling down the entire plate and—shame scalded her—even polishing off what remained in the package.

She wasn't seeing ghosts.

She was living a chocolate binge—a sugar-induced nightmare.

Sure of it now, she puffed her bangs off her forehead and tipped back her head to peer up at the long gallery's elaborate wood-inlaid ceiling. Calorie regret swung round into pure relief. Even so, she took a deep, ghost-banishing breath and began counting to ten, certain the spooks would be gone when she looked again.

Sadly they weren't.

If anything, they'd moved closer.

The nearest pointed a walking stick at her. "Begone, wench! If you—"

"Be warned!" A second, much more fierce-looking ghost elbowed the cane pointer aside. The shimmering blue mist around them darkened, even crackling when he swept the other spooks with a heated glare. "We are here to warn the lass, no' chase her away!"

Warn me? Mindy's blood froze.

Her eyes rounded. "Ahh, errr . . ." Her objections fizzled in her throat. This was bigger than chocolate hallucinations and grumbling frequent flyers.

She pressed a hand to her chest, not sure she could breathe. She recognized the ghosts from their portraits with little gold nameplates at the bottom of each heavy gilt frame. The first one—the *Begone* ghost—was Geordie MacNeil, one of Hunter's sixteenth-century ancestors. The other, the spook now aiming the sharp end of his sword at her, had to be Silvanus, a MacNeil chieftain of fifteenth-century fame. Legend claimed he'd outlived six wives and died not long before wedding a seventh, a great beauty who was said to have been more than half his age at the time.

No one knew much about Geordie.

And Mindy didn't want anything to do with either of them.

"You don't have to chase me anywhere." She didn't know how she managed to speak. She began backing away, still half hoping they were figments of too much chocolate. "I'm leaving just now and—"

"You're no' going anywhere." A deep voice boomed from the back of the long gallery. "No' until we've had a word with you. And then"—the blue haze parted to reveal Roderick MacNeil, another fifteenth-century laird, in all his formidable glory—"you can choose your path!"

Resplendent in full Highland dress, he sailed forward, kilt swinging about his knees, sword at his hip. He stopped right in front of her and gave her a sharp look before sweeping low in a gallant bow.

"Roderick MacNeil," he thundered unnecessarily as he straightened. "I am MacNeil of Barra, chief of that illustrious race! These other lairdlings"—he made a broad gesture with his arm—"answer to me. I—"

"We're all the MacNeil of Barra," another objected from deeper in the whirling mist. "Leastways we were in our own day and time!"

Beside him, Silvanus swelled his chest. "So I said just yestere'en. There be no' one o' us more lairdly than the other. That be the way o' it."

"Hear, hear!" Geordie rapped his walking stick against a table. "One for all and all for one is our creed."

Roderick spun around to glower at them. "If that is so, why must I tell the lass what we want of her?"

Silvanus huffed something unintelligible. Then he nudged the ghost hovering beside him until he, too, gave an inarticulate grunt.

Near the table, Geordie shuffled his feet, sending up eddies of sparkly blue mist. He didn't appear to have an opinion otherwise.

"Spineless women!" Roderick jammed his hands on his hips. "A blind newt would see why I am Barra!"

At the very back of the long gallery, someone snorted. It was a deep voice, richly burred, and sounded more amused than riled. The voice was also more distant. Different enough for Roderick's bushy red brows to snap together as he whirled to flash an annoyed glare at the farthest reaches of the haze-filled room.

But nothing except the mist moved there.

And only Bran of Barra's mute, oil-painted face stared back at them, his grin wicked as ever. He, at least—and Mindy was grateful—hadn't leapt out of his portrait frame like the others.

In fact, Mindy was quite sure that his portrait was just that.

A painted likeness, nothing more.

Even so, Roderick shook a fist at him. "You've been silent seven hundred years, *Cousin*. Dinnae think to thrust your nose in our business now!"

"Hear, hear!" Geordie rapped the table again.

Others rattled their swords and hooted agreement. Some tossed back their plaids and stood proud. All sent agitated glances down the room at the fourteenth-century chieftain's portrait.

Mindy could have kissed him.

He'd provided just the distraction she needed to start inching backward. Regrettably, she was having difficulty getting her legs to cooperate and managed only to bump into the doorjamb.

"Ho, lass!" Roderick's voice roared from just behind

her. "Where do you think you're heading? We haven't yet discussed our plans for you."

Mindy whipped around to find him towering over her. He stood with his legs planted apart and one hand resting masterfully on his sword hilt. Obviously adept at intimidation, he was using every inch of his big Highland body to his most fearsome advantage.

Mindy blinked.

When her jaw started to slip, Roderick grinned. "Didn't know that ghosts could move so quickly, eh?"

A ripple of hearty laughter from the other chieftains proved they appreciated his wit.

"I . . ." Mindy's tongue seemed stuck to the roof of her mouth. She tried not to quake when Roderick's grin vanished and he leaned toward her, coming so close that his curly-bearded chin almost tickled her own.

His gaze burned into hers, hot, blue, and terrifying. "Are you ready to hear us out?"

Mindy bit her lip to hold back the squeak that she was sure would be her only reply.

"Well?" He drew his sword with a real-sounding *zing*. "I've ne'er chanced to use this on a woman," he mused, eyeing the blade, "but there's always a first time. . . ."

"That sword isn't real." Mindy didn't know where the words came from. Maybe it was a touch of refuse-to-die airline bravura. She *had* been trained to face crash landings with a smile.

Nerves of steel and a saint's calm had been drilled into her for years.

In this case, it was likely desperation.

Either way, her daring had been a mistake because as soon as the words left her mouth, Roderick's eyes flashed dangerously. Stepping back, he flipped his sword high in the air, laughing as he caught it on the downfall and presented it to her, hilt first, to examine.

"See how real—or unreal—you find the blade, my lady." His voice thrummed with challenge. "I vow you'll change your mind about speaking with us thereafter!"

"I don't need to touch it." Mindy ignored her trembling knees and lifted her chin. He'd made her angry now. "You're a MacNeil. That counts more with me than if your sword is real or isn't. As a MacNeil"—she almost choked on the hated name—"you'll find a way to harm me regardless of the weapon you choose."

To her surprise, his brows snapped together and he spluttered.

He almost looked embarrassed.

But the moment passed quickly and he folded his arms, giving her his worst glower yet. "So-o-o!" He drew himself up to his full imposing height. "If that is the way the wind blows, you'll no doubt do our bidding."

"And what might that be?" Sheer annoyance kept Mindy's voice from cracking.

"We"—Roderick swept his ghostly friends with a regal glance—"want you to restore the tower to us."

"I'm selling the castle." Mindy was sure they already knew this. "Besides, you have it anyway. You live here, don't you? Glaring out of your portraits at everyone who dares to pass through the long gallery and—"

"You're no' telling her proper-like." Silvanus appeared at Roderick's elbow with a swirl of plaid and a scatter of whirling blue sparkles. "Tell her—"

"I'm getting to that part!" Roderick glared at him.

Mindy wasn't sure, but she thought Geordie sniggered.

He must have, because Roderick speared him with a dark look before turning back to her. Taking a deep breath—if ghosts could even do the like, though it seemed that indeed they could—he sheathed his sword and then once more planted his hands on his kilted hips.

"Hear this, lady, and think well before you reply," he began, watching from beneath his brows. "We would have you restore MacNeil's Tower to its original glory and"—he paused for dramatic effect—"we want you to return the castle to its rightful home."

Mindy stared at him. "The castle's rightful home?"

Roderick nodded meaningfully.

The other chieftains did the same.

A sick feeling began to spread through Mindy's middle. "I'm not sure I know what you mean." The lie made her heart pound and dried her mouth. She had a very good idea what he'd meant and the thought paralyzed her.

Still, she went for a bluff. "The Folly is in wonderful shape as it stands and—"

"The *Tower* is an abomination and shall remain so until it's returned to Barra!" Roderick's voice rose on every word. "You must take the castle back to Scotland for us. Stone by bleeding stone."

Mindy's eyes flew wide. "That's impossible. I—"

"It was possible to get the castle here!" Geordie shook his cane at her. "Taking it back should be no greater bother."

A chorus of ayes and foot stompings agreed with him.

Roderick folded his arms and grinned. "Well? What say you to our proposal?"

Mindy couldn't answer him.

The floor was dipping wildly beneath her feet. She was sure the walls were weaving. And a brilliant flash of dazzling blue light at the back of the long gallery was nearly blinding her. Blinking, she saw with horror that the blaze was Bran of Barra's portrait frame.

Worse, the builder of MacNeil's Tower no longer wore his roguish grin.

He was staring right at her, his proud oil-on-canvas face wearing a scowl more frightening than all his chiefly descendants put together.

If he, too, jumped down and *whoosh*ed up to her, she just might faint. After all, if the artist hadn't used poetic license, his sword was the longest of the lot's. Just now the blade's pommel stone burned with the same fiery blue as the portrait frame. He'd also unsheathed the sword and—it was very obvious—he stood clutching the blade's hilt in a white-knuckled grip.

He looked more than ready to use it.

Mindy shuddered. Her palms dampened.

But then the blue blaze vanished as quickly as it'd appeared. Once again, the long-ago chieftain smiled as if enjoying some private joke. His sword safely returned to the painted scabbard at his hip.

If he'd really been glaring at her, he was only oil and dust now.

Mindy blinked and shivered again, not surprised to find that the *ghostly* chieftains had pressed close. They'd circled her and now eyed her quizzically. Some had thrust the pointy ends of their swords into the blue mist at their feet and were leaning on the blades' hilts.

None of them seemed to have noticed the illumination of their forebear's portrait.

Their entire focus was on her.

"So, lass!" Roderick lifted a hopeful brow. "Will you agree to carry out our wishes?"

Mindy took a deep breath. She still couldn't believe she was conversing with ghosts. "I told you, I'm selling the castle. You'll have to find someone else. I'm moving to Hawaii as soon as the deal is inked."

Roderick's face fell. He went still as stone.

Geordie's jaw slipped. "Inked?"

"She means when she's sold the castle." Silvanus shot him an annoyed look, then turned back to Roderick. "But she'll no' be doing that, will she, now?"

Roderick gave a heavy sigh. "I was afraid it would come to this."

"Come to what?" Mindy was sure she didn't want to know.

"Our alternative plan should you prove disagreeable." Roderick stole a glance at the others, then cleared his throat. "We'd hoped you'd be more reasonable."

"I only want to leave here." Mindy was beginning to wonder if it wasn't the chili-hot sardines and garlic toast she'd eaten for lunch that had summoned them rather than the chocolate mint wafers.

Sardines and garlic seemed a more likely possibility.

It was a remote chance, but enough to keep her chin lifted. "That means"—she straightened her shoulders, as well—"I'll soon be out of here and you can be sure it won't be to fly to Scotland."

"A pity, that." Geordie looked down at his walking stick. "I dinnae think I'll care much for this *Hah-wah-ee*."

The others nodded in prompt commiseration.

Mindy felt sick.

She turned to Roderick. "What does he mean he won't care for Hawaii?"

"What he said, just." Roderick's tone was pure resignation. "If you'll no' be taking our castle back to Barra where it belongs, we've no choice but follow you wherever you go when you leave here.

"You've already seen how quickly we can move." A touch of pride lit his eyes. "We can also sift ourselves anywhere. So-o-o, if you won't comply with our—"

"You'll follow me to Hawaii?" Mindy stared at him. "Are you saying you'll *haunt* me?"

"Every last one of us, aye." Roderick glanced at the others, who all bobbed their heads. "We'll follow you to the ends of the earth if need be. And"—he made her a solemn bow—"we're prepared to do so for all your days."

Mindy felt her eyes widen. "That's madness. I-it's blackmail!"

Roderick spread his hands. "It is a drastic measure, to be sure. Nor something we do lightly."

Mindy didn't care. Images of cold mist, sheep, and constant rain flashed across her mind. Lukewarm toast and plates of steaming haggis, followed by black pudding—*blood sausage*—and rivers of tea when she was so a coffee person.

Long dark winter nights and summers that weren't.

Everyone knew Scots considered seventy degrees a major heat wave.

They drove left on roads that could only be called threads. Everyone you met claimed to be descended from Robert the Bruce. And—horrors—they sold fried Mars bars in the fish-and-chip shops.

Mindy felt under assault.

Her stomach began to hurt. "I don't want to go to Scotland."

"You can leave after you've done our bidding." Roderick waved away her objection. "We've been here, in this wretched *Pen-seal*-place, for centuries. We wish to go home."

"And to take our castle with us," Silvanus put in, eyeing her sternly. "We've watched o'er these walls all these many years, honor-bound to safeguard each stone. Now"—he put his hands on his hips, looking most decisive—"it's time for you to help us undo a great wrong."

"The choice is yours." Geordie lifted a finger significantly.

"You're not giving me a choice." Mindy's heart sank on the words.

Roderick flipped back his plaid, his grin triumphant. "We are giving you more. You will be spending time in Scotland, lass. *Scotland!* You'll see the grandest isle in the Hebrides, our own sweet Barra."

"Many would fall to their knees in gratitude." Silvanus's deep voice rang with pride.

"Hail Barra!" A round of cheers filled the long gallery. Everywhere, chests puffed and plaid folds were flicked and smoothed. Bearded chins lifted, while swords—and one walking stick—were thrust high in the air.

The ghosties enjoyed victory.

Mindy glared at them.

She didn't doubt for a heartbeat that they'd follow her to Hawaii.

They were MacNeils, after all.

One MacNeil had already made her life a misery. She wasn't about to see what a whole band of them would do if she crossed them. It didn't bear consideration. However she turned it, she lost.

She didn't have much choice except to do what they wanted.

She was doomed.

Bran knew he was in trouble when he cracked one eye to peer across his bedchamber at his sword. The eye crack had to be his thousandth since he'd sought his bed for the night. He refused to torture himself by counting how many times he'd tossed and turned. How often he'd punched and plumped his pillows didn't bear thinking upon, either. Yet no matter how penetratingly he stared through the darkness at his blade, he couldn't detect anything unusual.

More specifically, he couldn't catch the faintest glimmer of blue in the Heartbreaker's pommel stone.

The fabled gem appeared insultingly innocuous.

Yet Bran knew what he'd seen in the bailey.

And although the blazing heat that had scorched his side left no brand scars, his sword hip felt as if the skin should be blistered. He'd also swear that his veins ached from the fiery blast that had swept through them, igniting his entire body.

His head pained him so fiercely that even pressing his hands against his temples didn't ease the throbbing. And if he didn't know better, he'd think he'd swallowed a whole pailful of ashes.

His mouth was that dry.

Most damning of all, he could still see the American's startled blue eyes staring at him. Closing his own eyes helped him naught. If anything, each time he did manage to start slipping into a deep, much-needed slumber, he saw more than the woman's eyes.

He saw all of her.

And he saw her naked.

Fully unclothed in all her wondrous glory, she stood a few feet from where he'd propped the Heartbreaker against the wall. Tempting beyond reason, she shimmered in a shaft of glowing blue light that hid her most intimate secrets even as the luminous swirl of color taunted him with just enough glimpses of her curves and shadows to set him like granite.

"Odin's balls!" He flipped onto his back and snapped open his eyes.

Across the room, the blue mist swirling around the woman stilled and dipped just low enough to give him a clear view of her full, round breasts. They shone beautifully in the soft luminosity cloaking her, teasing him with their creamy, lush swells. Her nipples were taut, sweetly puckered and thrusting, as if she felt the cold, damp air streaming in through the shutter slats.

Or, saints help him, as if he'd been palming her breasts, rubbing his thumbs round and round their pink-tinted tips, making them tighten with excitement.

Bran scowled.

He wanted nothing to do with the woman, no matter that she had a lush and creamy bosom.

Wishing he hadn't noticed, he curled his fingers into the bedcovers, clenching his hands until his knuckles hurt. He swallowed hard, outraged that his sword's magic would summon the American here, into the sanctity of his bedchamber.

But furious or not, he was unable to look away.

A fierce lust slammed through him, scalding his blood and damning him with scorching need that made his loins pound and burn unbearably.

When the blue mist began to shift again, once more hiding her breasts, he released his fierce grip on the bedsheets and swiped an arm across his sweat-dampened brow. The mist was glowing even brighter now, whirling faster in glistening colors, sure signs—he hoped—that the vision would soon end.

Instead, the unholy glow parted again, this time presenting him with a quick glimpse of the tantalizing shadows at the apex of her thighs.

"Damnation!" Bran leapt from the bed, his control shattered.

To his horror, the woman jumped as if she'd heard him. Her gaze flashed to his, her startled blue eyes widening as she caught him staring at her nakedness.

She clapped one hand to her breasts and thrust the other one over the triangle of golden curls that—he was doomed—Bran couldn't stop trying to see behind her splayed fingers.

Naked himself, he snatched a bed cushion and held it strategically, hoping her surprise had kept her from noticing how much she affected him.

Unfortunately, the slashes of deep color across her cheeks said she *had* seen.

"You can't be here!" She finally spoke, the blue swirls circling her glittering more brightly than ever. "This—"

"Is my bedchamber and you're the intruder." Bran did his best to speak with chiefly authority. No easy task, standing mother-naked and clutching an embroidered and tasseled bed pillow in front of his groin.

He cleared his throat. "Begone and let me return to my night's rest."

"No." She had the temerity to argue. "As I was saying, this is my dream and *you* can't be here."

"I can be anywhere I wish." Bran glared at her, her boldness making him forget his dignity.

"Not in my dreams." She stood firm, her chin lifting.

He scowled at her, then flashed an even darker look at the Heartbreaker. The damned sword was a single blue flame, its light brighter than a thousand bale fires.

"No' in your dreams, you say?" Anger made Bran push away from the bedpost. A muscle leapt in his jaw and he narrowed his eyes, grateful that the blue mist hid her pert nipples from view.

He took a step toward her, his gaze locked on hers. "Did you know there are women who live and breathe to bed a Hebridean chieftain?"

"You're a ghost."

"Aye, so I am."

"A MacNeil."

"That, too." Clan pride flared in Bran's chest. "A greater race ne'er walked this earth."

"The MacNeils are—" She didn't finish, clamping her lips instead. Her lovely blue eyes glinted dangerously. "I am going to waken now. When I do, you'll no longer be here and I won't remember this nightmare."

"I have a better idea." Bran strode forward, drawn by the way her agitated breaths made her breasts jig on each inhale and driven by a mad urge to kiss her. "As you're here, and we're both naked—"

She vanished before he could reach for her. The room was empty as it'd ever been.

Bran tossed aside the bed cushion. Wheeling about, he scanned the shadows, but he knew she was gone. Nor did it surprise him to see the Heartbreaker leaning benignly against the wall, the blade's cold steel and crystal pommel stone gleaming dimly.

Bran scowled and rammed both hands through his hair. His heart thundered wildly. Cold sweat spilled down his brow and even his palms were slicked damp. Frustration and fury took care of the problem at his loins, but even as certain swellings receded, blood roared so hotly in his ears he could scarce hear himself think.

Though—he had to admit—at the moment, not thinking was a very good thing.

Every thought to have crossed his mind since the Heartbreaker's warning in the bailey sent terrible shivers slashing down his spine.

And he, Bran of Barra, Hebridean chieftain, appreciator of women, and Highlander to the bone, was not a man to be known for suffering shivers.

He was a lusty soul.

Broad grins, hearty laughter, and a ravenous appetite were his particulars.

He'd never been in love.

Not sure why that truth popped into his mind, he returned to bed and pulled a pillow over his head. A precaution should the closing of his eyes summon the naked American. He wasn't of a mind to see her again. Not this night or any other.

The Heartbreaker be damned.

The blade chooses its master.

His grandfather's words came back to him, bringing along a slew of other wisdoms credited to the half-mythic sword. Whispered tales of awe he'd heard in his early years as a lad. The most troubling being his grandsire's insistence that he couldn't promise the sword to Bran. According to clan belief, the Heartbreaker sought the hand to wield it, seeking a new MacNeil in each generation and magically placing itself in the path of the chosen.

But Bran hadn't cared for clan legend.

He'd wanted the sword. So he'd tagged after his grandfather always, begging to be the blade's next master. Until at the sage age of four-and-ten, he'd faced his first worthy opponent in swordplay—a well-loved cousin several years his senior—and upon drawing his blade to meet his cousin's challenge, he'd found not his own sword but the great shining Heartbreaker clutched in his hand.

The blade had been his ever since.

Leastways the ghostly sword whiling so innocently in

the shadows. Without doubt the true blade had sought other MacNeil masters through the ages, but Bran had always felt a special affinity with the sword.

Theirs was a special bond.

Even in ghostdom, he'd prided himself on keeping the Heartbreaker at his side.

Now he wished he'd ne'er laid eyes on the legendary sword. But he had and he could feel its powerful presence now, calling to him from across the darkened room. Not that he was going to risk another eye crack. He knew his bedchamber well enough to know there was a strange humminglike thickness to the air. A weird quality he'd noticed earlier, upon retiring, and one that seemed to intensify now.

Even the fat night candle on his bedside table gave off an odd hissing sound. And without looking, he knew the richly patterned tapestries on his walls were rippling with movement. He could hear the swishes and rustlings of their costly, heavy silk. A most curious phenomenon given that the wind wasn't all that strong and he'd taken care to bolt the room's window shutters.

Equally unsettling, he'd let the fire burn down, and the cold smell of peat-and-wood ash that filled the room was overlaid by a fresh, delicate scent unlike any he'd ever encountered except the few times ghostly business had forced him to sift himself into the realm of the present.

It was an exceptionally clean scent that he now recognized. The American's scent, lingering to torment him. Light as a sun-washed spring meadow and with just enough lily of the valley to make a man sigh in appreciation.

Bran favored a scowl to sighing.

He also did his best to ignore the bewitching fragrance. Unfortunately, the harder he tried, the more the scent wafted beneath his nose. He considered burying his face deeper in his pillow. As a ghost, it wasn't as if he needed to worry about harming himself.

But he did wish to do something to keep from breathing in the haunting perfume. Especially since he had a good idea what was causing the scent to remain.

The Heartbreaker surely felt his resistance and was enlisting every otherworldly trick in its steely, gempommeled arsenal to remind him of his destiny.

A fate he had no intention of claiming, so he rolled onto his side and pulled a hand down over his face before he could groan. Groaning, like shivers, was not a trait a Highland man acknowledged gladly.

It was a weakness to be avoided at all costs.

As were American women of the modern day, be they naked or otherwise.

No matter how delicious they smelled.

Or how they tasted . . .

"Hellfire and damnation!" Bran sat bolt upright and glared into the shadowy room, certain his sword would catch blue fire again any moment. Or worse, that the nameless American siren would reappear, this time without her mysterious veil of glittery blue light.

Next time—he just knew—she'd be naked without any such wizardry cloaking her. And then he'd be hardpressed to resist her.

That, too, he knew.

And the truth of it scared him to the marrow.

The sudden pounding on his door angered him. Muttering, he leapt from the bed and crossed the room in three long strides to yank the door wide and see who would dare intrude on his privacy. He'd pleaded head pains and given express orders that no one was to disturb him.

Of course, the grinning fool standing in the doorway didn't consider himself bound by such wishes.

Saor MacSwain thought much of himself.

In ghostdom as he had in life.

"You'd best have a good reason for bothering me." Bran gave his friend a soured look. "I was sleeping."

"Say you?" Saor cocked a brow and peered past him at the mussed bedsheets. "If you come back to the hall, I daresay you'll rest better thereafter."

Bran jutted his jaw. "This is my thereafter, if you've forgotten."

"Faugh!" Saor laughed. "I came to fetch you, thinking you've forgotten that Serafina is performing her dance-of-the-veils for us this e'en."

Bran blinked. He *had* forgotten Serafina's promise of a dance.

A dusky Saracen beauty who only rarely visited his hall, she was well received when she did. Her veil dance—and her willingness to delight Bran's manly friends in any manner they desired—made her one of the most popular and sought-after ghostesses in the other realm.

Bran admired her, too.

The last time she'd performed in his hall, she'd ended her dance on his lap. He could still feel how she'd slid her long, shapely legs around him. The sinuous rotations of her naked buttocks across his thighs and then the sleek silken heat of her wetness as she'd lowered herself onto him. He recalled, too, how her large, dark-nippled breasts had bounced and swayed. How, ultimately, she'd leaned close to rub them against his chest as she rode him.

Without doubt, she was the most skilled seductress he'd ever encountered. Just the mention of her name was enough to send a rush of heat pulsing into his groin.

Usually.

Tonight, the thought of her didn't even bring a single twitch.

His trusty male parts—and, indeed, all of him—remained as cold as the chill night air seeping in through the shutter slats.

A discreet downward glance proved it. Bed-naked as he was, there could be no mistaking.

Bran scowled. "Give Serafina my felicitations and my regrets." He reached to rub the back of his neck, hoping Saor would believe him. "The pain in my head this e'en is too great for even her *wonders* to be of service."

"You truly wish to stay abed? Alone?" Saor's grin faded. He flicked a quick glance down the dimly lit corridor, back toward the turnpike stair. "Serafina will no' be pleased."

"Perhaps these"—Bran flicked his fingers to produce two gold coins—"will sweeten her disappointment."

"Aye, and the sun will fall from the sky on the morrow." Saor looked skeptical, but he took the coins.

He also eyed Bran a bit longer, then shrugged and turned on his heel to sprint down the passageway. He vanished a few paces from the arched entry to the stair tower, apparently preferring to sift himself back into the hall rather than take the narrow, winding stairs.

Any other time, Bran would have thrown back his head and laughed. He certainly understood Saor's eagerness to return to Serafina's side.

But his own lack of desire to be there troubled him more.

Indeed, it took all his control not to slam his fist into

the doorjamb. Something he was even more tempted to do when he turned back to his room and caught the faint glimmer of blue winking at him from deep inside the Heartbreaker's charmed pommel stone.

"Hellfire and damnation," he growled, not for the first time that night.

If the sword heard him—or cared—it gave no sign.

Sadly, his gut told him plenty.

Disappointing, or even angering, Serafina was the least of his worries. In truth, his troubles hadn't even begun. And when they did, they'd be worse than anything he'd faced in seven hundred long years.

Much worse.

Gods help him.

Chapter 3

"Ghosts?"

Margo Menlove's voice rose on the word. Her eyes rounded and she grabbed Mindy's arms, squeezing tight. "A whole troop of them here at the Folly—bearded, kilt-swinging ghosts—and you didn't tell me!"

"I'm telling you now." Mindy broke free of her sister's grasp and went to stand beside the kitchen's antique refectory table. Its solidity soothed her. As did the ultramodern kitchen appliances lining the thick stone walls. Gleaming state-of-the-art ranges and refrigerators didn't smack of spooks and things that go bump in the night.

Better yet, the quiet hum of the dishwasher made it difficult to imagine the *zing* of a sword being whipped out of its scabbard.

The lingering scent of breakfast bacon helped, too.

Mindy doubted ghosts had much of an appetite.

Even so, she was grateful that no ancestral portraits hung in the huge barrel-vaulted space.

Only the massive double-arched fireplace hinted at the room's medieval origins, but she took care not to glance in that direction. The Folly's staff—invisible and discreet as in the Age of Victorians—took great pains in keeping the kitchen fire blazing, and its crackling, well-doing flames were just a tad too atmospheric.

Under the circumstances, that was.

Mindy shivered.

She also refused to think about the flicker of eerie blue light she'd seen earlier—a large man's silhouette reflected near the warm glow of the fire. Nor would she dwell on the faint skirl of pipes she'd heard coming from one of the kitchen's darker, more echoey corners.

Above all, she wasn't going to mention last night's dream. Margo didn't need to know everything. And she chose to credit the incident to nerves.

She rubbed her arms, determined to suppress the chills sweeping her.

No mean feat, considering.

Mindy swallowed, her gaze sliding briefly to the wall next to the kitchen hearth. A collection of the last century's cooking equipment hung there. Highly polished copper pots and kettles, preserving pans, and jelly molds winked brightly, attracting the eye. But nothing stirred. No dancing shadows and certainly no man's silhouette. But the fire glow did cast a weird reddish tint on the basket of aromatic juniper branches that the castle staff enjoyed tossing onto the flames to scent the room.

Even so, Mindy knew what she'd seen.

The big man's outline, insubstantial and fleeting as it'd been, had reminded her instantly of Bran of Barra. The castle's burly, fourteenth-century builder hadn't exactly accosted her as the other MacNeil ghosts had done, but he *had* glared at her from inside his portrait.

Heaven help her if he really had invaded her sleep.

Her pulse quickened just to remember.

She also recalled that his portrait sword was the

longest, most wicked looking of all Hunter's fierce oil-painted-cum-real-live-ghostie forebears. It might have been her imagination, but she was pretty sure the silhouette man had worn an exceptionally long blade low by his hip.

A chill sped down her spine.

Had there really been a time she'd romanticized men with swords? Foolish days when she'd secretly thought of kilted men with swords as walking orgasms?

She closed her eyes and bit her lip, knowing it was true.

Wishing it weren't, she trailed her fingers along the thick, age-smoothed edge of the table. A ploy to keep her sister from noticing that her hand trembled. She glanced toward the nearest window, not surprised to see rain beginning to pelt the ancient leaded panes. The stone mullion window surrounds already gleamed blackly with damp.

Mist curled through the nearby pines, hovering low, and making the dark woods look even bleaker than usual, the wet morning drearier than need be. Mindy stifled a grimace. For all intents and purposes, the Folly might already be on some godforsaken Scottish island.

Only Scotland, she was sure, would be much worse.

"You should have phoned me." Margo was in her face again. "I would've come right away."

Mindy started. "I didn't want to bother you."

"Bother me?" Margo's brows arched.

Mindy flicked a toast crumb off the table. "I knew you were busy."

She also knew that if she'd called Margo in the middle of her four-day Ye Olde Pagan Times–sponsored Gettysburg Ghostwatch Tour, she would've risked having her sister arrive on the Folly's doorstep with an entire busload of camera-happy, EMF-meter-toting paranormal zealots.

It would've been like living inside a goldfish bowl.

With the *Twilight Zone* theme music piped in to set the scene.

"You didn't want me showing up with ghost hunters in tow." Margo proved how perceptive she was. "That's why you didn't call me."

"And if it was?" Mindy flipped back her hair. "You know what I think about woo-woo wackos."

Margo laughed. "Does that include me?"

"You're my sister."

"Yes, I am." Margo tapped her with a French-manicured fingernail. "The very one who always smells candle grease and woodsmoke in here no matter"—she wrinkled her nose, sniffing—"how much bacon you fry for breakfast or how many gallons of Kona coffee you brew.

"This kitchen is trapped in the past and always will be." She glanced around, her eyes lighting with excitement. "It doesn't matter how many snazzy stainless steel fridges and whatnots you haul in here. This room is a portal—I've always known it."

Mindy flicked another toast crumb off the table.

It was an invisible one this time.

"The ghosts were in the long gallery," she argued, not at all ready to hear anything odd about the kitchen.

"Do you think they can't move around?" The gleam in Margo's eyes intensified. "I can feel whole battalions of spirits tracking through here. Maybe they're medieval servants, cooks, and little spit boys"—she looked around, warming to her topic—"or perhaps just hungry clansmen coming in to raid the midnight larder."

"That's ridiculous." Mindy rolled her eyes.

"Medieval Highlanders were big strong men." Margo sent her long-lashed gaze toward the closed door of the buttery. "I'm sure they had appetites to match."

"If they're here and hungry, they can have whatever they want as long as they leave me alone." Mindy folded her arms, starting to get cross.

Margo hopped up onto the table, swinging her legs. "The time for that is past. It's you disrupting their peace now. They won't be pleased to see you bringing in workmen and movers. Ghosts never like such things. The noise and—"

"The ghosts are insisting I do this!" Mindy's head was beginning to hurt. "They appeared to me. They demanded I have the Folly dismantled and—"

Several copper milk cans artfully arranged in a corner toppled over, crashing into an equally ancient butter churn. The clatter—with ensuing echo—was deafening and brought a huge grin to Margo's face.

"See?" She scissored her legs gleefully. "The castle spirits don't want you disturbing them. The Folly is their sanctuary. They're letting you know they want to stay here. They consider Bucks County their home now."

Mindy snorted. "The *Caspers* in the long gallery made it clear what they think of Bucks County and"— she glanced at the door arch, half expecting to see them huddled in the shadows, eavesdropping—"where they want to be. I'm taking them there, to Barra, and then I'm heading for Florida."

"*Florida?*" Margo sounded horrified.

Mindy quite agreed, but kept the sentiment to herself.

She did cross the kitchen to fetch a platter of locally made farmhouse Cheddar, sliced salami, and a loaf of crusty French bread.

"Here"—she plonked the tray down on the table,

next to her sister—"eat something before hunger puts any more crazy notions in your head."

"But . . . Florida?" Margo popped a salami slice into her mouth. "You wanted to go to Hawaii. Settle on Maui or, at least, Oahu's North Shore." She swallowed the salami and reached for another piece. "I even caught you scanning the Internet for homes in Haleiwa and Waialua. You—"

"My budget won't allow a North Shore rental, much less the kind of house I was hoping to buy." Mindy started to cut a piece of Cheddar, then set down the cheese knife.

Not surprisingly, she wasn't hungry.

She did frown. "Florida is my only option. It's sunny, warm, and affordable. I can stay with airline friends in Tampa until I've saved enough to rent a place of my own. If Global will let me start flying anywhere near my old salary, I should do okay.

"I'll visit Hawaii on my vacations." She shrugged, the prospect making her heart sink. "It won't be so bad. As long as I'm away from rain and cold mist, I'll be—"

"You'll be miserable." Margo jumped off the table. "I have a better idea. You stay here and let Ye Olde Pagan Times take advantage of your ghosties. Look how many people flock to our Gettysburg tours. The tours are booked solid months in advance, sometimes a whole year. A cadre of angry Highland ghosts in a real Scottish castle will make you a mint. And"—she waved a piece of bread in the air—"you'll be able to keep every dime of the fortune Hunter left you."

Mindy waited until her sister ran out of steam. "This might be a real Scottish castle, but it's in the wrong place. And the angry ghosts are going to be volatile, livid ghosts if I don't do what they want."

"But—"

"There aren't any buts."

"You're making a huge mistake." Margo adjusted the silk paisley scarf wrapped stylishly around her neck. "We could also call in some of the TV ghost-busting teams. Hollywood might even engage the place for film settings. Or you could lease turret rooms to recluse writers. The possibilities are—"

"A moot point." Mindy remained firm. "And the only mistake I made was helping Hunter with his seat belt."

"Then walk away." Margo proved she was just as relentless. "Let the castle fall to romantic ruin and take the money he's left you and run."

Mindy went to make more coffee. She needed caffeine. She wasn't about to tell Margo that she had tried to leave. Her sister would thrill to hear about how the ghosties had flanked the treelined drive down the castle hill. How they'd shaken their swords at her and, worst of all, how the three gang leaders, Roderick, Geordie, and Silvanus, had waited for her at the bottom of the road. Her car's headlights had picked them out standing in front of the wrought-iron gateway between the twin entrance lodges.

They'd armed themselves with long spears.

Deadly, wicked-looking, fourteen-foot-long, steel-headed lances that looked as if they'd come straight off the set of *Braveheart*.

Worst of all, just when she'd thought to plow right through them, the gate's remote sensor refused to work. She'd been effectively locked inside the property, much to the three ghosts' amusement.

The one called Silvanus had thrown back his head and laughed.

Then he'd disappeared into thin air.

Only to reappear in the backseat of her car!

She'd seen him grinning at her in the rearview mirror, the memory curdling her blood even now.

Her car radio had blared bagpipe music all the way back up the castle's graveled drive.

The radio wasn't turned on.

And—Mindy knew—her sister wasn't going to listen to reason. But she did understand cold, hard facts. Margo might dress like a model out of the pages of *English Country Living*, but Ye Olde Pagan Times paid her peanuts. Margo's chic look was pure good taste and a healthy dash of bargain hunting, combined with second-hand thrift.

So while Mindy waited for her coffee to brew, she scooped up an armful of papers and scribbled notes and carried them back across the kitchen. She dumped them on the table, then stepped back and wiped her hands.

"Here's why I can't run anywhere." She snatched a yellow-lined notepad and handed it to her sister. "I've told you how the ghosts threatened to follow me anywhere I go. These figures"—she tapped the top sheet of the notepad, indicating lines of numbers and her own looping script—"will show you exactly how much it's going to cost to have the Folly dismantled, transported across the Atlantic, and then reassembled on the Hebridean isle of Barra."

Mindy folded her arms, waiting as Margo scanned the jottings.

It didn't take long for the color to drain from Margo's face. "This is an astronomical sum."

"Uh-huh." Mindy nodded. "Once all the costs are tallied, not much will remain. Now you see"—she went to pour their coffee—"why I have to go back to flying and why I'll be moving to Florida and not Hawaii."

"But this is so unfair!" Margo waved aside the coffee Mindy offered her.

"Everything happens for a reason." Mindy took a sip of her own Kona blend. "Maybe it isn't my karma to be rich and independent and live the good life in Hawaii. Isn't that what you always say?" She set down her cup and summoned what she hoped was an untroubled smile. "That all our ups and downs are part of the big karmic cycle?"

"Yes, but—"

Mindy pressed a finger to her sister's lips. "No buts, remember?"

Margo swatted her hand away. "Well, it's just that—"

"No *it's just that*s, either." Mindy sighed inwardly. She knew better than to let her sister get on a tangent. "I love flying, anyway. It isn't as if—"

"These quotes can't be right." Margo frowned at the notepad. "You could send the castle to the moon and back for this kind of money."

Mindy shook her head. "I checked everywhere imaginable. Those figures are the most competitive and they came from the experts. One of the Global captains I know has a brother who works on the Acquisitions Committee at the Metropolitan Museum in New York. No one knows more about such things.

"They buy up everything from Tuscan villas to entire French palaces and bring it all back to New York, stone by stone. Apparently"—she paused to glance over her shoulder, half certain she'd felt someone standing behind her, listening—"they even keep secret warehouses throughout the city to hold such treasures until they decide what to do with them."

Mindy tucked a strand of hair behind her ear, remembering her phone conversations with the museum's luminaries. "The Metropolitan's board of trustees kindly recommended several removal firms best suited for"—she looked at her sister and forced a smile—"such a monumental task as I'm about to undertake."

Margo brightened. "Maybe the Metropolitan will want the Folly? Let them deal with—"

"The castle isn't for sale." Mindy drained her coffee. "It will be dismantled, each stone and every stick of furniture and what have you packed in straw, acid-free paper, and Bubble Wrap, then shipped *home* in at least ten thousand crates."

"I still say you're making a mistake." Margo glanced at the very spot where Mindy was sure someone invisible was standing. "Even Madame Zelda said it was your destiny to live in this castle. She didn't say anything about you getting rid of it. She—"

"That was in the early days when I'd just met Hunter." Mindy couldn't believe Margo would bring Ye Olde Pagan Times' resident fortune-teller into it. "Besides, we both know she only tells people what they want to hear. And"—she couldn't resist raising a finger—"her name isn't Madame Zelda of Bulgaria. She's Marta Lopez and she's Puerto Rican."

"She's accurate all the same." Margo helped herself to another salami slice and then slung her oversized leather handbag over her shoulder. "You did move in here not long after she read your tarot. And"—she went to the door arch, pausing just outside the shadows—"she was right about Hunter. She said your one true love would be a big, burly Scotsman who favored kilts and was a notorious ladies' man."

Mindy tried not to snort.

She started to remind Margo that the fortune-teller also said the Highlander would carry a sword, but she caught herself in time and just glared.

Glaring was good.

She did so until her sister waved an airy good-bye and disappeared into the narrow corridor's gloom. But the instant the tap-tapping of Margo's heels on the stone flags faded and she heard the castle door fall shut with a muffled *thunk*, the glare slipped from her face.

Damn her sister for reminding her of Marta Lopez/ Madame Zelda's predictions.

And double damn herself for remembering the bit about the sword.

Hunter wouldn't have touched one with a ten-foot pole.

He'd claimed they gave him the willies and he'd even considered selling the Folly's entire armory collection of medieval weaponry. Something he would surely have done if his parents' testament hadn't forbidden the sale of artifacts they considered part of their family heritage.

Mindy shivered, the fortune-teller's words echoing in her mind.

They were coming back clearer by the moment, reminding her of things she'd rather forget. Like how Madame Zelda's eyes had widened when she'd professed to see the Highlander's sword, claiming she'd never seen one quite that long.

Then she'd gone all coy. She'd smiled secretly and lowered her voice, looking at Mindy from beneath her lashes as she'd declared that other parts of this Scottish paragon would be extralong, as well.

The remembered words hit Mindy like a fist to the gut.

Hunter had been one of the least endowed men she'd ever seen.

He was tall and dashing. His smile wicked enough to

charm women out of trees. He knew his way around a mattress and was so skilled with his fingers and tongue that he should have carried a license. But big and burly wasn't an apt description.

However, the plaid-draped, coppery-haired man standing in profile to her near the kitchen fire, eating what looked like a beef rib, was definitely big and burly.

In fact, he defined the words.

At least this time he wasn't naked save for a medieval pillow.

Even so, Mindy felt her world begin to spin.

She blinked and knuckled her eyes, but he didn't go away. Far from it, he simply munched on his beef rib, staring into the fire all the while. Mindy pressed a hand to her breast, unable to look away from him.

Huge, powerfully built, and rough-hewn, he had the somewhat crumpled appearance of a man who'd just crawled out of bed. Or, she was sure in his case, off some scratchy medieval sleeping pallet. Without doubt, the thick, ancient wool of such coarse bedding, or even the prickly bits of straw on the floor, wouldn't have bothered him.

He looked that tough.

He was also a ghost.

Though there was nothing see-through, flimsy-whimsy about him. He had an air of brute strength, positively oozed power, and unless Mindy was mistaken, his nose was just a tad crooked. He looked real, solid, and—so far—wholly unaware of her presence.

His entire attention seemed focused on devouring his beef rib. An activity that disproved her assumption that ghosts didn't have appetites. This ghost clearly did. And he wasn't just any ghost, either. She didn't need to see the wicked-looking, overly long sword at his hip to speculate as to his identity.

She knew exactly who he was. He was Bran of Barra.

"Oh, God—it's you!" Mindy backed up against the refectory table, shock and recognition slamming into her like the punch from an iron fist.

The ghost whipped around to face her, his beef rib flying from his fingers. A torch—*a torch!*—flared on the smoke-blackened wall behind him and a shower of iridescent blue sparks burst from the crystal pommel stone of his sword. The bright glow of the sparkles, and the blazing torch flame, illuminated a kitchen that wasn't the one Mindy knew.

Bran of Barra knew it well.

Possession—and fury—stood all over him as he fisted his hands on his hips and gaped at her. "By the rood!" he roared, his warrior's body bunching with muscle. His stare flashed down the length of her, then snapped back to her face, his own wide-eyed and incredulous.

"You shred my last nerve, wench! Can a man no' eat in peace?" He shot a glance at the half-gnawed beef rib.

Mindy glanced at it, too, feeling sick.

Her heart might be racing, but there was nothing wrong with her eyes. It was plain to see that the rib rested on icky, matted rushes and not the kitchen's so-clean-you-could-eat-off-it highly polished stone floor.

She gulped.

Bran of Barra took a step forward. "I dinnae ken how you found your way in here, but you'd best be gone before someone else sees you." He came closer and flung out an arm, indicting the door arch.

It was an arch Mindy recognized, but one that appeared so different in the blackness of deep shadow and dancing medieval torchlight.

Bran of Barra looked even more medieval.

At least six feet four of pure Highland testosterone, he was simply overwhelming. His portrait's twinkling blue eyes and roguish grin didn't do him justice.

The dream image came close, but now . . . in a riled state, he was flat-out magnificent.

Mindy stared at him, mouth dry and knees knocking.

The words *dinnae ken*—and everything else he said in his rich, buttery-smooth burr—hung in the air between them. His voice was deep and real, almost tactile. It was a sensual touch sliding around her. The deliciously sexy Scottish burr mocked and taunted, making her pulse leap and igniting sparks of female awareness even as every living inch of her quivered and trembled with nerves.

She'd vowed to never again be moved by anything Scottish.

That she noticed his burr made her face flame and her head pound. Admitting that his rugged *I can toss you over my shoulder, carry you up the tower stairs, and ravish you* good looks were appealing was even more galling.

She'd been kilted and jilted once.

She wouldn't be hoodwinked again. Most especially, she wouldn't be fooled by a seven-hundred-years-dead Scotsman. Even if he did have a melt-her-panties burr, she was immune and would stay that way.

As if he knew, his eyes narrowed and—shades of *Twilight Zone*—his sword's crystal pommel stone began to glimmer with a pulsing blue radiance.

"Damnation!" He clamped a hand over the gemstone, his scowl turning fierce. "Away with you, whoe'er you are! There are others about who'd do more than just glower if they chanced upon you!"

It was the wrong thing to say.

Mindy straightened, heat scalding her cheeks.

No Scotsman, alive, ghostly, or otherwise, was ever going to *do* her again.

"I'm Mindy Menlove"—she lifted her chin to shoot daggers at him—"and I've already met the others, so you can't frighten me with them."

"What others?" He flashed a glance at the door arch, his brows snapping together as he scanned the shadows. "Was Saor one of them?"

"Say who?" Mindy blinked. She started to tell him about the long gallery of ghosts, but before she could open her mouth, he was right in front of her. His big body blotted everything except his broad, tartan-draped chest and shoulders that were almost indecently muscled.

The hot-eyed look he gave her *was* indecent.

So much so that her breath caught and her knees almost buckled.

She bit her lip and tried to scoot away, but he caught her wrist and jerked her close against him. So close, she could feel the rough weave of his plaid, the rock-marble hardness of his chest, and—she hardly believed it, considering—the soft brush of his breath on her cheek. She could also smell him. The bracing scent of cold, fresh air flooded her senses. It was a heady, outdoorsy scent laced with just a dash of wool, woodsmoke, and pure unadulterated man.

Intoxicating, and unlike anything in a bottle.

In fact, she was sure men would pay any price if such a scent were on the market.

Too bad the scent belonged to a man who wasn't a real, live man.

As if he sensed the thought, he circled his thumb across the sensitive skin of her inner wrist, his touch as real and warm as the living day. It also sent a rush of tingly shivers streaking up her arm.

Mindy's heart galloped.

He grinned.

"You're a ghost!" She tried to jerk free and couldn't.

His grip was like iron.

His gaze heated again and he stepped back just enough to sweep her with the kind of look that would have made her go all soft and hot under other circumstances. It did make her feel as though she should cover herself. For one crazy moment, she feared she might even be naked. After all, if she was standing here conversing with a ghost, who knew what else was possible? But then his eyes glinted with some indefinable emotion and he released her. He stepped back only long enough to brace his hands on the table on either side of her, effectively caging her within his arms.

"Aye, I'm a ghost." He sounded proud. "We've already discussed that. And it's no' me we're discussing. Saor, and others here, would plunder your sweetness in a trice. They're well-lusted, insatiable souls who'd waste no time showing you that lips as lush as yours are meant for kissing or that—"

"Kissing was the last thing the other ghosts wanted." Mindy swallowed. He'd brought his face so close to hers that he could easily kiss her now if he wished to do so.

She feared he might.

He'd certainly meant to in her dream.

As for now ...

She could see the rapid beat of his pulse at his throat. She also didn't miss the slight jerking of muscle in his jaw or the wiry, copper-bright hairs plainly visible where his plaid dipped low across his powerful chest. The hairs glistened like gold in the torchlight.

Swallowing, she tore her gaze away, forcing her mind to the bandy-legged, bushy-browed gallery ghosts with their scowls and shouted threats.

"The other ghosts yelled at me." She blurted the words, nerves making her voice rise. Chest hair was so her undoing. She took a deep breath, willing herself to think only of the crusty old ghosts. "They rushed forward to surround me, rattling their swords and—gah!"

She jumped, her eyes widening as an enormous gray beast streaked past them to pounce on the discarded beef rib. Clearly a dog—though much larger and more shaggy than any canine she'd ever seen—the animal hunkered down near the hearth fire to devour his bone.

He kept his gaze on them and as he did so, Mindy would've sworn he was grinning.

He was certainly in beef-rib-induced ecstasy.

"He's Gibbie." The sudden warmth in Bran of Barra's voice startled her. Actually, it would've melted her if he hadn't been, well, Bran of Barra.

Mindy frowned.

He was a Scottish MacNeil. And worst of all, he was a ghost. As was his dog, undoubtedly. Their relationship shouldn't matter a fig to her. But the way they were looking at each other squeezed her heart.

"He's yours?" She spoke the obvious. The dog's enthusiastic tail swishes and the devotion in his eyes proved their bond.

"Gibbie's been mine for over seven hundred years." Bran kept his gaze on the dog as he spoke, his expression softening. "He was mine in life and then"—he paused to shake his head, as if at a wonder—"when I was no more, he was there to greet me, tail wagging and happy as you see him now. We've been together ever since."

"So dogs do . . ." Mindy couldn't finish.

She blinked instead, and then swallowed against the rising heat in her throat. She loved dogs and had always wanted one. But flying wasn't conductive to having a four-legged friend. And Hunter wouldn't allow dogs at the Folly, claiming that he was allergic to dander.

Bran of Barra looked as if he could get high on the smell of wet dog and laugh out loud at the sight of muddy paw tracks on a just swept and polished floor. Even if the rush-strewn floor they were presently standing on looked mired by worse muck than mere mud.

Staring at that floor now, and at the furry beast blissfully cracking his bone, was enough to bring Mindy's world crashing down around her.

She might have been forced to accept ghosts, both see-through ones and this newest, muscle-ripped, and capable-of-grabbing-her-wrist-in-an-iron-lock-grip variety, but time slips or whatever altered the appearance of the kitchen was outside her belief system.

Time travel, sifting place, and whatnot belonged in novels. As did sexy Scottish ghosts and—it had to be said—their tongue-lolling, four-legged cohorts.

Mindy closed her eyes, sure she was losing it.

But when she looked again, nothing had changed. Bran of Barra was still crowding her space, trapping her against a kitchen table that, although of a similar size and sturdiness, was much less worn than the Folly's antique, age-smoothed refectory table.

And Gibbie the ghost dog was still gnawing happily on his beef rib.

Mindy took a deep breath and released it slowly. "So dogs . . ." She tried again, only to have the words jam in her throat.

"Aye, they do . . . wait for us," Bran of Barra confirmed, looking away from his dog to pierce her with another heated blue stare. "You can take a lesson from Gibbie. Something you'll heed if you're wise."

"If I'm wise?" Mindy bristled.

His swift reversal back to towering menace banished any burgeoning sense of sympathy she might've felt upon his dog's arrival. Especially with him clearly set to use the beast to frighten her.

"I think you're mistaken," she said, taking up a defiant stance.

She tossed back her hair, trying to pretend he wasn't a ghostly Highlander, but the Texan who'd once planted himself on a first-class armrest and refused to budge from an overbooked flight.

The memory of security carrying him off the plane gave her courage.

"Some might say I'd be wiser"—she lifted her chin, using her coolest tone—"to stop talking to a ghost."

"Aye, you would." To her surprise, he grinned.

Stepping back at last, he flicked his fingers to produce another well-roasted, succulent beef rib. "Ho, Gibbie!" he called, holding out the tidbit. "Show the lass how ravenous you are."

Gibbie leapt up and flew toward them, the gnawed bone forgotten. He slid to a skidding halt at Bran's feet, his entire body quivering with excitement.

In a blink, he plopped onto his haunches and raised his paw, raking the air.

"That's a good laddie." Bran of Barra gave him the new beef rib, which, along with Gibbie, disappeared in a flash as the dog nipped the bone, streaked across the rushes, and then—Mindy's jaw slipped—ran right through the solid stones of the kitchen wall.

Mindy's cool demeanor vanished like a puff of smoke.

Even so, she held her ground.

"If you did that to prove he's a ghost dog, you needn't have bothered." She hoped her voice didn't sound as shaky as she felt. "I already believed you."

"Ah . . ." Bran of Barra hooked his thumbs in his sword belt and rocked back on his heels. "But now you've seen how greedy MacNeil males are. How *ravenous* we can be when a tempting sweetmeat is dangled before us."

"Meaning?" Mindy was sure she didn't want to know.

He grinned and shrugged. But then he sent a pointed look at the door arch.

Mindy followed his gaze and understood at once. He didn't mean what she could see in the archway—the inky shadows and a single, smoking wall torch—but the noises issuing from beyond the kitchen's entry.

A low swell of raucous voices and other assorted up-roar, sounds that she hadn't noticed, rose from a near distance. But she heard now, her ears catching bursts of male and female laughter, the unmistakable *clink* of tankards, and the scrape of wooden bench legs on stone. It was the kind of mayhem one associated with medieval merrymaking.

And beneath it all—the realization struck terror in Mindy's heart—came the ceaseless roar of the sea, the sound of waves crashing over rocks and receding.

Mindy's blood chilled.

No one loved the ocean more than she did, but there wasn't any pounding surf anywhere near Bucks County, Pennsylvania. Nor did the waves she heard sound like any she knew. The noise was real and even recognizable, but more distant than if she'd pressed her ear to a seashell.

It was as if she was listening over a space that couldn't be measured in miles.

Like—Mindy swallowed—she was hearing through time.

A denial rose in her throat, but before she could form the words, a loud skirl of pipes and the scream of fiddles filled the chill, smoky air. Somewhere dogs barked and—she was sure—a woman screeched, then laughed. The sounds of vigorous dancing followed, stamping feet and lots of manly whoops.

Mindy began to tremble.

"Yon is no place for Americans." Bran of Barra spoke the words close to her ear, the soft brush of his lips against her hair almost a kiss.

"Begone, Mindy Menlove, before one of my men decides to prove it to you."

"You don't understand." She whipped around to argue, amazed her legs still held her. "I want nothing more than . . ."

The words died in her throat.

Bran of Barra was gone.

So were the floor rushes and the soot smears that had blackened the kitchen walls. Vanished, too, were the torches. And the only sound besides the patter of rain was the steady hum of the dishwasher.

That, and the racing of her heart.

A soft footfall behind her and—she started—the faintest rustle of wool.

"Remember Gibbie and his bone, lass." The words hushed past her. "You've been warned."

And she had.

Not that it mattered.

She was already up to her ears in paranormal madness and something told her ghost dogs, sounds of merrymaking, and waves that weren't there were just the beginning.

As for Bran of Barra . . .

He didn't fool her for an instant. It wasn't his high-spirited friends and their carouse that she needed to worry about.

It was him.

Chapter 4

Bran of Barra stood before his kitchen cook fire and wondered how in the blazes an American named Mindy Menlove had found her way into his keep. He couldn't shake the damnable feeling that her presence in his kitchens went beyond the sword's magic that made her shimmer inside the Heartbreaker's blue glow in his bailey and then—he shuddered—within his own bedchamber walls.

He ran a hand through his hair and cast a sideways glance at Gibbie, half hoping his longtime friend would provide an answer to the riddle. But the ghost dog simply wagged his tail, clearly expecting another meaty beef rib. Knowing Gibbie would keep his unblinking canine stare pinned on him until he produced one, Bran did just that. He flicked his fingers to conjure a succulent bone, which he tossed to Gibbie before letting out a long, defeated sigh.

If only his cares could be so easily remedied.

But a great mystery was afoot and he didn't have any answers.

Never before had a modern woman slipped into his world. He used all his skill and ghostly craft to keep Mac-

Neil's Tower as it'd been in his day. And just as he knew the tip of a sword from its hilt or a clump of heather from a thornbush, he'd damty sure know if he'd sifted himself into her time. But he hadn't gone anywhere. The lass had appeared in his kitchens. Here at MacNeil's Tower and on his own beloved Isle of Barra. And, this time, she'd done so without being swathed in a mysterious blue light. Somehow she'd breached the delicate veil that hid his realm from the living.

It was an action that struck terror into his heart. He stroked his beard and felt his pulse skitter, his gut tighten and twist. That her fresh and delicate lily-of-the-valley scent lingered in the air to taunt him only made it worse. But he was most especially alarmed because he was certain that she wasn't just any American female.

She was the lass he'd seen twice now.

Bran swallowed hard, not at all pleased that his life, for want of a better word, had gone so disastrously awry. Yet there could be no doubt that Mindy Menlove was the vision maid shown to him by the Heartbreaker's unholy magic.

And unless he'd lost his fine ear for accents, she hailed from that *Pen-seal*-where'er place that boded such ill for medieval Highlanders.

As a Hebridean Highlander—a braw and respected chieftain of the Isles—he would surely prove even more irresistible to such a female. There wasn't a woman born who didn't melt in the presence of an Islesman. He couldn't imagine Mindy Menlove would prove immune.

Most especially with a name like Menlove, by all the tartaned saints!

Bran felt a chill sweep clear to his toes.

Dread seized him and it was all he could do not to

hunch over, brace his hands on his knees, and gulp deep breaths of air to stop the roiling in his innards.

Not that anyone could fault him for such unmanly behavior.

He had ample reason for concern. After all, every one of his ghostly friends who'd had their heads turned by a modern woman had fallen under the spell of a lass of her ilk.

There'd been no exceptions.

Even now, after he'd managed to sift himself away from her, the Heartbreaker's pommel stone still glowed with a soft blue light. And—he was loath to admit it— the crystal seemed to be grinning up at him, almost looking pleased.

Its blue shimmer danced over the kitchen's thick, smoke-blackened walls and even reached into the corners and other dark places of the room, tinting the shadows and casting everything in a glittery, magical light.

Almost as if the fairies and no' one mere American female had laid claim to his home.

Bran shuddered.

The gemstone's luminance was a terrible confirmation of the maid's significance.

Not that he'd deny her appeal. As a Highlander still possessed of the same heated red blood that had made him so lusty in life, he'd have to be blind not to have noted her charms. But he did allow himself the satisfaction of letting his brows snap together in a dark frown.

He could still see the wench before him. His sharp mind's eye captured the cheeky tilt of her chin and her flashing blue eyes. He recalled how she'd tossed back her shining blond hair and then parted her lips ever so provocatively when he'd glared at her. Almost as if she'd expected him to sweep her into his arms and kiss her.

Bran snorted.

Truth was, he *had* almost kissed her.

He'd been tempted to do more.

"Odin's balls!" He growled his favorite curse to the empty room.

He could feel her sweetly curved lips beneath his, knew exactly how her tongue would slide against his in a sinuous, silken tangle. He knew, too, how she'd press herself into him, letting her lush breasts rub against him as she slipped her arms around his neck and tunneled her fingers through his hair.

Bran's mouth went dry and his hands itched to touch her again. He *had* touched her! And it'd been a great mistake because he could recall the smooth warmth of her skin, the gentle beat of her pulse. He imagined holding her wrist now, perhaps replacing his circling thumb with kisses.

Kisses and nuzzles that would lead to . . . Scowling fiercely, he broke off the thought before he drove himself to madness. Without doubt, there was something in the water in *Pen-seal-landia* that turned the womenfolk into sirens. They were living, breathing vixens that no man, alive or otherwise, could resist.

Now he, too, was in danger of being snared by one.

Trouble was, unlike his chiefly friends who'd thrilled to have such females fawn and gush all over them, he enjoyed being a ghost.

He didn't want some American temptress whisking him into her day.

He—Bran of Barra, Hebridean chieftain of great acclaim—was a ghost by choice and with pride.

Yet it weakened his knees to think he couldn't visit his kitchens in the small hours without having an American female materializing before his nose. Havers, but she'd startled him, ruining his night's peace, and stealing his appetite.

Well, she hadn't quite taken his appetite.

He *did* have a voracious one.

And he was still hungry, praise Thor and his thunderbolts!

Beginning to feel better, he cocked his ear, pleased to note that the revelry in his hall remained loud and raucous. The kitchen's thick stone walls blotted much of the noise, but he could still hear the wild skirl of pipes and the vigorous strains of a fiddle.

Just as the occasional hoot and whoop reached him, the joyous burst of female laughter, and—he grinned—the energetic stamp of dancing feet as his friends jigged and whirled to Highland reels.

It was good that they were enjoying themselves.

Bran's grin widened and he rubbed his hands together, determined to do the same.

Only at the moment, his greatest desire wasn't to join the carouse in his hall, but to eat. He might have devoured several fish-and-eel pies and even an entire platter of oysters before he'd sought his bed, but his stomach felt empty now.

Indeed, it rumbled as if he hadn't eaten in days.

So he flexed his fingers and then wriggled them, using his ghostly magic to fill both his hands with perfectly roasted beef ribs, each one meaty, dripping with juices, and smelling delicious.

His mouth began to water.

Like Gibbie, he did love his beef ribs.

But before he could take the first bite, there was a

screech and a crash somewhere above him. Bran scowled and sprinted for the kitchen's torchlit entry, his beef ribs still clutched tightly in his hands. Unfortunately, the moment he gained the archway, Saor came thundering down the stair tower's winding stone steps.

The two men collided.

Bran's beef ribs went flying.

Gibbie and two of the other castle dogs came running. They leapt to catch the bones in the air before they could land on the stone-flagged floor. Only one beef rib escaped their snapping jaws and skittered into the shadows, leaving a trail of grease in its wake.

Bran stared after the disappearing rib and then whipped around to glare at his friend. "God's bones, MacSwain!" Bran roared the words, not caring who heard. "Have you lost your wits?"

"I . . . ah . . . errr." Saor shoved a shaky hand through his hair, glanced over his shoulder.

He'd gone white as a ghost.

Truth be told, he looked as though he'd seen one.

Bran stepped back and jammed his hands on his hips. His mood was now thoroughly ruined. "Have done—out with it." He decided to speak plain. "You look like you've seen a bleeding ghost!"

Bran expected his friend to laugh.

Instead, Saor threw another glance behind him. When he turned back to Bran, he pulled a hand down over his face, knuckled his eyes. "It wasn't me." He leaned close, his voice low. "Did you no' hear the cry and thud abovestairs just now? It was—"

"I heard, aye. But I thought it was you careening down yon steps." Bran flashed a glance at the stair tower's darkness. "Thought you hit your elbow or something and shrieked like a woman."

"Would that I had." Saor's brows drew together. "But you almost have the way of it."

"You stubbed a toe rather than smashing an elbow?" Bran couldn't resist.

The look Saor gave him dashed his levity. "Nae, you loon. I meant the crash and the cry did come from a woman. It was Serafina. She saw three ghosts in the long gallery."

Bran snorted. "Last I looked"—he thrust his arms out to the sides and pretended to examine them—"there isn't anyone at MacNeil's Tower who isn't a bogle!"

He refused to tell Saor about Mindy Menlove.

She was his business alone.

So he feigned an expression of innocence and cleared his throat. "We're often visited by newcomers to our realm. If I dare say it myself, we're renowned for our hospitality. Thon three ghosties will have heard of our revelries and feasting and decided to drop in."

"They weren't just any ghosts. No' like us, anyway. They were"—Saor craned his neck to peer at the nearest window arch as if he expected to see the three ghosts staring in at them—"well, see-through!"

"Humph!" Bran's lips twitched. "Any one of us can appear that way if we wish. It's one of the first intricacies of ghostdom to be mastered."

"There's more." Saor sounded truly alarmed. "Serafina said they were MacNeil chieftains. But they weren't any MacNeils she'd ever seen here before. She doubted they were of our own fourteenth century. In her well-traveled estimation, she believes they were haints of fifteenth- or even sixteenth-century ilk."

"All the better." Bran folded his arms and grinned. "If they're MacNeil chieftains who lairded it after me, they can tell me how the clan fared after my, er ... ah ... demise."

"Aye, and that's what fashed Serafina." Saor almost choked on the words. "She claims they were stomping up and down the long gallery, ranting and raving because the keep was no more. She said—"

"She misheard them." Bran waved away such foolish prattle. "MacNeil's Tower exists sure as the day is long. In this realm or in any other day, these stones still stand."

He shot a glance at the window, reassured by the drizzly rain gusting past the stone-edged arch, the crash of the surf on the rocks beyond the castle walls.

"This tower will stand a thousand, even two thousand years. That I know!" He crossed his arms again, sure of it.

He just wasn't going to tell his roguish, dazzle-every-woman-he-met friend how he knew.

It stood to reason that Mindy Menlove was an American tourist who'd been poking about the keep in her own day. Everyone knew such folk loved nothing better. The wench was no doubt one of the moony-eyed ones. The worst of the lot, who thought old castles and mist-hung hills were romantic. To be sure, she'd been snooping about, oohing and aahing, when some glitch in the veil between the times had allowed her to suddenly appear in his world.

That she'd done so was clear proof that his tower yet stood.

Bran's chest swelled on the thought.

His heart squeezed.

He did love his home.

But he wasn't going to get misty-eyed in front of Saor, so he flipped back his plaid in a most manly flourish and hooked his thumbs in his sword belt. "I'd like to speak with these three ghosties," he announced. "If they are MacNeil chieftains, they deserve a proper Barra welcome.

"Go fetch them down to the hall." Bran nodded, ending their discourse.

Saor didn't budge. "That's no' possible. They're gone."

"Eh?" Some of Bran's beneficence faded. "What do you mean, they're gone?"

"They left in a huff." Saor rubbed the back of his neck, looking miserable. "That's why Serafina cried out and dropped the jug of scented oil she was carrying. She was offended because the three chieftains didn't pay her any heed. Recognizing their worth, she said she smiled and started to invite them to the hall, but"—he paused dramatically—"they were arguing so heatedly amongst themselves that they told her to 'stop batting her lashes at them and step out of their way, that they were about important business and had no time for her.'"

"No time for Serafina?" Bran could scarce believe it. Men had fought to the blood for an hour of the seductress's attentions. "You are certain?"

Saor nodded. "Aye, that's what they said, just. Then they scowled at her and vanished."

"I see." Bran tried hard to do so. "Perhaps the three ghosties weren't here because of our warm fire and fine viands at all. Could be they were walking the long gallery in their own time and Serafina just happened upon them." He nodded sagely. "I have heard and seen stranger things."

Saor shrugged. "Could be," he agreed. "I once stumbled across a prune-faced MacNeil widow woman in the undercroft. She, too, was of a different century than ours and"—he shuddered—"the glare she gave me made me full sorry I'd somehow sifted myself into her time."

He rubbed his arms as if the memory had the power

to give him chills. "Barra's a fair place, but the layers betwixt the ages are thinner here than elsewhere."

"Aye, 'tis all too easy for one like us to land where he shouldn't!" Bran nodded again, aware that it was so.

"I think you should go see to Serafina," he suggested. The Saracen beauty could be temperamental. "I'll no' have her moods ruining the high fettle of the others. Folk dinnae come here for intrigues and mayhem."

"As you wish." Saor couldn't quite keep the smile out of his voice.

Bran knew his friend had a weakness for the dusky-skinned temptress, with her raven locks and exotic perfume. The speed with which Saor turned and flew back up the stairs, taking them two at a time, proved it.

Bran frowned.

There'd been a time when he, too, would have raced to Serafina's side.

Indeed, he might have knocked Saor out of the way to get there.

Now . . .

His scowl deepened and he flicked his fingers. Not to conjure a beef rib—though he was still mightily famished—but to snatch a brimming cup of ale from the kitchen's cold, smoke-tinged air.

He quaffed the frothy brew in one quick gulp.

He should help himself to an entire ewer of ale. Or perhaps a bracing swig of *uisge beatha*. The fiery Highland spirits would surely banish the gooseflesh that was beginning to prick his nape. *Uisge beatha* was, after all, Scotland's cure-all for every ill known to man.

But he, Bran of Barra, prided himself on taking matters into his own hands.

He didn't need to toss down a bolt of firewater to bolster his courage.

A Barra MacNeil feared nothing.

So he swiped a hand across his mouth, ensuring that no ale flecks clung to his fine red beard, and then prepared to do what he'd never done before.

Take a peek at modern-day Barra.

Even if the thought soured his stomach and was as appealing as tumbling, naked, in a patch of stinging nettles.

He was anything but a fool and he'd sifted himself in and out of other Highland locales often enough over the centuries to know that keeps like his didn't fare well through time. Almost all once-mighty abodes lost their roofs. Many saw good, solid walls crumble and sag. And some were reduced to shameful piles of rubble.

Praise God, he knew through Mindy Menlove's appearance that his tower yet stood.

An American tourist wouldn't be interested in an out-of-the-way place like Barra otherwise.

Even so, if three MacNeil chiefly ghosts and Mindy sent-to-tempt-him Menlove had all pierced the carefully wrought shields he kept around his beloved fourteenth-century keep, it followed that great activity must be going on in Barra of modern times.

Bran put back his shoulders and took a deep breath.

It was his duty to discover what was amiss.

Eager to be about it, he closed his eyes and concentrated on sifting himself into his bailey. But not the bustling courtyard of his own day, a colorful, noisy place he knew and loved so dearly that it sometimes hurt his heart just to stride across its cobbles.

Nae, he sifted himself to whatever was left of his bailey in Mindy Menlove's time.

He knew he'd made it when he could no longer feel the cobbles beneath his feet.

He was standing on grass.

Bran swallowed. His heart began galloping. He wasn't quite ready to open his eyes, but the chill, briny air comforted him. Also familiar was the sound of the wind churning up the sea beyond his curtain walls. They were noises he knew and loved and that meant home.

It didn't matter the century.

Or that his courtyard had lost its cobbles somewhere in the long passage of time.

A buffet of wind tossed his plaid, reminding him of why he'd come here. So he drew another deep breath and opened his eyes. Unfortunately he saw nothing but blowing mist and—if he wasn't mistaken—a few straggly clumps of heather.

Whatever remained of his walls was hidden behind the drifting sheets of mist. Chills sped down his spine and for one maddening moment, he wondered if he'd sifted himself to the wrong place. But the cold, damp air was so thick with the smell of the sea, and the ground—with or without cobbles—was his.

That, he knew to the roots of his soul.

It was just a matter of getting his bearings and then peering through the damty fog.

He took a few steps forward, mindful of any tumbled stones or suchlike he might encounter. But when the mists did part long enough for him to see more than a few feet in front of him, he realized he needn't have bothered. Nothing surrounded him but the heather-and-bracken-strewn ground and the tossing, whitecapped sea.

MacNeil's Tower was gone.

Bran blinked and turned in a disbelieving circle. He didn't want to accept the truth before his eyes. But it was there all the same. And the brittle horror of it was worse than anything he'd ever dared imagine.

His home had been wiped from the earth as if it'd never existed.

Not a single stone remained.

Only the cold night, the waves, and the eerie, wind-driven mist looked on as terrible pain pierced his heart and punched holes in his soul. Anguished, he threw back his head to roar denial, but a scalding thickness closed his throat, cutting off his cry.

He did fist his hands, barely aware of the soft drizzle beginning to fall. The chill droplets clung to his hair and rolled down his face, but did nothing to cool the burning agony inside him.

He'd expected at least one ruined wall.

Tears blurred his vision, but like all Highlanders, he was man enough not to hide his feelings. He did bend to scoop up handfuls of damp, loamy-smelling earth, clutching the peat to his chest as if doing so might make his home rise up out of the whirling mist.

But nothing stirred except the sudden blur of gray racing toward him across the springy turf.

Bran's heart gave a leap.

It was Gibbie.

The dog hurtled into him, almost knocking him down. Bran dropped to his knees and reached out, pulling his old friend hard against him. He rumpled Gibbie's shaggy coat and rubbed his ears, some of the pain in his heart lessening.

"Ach, laddie, did you follow me here, too?" Bran lowered his head, pressing his cheek against the great beast's rain-dampened shoulder. " 'Tis no' a fine place for us just now, our Barra. But I'm glad to be seeing you!"

As if that was all that mattered—and Bran supposed that, to Gibbie, it was—the dog barked happily and pressed closer to him, slathering Bran with kisses.

"Come, you, let us be away." Bran pushed to his feet and forced a grin, not wanting Gibbie to see his distress and think he was upset because the dog had joined him.

In truth, Gibbie was his salvation.

As was his ability—praise the saints—to sift them both back to fourteenth-century Barra, where they belonged. In their own merry keep with a roaring fire, jovial friends, and all the finger-flicked beef ribs their ghostly hearts desired.

And as Bran reached down to curl his fingers around Gibbie's collar—just to be sure he didn't lose him on the way home—he vowed to never again visit Barra of modern times.

Once had almost undone him.

He wouldn't make the same mistake twice.

The first thing Mindy did upon walking into Newark Liberty International Airport a month later was to throw away the six outdated Scotland guidebooks and several faded and well-thumbed maps of the Highlands and the Isles that Margo had insisted on giving her as must-have reading material for the flight to Glasgow.

Margo Menlove had never been to Scotland. But as a die-hard Scotophile, she had a ton of tartany paraphernalia clogging her tiny apartment and considered herself an authority on all things Scottish.

She meant well.

And her eyes had flashed with such excitement when she'd dug her treasures out of her oversized handbag and presented them to Mindy.

Margo just didn't understand that Mindy wasn't going to Scotland as a tourist.

She wasn't one of the gazillion genealogy-obsessed Americans whose ancestors emigrated from Scotland two hundred years ago and viewed their package-deal see-Scotland-in-seven-days coach-bus tour as a journey that was taking them home.

She wasn't into cold, rain, and sheep.

Nor was she a Kilt-o-maniac.

Not anymore, anyway.

She was going to Barra for one reason only. And her greatest wish was to leave as quickly as possible. Though she would be sure she took time to pick up some nice newly printed guidebooks and maps for Margo's collection. Perhaps, too, a nice length of heathery-colored tweed that Margo could no doubt whip into something stunning.

Mindy smiled. She wished she had her sister's sense of style. But having spent her entire adult life wearing an airline uniform left her a bit spoiled. To her, a top was a top was a top. And as for some women's passion for shoes, well, she just didn't get the thrill.

She paused to let an air crew hurry past, the flight attendants smartly elegant in stewardess blue and with well-polished heels to match. Looking after them, Mindy felt a pang as they disappeared into the crowd, the rattle of their wheeled crew luggage and the *click-click* of their heels bringing back memories.

She looked down at her own shoes, bought especially for this trip, and almost laughed out loud.

Thick-soled black leather walking boots too bulky for her checked bag, they were like nothing she'd ever worn before. She hoped they'd protect her from turning an ankle in some godforsaken Hebridean bog.

Nothing else mattered.

Except perhaps getting checked in and to the gate before she changed her mind and made tracks straight for Global's Newark crew lounge, friends she missed, and—one could dream—a fast ticket to her old job!

She *was* tempted.

Especially when—nearly an hour and much hassle later—she reached the boarding gate and had the bad luck to sit down next to a talker.

"We're going on a history and heritage tour," the middle-aged woman gushed, her eyes lighting with the zeal of a die-hard Scotophile. "We're all Scottish"— she indicated the little group standing close by, all wearing badges proclaiming their names and that they were on a Celtic Twilight tour—"and we'll be visiting the ancestral castles of each one of us.

"Treading in the footsteps of our forebears and"— she heaved a great sigh, getting misty-eyed—"breathing in the air of our native land."

Mindy nodded. She wished she'd noticed the woman's KISS ME, I'M SCOTTISH pin before she'd sat beside her. Years of suffering Margo's endless pining for the Highlands had put her off such people. She started to say something, anything, to be polite, but before she could, the woman leaned close.

"You must have Scottish roots." She pulled a card from her jacket pocket and pressed it into Mindy's hand. "I have an online business that sells Scottish memorabilia. We do everything from T-shirts and coffee mugs emblazoned with your clan name and crest to teddy bears wearing your own family tartan."

"I'm not Scottish." Mindy resisted announcing that she, like the woman herself, was American. "But—"

"I must tell you"—the woman spoke right over her— "we're ending our trip with a gala weekend at Raven-scraig Castle near Oban. They have a state-of-the-art genealogical research center called One Cairn Village where we can reference everything we learn on the tour. They even do—"

"Ravenscraig Castle?" Mindy's heart sank.

She'd booked her first night in Scotland at the castle hotel. It'd caught her eye because of its proximity to Oban, where she'd board the CalMac ferry to Barra. And because a castle hotel sounded luxurious and she deserved a night of pampering before stranding herself on a rocky Hebridean island that surely lacked most modern conveniences.

But she'd somehow overlooked that Ravenscraig had a genealogy center. The place would be overrun with history buffs and ancestral enthusiasts.

Mindy shuddered.

The *talker* was just warming up. "Yes, that's it. Ravenscraig Castle. It's owned by a real laird, Sir Alexander Douglas, and his American wife. I believe her name is Lady Mara. They're known throughout the Highlands for their medieval-reenactment festivals and—"

"Medieval reenactment?"

"Oh, yes. Their 'Medieval Dayes' weekends are supposed to be fabulous. Very authentic, but"—she gripped Mindy's arm, speaking with as much relish as if she were talking about attending a tournament at Buckingham Palace—"they're just as famous for the genealogy research they sponsor. They even give out certificates verifying one's roots. And in some cases where they have connections with the lairds, they present you with a land deed for a square foot of your own home glen!"

Mindy gulped.

It just kept getting worse.

Genealogy nuts were bad. The thought of arriving at

the castle hotel in the middle of a medieval reenactment was off-putting enough for her to break out in hives.

She'd had her fill of medieval lately and didn't want any more. Thousands of numbered and packed-in-straw castle stones were more than anyone's share of the Middle Ages. Now that those stones were on their way to the Auld Hameland—and very likely there already—she should be able to consider her part in their history a done deal.

In fact, when a Global PA announcement rang through the concourse calling passengers to board a flight to St. Croix, Mindy decided those now-in-Barra stones were enough. She wasn't doing anything else and neither was she flying to Glasgow, getting in a rental car, and driving left through heather and mist.

Her heart was *not* in the Highlands.

It was on a sunny beach where the sand burned her feet and the smell of cocoa butter tanning oil scented the air.

Almost tasting the tropics, she sprang to her feet. Unfortunately, her seat companion leapt up, as well. Once more the woman grabbed her arm, holding tight.

"I forgot to tell you the best part about Ravenscraig." She sounded excited enough to burst. "The castle's One Cairn Village isn't just a research center. It also has its own Highland village with self-catering cottages for visitors, a gift and tea shop, and even a memorial cairn to the MacDougalls, who originally built the castle.

"It's said"—she stepped closer, her eyes blazing even brighter than before—"that the village could be right out of *Brigadoon*!"

"I'll keep that in mind." Mindy broke free and hastened from the waiting area.

She wasn't going to be *Brigadoon*ed anywhere.

"Don't be long," the woman called after her. "They'll be boarding soon."

"Without me," Mindy muttered to herself as she hurried down the concourse, dodging passengers and air crews going in the other direction.

She was good at zipping through busy airports.

But she stopped short when she reached the end of the concourse. It opened very near to one of the security checkpoints and—her blood ran cold—the three ancestral ghosts from the long gallery stood there glaring at her.

"O-o-oh, no!" Her cry caused several businessmen to stare at her.

They, of course, didn't see anything amiss.

Mindy frowned as the men hastened past her. It didn't surprise her that they thought she was nuts.

She knew enough from Margo and other paranormal enthusiasts at Ye Olde Pagan Times to understand that—if one believed such things—ghosts could make themselves visible, or not, to anyone they chose to visit.

Though there were always sensitives who saw them, regardless.

Wishing she didn't see them, Mindy shook her head. "Oh, no," she repeated, her chest tight with dread.

"Och, aye." The ghostie called Roderick whipped out his sword and shook it at her.

Geordie did the same with his walking stick.

Silvanus only grinned. He also had the cheek to cut her a jaunty bow.

Then before she could make a run for it—something she *did* consider—the other ghost chieftains from the long gallery appeared behind them, each one brandishing a sword or spear and looking as if he'd just stepped off the *Braveheart* set.

When they rushed forward, their weapons lowered and their clan battle cries splitting the air, Mindy changed her mind about escape.

As if they knew, they vanished at once.

Well, all except Silvanus.

That one suddenly appeared at her side. "You made the right choice, lassie," he said, winking at her. "You're going to love Scotland."

And then he, too, was gone.

". . . Ladies and Gentlemen, this is the final boarding call for Continental flight sixteen to Glasgow. Will all passengers not yet on board please come immediately to Gate C-127."

Mindy heard the announcement and bit back a groan.

It was now or never.

But one thing she knew as she hastened back to the boarding gate, this time going with the fast-moving stream of concourse passengers.

She was not going to love Scotland.

Chapter 5

Nearly seven hours and an Atlantic crossing later, Mindy woke from a fitful sleep. Years of flying on duty—she'd preferred working night flights—made it next to impossible to rest well on planes. Nor was her coach window seat very conducive to deep slumber. But even if the space allotted would cramp a six-year-old and the pillow that was supposed to make her more comfortable could have passed for a very thin washcloth, she hadn't wanted to splurge on business class.

It stung enough to pay full fare.

She was, after all, used to flying first class for next to nothing.

She also had an infallible instinct for when a plane was about to begin its descent. As if to prove her nose for imminent landings was still sharp, the sound of the engines shifted even before she'd fully cracked her eyes. Moments later, the captain's voice came over the loudspeaker, wishing the passengers a good morning and informing them that they'd just passed over the coast of Ireland. He then told his cabin crew to prepare for arrival in Glasgow.

Glasgow.

A burst of cheers and clapping rose from a few rows behind her. The *going home* passengers booked on the Celtic Twilight tour.

Mindy didn't share their enthusiasm. She did feel her mouth go dry and her palms dampen. Never had a city name struck more dread in her heart. And she wasn't even staying there. She had no ties to Glasgow at all beyond landing at its airport and picking up her rental car.

But Glasgow meant Scotland.

Mindy shivered. She didn't believe in such things—though she had become a firm believer in ghosts—but she couldn't shake the weird sensation that Scotland was waiting for her. She could almost feel it lurking down there beneath the fast-descending plane like some great hulking beast ready to pounce on her the moment she arrived.

Hoping to dispel the feeling, she pushed up the plastic window shade, intending to glare down at the Hebrides, which, she knew, they had to be speeding over about now. But the chain of islands that curved along Scotland's west coast wasn't down there.

Nothing was.

She saw only what looked like an endless sea of cotton batting. Gray cotton batting as far as the eye could see. *Rain clouds.* Mindy pressed her forehead to the window, straining to make out something anyway. Anything she could spot to prove that she wouldn't be spending her time in Scotland living in a world of uninterrupted gloom. Unfortunately, when she did find a break in the cloud cover, it was to see sheets of rolling mist drifting across a sea that could only be called inky black. She also caught a flash of creamy white breakers and two barren islands that were so tiny they were little more than seabound rocks.

Empty, silent, and clearly uninhabited, they did have steep, dark cliffs. Deep and narrow inlets that made them even more forbidding. Secretive-looking caves in the high-walled sides of those inlets lent the isles an air of mystery. They were nothing like the Hebrides of song, beautiful, ethereal, and heart-wrenchingly romantic.

Those two specks of jagged rock were the real deal. And seeing them at their brooding, mist-shrouded worst only confirmed what she already knew.

Scotland was so not her kind of place.

Two hours later as she drove—drove left!—through sheets of teeming rain along Scotland's supposedly scenic A-82, she was ready to carve that opinion into stone. Thankfully her rental car was small. Otherwise she would have had serious problems navigating the pencil-thin road that ran in a series of hairpin twists and turns along the western shore of Loch Lomond, which she assumed was somewhere to her right.

She couldn't see the famous loch through the curtains of rain.

An interminable downpour that, at the very least, worked wonders for her jet lag.

There wasn't anything more powerful than a fear of hurtling off the road and into a loch she couldn't see to keep her eyes peeled and her every sense alert.

Anger kept her going, too.

Driving left was worse than she'd expected. It was a living nightmare surely designed to keep down the influx of right-driving tourists. But she'd be damned if she'd concede defeat by heading back to the airport and returning the car. So she kept her hands tight on the wheel, gritted her teeth, and tried very hard not to cry out each time a coach tour bus zoomed up behind her. Even worse were the rolling houses on wheels, otherwise known as *recreational vehicles*, that kept roaring past her from the opposite direction.

She'd stopped counting those buggers when she hit twenty.

Who knew all the blasted road-hogging nightmares called Scotland's A-82 their home?

She knew it.

And she also knew that if she stopped at one more promising-looking inn or bed-and-breakfast only to be turned away with a "Sorry; we're booked full," she was soon going to have a major nerve meltdown.

She did *not* want to spend the night at Ravenscraig Castle.

Regrettably, it was beginning to look as if she had no choice. And no way was she sleeping in her car. It didn't matter that if she left the A-82, she'd no doubt find herself surrounded by hills and moors that went on forever with no sign of human habitation and no one to object to an exhausted and irritable American woman roughing it for the night.

No, that wasn't for her.

Even bonny Scotland had ax murderers, she was sure.

She already knew it had ghosts.

Bran of Barra came to mind.

But thinking of him only made her flush. She was certain that the big, burly Highland ghost with the slightly crooked nose and lopsided grin had almost kissed her. And *that* just served to rile her even more.

She didn't want to think about spooks.

And she especially didn't want to think about kissing one of them.

So she set her jaw and kept going, trying to ignore

the horrors of left driving, the wind buffets that could easily rival a hurricane, and the ceaseless drumming of rain on the roof of her car. She also did her best not to start laughing hysterically at the image of Scotland as portrayed on all the travel posters. She saw nothing of the castles and kilts and bagpipers playing their hearts out on some lonely, heather-covered hill.

In fact, if the rain didn't soon lessen, she'd need swim goggles to see anything at all!

She was also lost.

At least she thought she was until she reached the junction of Crianlarich. The tiny blink-your-eyes-and-it's-gone village was the crossroads where the rental-car agent had told her she'd need to start watching for the A-85 turnoff. That road would veer west, taking her through Glen Lochy and the Pass of Brander toward Gateway-to-the-Isles Oban and then straight to—the name sat like an iron weight in her stomach—Ravenscraig Castle of genealogy and medieval-reenactment fame.

Two strikes against the place in her jaundiced opinion.

She refused to think about the *Brigadoon* slant.

But then, after what seemed like an endless stretch of twisting coast road, she spotted Ravenscraig's double-turreted gatehouse. She also saw an enormous gray dog sitting just inside the entryway's tunnellike arch. Shaggy and fearsome-looking, the dog appeared to be watching the road. That wouldn't have bothered her normally—she loved dogs, after all—but this one had glowing amber eyes that she'd swear were staring right at her. Yet when she slowed the car, he stood and loped away into the deep woods behind the gatehouse.

Mindy blinked.

She didn't think Scotland still had wolves, but it wouldn't surprise her.

The dog, or whatever it'd been, certainly could have passed for one.

She shivered, chilled despite the heavy all-weather jacket she'd bought for the trip. A Barbour waxed jacket that Margo had insisted was a *classic* and an absolute must for travel in Britain.

It did make her feel rather posh.

Especially with the apricot cashmere turtleneck and matching paisley scarf that Margo had made her pick up to go with the jacket. As long as she ignored her clunky walking boots, she could have stepped out of one of her sister's *English Country Living* magazines.

Quite a turnabout for a girl who dreamed of living in a bikini and pareo.

She could have laughed, but . . .

The wolf-dog creature had put a major crimp in an already bad day. His penetrating stare made her feel as if he'd been waiting for her.

Not just watching the road, but looking for her.

Mindy blew a strand of hair off her face, determining not to worry about it.

At least Ravenscraig seemed to greet her kindly. The gatehouse's wrought-iron gates stood wide, and—she couldn't believe it—just as she approached and swung into the imposing entry, the rain stopped.

It still drizzled. But she wouldn't expect anything else from such a cold wet place as Scotland. At least now she could see where she was going without the windshield wipers swishing back and forth at light speed. Too bad the first thing that caught her eye was a sign indicating the way to One Cairn Village.

Curiosity made her stop. She let down the window and was immediately treated to a blast of chill air that smelled of pine, damp loamy earth, and the sea. In fact, she was sure she could hear distant waves crashing over rocks.

Mindy's pulse leapt. She remembered from booking online through the castle hotel's Web site that Ravenscraig stood on a bluff.

She did love the sea.

Too bad—in this dark and misty setting—the sound of pounding surf only reminded her of the spooky old Celtic tales she'd heard at Margo's Ye Olde Pagan Times. Strange, hair-raising stories of long Atlantic rollers rising up to shape-shift into fiery-eyed, horselike sea serpents as the foaming waves raced to shore.

Mindy frowned and jabbed the button to raise the window again, blotting the sound.

It was a good thing she didn't believe in shapeshifters.

Now, ghosts . . .

Her scowl deepened and she tapped the accelerator, glad to drive away from the turnoff to One Cairn Village. She might not have seen the village—clearly it was nestled too deep in the woods to be spotted from the main drive—but she'd felt its power.

A *weird* something that lifted the fine hairs on her nape and made her almost feel as if she'd entered an older, forgotten-by-time kind of place when she'd left the coast road and passed through Ravenscraig's gatehouse.

At least she hadn't seen *them* anywhere.

The Long Gallery Threesome, as she now thought of the trio of ancestral ghosts from the Folly.

But when she drove out of the trees and caught her

first glimpse of the castle hotel, she was sure they'd be here somewhere. Ravenscraig could have leapt out of the pages of a fairy tale.

It had to be a haven for ghosts.

Mindy swallowed, unable to take her gaze off the castle. The Folly was—and would be again—a sturdy, square-shaped medieval tower. This place looked like a castle confection suitable for Disney World.

It was tall, parapeted, and built of pink sandstone that gleamed red from the recent rain, with narrow-slit windows that seemed to stare at her from across a sweep of well-manicured lawn. Mist rose from the grass, hovering low and adding to the sense of otherworldliness. And— she wasn't at all surprised—dark rain clouds filled a huge swath of sky directly behind the castle, proving that Ravenscraig indeed perched on the very edge of a cliff.

Not that it should matter to her where the castle stood.

All she wanted was a clean and comfortable bed, a hot shower, and, in the morning, a substantial breakfast to see her through to Barra.

She did like to eat.

So she followed the curving drive around the lawn toward the two rounded towers that guarded the castle's massive iron-studded door.

A door that swung open the instant she stopped in front of Ravenscraig's broad stone steps. Mindy's heart leapt to her throat. For one crazy moment, she expected the Long Gallery Threesome to rush out, yelling their slogans, swords and walking stick at the ready.

With great caution, she climbed out of the car, her gaze pinned on the castle door.

But the only *souls* to rush to greet her were three dogs.

Two lively Jack Russells who flew down the steps at breakneck speed and a border collie whose slower gait and whitened muzzle marked him as a senior dog.

The wolfish beast was nowhere to be seen.

Before she could be grateful for small miracles, a gnomelike man in a kilt appeared on the steps. His bushy white brows snapped together in a fierce scowl when he saw the three dogs sniffing and crowding her. When the two Jack Russells started jumping on her, he hobbled forward, waving his arms like a windmill.

"Away with you, you pesky buggers!" His blue eyes flashed as he scolded them. "Dottie, Scottie, get down!" He shook a fist at the Jacks. "That's no way to greet our guests!

"And you, Ben . . ." He started after the border collie. "You ought to know better!"

The dogs ignored him, now running circles around the car, each one barking a storm. Even Ben, the aged border collie, kept pace, his plumed tail held high in excitement and his pink tongue lolling.

It was canine chaos.

Mindy laughed.

Until the old man's swinging kilt and his thick burr reminded her where she was. This was Scotland—very near to the Western Isles and the MacNeils' beloved Barra—and she shouldn't be finding anything here to laugh about.

Not even Scottish dogs.

No matter how amusing she might find them.

As if they wished to change her mind, the three dogs rushed her again, frisking around her feet and wagging their tails. The border collie pressed close and slurped her hand. Not to be outdone, the two little Jacks pounced on her calves, their wet noses cold on her knees. They, too, kissed her, and then they all took off, bounding across the lawn toward a thick hedge of rhododendron.

"Oh, my!" Mindy brushed at her pants legs. "They—"

"You pay them no heed, lassie." The old man glared after the dogs. "Pampered, worthless beasties, they are. Good for naught but stirring mischief! We'll have your clothes cleaned. We have a fine laundry service and—"

"No, no." Mindy wished she hadn't swiped at her pants. "I love dogs and there isn't a speck of dirt. Even if there was, I wouldn't—"

"You'll be Miss Menlove." He cocked one of his extraordinary brows, peering sharply at her. "We've been expecting you. I'm Murdoch MacEwan, house steward. Welcome to Ravenscraig.

"We're always pleased to have American guests." He thrust out a hand, almost crushing her fingers in a grip that seemed much too strong for such a wizened little man. "You'll enjoy your stay with us. Our genealogy center—"

"I'm not here to trace my roots." Mindy could've bitten her tongue. She hadn't meant to be rude. "I mean ... I'm not Scottish. I'm not even sure where my ancestors came from, though I think they were English."

"English?" Murdoch MacEwan's eyes narrowed ever so slightly.

Mindy wished she could sink into the graveled drive.

Who would've thought the Scots would still harbor historical grudges?

But the steward had definitely bristled.

"If you'll come this way"—he turned back to the castle's low steps—"I'll take you through to the reception and then see to your car and luggage."

"Actually, I'm from Bucks County, Pennsylvania." Mindy followed him up the steps, feeling a ridiculous need to explain. "It's near Philadelphia. We like to think America was born there. There are also many Colonial and Revolutionary battlefields nearby where we fought the English and—"

"Philadelphia, you say?" The little man swung round, his entire face lit like a Christmas tree. "Herself is from Philadelphia," he said, beaming. "Lady Mara, our very own lady of the castle."

Mindy smiled back, thankful—as so often—that her airline training also taught her how to change awkward topics in the blink of an eye.

"I'd heard that she was American." That much was true. "I'd love to meet her," she added to be polite, not quite sure she did want to have to make small talk with an American who obviously must love Scotland and had even married a real live Highland laird.

They would have absolutely nothing in common.

Or so she thought until Murdoch left her alone in the dark-paneled entry. He hurried away, disappearing up a spacious open staircase at the end of the corridor, having promised to return with Lady Mara. He wasn't gone two seconds before Mindy felt chilled from the inside out.

It was the same shiver of awareness she'd often had at the Folly.

As if someone was watching her.

Rubbing her arms, she was sure Lady Mara would recognize the sensation. That much they did share. Anyone who lived in such a historical old place likely knew the feeling. And it was getting stronger the longer she stood in the echoing silence of the foyer.

She started pacing, but then stopped to peer into a

vast, shadowy room that could only be the castle hotel's erstwhile great hall.

As in the entry passage, standing suits of armor gleamed from niches set at intervals along the room's walls. An incredible array of medieval weaponry dazzled the eye, with swords, lances, and shields seeming to occupy every inch of display space.

The room also boasted an impressive painted beam ceiling and even offered stunning views of the sea through a wall of tall, arched windows. Or so Mindy assumed, as, at present, thick clouds and rolling mist were all that could be seen out the ancient glass panes.

But none of that was responsible for the déjà vu moment she'd experienced on peering into the great hall's shadow-hung gloom. Everyone knew there was a sense of kinship shared by those who lived in ancient places.

Yet this was more.

It was the kilted man standing near the room's massive hearth, his broad, plaid-draped back to the door.

Big, burly, and with a shock of fire-burnished hair skimming wide-set, powerful shoulders, he had an air of the *medieval* about him. Power and pure masculine strength poured off him so that even in front of the enormous hearth—a fireplace large enough to roast two whole oxen—he dominated the space, seeming to tower over everything around him as if he were, well, larger than life.

He could have been Bran of Barra.

No, it *was* him.

Mindy's jaw slipped. She took a step forward, and another, her heart thumping. Her mouth went dry, so badly she might have swallowed a spoonful of chalk. As if he knew, the ghost turned slowly around, his blue gaze locking with hers. Recognition flashed across his face and he gave her a wickedly intimate smile.

Mindy put back her shoulders, not about to return it.

I told you no' to come here.

His words slid past her ear as if he were standing right beside her. His voice . . . it was sinfully provocative. Mindy tried to remain unaffected. But the silky-smooth tones lingered, taunting everything female inside her.

No man—corporeal or otherwise—should speak that way.

Annoyingly, Bran of Barra did.

Deep, low, and richly burred, his soft Highland voice would have melted her had she heard it B.H.

Before Hunter.

As things stood, she was supposed to be immune to Scottish charm. So she lifted her chin and glared across the shadowy room at him. No way was she crossing the threshold. They were on his turf now, after all, and that might give him some supernatural advantage.

Mindy swallowed, hoping it wasn't so. "You warned me to stay away from your friends at the Folly," she shot back at him, taking satisfaction in his immediate frown.

The way he blinked on the word *Folly*.

Pleased, she put her hands on her hips. "You said nothing about Ravenscraig. In fact, I'm surprised you're even here. Or are you following—"

"He's a ghost, you know."

"Agggh!" Mindy spun around to find a tiny whitehaired woman peering up her. Birdlike and wearing a frilly white apron, she smiled sweetly.

"Married our own Lady Mara, he did," she chirped, her bright blue eyes taking on a mischievous, childlike gleam. She clutched a wicker basket of gift-boxed soaps and candles, hitching the basket on her hip as she stepped closer. "His name is Lord Basil and—"

"*Innes.* You know that's Alex in there." A young woman with flaming auburn hair and a Philly accent reached to take the basket from the old woman, stirring a waft of herbs and lavender as she hooked it on her own arm. "He's discussing our plans for the Autumnal Ancestral Ball with his friend Hardwick." She gave Mindy an apologetic smile, her gaze flicking to the open doorway to the great hall. "Lord Basil isn't with us any longer."

"He was just there." Innes smoothed her apron with an age-spotted hand. "He was talking to thon young lassie, wasn't he, miss?"

She turned a hopeful gaze on Mindy. "He said you shouldn't be here."

"Innes!" The American—surely Lady Mara—took the old woman's elbow and started guiding her away. "Shouldn't you be in the tea shop?" She glanced over her shoulder at Mindy. "Innes runs our tea and gift shop down in One Cairn Village. She's our resident soap and candle maker."

Mindy ignored them both, too gob-smacked, as the Brits said, to see two men in deep conversation near the great hall's fireplace.

Bran of Barra wasn't with them.

He'd vanished as if he'd never been there.

And in his place—exactly where he'd been standing a moment ago—these two new men were talking away. As if they'd been there all along, discussing, she now knew, an upcoming ancestral event.

That thought alone gave her another chill. Hoping it didn't show, she stared at the men. Both were tall and well built, and had an air of the medieval about them.

But their jeans, heavy work boots, and thick Arran sweaters marked them as twenty-first century.

Both turned to smile at her.

One had dark, shoulder-length hair and flashing eyes that gave him the look of a pirate. The other was slightly taller and had shining chestnut brown hair that, like the other man's, just brushed his shoulders. He also had dimples. And the greenest eyes Mindy had ever seen. When his sea green gaze slid to Lady Mara, turning all warm and adoring, and he lifted a hand in greeting before turning back to his friend, Mindy guessed that he was Alex.

Sir Alexander Douglas, as the castle brochure called him, which would make him the Philadelphian's Highland laird husband and master of Ravenscraig.

But his fine manly beauty left Mindy cold.

Even if in some hidden-away corner of her heart, she'd give anything to have a man look at her the way she'd just seen him look at his wife.

Dinnae think I'm no' here just because you cannae see me.

Mindy jumped.

Bran of Barra's rich burr was even closer than before. He also sounded amused. She could almost see the corner of his mouth lifting. She *did* feel his hand press her cheek, cradling her face. Her heart stopped and her breath snagged in her throat. His touch felt good, his fingers strong and warm as they brushed—no, as they caressed—the sensitive hollow behind her ear.

Then his lips were there, too. And his hands moved to her shoulders, gripping her firmly as he leaned in to nuzzle her neck.

Mindy shivered. The man knew how to neck nuzzle.

For a beat, she was whisked back to the times she'd

pinned her gaze on his portrait in the Folly's long gallery, letting his image help her flit past the other paintings. His roguish grin and twinkling eyes had reassured her that he would protect her from the other ancestrals if they leapt down from their gilded frames. He'd been her hero.

Now...

His teeth lightly grazed her earlobe, sending ripples of delicious chills all through her. She bit back a sigh, resisting the urge to angle her neck and offer more of herself to his attentions.

You should have heeded my warning, Mindy Menlove. 'Tis too late now.

"So sorry I was late in greeting you!" Lady Mara's American voice filled the entry passage, as did a chill, damp wind as she closed the castle door behind her.

Mindy started. Her nerves were jangled and—heaven help her—her skin actually tingled from Bran of Barra's neck nuzzle, the surprising softness of what she was sure had been his beard.

She knew her face was flaming. Smoothing her hair, she attempted a smile, hoping she didn't look as if she'd just shared an up-close-and-personal moment with a ghost.

The other woman was hurrying forward, her pretty face flushed from the cold. Blessedly, she didn't look at all suspicious. "Sorry," she said again, smiling. "I had to find someone to take Innes back to her tea shop. She gets confused at times. Lord Basil was the husband of Ravenscraig's former owner, the late Lady Warfield. Poor Innes often mistakes other men for him.

"But, anyway"—she reached Mindy, thrust out her hand—"I'm Mara MacDou—I mean Mara Douglas. Welcome to Ravenscraig."

"Mindy Menlove." Mindy took her hand, not missing that she'd almost called herself MacDou-something. *A Scotophile!* No wonder she ended up living in a Scottish castle and married to a man Margo would call a hot Scot.

But she did seem nice.

And like Margo, she looked as if she belonged in a glossy English country home-and-style magazine. She had on a short tweed skirt Margo would kill for and a silky-light, elbow-length sweater of palest blue. She'd slung an expensive-looking cardigan in the same shade around her shoulders, adding a dash of Euro chic. Her low-heeled beige shoes looked Continental, too. Most likely, they were Italian.

She gave Mindy an open smile, her greeting warm and genuine. "If you'll come this way"—she indicated an open door near the foot of the sweeping staircase— "I'll see you signed in and settled. I'm sure you would've enjoyed one of the village cottages, but we're full up with two coach tour buses of Canadian Camerons.

"We've given you the Havbredey suite in the Victorian Lodge's Coach House." She glanced over her shoulder as she led the way to the reception. "I don't think you'll be disappointed. The Havbredey is—"

"Havbredey?" Mindy blinked. For some reason the name made her pulse quicken.

"It was Old Norse for the Hebrides," Lady Mara informed her. "The name means 'Isles on the Edge of the 'Sea.' It's a quite apt description." She lifted a friendly brow. "You wouldn't happen to be going there, would you?"

"To the Hebrides?" Mindy nearly choked. "No," she lied, sure the woman could tell. "I'm here on business and won't be staying long."

She wasn't about to say more.

If she did, she feared the whole story—including Bran of Barra and the Long Gallery Threesome—would tumble out. Especially if she admitted she was headed to the Isles. Jet-lagged as she was, she might even babble Hunter's role in the tale.

Mindy shuddered, just imagining.

Mara Douglas seemed down-to-earth. Not the kind of woman who would have fallen for Hunter-the-jerk and his seat belt ploy. Mindy didn't want her to think she was one of those mad-for-plaid Americans who lost their heads—and likely a lot more—at the first flash of a kilt.

Nor did she want to sound crazy if she mentioned the Folly and its ghosts.

"A shame you won't be here long." Lady Mara showed her to a tartan-covered desk chair, handed her a check-in form. "You see . . ." She gave Mindy a curious look. "There were one or two other coach-house suites available, but something just told me the Havbredey was for you."

Mindy had to bite her tongue to keep from asking for one of the other rooms. "I'm sure I'll love it," she fibbed again.

A room called *the Hebrides*—regardless of the language—gave her the willies.

It reminded her too much of why she was here.

Not to mention *him*.

Bran of Barra.

The ghost whose mere neck nuzzle had made her tingle clear to her toes.

"Are you all right?" Lady Mara was eyeing her strangely. "You look a bit peaked."

"I'm just exhausted from the trip." Mindy finished

scribbling her name and address on the hotel form. "Was the auburn-haired man in the great hall your husband?" She stood, grasping at anything to change the subject. "I heard you were from Philly and married a—" She broke off, reddening.

"A Highland chieftain?" Lady Mara didn't look offended at all. Far from it, her eyes sparkled with amusement. "It's every Scotophile's dream, isn't it? Getting swept off your feet by a braw Scottish warrior." She laughed. "Thing is, even though I was born a MacDougall and my father has to be the greatest genealogy buff on the planet, I never had any desire to come here.

"I was in the travel industry and ran tours to England." She reached to adjust the cardigan around her shoulders. "I lived and breathed to be in London. Harrods Food Court, shopping at Liberty's, or a stroll through Hyde Park could keep me on an adrenaline rush for days." She shook her head as if remembering. "Oh, yeah, I was a die-hard Anglophile. I even started my tour business just to spend time there on the cheap."

Mindy stared at her, disbelieving. "I was a flight attendant. In fact, I'll be going back to flying after this trip."

"Will you, now?" Mara MacDougall Douglas suddenly sounded very Scottish.

But then she shrugged lightly, her eyes twinkling again. "Perhaps it's a good thing you won't be around for our upcoming Ancestral Ball. Some of Alex's friends can be quite charming. You saw one of them with him in the great hall. But he's out of the running. He's married and lives up in Sutherland, where he and his wife help run Dunroamin Castle, a residential care home that's in her family.

"She, too, came here on business, meaning to just stay a summer." Lady Mara glanced at her fingernails, a smile tugging at her lips. "But then—"

A soft rap at the door interrupted her. Mindy glanced around to see a strapping young Highlander in a kilt hovering on the threshold. Light from one of the office's wall sconces gleamed on his hair, showing it to be an even brighter red than Lady Mara's.

"Murdoch said a new guest had arrived for the Havbredey." His soft Highland voice was friendly. "He sent me to take her there. I've already seen to her car and luggage. And"—he glanced at Mindy—"I've laid a fire in the suite's lounge and set out a welcome dram."

"Excellent, Malcolm." Lady Mara nodded. "Be sure to take her through the village on the way." She smiled as she handed Mindy a key. "One Cairn Village might be our own modern incarnation of Auld Scotland, but we like to think it holds some Highland magic.

"Celtic whimsy and all that, you know?" She winked. "I think you'll like it."

"I'm sure I will," Mindy lied for the third time since meeting Mara MacDougall Douglas.

Worse than that, as she followed kilt-wearing, rosy-cheeked Malcolm out of the reception and back down the castle's entry passage toward the door, she had the strangest feeling that if she set foot in the mock Highland village, she'd never see America again.

The hairs had lifted on her nape when she'd driven past the turnoff to the village. Even then, safely inside her car, she'd felt the place's power. It might have been the darkness of the woods or the lingering drifts of mist that curled through the trees.

She knew odd things were said to happen in Scotland.

And if she considered her own Scottish track record, she might be heading for trouble.

In fact, now she was certain of it.

Chapter 6

"Aye, well, that's you, all set." Malcolm stepped out the door of the Havbredey suite, but didn't yet descend the stone steps that led down the side of Ravenscraig's Victorian Coach House. Instead, he hovered on the landing, clearly meaning to be helpful.

He peered up at the night sky, where the moon was just sailing out from behind dark, fast-moving clouds. "The weather will be turning before an hour, true as I'm standing here. Are you sure you'll no' be wanting me to fetch you for tea after you've had a chance to freshen up?

"You'd get drenched if you tried to walk back to the castle or even the village once the rain starts." He hunched his shoulders against the quickening wind, flashed another glance at the clouds. "There's a full buffet in the castle dining room or"—his chest seemed to swell—"a fine Highlander's tea served at the back o' Innes's shop. She does a wicked tuna sandwich on homemade bread, served with her own soup, chicken vegetable today. Or you can have fish-and-chips, the best this side of Oban."

Mindy forced a smile and shook her head. "I'm fine, thank you. All I want is to sleep."

"You're sure?" He arched a ginger-colored brow, looking concerned.

"Absolutely." Mindy let her smile brighten and started inching shut the door. She didn't want to seem unappreciative, but she was getting very close to telling him that what she really needed was an aspirin.

Or several.

She'd worry about food later.

After she'd put Ravenscraig Castle behind her. The place was too eerie and too old, and had too many men who could be medieval crowding its ancient walls. Not to mention that *he* was here.

No way had she imagined Bran of Barra.

The rough-and-ready Hebridean chieftain wasn't the kind of man a woman overlooked. Ghost or not, he was the type who strode into every room with a flourish, drawing eyes and making the space his own. Resplendent in his kilt and with a proud jut to his chin, he'd attract female notice at a hundred paces, regardless of the dimension.

Mindy's brow knit. He *had* been in the great hall. And he'd definitely been in the foyer with her, invisible or not. She still sizzled from the encounter, drat it!

Even now, she could hear his husky voice at her ear, feel his breath teasing across her skin and his firm jaw moving ever so softly against her neck, making her shiver and reminding her she'd always been drawn to big, strong men with gentle hands. Such men could melt her in quick time.

Mindy released a slow, trembling breath. It wasn't in her best interest to think about how easily Bran of Barra could seduce her if he wrapped his powerful arms around her, pulled her close against his huge, muscle-packed body.

Or what would happen if he kissed her.

For now, she'd put him from her mind and just be glad that Malcolm had finally turned and thumped back down the steps, leaving her alone. Not that he wasn't a nice young man, courteous to a fault and, without doubt, dedicated to the castle hotel.

He was.

But genial or not, his tour of One Cairn Village had quainted her out.

And his long, detailed history of the MacDougalls, the original builders of the castle, had given her a raging headache. He'd taken her through the centuries, clear back to the days of Robert the Bruce!

Images flashed through Mindy's mind. She could almost see Scotland's warrior king thundering into the mock village, riding a great black steed. Men would cheer and rush to surround him, each one eager to join his army. The women would vie for his attention, pushing and shoving to thrust themselves to the fore, then swooning if he glanced their way.

Margo—if she'd been there—would have climaxed on the spot.

Mindy smiled, sure of it.

Her sister could get more excited about Robert Bruce than some women did over Hollywood heartthrobs. And yet *she* had gone all tingly when a ghost had rubbed his seven-hundred-year-old beard against her neck!

Mindy frowned again and yanked off her heavy waxed jacket, tossing it onto a chair.

It had to be the jet lag.

She'd been up well over twenty-four hours now. Sleep deprivation did weird things to people. Not to mention crossing five time zones and . . .

Landing in a place where even the American owner spoke of Highland magic!

She shuddered and rubbed her arms, suddenly cold.

Not that anyone could blame her.

Walking through One Cairn Village in the misty gray of evening and with the village's cluster of thatched, whitewashed cottages had felt like slipping into the pages of a history book. Though she doubted a real fourteenth-century village would have been so neat and tidy. One Cairn Village's cottages had each winked with a pretty bright blue door and candles had flickered in the windows, though Malcolm had told her they weren't real. They were electric lights made to look like candles.

But the late-autumn flowers and heather that bloomed everywhere, decorating door stoops and edging the footpaths that curved through the village, were real. As was the large memorial cairn with its tall Celtic cross at the very center of the village.

Dedicated to long-ago MacDougalls, or so Malcolm had claimed, the cairn and its ancient-looking cross had given her the chills. As had the thin blue threads of peat smoke rising from the low chimney stacks of the cottages. The smoke seemed to hang in the air, giving the village an earthy-rich, old-timey smell.

Too bad she was done with old-timey.

One Cairn Village's Celtic whimsy existed, no doubt.

It just wasn't her cuppa.

Unfortunately, she was stunned to find that the Havbredey suite was. Airy and light, it was nothing like she'd expected, proving to be one great open space. Highly polished hardwood floors with a scattering of cream-colored woolen rugs struck an inviting note, while the pine furnishings went well with the plain walls. Floor-length curtains in the same off-white shade as the rugs framed a tall window near the hearth, where a comfortable-looking tartan sofa was drawn up to catch the fire's warmth. A flight of narrow pine stairs at the back of the room led up to a small loft bedroom.

The bathroom, also upstairs, was a hedonist's dream. All honey-gold marble with black accents, it offered a corner whirlpool bath and a separate glass-enclosed shower, and was crammed with an amazing assortment of the finest bath oils, soaps, and scented lotions.

The only thing she'd change would be to ditch the large spray of white heather and red rowan berries in a vase on the vanity. She'd replace the oh-so-Highlandy display with something Polynesian. A tasteful arrangement of bird-of-paradise came to mind. Or perhaps she'd choose wild orchids and frangipani.

Otherwise, she'd loved the suite on sight. Her breath had caught the instant Malcolm swung open the door. Even the plaid sofa and the several large black-and-white photographs of the Hebrides couldn't detract from the immediate sense of welcome and belonging.

She could see herself curled up before the fire, listening to the wind howl outside as she sipped hot chocolate and lost herself in a good cozy mystery.

It was the kind of place she could have stayed in forever.

And that scared her more than if a troop of glittery-winged, green-gowned faery folk had popped out from behind the village's memorial cairn to wave their sparkly wands at her.

She didn't want to like anything here, yet . . .

"Enough!" She gave herself a shake and crossed the room to the sofa—deftly pretending it wasn't tartan—before she turned into one of those people who constantly yearn for a pot of tea and scones.

Or should it be shortbread and whisky?

Sure she didn't want to know, she dropped onto the

sofa and reached for one of the books on the pine side table. Past her second wind, she hoped a bit of reading would help her fall asleep.

Unfortunately, the first book she grabbed was *Rivers of Stone: A Highlander's Ancestral Journey* by Wee Hughie MacSporran. Half-afraid the title might summon the Long Gallery Threesome, Mindy slapped the book back onto the side table and reached for another.

This one's cover bore a color, full-sized photo of a tall, rather portly Highlander in a kilt. Obviously the proud author of this *A Highlander's* series, Wee Hughie MacSporran had rosy red cheeks and thinning auburn hair, and beamed from beside the world-famous Bannockburn statue of Robert the Bruce.

Mindy eyed the cover photo, thinking the man looked rather like a kilted teddy bear. But it was the title that made her toss the book back onto the pile: *Royal Roots: A Highlander's Guide to Discovering Illustrious Forebears.*

Not caring when the book slid across the little table and landed on the floor, she drew her feet up beneath her and then shuddered.

Were all Highlanders so ancestral-crazy?

Frowning, she was about to reach for the third and last book when her cell phone rang. The caller ID said *restricted*, but it could be only Margo, so she flipped it open and took the call. "Hello?"

"Mindy!" Her sister's voice came through the line. "You're in Scotland! How are you? What are you doing now?"

Mindy pulled a tartan throw over her knees and glanced at the hearth. The fire was already dying down and the room was beginning to chill.

No, it was turning icebox cold.

Mindy frowned. "What am I doing?" She cast another look at the peat embers. They resembled charcoaled marshmallows with just a hint of orange glow. "I'm relaxing by a crackling fire, sipping single malt, and romanticizing about my journey to the Isles tomorrow."

"O-o-oh!" Margo's excitement was palpable. "I knew it! There one day and you've fallen under Scotland's spell. It happens to everyone. I told you—"

"Sorry. I lied." Mindy shifted on the sofa. "But I am curled up before a peat fire. Sadly, it's little more than a clump of smoldering ash just now. I'm not drinking whisky, though I could be if I wanted. There's a small welcome bottle and a glass on the bedside table.

"Otherwise, I'm in a darkened suite in a Victorian coach house on a wet and windy night in the middle of nowhere. If you ignore the wind"—she glanced at the night-blackened window and shuddered—"it's very still and quiet. And although I wouldn't have believed it, it's getting colder and eerier with each passing minute."

"But have you seen any mist?" Margo's enthusiasm wasn't dampened. "They say it rolls down the braes and clings to the corries. They—"

"I don't know what a corrie is, but—"

"It's a cleft in the side of a mountain, sort of like a deep and narrow ravine," Margo the Scotland expert explained. "A brae is the hillside itself and—"

"I don't care what they are." Mindy glanced at the dark window again. The wind gusts were starting to rattle the panes. "If there are braes and corries out there, I didn't see any. Your mist was everywhere, pea-soup thick and blotting any heathery hills or romantic castle ruins that might have enchanted me."

"You'll come around!" Margo laughed. "I'd dare anyone to go to Scotland and not fall in love. No way is my own sister going to be the one exception."

Mindy pinched the bridge of her nose and tried not to sigh. "Actually," she began, feeling a pang of sisterly guilt because Margo truly did love Scotland, "my suite is quite nice. It's got two levels and is airy. I could see it in Hawaii or Florida if I switched the pine furnishings and tartan for tropical prints and bamboo. Get rid of all the photos of the Hebrides and replace them with Maui sunsets.

"The suite is called the Havbredey"—her tongue twisted on the word—"and it means—"

"I know what it means, you goose!" Margo laughed again.

"I should have known."

"Yes, you should have. I can tell you all kinds of things about Scot—"

Margo broke off abruptly and Mindy could hear the murmur of voices in the background. Then the creak of a door followed by the distinctive tinkle of the wind chimes that announced new customers at Ye Olde Pagan Times.

"I'm back." Margo was on the line again, sounding a bit breathless. "Anyway, it's about the Hebrides that—"

"Are you at work?" Mindy knew Margo's boss, an eccentric old woman named Patience Peasgood, though nice, wouldn't appreciate Margo chatting overseas on work time. "You can call me when you get off. I'll hear the phone, even if I'm asleep. I don't want Patience—"

"That's the best part!" Margo almost shouted the words. "It was Patience who told me to call you. She and Madame Zelda insisted—"

"You mean Marta Lopez." Mindy rolled her eyes. "The Puerto Rican tarot reader."

"She's good whether you like her or not."

"Ice cream is good, too, but look what happens if you eat it all the time."

"You're just jet-lagged. Listen—"

"I'm all ears." Mindy settled back against the cushions. "What's up?"

"I'm flying over to see you!" Margo's voice swelled with glee. "Can you believe it? Patience gave me unpaid leave to come and—"

"I'm not even there yet." Mindy tightened her grip on the phone. "Not in Barra, anyway. I'll be staying at one of the island's best hotels and you know how hard it was to get a booking. The lady said they were full up and—"

"Don't worry! I don't mean now." Margo would be waving a hand, Mindy knew. "Patience put some strings on my leave, but that's no bother. She's looking for another girl to help out afternoons and weekends. As soon as she finds someone suitable, she said I can have the time off to fly over and join you. Unless business gets too busy and then . . ."

Mindy listened to Margo rattle on. Her chances of coming didn't sound that solid. Even so, a wave of dread crashed over her at the thought of her ghost-busting enthusiast sister appearing at Barra.

"That's wonderful!" Mindy hoped her voice didn't come across as squeaky.

But she knew it did.

"Don't be so alarmed." Margo's reply proved it. "My trip might not even happen. But if it does, I promise not to embarrass you."

"I didn't mean that. . . ." Mindy combed a hand through her hair, unable to finish.

Margo already had embarrassed her—or would have—if Mindy wasn't always one step ahead of her.

Feeling sweat bead her brow, Mindy glanced at her hand luggage, on the floor near the suite's large four-poster bed.

A super-duper ghost-detecting device was tucked into the side pocket of the carry-on. The latest in spook-sleuthing technology, according to Margo and everyone at Ye Olde Pagan Times, the thing was an EMF reader.

Designed to pick up fluctuations in electromagnetic fields where ghosts were believed to gather, the EMF meter had all the bells and whistles. It included a shrill alarm tone that sounded if the registered paranormal activity proved to be especially strong.

The only reason Mindy hadn't pitched it at Newark was that Margo had it on loan from Patience Peasgood. After Mindy's trip, it had to be returned to the shop.

So Mindy had done the only reasonable thing and removed the batteries.

Thankfully, no one in security had found the EMF meter, demanding answers to questions that would only make her look goofy.

If Margo came to Barra, she'd be weighted down with several more such devices. Not to mention infrared thermometers and cameras and whatever else practicing ghost hunters carried around with them.

People would notice.

And Mindy wouldn't be just embarrassed.

She'd be mortified.

"I know what you meant." The hurt in Margo's voice brought back Mindy's stab of guilt. "I won't bring any equipment except my diggy camera. You already have a good EMF reader there. That'll be enough.

"And don't worry." Margo laughed again. "I won't do an EVP session or anything."

Mindy closed her eyes. She was sure trying to catch

ghostly voices on a tape recorder would be one of her sister's first attempts to attract Highland spirits.

"I'll hold you to that." Mindy's plaid throw slipped and she reached to tuck it around her knees again. "No woo-woo weirdness and I'll be glad to see you."

That, at least, was true.

She did love Margo, despite her penchant for the strange and unexplained.

But having Margo underfoot, mooning around and waxing poetic about the Scottish Highlands, just so wasn't on Mindy's agenda for this trip.

Everyone knew the Scots thought Americans were a bit overly dotty about Scotland. Just as it was well-known that the Highland telegraph was alive and working better than ever, even in these age-of-the-Internet times.

Margo would have everyone in the Isles thinking they'd both gone around the bend. The verdict would spread like a fire on the moor. They'd be branded as certifiable, which might even leak back to Global, hurting Mindy's chances of returning to her old flying job.

Airlines took a narrow view of anything that even fringed on unbalanced.

"Madame Zelda did a reading for me," Margo gushed on. "She's certain I'm fated to make this trip. But if you'd rather I didn't . . ."

"No, no!" Mindy bit her tongue to keep from reminding Margo that if she'd revealed her dreams to the fortune-teller, of course, Madame Zelda would say they'd come true.

Hoping to change the subject, Mindy glanced around the dimly lit room. Her gaze fell on a large gift bag bearing the tartan-ribboned thistle design of One Cairn Village. The package sat on an old-fashioned trunk at the foot of the bed. Mindy hurried there now, snatching up the bag and pulling out a gorgeous length of tweed, purchased for Margo in Innes's tea and gift shop.

"Of course, you must come." Mindy hugged the tweed to her, wishing Margo could see it now. "I picked up some stunning tweed for you this afternoon. It's—"

"Tweed?" Margo's voice rose with excitement. Her Highland vacation plans took a backseat to style. "You bought genuine Scottish tweed for me?"

"I did." Mindy smiled, glad she'd splurged. "It was made right here at Ravenscraig Castle, where I'm staying. It's called Kiss o' Heather and is all purply mauve with a touch of pink. You'll love it."

"I already do." Margo paused. "Is there enough to make a skirt?"

"There is." Mindy returned to the sofa. "That's what I thought you could do with it."

"O-o-oh!" Margo sounded like she might jump through the phone. "I can't wait to see it. Thank you and—oh, here come more customers.

"Gotta go!" She hung up just as Ye Olde Pagan Times' wind chime began to tinkle.

Mindy stared at the dead phone. She rubbed her eyes, feeling as if she'd been caught up by a cyclone. Margo on a Scotland roll could exhaust anyone. Mindy just wished she hadn't gone on about the woo-woo stuff.

Especially with the wind shrieking round the eaves and making weird *whoosh*ing noises in the chimney. It didn't help that the night sky—what little of it she could see through the window—no longer looked cold and gray, but was now cold and black.

Pitch-black. The kind of darkness she was sure couldn't be found on the other side of the Atlantic Ocean.

And thanks to her sister, she now imagined that inky emptiness teeming with all kinds of dangers. If ghosts existed—even back home in New Hope—then who knew what creatures roamed Scotland's hills after nightfall?

She'd already seen a dog that could have been a werewolf!

Shivering, she puffed her bangs off her forehead and snatched another book off the side table. Better to read about someone's ancestral beanstalk than worry about Celtic beasties that might—or might not—be prowling through the woods beneath her window.

Determined to bore herself with Wee Hughie's genealogical wanderings, she glanced down at the book in her hand. It *was* another volume of the author's *A Highlander's* series. But this one was titled *Hearthside Tales: A Highlander's Look at Scottish Myth and Legend.*

A bad artist's rendering of Nessie graced the cover.

"Ack!" Mindy dropped the book as if it'd been a hot potato.

She was not going to read about the very creatures she was trying to put from her mind. What she needed was a good hot shower or a long soak in the luxurious marble whirlpool. There was nothing better than modern-day niceties to banish things that went bump in the night.

But the instant she stood, the wind dropped and the room went eerily quiet.

Even the air felt different, turning thick and heavy.

"Pah! It's nerves, Menlove, pure nerves," she muttered, starting across the room.

She didn't make it halfway to the bathroom before a piercing howl stopped her cold. Heart racing, she clapped a hand to her breast, listening as the sound ended on a haunting, high-pitched wail.

It was the kind of mournful tone Margo would call otherworldly.

Mindy was sure it was a hybrid owl.

Certain she wouldn't get any sleep until she knew, she went to the window, peering through the glass until her eyes adjusted to the darkness.

When they did, she could make out one or two pin-pricks of light from One Cairn Village on the other side of the wood. Closer to the Victorian Lodge Coach House, she spotted several large outcroppings of rock. Nothing stirred except the soft mist drifting through the trees.

Mindy breathed a sigh of relief.

Even if she hadn't seen the owl, everything looked as it should. Until something huge and dark loped past directly beneath her.

"Gah!" She jumped and the creature stopped, swinging round to stare up at her with glowing amber eyes.

It was the wolf-dog from the gatehouse.

He, rather than a mutant owl, must've made the bloodcurdling howl. And—Mindy's heart stopped as she stared back at him, unable to look away—she now knew why he'd given her such goose bumps.

She knew him.

Or rather, she remembered him.

He was Gibbie.

Bran of Barra's ghost dog that she'd seen the night the Hebridean chieftain had appeared right in front of her in the Folly's kitchen.

Then, as now, the two were inseparable.

Both watched her from near the edge of the wood. Gibbie stood where he'd swung around to stare at her, and his master was right beside him, where he'd mani-fested out of thin air, appearing in the wink of an eye.

Mindy gulped and twitched back the curtain to get a better look. It was frightfully dark and a thin autumn rain was just beginning to fall. Droplets were splattering the window glass, running down the panes.

But she wasn't mistaken.

Bran of Barra was down there.

The glint of his coppery red hair shone in the moonlight and his plaid whipped around him, caught by the wind just starting to gust again. Shadows cast across his face made it difficult to see his expression, but she could feel both anger and passion radiating off him.

He was certainly staring right at her.

Every instinct told her to draw back from the window. Or at least step behind the curtains, shielding herself from his bold, assessing stare.

But she couldn't look away.

Bran of Barra and his dog stepped closer. So near, she could see raindrops glistening on his hair and shoulders. He reached down to stroke the dog's ears, but his gaze never left her face.

He watched her with a look that made her insides quiver.

It wasn't the kind of look modern-day men gave women. It was the kind of piercing, oh-so-uncompromisingly male perusal that only bold, take-charge men of times past fixed on a woman when they wished to seduce and unsettle.

And it was working.

Ghostly or not, his strength wove a seductive spell around her. And the way he sometimes let his gaze drop to her lips, as if contemplating how best to plunder them, well, those heated looks filled her with tingly anticipation. Mindy could feel her entire body flaming.

She shouldn't think about his kisses.

She did straighten her back, not wanting him to see how much he stirred her.

He angled his head and she was sure his lips were twitching into a smile. But then he glanced at the dog and strode another few paces toward the coach house, his faithful companion at his side.

Mindy stood frozen, trying to pretend he and his beast were nothing but a swirl of mist. Well, two swirls. In the darkness of night, many things could take on the shape of a man and a dog. Such an error was especially possible when those swirls were seen by someone beyond exhausted.

It was just a pity that the dog's luminous golden eyes and the bright blue sparks dancing around the pommel stone of Bran of Barra's sword torpedoed her mist-swirl theory.

She doubted even Highland fog came in colors.

Whitish gray was pretty much worldwide standard.

Mindy swallowed. Her pulse raced and she could feel her nerves prickling. But when Bran of Barra took another leisurely step in her direction and she leapt backward, tripping over Wee Hughie MacSporran's book and landing with a painful *thump* on the polished floor, she got mad.

She jumped up, kicked Wee Hughie's book into a corner, and marched back to the window. She whipped back the curtains, prepared to glare down at the lout and tell him just where he and his wolf-dog could go.

But in the short time it'd taken for her to fall and scramble to her feet, the heavens had opened. Just as Malcolm predicted, great sheets of rain were blowing across the clearing beneath her window. In fact, it was pouring so hard that she couldn't even make out the pines that marked the edge of the wood.

Somewhere thunder boomed and a jagged bolt of lightning flashed across the sky.

Bran of Barra and Gibbie were gone.

Frowning, Mindy opened the casement and leaned out. But the only thing to greet her was the gusting wind and rain. Bran and his beast really had vanished. And the instant she realized she'd called the ghost *Bran*, she closed the window so fast she almost cracked the glass.

She was not going to get first-name personal with a man who wasn't there.

No matter how real he might appear.

Or how sexy.

But despite her attempts to put him from her mind and go to bed in her best I-am-not-affected-by-him attitude, she found herself moving about the room, turning on lamps, overhead lights, and even the television. Not that it helped much to create a nonghostly atmosphere with the ceiling lights recessed and muted and the table lamps designed to look like old-fashioned oil lamps.

The TV wasn't very soothing, either, as the only program that came on without snow and static was a 1950s film in Gaelic.

Mindy didn't want to look too closely, but she strongly suspected it was *Brigadoon*.

When Gene Kelly strode onto the screen, she was sure.

"Not for me." She grabbed the remote off the coffee table and clicked.

The screen went black just as Bran of Barra appeared in front of her, his great shaggy dog at his heels and a grin on his face.

"Gah!" Mindy jumped. The remote went flying from her fingers.

Bran of Barra waited until it landed with a *clack* on

the hardwood floor, and then planted his hands on his kilt-covered hips.

"So-o-o, lass, we meet again." He looked about the room, one brow arched, appraisingly. "I'm thinking it's a pity you're staying in these fine lodgings. Such comfort will soften you, it will. You'll no' find Barra as hospitable. 'Tis a cold, windswept place where giant waves pound the cliffs and the gales are strong enough to blow you away in a wink. It won't be at all to your liking.

"If"—his gaze snapped back to her—"that's where you're heading."

Mindy suppressed the urge to laugh. If she weren't so unsettled—which she knew was his point—she'd no doubt bust a gut. As it was, she tilted her head to one side and jammed her own hands on her hips.

"Where I'm going is my own business." She kept her voice cool, glad certain ghost-hunting, the-star-is-psychic-and-speaks-with-the-Other-Side TV shows made it seem halfway normal to converse with him. "As for Barra, you needn't bother trying to convince me I won't like it. I already know that very well myself."

To her surprise, he blinked, looking almost offended.

"Barra is the pearl of the Hebrides." His chest swelled and his voice rang with pride. "Though I'll own it's possible that only a Barrach can fully appreciate the isle's true worth and many splendors."

He folded his arms, eyeing her as if he expected agreement.

When she said nothing, he set his lips in a hard line and flicked an invisible speck of lint from his plaid.

He was clearly peeved.

His dog began shuffling around the room, sniffing at furniture. He passed close by her once, his cold nose bumping her hand and his plumed tail swishing a few times, as if they were friends.

Mindy refused to be distracted.

Nor would she admit that how people felt about dogs was one of her measures of a person's goodness. Bran's devotion to his dog appealed to her strongly. And that the dog loved him so much in return also said bundles.

She'd withdrawn from more than one potential relationship because the man hadn't liked dogs. The way Bran of Barra's whole expression softened when he looked at Gibbie made so much seem insignificant.

Like his ghostly status. Even his name—*MacNeil*.

But she didn't want to fall for him.

She put back her shoulders, chin lifted. "Why are you following me? Why don't you want me—" A fierce gust of wind rattled the windowpanes, cutting her off.

Bran of Barra paid the screaming wind no heed.

He did raise one auburn eyebrow. "Want you, my lady?"

"I meant"—Mindy ran a hand down the front of her sweater, sure it'd shrunk two sizes since he'd *popped* into the room—"why don't you want me on Barra? The other ghosts—"

"The other ghosts are no longer your concern." His mouth almost twitched into a smile. "I am."

"Every one of you is a problem for me."

"Nae, you err." He set his hand on the hilt of his sword. Its crystal gemstone was glowing blue. "My friends have naught to do with this. You heard them in my hall. They only wish"—he glanced at the darkened window—"peace to enjoy their days and make merry as they will.

"I warned you once that their passions are dangerous if roused. Now it is me you must be wary of. If"—he closed his fingers around his sword's pommel stone, hiding the crystal—"you visit my hall again."

"I'm not afraid of you." Mindy felt her temper rise. "And I'm used to trouble."

"Ahhh, but I haven't yet begun to make trouble for you, Mindy-lass. I promise you"—he spoke softly, his deep voice sending shivers all through her—"you'll know when I do."

Mindy bit her lip, not doubting him.

She took a step backward.

He looked too real. Everything about him was too much like the braw Scottish warriors she'd fantasized about in the years before Hunter. His voice, that accent . . .

The *look* he was giving her set her heart racing.

Even more alarming, the room suddenly felt much smaller. Bran of Barra, already one of the tallest, most commandingly built men she'd ever seen, now appeared even bigger. He seemed to grow in power and stature, a muscle-ripped bear of a man whose intense gaze was searing her.

Mindy swallowed.

She was quite sure there was no man like him anywhere. Not in her world or his, nor anyplace in between. He was a force of nature. And he was coming at her with slow, sure steps that made it hard to breathe.

No, it was the heat in his eyes doing that.

He meant to kiss her.

"No-o-o!" She scooted around the sofa, putting its bulk between them.

He laughed. "Och, lass, do you truly think you can escape me so easily?"

On the words, he was right beside her. But rather than ravish her, he merely lifted a hand to brush his knuckles down her cheek. It was the lightest of touches, but it sent tingles rippling along her nerves, making her go hot and shivery all over.

"It willnae be good if you go to Barra." His gaze moved over her face, then dropped to her lips. "Stay away." He lowered his head, kissing her so gently she could barely note the coolness of his lips before it was over.

And—damn her—she wanted more!

She felt herself trembling, and shame scalded her. She didn't need this. Putting up a hand, she backed away and this time he didn't follow.

"You see, sweet"—he was suddenly across the room where his dog lay before the hearth—"the kind of trouble you'll bring on yourself if you act unwisely."

Mindy glared at him, angry.

He had the gall to shrug. "Go home to your America and rest easy that you'll no' be missing much. There isn't a stone left on Barra to see."

"There is now." Mindy tossed her hair. "I know because I had them sent there!"

She angled her head, ready to savor his shock, but empty air stared back at her. She whirled around, sure he'd be behind her, grinning. But he wasn't. He was gone. Certain she'd never been more shaken, she dropped onto the sofa.

She'd wanted him to kiss her.

A ghost!

Feeling both hot and cold—and still maddeningly excited—she pulled the tartan rug over her, adding two plump pillows for good measure.

She was so sleepy.

If she just closed her eyes—

Brrrrring! A loud siren tone filled the room. The

shrilling grew louder, hurting her ears. She leapt up, tripping over the bedcovers as they tangled around her legs. She stumbled forward through the dark, trying to find the bedside lamp.

The sound was too shrill for her cell phone. Mindy tried to shake off the fog of drowsiness, feeling confused.

Until she remembered that Margo's all-the-bells-and-whistles EMF Spook-o-meter was in her bag. She grabbed her purse, pulling out the ghost-busting device just as the siren dwindled to silence.

She frowned at the small contraption, remembering too late that she'd discarded its batteries before she'd left Newark Airport.

In that moment, the *brrrrring* noise went off again. Only this time it wasn't as loud. And it certainly wasn't the EMF meter.

It was the alarm clock on the nightstand.

She'd set it for six a.m. so she wouldn't miss Ravenscraig's full Scottish breakfast, served in the castle dining room from seven to nine. Margo's ghost-hunting device hadn't gone off at all. She'd been sleeping and dreamed everything. Most likely, Bran of Barra's visit, too.

She sank onto the edge of the bed and rubbed her hands over her face, trying to remember undressing and slipping beneath the covers. She couldn't, but she did recall every detail of her dream encounter with Bran.

She should be glad it hadn't been real.

Instead she was almost sorry. And that could mean only one thing.

Trouble.

Chapter 7

Bran of Barra had never felt more like a scoundrel.

Nae, *scoundrel* wasn't quite odious enough. Scowling, he paced his rain-washed bailey, searching for a more suitable epithet. When it came, he revolted at the description, but couldn't deny its blistering aptness. He wasn't a mere lout. He was a cloven-footed, ring-tailed arse.

He paused, wincing.

For a proud man who considered himself as having a way with the ladies, it didn't sit well with him that he'd deliberately set out to intimidate Mindy Menlove.

That he'd had little choice did nothing to banish his guilt.

Equally damning, when he'd sifted himself back to Barra—returning to the cold and misty forecourt outside his keep and not the cheery warmth of his hall—he'd revealed that he'd turned into a coward, as well.

Never in all his long centuries of making occasional forays from Barra had he hesitated to remanifest in his crowded, boisterous hall. He relished the cozy familiarity and all the well-kent faces waiting there to greet him. Souls who—if he'd reappeared in their midst—would immediately see that something was amiss.

They'd hound him good-naturedly, not relenting until they pried the truth from him.

So for the first time in his afterlife, he found himself avoiding his own hearthside.

His frown deepened.

Furious, he strode across the bailey and climbed onto the curtain wall, where he glared across the night-blackened water at the dark smudge of hills rising behind Barra's inner shore. For once, he regretted that he'd built his tower on its own rocky little isle in the middle of the bay. It would suit him fine to be up on the larger island's highest peak, letting the icy sea wind blast away his cares.

He fisted his hands on the cold ledge of the wall. He was fooling himself and knew it well. Even the fiercest gale wasn't strong enough to chase the lass from his mind.

Her hold on him appeared as inescapable as a flood tide he couldn't outrun.

Bran shoved a hand through his hair and glanced at the heavens. Although a light drizzle fell, there was no sign of the teeming rain that had drenched Ravenscraig, and a sliver of moon peeked through the clouds.

Gibbie was leaning into him, his great bulk heavy against Bran's legs. He reached down to pat the dog's head, glad for his company. Thin wisps of mist curled around them, chill and damp. And below the curtain walls, huge waves crashed over the rocks, filling the air with spume.

It could have been an ordinary night, if only . . .

"Damn American." Bran felt his jaw clench.

He wished she'd been afraid of him. Experience had taught him that most moderns feared the unexplained, men and women alike. It didn't matter if ghosts appeared solid, as Bran prided himself on being able to do. The cold shivers rippled down their spines all the same.

Yet Mindy had faced him with courage, even challenging him, his right to be at Ravenscraig. A place he visited not infrequently, as did many others of his ilk.

Ghosts knew where they were welcome.

Just as Mindy knew when she didn't wish to be bothered.

The image of her lifting her chin and flipping back that shining blond hair flashed across his mind. As did the sparking anger he'd seen in her eyes and—damn his blundering hide—how she'd nipped around the sofa and tried to ward him off when he'd meant to kiss her.

Nae, he corrected, he'd planned to swing her up into his arms, hoist her over his shoulder, and carry her to her bed, hoping she'd faint from fright before he was forced to toss her onto the mattress and pretend he was about to have his way with her.

But she hadn't swooned and her bravery—something all Highlanders honored—had stirred his admiration.

Gods pity him.

The last thing he needed was to feel sympathy for her.

That esteem had ripped his intentions to shreds so that he'd stared at the pulse leaping at the base of her throat and felt the ridiculous urge to soothe her. He could have pulled her to him, crushing her mouth beneath his.

Instead, he'd smoothed his knuckles down her cheek and brushed his lips against hers so lightly that the intimacy of the kiss had set his heart to thumping in a way it'd never done before.

He'd never kissed a woman with such care.

Nor had he ever stomped about in the misting rain,

hours later—in truth, centuries apart—and tortured himself with recollections of how very soft her skin was. Or how much her sweet, lush lips tempted him, blinding him to reason and making him wish . . .

He leaned harder against the wall and sighed.

Gibbie gave a disgusted groan and trotted away to investigate the shadows and smells on the far side of the bailey, clearly finding them more interesting. But as soon as he disappeared into the mist, a firm hand clamped down on Bran's shoulder.

He started and reached for his sword, but a familiar laugh stopped him.

Saor MacSwain lifted his voice above the wind. "Since when do you return from Ravenscraig looking as if you'd swallowed a jug of soured ale?"

"Perhaps I have?" Bran whirled to glare at the other chieftain, the only soul who'd dare disturb him when he so obviously desired to be left alone.

To emphasize that point, he turned back to the wall and stared down at the sea. "Truth is I do regret making the journey. I doubt I'll visit our old friends again."

"The devil you say!" Saor stepped closer and angled his head to peer into Bran's face. "What will come of Ravenscraig's Ancestral Balls if you weren't there to add a dash of honest Highland authenticity? The visitors who recognize you as a ghost are thrilled to have their belief confirmed that all Scottish castles are haunted. And the ones who see you as a man"—he flashed a wicked smile—"perhaps the many American lassies who stay at Ravenscraig, well, they—"

"They can content themselves with the other Highland ghosties who beat a track through the heather to attend such fests." Bran gave his friend a narrow look. "I have far more weighty matters on my mind than playing the gallant to kilt-crazed tourists."

Saor arched a brow. "What, then? Are you fashed about the three MacNeil chieftains Serafina—"

"This has naught to do with Serafina or thon ghosties, whoe'er they were!" Bran scowled.

It had to do with a modern female he wasn't about to mention.

And—the thought jellied his knees—it was about something so incredible, he'd been doing his damnedest not to think on the possibility, because if it proved true, the wonder of it might just stop his heart.

"Och, well . . ." Saor considered his fingernails. "If no' our lovely little Saracen or our mysterious visitors, it can only be a wench plaguing you." He looked up quickly, his dark eyes glinting with amusement. "A maid I've yet to meet, I'm thinking."

Bran kept his mouth clamped in a tight, hard line.

Saor looked ready to split his sides. "Perhaps 'tis I who should sift myself to Oban and see what fetching lassie has turned your head."

"You'll no' be going anywhere." Bran shot out a hand to grip Saor's arm. "And"—his brows snapped together—"do you truly think I'd be scowling so fiercely if some bonnie bit o' fluff had caught my eye?"

Saor jerked free, grinning. "Aye, that I do!"

"Well, you're wrong."

To Bran's annoyance, his friend threw back his head and howled with laughter.

Ignoring the lump's hooting, Bran folded his arms. "If you must know, you long-nosed gawp, my foul humor has to do with Barra."

"You?" Saor stopped laughing.

"Nae, it isn't me. Though . . ." Bran glanced across the bay to the dark outline of the island that was as much a part of him as the air he breathed. He *was* Barra. And in so much more than his mere title.

There were times he'd walked across those hills and moors, or along the Traigh Mhor, Barra's great cockle strand, and would have sworn he felt the isle's heart beating steadily beneath his feet.

He swallowed, remembering.

Saor followed his gaze. "The isle, then?"

"Close, but I mean this wee rocky islet where we're standing." Bran flung out an arm, gesturing to the quiet bailey and the sturdy gray bulk of his tower. "It's my home that's troubling me. Yon keep that is my pride and that gives refuge to my friends."

Saor leaned back against the curtain wall and crossed his long legs at the ankles. He didn't say anything, just lifted one brow, waiting.

"It's gone, my friend." The admission tasted like ash on Bran's tongue. "MacNeil's Tower is no more. This"— he flicked a hand in the direction of the keep, knew the other chieftain would understand he meant the world he kept alive through ghostly contrivance—"is all that remains.

"A conjured shadow of what once was." Pain sliced through Bran like a knife. "Nary a stone remains in the day of the moderns. Not one crumbled bit of walling nor even a lichened piece of rubble."

Bran felt his throat thicken, but he didn't shame his feelings.

He loved Barra that much.

"It's all vanished, Saor. This spit of a rock, wiped clean as if my tower never stood."

"How can you know?" Saor was staring at the keep,

his gaze on one of the narrow slit windows. Dim yellow light glimmered there, showing that one of Bran's friends had claimed the room for the night.

"You swore you'd never visit Barra in the present day." Saor glanced at him, questioning.

"Well, I did."

Saor's eyes rounded. "When? I didn't notice you'd slipped away."

Bran snorted. "Do you think I'd tarry long? Seeing what I did, or"—he shuddered—"I should say, what I didn't see!"

"You didn't say when you went."

"Does it matter?"

"I'm curious."

"It was the night you told me about Serafina and the three MacNeil chieftains. The ghosties who weren't knocked sideways by her charms." Bran flicked his fingers to conjure a cup of ale, took a deep swig, and tossed the cup aside.

It disappeared before it hit the cobbles.

He wiped his mouth, remembering the night was the same e'en Mindy had appeared in his kitchens.

"With so many odd goings-on, I reckoned something must've stirred an interest in Barra." He kept as close to the truth as possible. "It seemed likely such a disturbance would have happened in the present time. As chief, I saw it my duty to have a look."

Saor gave a low whistle. "Now you know why our mothers e'er preached that it did no good to peek beneath rocks."

"Aye, that is the way of it."

"Then why did you go sifting yourself off to Ravenscraig?" Saor rubbed his brow. "I'd think you'd have had enough of the modern world for a time."

"Pah!" Bran turned to gaze out at the sea again. "That place is as familiar as our own isle-strewn waters. Alex was once one of us, if you've forgotten. I wanted a distraction and having a good craic about Ravenscraig's next Ancestral Ball seemed a good one."

"Then why did I find you looking so grim?"

"Because"—Bran spun around—"I heard some interesting tidings from a guest there."

"A female guest?"

"It doesn't matter," Bran snapped, realizing too late that his curt tone confirmed Saor's suspicions.

"What's important"—he felt a rush of emotion—"is that I was told the tower's stones have been returned to Barra."

"Havers!" Saor stared at him. "You're no' making sense. First your guts twist because the tower's gone and now you're for telling me it's back again."

Bran curled his hands around his sword belt so he wouldn't ram them through his hair. "I cannae say if the castle stands or not. Nor do I know if the woman spoke true. Or if she did, what was done with the stones upon their arrival here.

"Sakes, where did they disappear to in the first place?" He flashed a glance at the keep, unable to keep the frustration out of his voice. "We've both seen enough present-day ruins of once-mighty strongholds to know that even when they fall, something remains.

"Yet"—he frowned—"when I sifted myself to modern Barra, it was as I told you. I found myself surrounded by desolation without even a speck o' dust remaining. I say you again, even if MacNeil's Tower fell, those stones should have been lying about. They didn't sprout wings and fly away. So where did they go and how—"

"Why didn't you ask the lassie?" Saor made it sound so simple.

Bran took a deep breath and knew he was about to embarrass himself. "Because, you loon, I was so startled when she mentioned the stones that I accidentally sifted myself back here."

"Then perhaps you should return?" Saor leaned back against the wall again and folded his arms. "Go back to Ravenscraig and find peace. Or"—he angled his dark head—"hie yourself to present-day Barra and have another look."

Bran snorted.

"You already went once," Saor pressed. "Another peek won't matter now."

Bran glared at him. "I'm needed here."

"Och, aye." Saor stretched out a hand to rub Gibbie's ears when the dog joined them. "There isn't another bluidy soul amongst us able to use a wee bit o' ghostly trickery to maintain the good life we enjoy here."

Gibbie sat and barked, clearly in agreement.

Bran scrubbed his hands over his face and ignored both of them.

It *was* a poor excuse.

But he couldn't risk the damage to his heart if he returned and had to suffer discovering that his beloved home had indeed faded from memory.

As for seeing Mindy again . . .

Bran glanced at the Heartbreaker's pommel stone and then away. Praise God the charmed crystal hadn't chosen this moment to blaze blue and torment him with jabs of white-hot pain to his side.

But he was struck with sudden inspiration.

"Oho—I've an idea!" He grabbed Saor's arm, gripping tight. "You can sift yourself to modern Barra. Have a wander about, and see if the lassie was telling tall tales or if she really did have my stones sent back here!"

"Me?" Saor's bluster left him. "I cannae—"

Gibbie barked again and looked up at Saor with an adoring doggy grin, his tail swishing back and forth across the wet cobbles.

"Bah!" Bran released him and stood back, pleased. "You just praised your own skills, man. Even Gibbie"—he jerked a look at the dog—"knows you're just the one to find out the truth for us."

"I meant to say I cannae sift myself anywhere just now." Saor cleared his throat, threw a glance at the darkened keep. "I told Serafina I'd join her—"

Bran laughed. "You've been out here with me too long for her to have waited. That one's hotter than a glowing coal snatched off the fire. She'll be warming someone else's bed about now and well you know it."

Saor's scowl said he did.

He began to pace. "I'll no' stay long, mind. Only a quick peek and I'm out o' there. Thon modern time is too crowded and loud for my liking."

Pausing to swipe a raindrop from his brow, he glanced at Bran. "Have you e'er seen or heard"—he shuddered—"those things they call leaf blowers?"

"You'll find Barra still as the grave."

"Fie, man." Saor whipped about to glare at him. "If you're so sure nothing's there, why ask me to go?"

"Because I am Barra and can." Bran thrust his chin, unbending.

It wasn't often he pulled chiefly superiority.

"And because"—he turned away, not wanting Saor to see his expression soften—"you are the only one I know will tell me true."

He'd lost his other trusted friends to Americans!

Feeling a sudden pang of loss, he clasped his hands behind his back and waited for Saor to argue. He kept his gaze fixed on the bay, where gusting wind was sending up spray from the choppy, whitecapped waves.

Behind him, all was silent.

Bran's conscience began to twitch and squirm. The Barra MacNeils might be, well, *the Barra MacNeils*, but as chief of the MacSwains, Saor claimed a long and proud bloodline of his own. Bran shifted and let out a long breath. He shouldn't have lairded it over his friend.

Wishing to make amends, Bran turned, but Saor was already gone.

The bailey was dark and empty.

Only Gibbie remained.

And his tail was wagging, his excited gaze fixed on a spot of nothingness that still crackled with the *air shimmers* left by Saor's swift departure.

"So he went, eh, Gibbie?" Bran didn't bother to say where.

The dog knew.

And since the beast—who Bran suspected was as intuitive as any Highland seer—didn't appear troubled, he hoped his friend would return with good tidings.

Bran refused to consider anything else.

But when the waiting stretched into what seemed an eternity, he began to have some doubt. Saor wasn't a MacNeil, but he loved Barra and Bran's tower with the fullness of his heart.

He was a MacNeil in spirit.

And as such, he'd be as troubled as Bran to see their well-loved bit of home reduced to nothing more than an echo in the dark.

Saor would return at once.

Unless . . .

"Odin's balls!" Bran's pulse leapt. Were he a lesser man, he would shake all over. As it was, he clapped one hand to his plaid-draped chest and clenched the other into a tight, painful fist.

There could be only one reason for Saor's tardiness.

Mindy hadn't lied.

The air shifted then, a mere ripple quick as winking, and Saor appeared. "You heard rightly," he announced. "Barra, this wee islet in the bay is mounded with stones. I gave them a good keek, and am sure they're your own. And"—he grinned—"from what I saw of them, they're looking no worse for centuries of wear."

Bran stared at him. For a moment, he couldn't breathe or speak. A wave of light-headedness gripped him and he heard the roar of blood in his ears.

He felt his chest tighten. "The tower's stones . . ."

"And the ones from the walls and the chapel, the outbuildings, and the saints only know what else." Saor rolled his shoulders. "There were that many piled hither and thither. I think I even saw the old stone bollard we used to moor our galleys."

Bran's heart squeezed. He'd stolen his first kiss next to that bollard.

As if Saor read his mind, he planted his hands on his hips and laughed. "Scarce recognized it, I did. Stone's gone shiny as a bairn's behind. Belike centuries of Mac-Neils used it, wearing it smooth with their mooring lines."

"And did you see the lass who told me about the stones?" Bran had to know. "She's a fetching wench. Sun-bright hair cut close to her chin and deep blue eyes. She's"—he tried not to grimace—"an American."

Saor's brows lifted, but he shook his head. "I saw

nothing but piles o' stanes. And"—he frowned—"the blackness of a pit."

"A pit?" Bran blinked.

"Aye, so I said." Saor's eyes glinted in the darkness. "That's why it took me so long. I manifested in the bottom of a great yawning void and thought I'd landed myself in the Dark One's own torture chamber.

"I stood still for the longest time, no' wanting to even sift myself away lest the stir in the air attract that one's attention. But then"—his smile returned—"my eyes adjusted to the dimness and I saw where I was."

"And where was that?"

"Deep inside the ruins of the ancient broch you built your stronghold upon."

"What?" Bran's jaw slipped.

Saor clapped him on the shoulder. "Dinnae tell me you've forgotten? At the time, you'd said that if the Auld Ones who stayed on Barra when these isles were young deemed this islet a good place for their broch, you'd call it a meet site for a MacNeil castle."

"I ken what I said"—Bran's insides were beginning to quiver—"but that broch was underground even in our day. Part of it was our foundation and basement, the rest filled in with earth and rubble."

"Well, it's not filled in now."

"But, why . . ."

Bran let the words trail away, not wanting to make the connection dancing on the fringes of his mind. Doing so would see him even more bound to a certain bonnie American, and his sense of self-preservation warred against deepening any possible ties to her.

"I'll tell you what I think." The excitement in Saor's voice showed he didn't share Bran's hesitation. "Having seen what I did, it's clear that someone, perhaps this *fetching wench* of yours, hasn't just returned your tower's stones simply to toss them onto the ground.

"Whoe'er is responsible means to rebuild the castle. And they've already started by digging the old foundation." He grinned again. "That was the pit I landed in. The old broch ruin, waiting to support your restored tower, just as it did in the past."

Bran swallowed. He was certain Saor was right.

It was the last thing he'd expected.

And the very idea was making his eyes burn with a blinding, stinging saltiness that had nothing to do with the spray-filled air and everything to do with an American he'd now have to find at the soonest and tender his thanks.

His sense of chivalry demanded it.

As did his position as chief.

In truth, such an encounter might be quite pleasurable. Indeed, the notion was becoming more so the longer he thought about it.

Feeling better already, even buoyant, he grabbed Saor's elbow and pulled him across the bailey to the tower. "Come, my friends—" He glanced over his shoulder at Gibbie, trotting faithfully behind them. "It would seem we have some celebrating to do!"

He didn't mention that he hoped a full belly and a good night's sleep thereafter would help him prepare for his meeting with Mindy.

His seduction of her.

The thought came from nowhere.

But as he threw open the tower door and stood back to let Saor and Gibbie enter his keep, he knew he liked the idea very much.

It could happen.

He glanced down at the Heartbreaker, this time eyeing the crystal pommel stone without dread. Until he remembered one disturbing detail that put a most troubling pall on his burst of high spirits and optimism.

For all her good deeds and beauty, the American had one serious flaw.

She'd claimed she detested Barra.

Dimensions away, but closer than Bran would have believed, three souls who did love Barra stood outside the imposing Oban Ferry Terminal and eyed the arriving passengers with growing trepidation. It wasn't as if they had much experience with Caledonian MacBrayne—affectionately known as CalMac—and their business of ferrying good folk here and yon throughout the whole of the Western Isles.

Geordie, Roderick, and Silvanus—being of an age when said waters were plied only by sleek birlinns and galleys, those magnificent greyhounds of the seas—were more than willing to leave the business of transporting moderns to those more at ease with such bustle.

CalMac was doing fine so far as they could tell.

But it was late afternoon and Mindy Menlove was booked on the soon-to-be-departing ferry to Barra.

Alarmingly, she had yet to arrive.

And that did concern the Long Gallery Threesome.

"I told you both we shouldn't have let her from our sight." Silvanus glared at the other two ghosts from beneath angry brows. "If you'll recall"—he puffed his chest—"I wanted to hie myself into her car. Just to make certain she didn't lose her way, mind!"

"You're the one who needs to mind." Geordie raised his walking stick and shook it at him. "Last time you planted yourself inside her automo-*beel*, back at the Folly, she nearly drove off the road and into the trees!"

"She wasn't expecting me, was all." Silvanus put back his shoulders. "This time I'm sure she would have appreciated my assistance."

"Pah-phooey!" Geordie lowered his cane and leaned on it. "You were e'er one to do as you pleased, having no care for the rest o' us."

"Quit your bellyaching, both of you." Roderick stepped between them. " 'Tis keeping an eye on the crowd we need to be a-doing, not fussing amongst ourselves. If you keep at it, we may miss her when she arrives."

"If she does," huffed Silvanus.

"She will." Roderick folded his arms, his sharp gaze on the endless stream of ferry passengers. "See all these busy folk, eager to visit our own fair Barra! Warms the cockles, it does, eh?

"So many souls come from near and far." He preened a bit, smoothing his plaid. "The lass will be here soon, too. I feel it in my bones."

"My bones say she's turned tail and run off to her *Haw-wah-ee*." Silvanus began strutting back and forth in front of the ferry terminal's glass-doored entrance. "It's rained since she's been here and she's made it plain what she thinks of cold and mist."

"But this is *Scottish* mist!" Roderick made a lofty gesture that took in the waterfront and the great hills encircling the town.

Highland mist was everywhere, rolling gently down the braes and hovering above the choppy water in the bay. Billowing curtains of it, soft and gray, drifted along the road, taking the sharp edges off modern buildings and damping the noise from cars and hurrying people.

Roderick hadn't seen such mist in years and the sight almost overwhelmed him.

He cleared his throat and dashed at his eyes. "Dinnae

tell me the lass willnae be enchanted by our Hameland. I do believe she already is."

Silvanus hooted.

Geordie shook his head. "Herself is lost, I say you." He lifted his walking stick again, this time pointing at the town. "Or have neither of you noticed how many roads be blocked with 'Men Working' and 'Diversion' signs? I may no' be an expert in modern times, but even I know that a soul can get confused right quick if the path a body means to follow suddenly ups and goes another way!"

Silvanus and Roderick exchanged glances.

"All these other tourists found their way here." Silvanus slid a look at the growing crowd. "If she means to catch the ferry, she'll be on it. Not"—he stuck out his chin—"that I believe she wishes to be here!"

"Hah!" Geordie struck his most superior pose. "You're both blind as bats! Yon folk aren't tourists. They're Highlanders and Islesmen, just like us. Several centuries removed, of course."

"So they are." Silvanus rubbed the back of his neck, frowning. "I wonder what they want on Barra."

"And why shouldn't they visit Barra?" Roderick shot him a dark look. "Can you name a fairer isle?"

"'Tis passing strange and you know it." Silvanus glared at him. "Even in our day, the only folk who came to Barra were our own—"

"There she is!" Geordie pointed at a small blue car inching toward the ferry terminal.

Mindy could be seen at the wheel, her hands white-knuckled and her face grim.

Silvanus whirled on Roderick and Geordie. "I told you she's miserable here. Just look at her!"

"She's here. That's all that matters." Roderick stood

straighter, smoothing his plaid. "There's time aplenty for her to come around."

"And you think our welcome-to-Barra greeting will impress her?" Silvanus didn't bother to hide his skepticism.

"I thought it was a warning?" chimed Geordie.

"You're both wrong." Roderick cast a glance at the mist-hung bay, his heart already thundering with excitement. "What we are about to do is make a flourish."

Silvanus rolled his eyes. "I say it's a mistake."

Roderick slung his arm around Geordie's shoulders. "You're outnumbered. Geordie sides with me."

Silvanus glared at them both, not missing that Roderick's foot was jammed hard on Geordie's toes.

Pretending not to notice, he strode forward and slapped Roderick on the back, most vigorously. "Then let us be away to attend our *surprise!*"

But as they all three turned and headed down the road to the bay, kilts swinging, Silvanus vowed that when all was said and done, he'd make it up to the lass.

A flourish, indeed.

If she spotted them through the thickening mist, she might never be the same again. And it would all be their interfering fault.

Silvanus frowned. Aye, he'd have to do something good for her and he would.

Somehow, someday.

Chapter 8

It was by the skin of her teeth that Mindy made the Barra ferry. But now that she was on board—her rental car wedged in place between a battered van and an RV, both belonging to the other stragglers who'd arrived at the last minute—she found she couldn't move.

Her hands clutched the steering wheel in a death grip and her knees shook so badly, she doubted her legs would ever support her again. At the very least, not until she recovered from her driving-around-Oban-and-trying-to-get-to-the-ferry panic and could breathe again.

It hadn't even been that she hadn't found the ferry.

She had.

She'd seen it from afar—after all, a giant black-and-white Caledonian MacBrayne ferry wasn't easy to miss—but who would have guessed that every road leading to the ferry terminal would be barricaded and that the alternative—*diverted-traffic*—route would be a maze of one-way streets and confusion?

Spindle-thin one-way streets that seemed only to lead her farther away from the place she was trying so hard to reach.

It'd been a harrowing experience.

And it'd been made even worse by having to go through it while driving left.

She hated driving left.

The only thing she disliked more was making a spectacle of herself. And she was doing a fine job of that now. She didn't need to look into the rearview mirror to know that her face was glowing tomato red or that her eyes glistened with unshed tears of frustration.

The glances the van and RV drivers and their passengers had given her as they'd hopped out of their vehicles and exited the ferry's parking hold had been telling.

And if their looks weren't enough, the stares of the black-and-yellow-jacketed ferry workers who'd waved her aboard said everything.

They thought she was mad.

And, Mindy admitted, she was beginning to believe that she was.

Why else would she be here?

She frowned and puffed her bangs off her forehead. It'd been a mistake to keep driving in circles when she realized how close she was to missing the ferry. What she should have done was seize the moment, view it as fate, and turn around to head back to Glasgow and the next available flight to Newark.

Or, for that matter, any US-bound plane she could catch.

Instead, she'd kept on, even stopping to ask directions from an old man walking a dog.

Unfortunately, he'd known exactly how she could reach the ferry.

And now . . .

Mindy took a deep breath. She wouldn't have believed it possible, but the knocking in her knees was finally beginning to lessen. Grateful, she slid a glance at the three black-and-yellow-jacketed ferrymen, relieved to see that they had turned away and were no longer staring at her.

If she was quick, she could escape to the ship's upper level.

She could stand at the rail and let the chill wind blast the heat out of her cheeks. Or, perhaps a better idea, she could lose herself in one of the lounges or claim a quiet spot in the cafeteria.

She just needed to slip out of the car and sprint up the stairs.

It was now or never.

But when she leaned down to grab her purse—it'd slid off the passenger seat—she bumped into something that set off the car alarm.

Bleep, bleep, bleeeep!

"Oh, no-o-o!" Her heart stopped.

The noise was deafening.

"Oh, God!" Frantic, she jerked back up and fiddled with the key. When it wouldn't budge, she began pressing every button she could see until, at last, she jabbed something that stopped the bleeping.

"Having problems, lassie?" One of the workmen opened the car door, peering in at her.

"No, I . . ." She couldn't finish. There was no point in lying when it was painfully obvious that she was about to expire from stress.

"Right, then." The man stepped aside as she clambered out of the car. He glanced at his mates and then looked back at her, his weather-beaten face sympathetic. "You've got five full hours before we arrive in Barra. That should be long enough to get o'er whate'er it was that wasn't bothering you.

"If I were you, I'd be for having a wee dram abovestairs." He indicated the stairwell only a few yards behind him, smiling. "A good swig and you'll be feeling better in no time."

"I—I'll do that, thank you." Mindy forced a smile, knowing it was a shaky one.

It was the best she could do.

The man's own smile was crooked, reminding her of Bran of Barra's lopsided grin.

On the thought, her pulse skittered. Before she could flush any redder, she hitched her bag onto her shoulder and hastened to the steps, hurrying up them as fast as her wobbly legs would carry her.

She would have a dram.

In fact, she might even have two.

But when she finally located a lounge, it was to discover that the entire carpeted, large-windowed area was standing-room only. Men stood four deep at the bar and although there were quite a few sofas and little round tables, each one boasting at least four chairs, there wasn't an empty seat anywhere to be seen.

The cafeteria was worse.

Even from the door, she could see that every table was occupied. And the line snaking past the serve-yourself buffet-style offerings looked so long she doubted she'd get through it before the ferry docked at Barra.

Mindy sighed.

Who would have guessed so many people would want to visit a tiny island in the Outer Hebrides?

You'd think they were giving away something.

Sure she didn't want any of it, whatever it might be, she pulled a scarf out of her jacket pocket, tied it around her neck, and went in search of exit stairs to the outside promenades. It was clear that most of the passengers— Scots, not tourists, from the looks of them—were more keen on staying inside than facing the cold wind on the decks.

And as she wasn't feeling very sociable, that was where she supposed she should be.

So she elbowed her way through the ferry passengers thronging the corridors until she found the nearest exit to the outer decks. Escape in sight, she shot a last frown at the teeming ship's lounge, then wrenched open the door and stepped out into icy, biting wind.

It was a grave mistake.

Not because the gusting wind threw freezing spray at her. Nor did it bother her that within two seconds of stepping outside, her eyes were tearing and her fingers felt like Popsicles.

What stopped her in her tracks—and stole her breath—was the shock of exhilaration.

It hit her full force.

And it was so unexpected, so unwelcome, that she could only lurch across the pitching, rolling deck, grab the rail, and look about her, slack-jawed and wide-eyed.

They hadn't even left Oban Bay—fishing boats bobbed everywhere and she could still see the town and the headlights of cars moving along the coast roads—but already she felt a prickly kind of freedom that caught her totally unawares. Cold, windy, and gray, especially when *wet*, just wasn't her idea of happiness.

And yet . . .

The choppy, whitecapped water, so roughened by the fast-moving current, and the many seabirds screeching and wheeling above, even the chilling rain driving into her face—it was all just so wild.

As if time as she knew it hadn't yet happened.

And—she couldn't believe the thought crossed her

mind—as if the brash, modern world she knew and had always loved didn't matter here.

The dark cliffs crowding the bay, swells surging against them, said as much. High above, a crescent moon was just beginning to cast its glimmer on the blue-black water, adding to the entrancement. It was a lonely, sea-washed world that wasn't supposed to affect her.

She wasn't her Scotophile sister.

The Hebrides, especially, should repel her.

Instead, her heart thundered and her grip on the rail turned white-knuckled. She sensed a strange power— a fierce, stark beauty—in the elements around her that left her feeling slightly faint.

These churning seas, the rocky headlands, and the empty shores had nothing to do with the Hebrides of song—those celebrated, gemlike isles Margo could wax poetic over for hours, getting misty-eyed about sparkling turquoise and amethyst water, white cockleshell strands, and glittering bays.

Margo would no doubt also mention Bonnie Prince Charlie, Culloden, and the anguish of Scottish exiles scattered the world over, ever yearning to return.

Mindy huddled deeper into her heavy waxed jacket, certain she wasn't looking out at her sister's romanticized Scotland—a sentimental, tartan-draped wonderland she'd put together from watching *Braveheart* and reading romance novels.

This before her was the real deal.

It was Bran of Barra's world.

A vast, rapturous place of tides, cliffs, and reefs that gave meaning to the old adage that you are where you live. Each soul ever born, hewn and molded by—

"'Tis a wide-open, edge-of-the-world place, eh?" a reedy voice trilled behind Mindy.

Starting, she spun around.

She wished she hadn't when she saw the tiny old woman peering up at her. Birdlike and with a piercing blue gaze, the wizened woman was dressed in black and had a whir of frizzled white hair. She could have been the witch who shoved poor Hansel and Gretel into the oven. At the very least, she might easily belong in another time.

Mindy blinked, feeling a flutter of unease.

But the woman's eyes were bright, twinkling even, and she *was* smiling.

"I'm most partial to the Hebrides," she announced, joining Mindy at the rail.

A move that quickly revealed that although she did look like a crone straight out of a rather grim fairy tale, her black *cloak* was nothing more sinister than a dark-hued waxed jacket. And her boots weren't old-fashioned or wicked-witchy-ish at all. They were simply sensible footgear, thick soled, high ankled, and tied with red plaid laces.

Mindy's first-glance assessment had been erroneous.

Even so . . .

There was *something* about the woman.

Mindy shivered and narrowed her eyes, trying as surreptitiously as possible to discover if she could see through the woman.

She couldn't.

But relief didn't sweep her.

It remained odd that the woman appeared just when Mindy was feeling as if she'd entered into a bold new world. A place that had captivated her as soon as she'd stepped on deck, and—her heart skittered—she wasn't sure what to make of her sudden, inexplicable enchantment.

The old woman tutted. "These isle-strewn waters"—

she made a grand gesture, taking in the tossing waves and the dark smudges of islands—"formed the men who rule here."

Mindy blinked. *"Rule?"*

She could have bitten her tongue, giving the strange woman the perfect in to pursue what was turning into a very bizarre encounter.

"Hold sway, my dear." The woman glanced at her. "The Lords of the Isles and all the bit chieftains, each one living like a king in his own wee realm. Only men"—the crone turned back to the rail, her expression almost proprietorial—"strengthened by cold seas, high wind, and long, dark winters could be so grand.

"There be none like 'em anywhere." The woman nodded smugly. "Nowhere worth being, that is!"

"You're from here?" Mindy could feel her ill ease returning, a growing urge to inch away from the woman and dash back inside the crowded ferry. "I can see the Hebrides are quite an impressive place."

"Ach!" The woman cackled. "I live on Doon. But all these isles have their charm." She gave a little sigh, pressed a knotty hand to her breast. "Wait until you see them on a fine summer's day. That's when—"

"I won't be here in summer."

"Nae?"

"No." Mindy folded her arms on the rail. "I won't even be here in the spring. I'm traveling on business and will be leaving as soon as possible."

The woman raised a scraggly brow. "Is that so?"

Mindy nodded.

"Then you won't be seeing thon water when it turns all clear and amethyst. Or"—the crone gave her a mysterious smile—"how the sun can gleam on our white cockleshell strands and set our bays aglitter?

"The Hebrides of song and legend—"

"Are you a mind reader?" Mindy blurted the words before she could catch herself.

It was too weird that the woman repeated her thoughts about *Margo's Hebrides* almost verbatim.

But the crone only laughed delightedly. "I'm but an auld woman who loves her home. It pleases me when these isles are appreciated." She turned a benevolent gaze on the water. "Most Americans come here in search of—"

"I'm not here as a tourist." Mindy eyed her again, half certain that if she stared hard enough, this time she'd be able to see through her.

Again, she couldn't.

But she did frown. "I know many Americans dream about visiting Scotland. But"—Mindy kept her tone neutral, not wanting to offend—"I'm not one of them. And I'm not looking for anything."

"Perhaps you should be?"

"I—"

Mindy's breath left her in a rush. The old woman wasn't transparent, but there *was* a man standing at the rail a few yards behind her.

A kilted man.

And Mindy was certain he hadn't been there before.

He stood in shadow, his chin lifted proudly and his gaze on the sea, but he didn't need to be looking Mindy's way for her to recognize him.

He was Bran of Barra.

And here—in his element, his powerful silhouette limned against the rolling sea and dark clouds—he was magnificent. Glorious in a way no modern man could rival. Wind lifted his hair and tore at his plaid, but he stood tall and unbending, as if the gusting spray and damp didn't even faze him.

She surely looked like a bedraggled wet hen.

He was breathtaking.

And he wasn't just hewn of this wild, watery world. He was its master and wasn't shy about proclaiming his supremacy. It thrummed through every brawny inch of him and shimmered in the air around him, leaving no doubt that he ruled these dominions. And that he loved them with a fierceness that almost fringed on unholy.

Mindy swallowed, her heart thumping madly.

When he turned his head and looked straight at her, she almost choked. She did flush. A great wave of heat swept her, starting at the roots of her hair and tingling through her, clear to her toes.

"So-o-o, Mindy-lass, tell me true." He didn't move, but his voice came as close as if his lips had brushed her ear. "Are you awed yet?"

"I think . . . I mean . . . ," she spluttered, horrified that she'd almost called him a rogue.

This *was* the twenty-first century, after all.

She shot a look at the old woman, but she was staring out to sea, her gaze fixed on the beetling cliffs of an island off to their left.

She didn't seem to notice Bran of Barra's presence.

Mindy was all too much aware of him.

Trembling, she started toward him, but the ferry pitched then, the violent dip and slide knocking her hard against the rail.

"I thought I dreamed you!" She clutched the slippery railing, fighting for balance. "And, no, you don't awe me," she lied, glaring at him. "I think you're—"

"Oho, what's this?" He held up his hands. "I didn't mean my own self. I wanted to know"—his blue eyes sparkled and he flashed one of his crooked smiles—"if you've fallen under the spell o' my isles."

"I don't believe in spells."

"But you believe in dreams."

"I didn't say that."

"Ah, but you didn't have to." He took a step forward, his smile turning deadly. "I saw it in your eyes when you spoke of our kiss."

"I didn't say anything about that!" Mindy felt her face flame. She *had* meant the kiss when she'd said she'd thought she'd dreamed him. "And it wasn't a real—"

She broke off at the sound of a titter behind her.

She'd forgotten the strange old woman.

Wheeling around, she started to tell the woman from Doon to mind her own business, but the rail where the woman had been standing was empty. There was nothing there except shadows and flying sea spray. Equally alarming, if the old woman had tottered back inside, she'd have had to pass Mindy on her way to the exit door.

And, of course, she hadn't.

"Oh, God!" Mindy clapped a hand to her cheek. "She really was a witch! Or a ghost—"

"A ghost? Where . . . ?" A tall, lanky youth stood staring her, slack-jawed.

His friends—a cluster of teens, similarly agog—crowded in the open exit doorway, gaping at her with startled, round eyes, though one, a spiky-haired youth with a stud in his nose, was most definitely smirking. The girl next to him, a tiny redhead dressed in black and with her eyes heavily kohled, jabbed him in the ribs. "I didn't see a ghost, but I did see the Goodwife of Doon! She travels about working spells and doing good, like in olden times. I know because my mum knew someone who begged her assistance once when their wean was doing poorly and no doctors could help. Folk in our village believe her magic is real.

"I recognized her just now because I saw her leaving my mum's friend's cottage." The girl tucked her hair behind an ear, her chin jutting out in challenge.

"More like you were nipping in your da's whisky if you're telling me you just saw an old woman who wasn't there!" The spiky-haired youth swaggered to the rail, laughing.

The girl followed, clearly bent on arguing.

Mindy ignored them and whirled back to Bran. But like the crone, whoever she might have been, he, too, had vanished.

Or so she thought until she summoned her best I-am-above-this mien, crossed the deck, and pushed through the gawking teens to reenter the ferry, only to feel a strong, familiar, and entirely invisible hand clamp down on her shoulder.

When she also felt Bran of Barra's—likewise incorporeal but oh-so-sexy—beard tickle her neck, the world began to spin in a way that had nothing to do with the rolls and plunges of the ferry.

She froze.

Who knew that the mere touch of a seven-hundred-year-old beard could turn a girl's knees to water and make her head feel light?

As if he was well aware, Bran of Barra chuckled.

He came closer, the heat of him against her back sending shivers all through her. She drew a quick breath and tried to scoot away, but her efforts only caused him to slip his other hand into her hair and lean down, brushing his lips along her jaw.

"You shouldn't have said our kiss wasn't real, Mindy-lass." His breath feathered across her cheek, electrifying her. "You leave me no choice but to prove to you that it was. And"—his tone dropped meaningfully—"to show you that such a soft kiss as I gave you was only a prelude to deeper, much more passionate kisses."

She felt his thumb rub across her lower lip. Before she could gasp, he took her face in his hands. They were big, warm, and strong against her cheeks. Then his mouth slanted across hers, his lips cool, firm, and determined. Her heart slammed against her chest—the kiss felt so real, so wonderful—but when he tightened his grip on her face and started probing with his tongue, seeking to deepen the intimacy, she knew she was in danger. Mindy jerked free. "I don't want your kisses!"

"Ah, but you will."

"Oh, no, I won't." She glared at him.

"You'll do more than want them, Mindy-lass. I say you'll crave them."

The supreme confidence in his voice—his disturbingly Scottish voice—made her heart race. "Never," she snapped before remembering no one else could see him.

And, worse, that everyone could see and hear her.

People were staring.

Mindy took a deep breath to settle nerves that were beginning to unravel. She stood straighter and tugged at the front of her jacket, adjusted the scarf she'd knotted around her neck.

Anything to achieve a sense of balance.

She didn't stare at other people. And she really disliked being the object of such gawking.

"Look here." She would have poked Bran of Barra in the chest if she didn't want to risk looking even sillier. "I don't think—"

Lout that he was, he laughed. "Never fear, sweetness." The words came close to her ear again, though this time he wasn't touching her. "I know fine that this isn't the place for us to enjoy ourselves.

"We'll meet on Barra." He did touch her then, reaching to smooth a hand over her hair. "And when we do, you'll never again doubt my amorous capabilities. I'll kiss you until the earth shakes beneath your feet. Or"—he laughed again—"at least until your toes curl!

"Be sure of it!" Leaning in, he gave her a hard, fast kiss on the cheek.

She knew instinctively that he bowed slightly when he stepped away from her. She was also sure there'd be a wickedly annoying smile twitching about his lips. And that his dancing blue eyes would show that he knew he dazzled her. Then, as qucikly as he'd appeared, he was gone, taking his devilry and laughter with him.

Mindy leaned back against the wall, breathless.

Kiss her until her toes curled! The man—no, ghost—was an unmitigated, arrogant, and insufferable scoundrel. But his teasing blue eyes and that deep, buttery-rich burr made him beyond dangerous.

Mindy bit her lip. Had she really believed she could remain immune to a Scottish accent?

There wasn't a woman alive who could!

Even now, those soft, lilting tones echoed in her mind, seducing her with each deliciously rolled *r* and all that honeyed richness that made Scotsmen temptation walking.

And Highland Scots were the worst!

They should be outlawed.

Mindy swiped a hand across her brow, certain the dampness there had nothing to do with the flying spray that had been blowing along the ferry's outer deck.

Hunter the cad's seven-hundred-year-old ancestor had gotten to her.

His promises—about kisses, no less—conjured a whirl of images that set her entire body tingling.

She could hardly stand for the hot rush of sensation whirling through her. She didn't need *curled toes* to add to her misery. The last thing she wanted was to be kissed by Bran of Barra.

He didn't need to convince her of his seduction skills.

That he had them was a given.

Just remembering the feel of his soft, warm breath against her skin—his hand gripping her shoulder so firmly, the other tangled in her hair, his fingers caressing the back of her neck—ignited everything feminine inside her, sweeping her with fierce, undeniable desire.

She was on the road to madness.

And she didn't need him making the earth tremble beneath her.

It already did.

Determined to do something about that shaking, she pulled herself together and pushed away from the wall before someone mistook her limp-noodled posture for a bad case of mal de mer. Or, worse, an overindulgence in drams.

She hadn't touched a drop of fine Highland single malt, but now seemed like a very good time.

Especially when, upon entering the nearest lounge, she found that the men crowding the bar now stood only two deep rather than four. Unfortunately all the seats still seemed to be taken, and now that they'd been under way for a while, the whole dimly lit area smelled strongly of fish-and-chips, damp waxed jackets and woolens, and spilled ale.

But the ferry cafeteria had looked even more crowded and no way was she venturing on deck again.

She didn't want to give Bran of Barra another chance to catch her alone.

And the risk of running into the strange old woman from Doon again—wherever Doon might be—was just another excellent reason to treat herself to a brisk swig of Scotland's most famed libation.

Somehow she didn't think either one of them would accost her in the busy pub. So she put back her shoulders and tried to pretend that the people thronging the lounge weren't Scots on a ferry to Barra, many of them giving her sidelong, how-do-you-fit-in-here looks, and imagined they were airline passengers and on one of *her* flights.

Feeling instantly better, she threaded her way through the crowd and even managed to get close enough to the bar to order a "Jacket Potato with Bangers 'n' Beans," glad she'd had enough UK layovers to know that bangers were sausages. As for her single malt . . .

There were so many bottles lining the glass shelves behind the bar!

But one—*Laphroaig*—jumped out at her. Margo's favorite, and pronounced *La-froyg*, it was the only one she recognized, remembering that her sister insisted that although the whisky was an acquired taste, no other was as smooth and peaty, almost tasting like a smoky turf fire.

Mindy eyed the bottle, hesitating.

She was wet and cold from being on the promenade. Her heavy waxed jacket, against all advertising claims, had let the damp seep through to chill her. And despite her sturdy, equally high-dollared hill-walking boots, her socks felt waterlogged and her toes were frozen. She didn't care to acknowledge that her hair was soaked and plastered to her head, her bangs dripping. As for what her makeup might look like . . .

She shuddered and tried not to think about it.

She *could* use a dram.

But—she recalled Margo's sighs of rapture when-ever she spoke of her favorite whisky—anything peat flavored and smacking of turf fires might be just a touch too Highlandy for her taste.

"Dinnae ken your whisky?" The many-earringed, ponytailed barkeep flickered his eyebrow at her. "Most Americans order Glenlivet or Famous Grouse." He smiled, already reaching for the latter. "You'll like—"

"I'll have Laphroaig." She looked him straight in the eye. "I appreciate its smoky flavor."

The man looked at her with new respect. "Not many tourists ask for that one, much less"—he turned away to take the bottle from the shelf—"pronounce its name correctly."

Mindy tucked her hair behind her ear and smiled, looking on as he poured her a generous measure.

He flashed a glance at her, a much warmer one this time. "Water or soda?"

"Neat."

"Nothing at all?"

"I prefer it as is, thanks." Mindy paid and found a seat against the windows. She took a sip of her Laphroaig, feeling extraordinarily proud of herself. It felt good to have put a crimp in the barkeep's opinion of Americans, even if she'd had to borrow Margo's Scotophile knowl-edge to do so.

The result was gratifying.

Even the Scots in the lounge had stopped giving her sideways, narrow-eyed looks. And the mist blowing past the lounge's large windows had thickened into what she knew the locals called sea haar. The consistency of pea soup, the fog now blocked all views of the rolling Hebridean sea and the dark, picturesque isles that kept looming up out of nowhere.

Mindy shifted in her seat, pleased.

She didn't want to do scenic.

Impenetrable fog suited her better. Enough quivers had run through her when she'd gone out on the deck. Her whole safe world, everything she felt—or, better said, didn't want to feel—about Scotland, tumbled down around her when she'd walked into that wild, romantic seascape.

And that was before Bran of Barra made an appearance.

His arrival only worsened things.

He'd looked so perfect, so right, against the rugged backdrop of churning, rough-watered seas and all those steep, black-glistening cliffs. The deeply indented bays with sweet little stretches of gleaming sand beaches. Hauntingly atmospheric places where she was sure few, if any, men had ever set foot.

Off-the-map, unfrequented places where Bran of Barra could stand with his legs braced apart and his hands on his hips, his plaid snapping in the wind, and no one—not one living soul—would dare challenge his right to be there.

He was that kind of man.

He wore remoteness well.

And seeing him as she had, on the ferry deck, yet still in his untamed, almost legendary surroundings, had stirred her attraction to him so fiercely that she wondered she hadn't gone up in flames.

She shivered.

She could still see him, feel his gaze locking with hers and how easily he'd seduced her with one look, sweep-

ing her up into his bold, larger-than-life passion and undoing her resistance with promises of toe-curling kisses.

Kisses she knew would only lead to . . .

"Agggh . . ." The sigh escaped her before she could
stop it.

She glanced around, but no one seemed to have heard
her. Grateful, she snuggled deeper into her jacket, welcoming the dense sea haar that blotted his world from
view. It was easier here, in the crowded ferry lounge, to
just drift and think of other things.

So she leaned back and quietly sipped her Laphroaig
until the empty dram glass slipped from her fingers to
land with a little *clack* on the table, roll across its polished surface, and drop to the floor.

Mindy started, and then blinked to notice that the
lounge was nearly empty. Only a few other ferry passengers remained, and from the looks of them, they were
dozing. The ponytailed barkeep stood with his back to
her, busying himself polishing ale glasses over a sink of
steaming water.

It was very quiet.

A glance at her watch proved what she wouldn't have
believed otherwise: she'd fallen asleep.

They'd soon be arriving at Barra.

And, she recognized with alarm, it hadn't been dropping her dram glass that had wakened her. It'd been
a strange gonglike noise she could still hear, beating
steadily, even though the other passengers and the glass-
polishing barkeep didn't seem to notice.

A chill rippled down her spine.

Her nape prickled.

She didn't want to hear noises that no one else did.

It was bad enough being attracted to a ghost and having conversations with little old ladies in black who, if

not exactly ghostly, weren't your run-of-the-mill grand-mothers next door, either.

"Oh, man." Very carefully, she leaned down to retrieve the fallen dram glass. When she straightened, something caught her attention from the corner of her eye.

It was something outside the windows.

And it was terrifying.

Mindy's heart stopped. Disbelief slammed into her as a high-prowed medieval galley shot past the slower-moving ferry. The ghost galley's flashing oars sent up clouds of spume as it sped into the mist only to whip around and race by the windows again.

"O-o-oh, no . . ." Mindy stared, her blood icing.

That it was a ghost ship was beyond doubt.

Roderick, Silvanus, and Geordie stood beaming at the stern, their arms raised in proud salute, basking in their flamboyant display.

Mindy also recognized the gong-beating helmsman. He was one of the *ancestrals* from the Folly's long gal-lery. As were the oarsmen who so tirelessly kept the gal-ley flying back and forth beside the ferry.

On their fourth pass, Silvanus grabbed Geordie's walking stick and thrust it high, using the cane to make great, sweeping circles in the air above his head. Some of the ghosties whooped, their cries rising above the rhythmic drumming of the helmsman's gong.

Mindy's blood began to roar in her ears. She knew what they were doing.

They were welcoming her to Barra.

And, as always, only she saw them.

She swallowed.

The twinkle in Silvanus's eyes almost got to her. As did the excitement, and pride, that shone on the faces of the other ghosties. If the gong beater swelled his chest even the slightest bit more, he'd surely explode.

He looked that victorious.

They all did.

And she should turn away from the window, rest her hands flat against the solidity of the table, and take deep breaths as she imagined how wonderful it would be to soon slip into her bed at the inn. How, once there, she'd pull the covers up to her chin, forgetting the Long Gallery Threesome and their zealous friends.

Instead, she kept staring at them and had to struggle against returning their waves.

Their enthusiasm was infectious.

And she had the strangest feeling that it wasn't just that. Scotland—or, at least, the Hebrides—seemed to have a behavioral and mind-altering effect on her.

She should be horror-struck.

She *was* appalled.

But what infuriated her was to find that she was watching the ghosties—otherworldly beings, for heaven's sake—as if their performance were commonplace.

Mindy shuddered. There was nothing at all ordinary about being greeted by a band of medieval Highland warriors in a ghost galley beating up and down past the windows of a modern-day ferry.

The sight should send her fleeing.

It was every bit as bizarre as if little green men in a round, silver saucer had suddenly appeared outside the plane windows on one of her work flights.

There wasn't that big a stretch between Martians and ghosts.

Yet . . .

She leaned closer to the window, pressing her forehead against the cold glass to see better through the fog. She shouldn't want to see the ghost galley more clearly. But something had happened to her somewhere between landing in Glasgow and driving left onto a Barra-bound ferry.

Something indefinable.

And now, watching the Folly ancestrals having such fun with their *flourish*, as Margo would call their antics, only reminded her that Bran also planned to give her a special welcome-to-Barra greeting.

Mindy's breath caught. Her pulse skittered just from remembering his words. How his eyes had smoldered and his grin had turned so utterly wicked as he'd spoken his warning.

His next kiss wouldn't be innocent. It would be nothing like the first one, a light and fleeting, brush of his lips across hers.

Nor would he let her pull away as she'd done in the ferry corridor.

The next time there'd be no escaping.

He'd appear out of nowhere, grab and crush her in a breath-stealing, big-burly-man bear hug, kissing her passionately. And then, like the rogue that he was, he'd set about proving his prowess.

And then she'd be in deep trouble.

Because she strongly suspected she wouldn't be able to resist him.

Chapter 9

The mist was swirling thicker than ever when Mindy finally drove off the CalMac ferry at Barra's Castlebay pier. In fact, the mist—no, sea haar—was so impenetrable that she hadn't even been able to catch a glimpse of Bran's stony islet as the ferry passed the castle site on its way to the dock. Lights did flicker dimly along the town's waterfront, but whether the yellow-glowing pinpricks belonged to cottages, shops, or even a fleet of fishing boats was something she just couldn't tell at this point.

She did know that everyone leaving the ferry seemed to be going to the same place.

And when she considered how small Barra was, and the very explicit directions she'd received, it appeared as if that place was her destination.

The Hebridean House Hotel.

A family-run, four-star country-house hotel only a few minutes above the main village of Castlebay. According to Mindy's source—a Scotland-loving airline friend who, unlike Margo, had actually been to Scotland and even made frequent return visits—Hebridean House was the best place to stay on Barra.

The rooms were spacious and comfortable, fireplaces

were kept lit, the food was excellent, and the views divine, or so Mindy's ex-colleague enthused. There was also a pub with great real ale where locals often held impromptu music sessions.

Best of all, the bathrooms were modern and, Mindy had been assured, she wouldn't have to worry about learning how to operate fiddly showers that were next to impossible to get just the right temperature.

She'd fall in love with Hebridean House.

But now, as she inched her way through the cold, wet night, following a long string of red taillights through the tiny seaside village and up the hill to the large and rambling hotel, she had serious doubts.

With the exception of ghosts, Mindy had expected Barra to be a wild and empty place. The kind of grandiose nowhere that looks haunting in oil paintings, but where, in real life, she'd find nothing stirring but the ripple of wind on the sea, and, maybe, the occasional bark of a dog.

Far from it, the isle struck her as the Grand Central Station of the Hebrides.

Barra hopped with activity.

And she hadn't been mistaken. Everyone was headed to her hotel.

Mindy shuddered and gripped the steering wheel tighter. At least she doubted Silvanus, Roderick, Geordie, and the others would abandon their galley to waylay her in the lobby of an overcrowded Victorian-era country-house hotel. She hadn't seen them since the ferry had slowed its engines and made for the Castlebay pier.

Bran was a huge question mark.

She couldn't be sure, but she might have caught glimpses of a huge, shaggy dog loping alongside the road next to her slow-moving rental car.

If so, the dog could be Gibbie.

She narrowed her eyes and tried to peer deeper into the rolling mist. She'd almost swear that when the fog thinned a bit in places, she'd spotted the large, burly figure of a man walking swiftly a few yards behind the dog. Even more telling, she'd also seen at least one or two strange bursts of brilliant blue light, each odd flare coming from near the striding man's hip.

Bran of Barra's sword had a gemstone that glowed. She'd seen the blade's pommel stone shoot blue flames more than once.

He could be following her.

The possibility made her heart pound. Although she would have guessed that, like the *ancestrals* from the Folly, he'd choose to avoid confronting her in a place as jam-packed as the Hebridean House appeared to be.

Not especially pleased about the crowd herself, she pulled into the hotel's car park—a surprisingly large one—and began what she feared would be a fruitless search for an empty parking space.

People were everywhere.

Circling cars, many from the ferry, cruised slowly past, going round and round, as drivers and passengers kept an eye out for a place to park. Finally, after turning and heading a bit back down the narrow, twisting road, she found a semisheltered spot near a drystone wall.

Gusty wind nearly blew her off her feet when she climbed out of the car, but the damp and darkness gave her energy she didn't know she had, and she marched up the road, reaching the car park with what seemed like only a few quick steps.

She ignored the hotel bar, located to the side of the building and indicated by a hand-painted sign over its red door, reading THE HERRING CATCHER, EST. 1878.

Though surely reeking atmosphere and age, the pub looked—and sounded—filled to bursting.

Not surprised, she made straight for the Hebridean's main entrance, where even more people were streaming across the threshold.

When she got there, she saw why.

A poster was tacked to the door: *Do you have a tale to tell? If so, the Highland Storyweaver wants to put you in his next book!*

Mindy stopped to read the smaller print near the bottom of the advert. A quick scan explained that Wee Hughie MacSporran, Highland historian and author, was staying at the hotel to give readings, do signings, and—the surefire reason for the mob—he was searching for *tall tales* to include in his upcoming book, *More Hearthside Tales: A Highlander's Look at Clan Legend and Lore*.

"He's writing a history of local family tradition and myth." A little man appeared at Mindy's elbow. He had tufted ginger hair and was sporting a Harris Tweed jacket that smelled of mothballs. "The book is a follow-up to his best seller *Hearthside Tales: A Highlander's Look at Scottish Myth and Legend*.

"That's this one." He held out the volume for Mindy's inspection. "It was such a hit that he's expanding the new book with tales from the Hebrides. That's why we're all here." The man glanced around, his cheeks glowing as he surveyed the milling crowd. "We're come to share our family legends. And, we hope, to have him put our stories in the book."

"I've heard of him." Mindy eyed the heavyset Scotsman on the book cover. She recognized him because he'd reminded her of a kilted teddy bear. "His books were in my room back at Oban, at Ravenscraig Castle."

The man waved the book importantly. "Wee Hughie is known and respected throughout the Highlands. Even the visitor centers at Culloden and Glencoe carry his work.

"And"—he leaned close, lowering his voice—"if he uses my story in *More Hearthside Tales*, I intend to write my own book. My family has a Selkie ancestress and I can trace my lineage directly to her."

He stepped back, chin lifting. "There'd be lots of folk what would be keen to hear my tale."

"I'm sure." Mindy tried to edge past him.

He gripped her arm, leaning in again. "I'm hoping MacSporran will introduce me to his editor."

"I'll keep my fingers crossed for you." Mindy broke free and almost sprinted for the reception.

"I have a room." She lifted her voice, trying to catch the eye of a harried-looking woman in a blue cardigan sweater with a red Hebridean House crest. "Mindy Menlove. I reserved by e-mail."

"Menlove?" The woman turned to face her. "I don't recall such a name."

"I have a confirmation." Mindy began rummaging in her bag. "Here it is." She pulled out the crumpled e-mail, placing it on the desk. "You can read it."

"Hmmm." The woman snatched the paper. "This is from us, to be sure," she said, her brow wrinkling. "But I still don't think we have you booked. There must be some error—"

"But there can't be." Mindy grabbed the e-mail, pointing at the date. "It says right here—"

"Och, I can see that, right enough." The woman edged her glasses up her nose. "It's just"—she cast a glance at the people thronging the lobby and the sitting room beyond—"things have been a bit confused lately.

"We're quite full, you see." She looked back at Mindy, shrugging. "If you don't have a reservation . . ." She let the words trail off meaningfully.

"But I do."

The woman raised a doubtful brow. "I'd remember a name like Menlove."

"Can you at least check?" Mindy could feel her face heating. "I'm sure I'm in your computer."

The woman's lips thinned. "Lassie, since thon writer checked in"—she glanced at a poster on the wall behind her desk; it was the same one as on the door—"everyone in the Outer and Inner Hebrides has made a booking with us. Some folk have even come so far as from Loch Ness." She adjusted her glasses again. "Family that claims Nessie swims past their back garden wall each third full moon. Like everyone else, they're keen to have their tale told, get in a book, and become famous."

"I'm not here to find fame." Mindy was getting angry now. "I just want a room."

"Ah, well . . ." The woman went to the far side of the reception desk and reached for a thick red ledger. "I still dinnae see your name," she said, flipping through pages covered with illegible scribbles.

Mindy tucked her hair behind an ear. "Can you please check your computer?"

The woman gave Mindy an over-her-glasses look and closed the ledger. Without a word, she moved to stand before the computer keyboard, her fingers clacking with tap-tapping efficiency across the keys.

"Hmmm . . ." She glanced at Mindy again. "I'm afraid I still don't have you."

Mindy stared at her and then at the people standing about in small groups in the lobby. The sitting room looked as jammed as a sardine can.

She turned back to the woman. "I came all the way from America. I've brought stones from a castle and—"

"Och!" The woman's face lit up. "So you're *that* American? Well, then!" She stepped back, smoothing her hands on her cardigan. "That does change things."

"You have a room?" Mindy didn't care that bringing the stones seemed to impress her.

"Michty me, I do be wishing I did." She worried her lip, considering. "But . . ." She stared into space, tapping her chin with a finger.

"I don't need anything fancy." Mindy was getting desperate. "I'm so tired I could sleep in a broom closet. As long as the bed's clean and there's a bath."

A private bath was essential.

Mindy stood straighter. She wasn't prepared to share a down-the-hall bathroom with countless want-to-be-in-a-book, fame-seeking Scots.

But the look the woman gave her said she might not have a choice.

"So you don't have anything?" Mindy hitched up her bag, which was beginning to slide off her shoulder. "Not even a small room with a private bath?"

"Och, there is something. And there is a bath." The woman hesitated. "It's just—"

"Just what?"

"It's not here."

Mindy blinked. "What do you mean it isn't here?"

"Exactly what I said, my dear." The woman looked embarrassed. "We really are booked up. So many people here to meet the author," she said, her voice apologetic. "The other hotels and inns are all full, too. Even the smaller bed-and-breakfasts.

"But there is a small self-catering cottage down on the other side of the village." The woman began tapping her chin again. "It's called the Anchor and is just past an old stone jetty that no one uses anymore."

"I'll take it."

"It hasn't been cleaned or aired."

"I don't care." Mindy did, but she also wasn't going to sleep in her car.

"Well . . ." The woman threw a look at the door. "I think Jock, the owner, is over in the Herring Catcher tonight. I'll just go make sure he doesn't mind you staying there."

She came around the desk, all brisk business again. "If he says it's fine, you'll find the key above the door. Or"—she smiled—"it may well be unlocked. We don't much worry about such things on Barra."

"I'm sure." Mindy leaned against the desk, looking after the woman as she strode across the reception and out the hotel door.

It was then that she saw him.

He stood near the hearth on the other side of the reception, looking as if he were there to enjoy the fire's cheery warmth. But there was nothing casual about the way he leaned against the door to the nearby sitting room, his arms folded and his gaze burning into her.

His big, shaggy dog sat beside him. Gibbie, too, stared at her. But the dog's expression was friendly. He even looked as though he were grinning.

His tail swished, seeming to prove his delight in seeing her.

Bran of Barra was clearly delighted, too.

But the heat in his eyes indicated a very different kind of pleasure from that of his canine companion.

Mindy swallowed hard.

Everyone filing in and out of the Hebridean House's busy lobby seemed to fade away. Even the noise lessened, until the only sound Mindy heard was the hard thumping of her heart and the rush of her pulse.

Bran of Barra's lips twitched.

He also wasn't wearing his kilt.

Mindy blinked, unable not to stare. Never would she have believed that worn corduroy trousers and a bulky fisherman's sweater could be so sexy. But the rough-edged, windblown look suited him. With his hair in a ponytail and his beard neatly trimmed, the effect was devastating.

Nor did it hurt that he stood head and shoulders above every other man in the room. Tall men, especially big, brawny ones, had always been her weakness.

Mindy pressed a hand to her breast, sure she couldn't breathe.

Bran of Barra's lip twitch spread into a grin.

Gibbie's tail wagged faster.

When the dog barked—loudly—and no one else in the reception noticed, Mindy realized that, again, she was the only the one who saw either of them.

Not that it mattered.

He was there just for her and his appearance couldn't have been more effective if a high-paid Hollywood publicist had styled and posed him.

No, that was wrong.

Bran of Barra was the kind of man who'd laugh in the face of any such staged artifice. And it was his incredible earthiness, and the way his gaze fixed—and stayed—on her, that was making her feel so hot inside.

He absolutely knocked her sideways.

And before she even knew she'd crossed the room, she found herself standing before him.

"Why are you dressed like that?" She looked up at him, feeling silly because that was the only thing she could think to say.

"You disapprove?"

"No, I—"

"Mindy-lass." He straightened and reached for her hand. "You are in the Outer Hebrides. There are folk here who"—he glanced about—"despite your modern times, still see things others can't, including ghosts. So I chose to appear in a manner that won't attract too much attention."

Mindy almost choked.

His hand felt warm and calloused. His grip was strong, firm, and masculine, in a way that went through her like a bolt of high-watt electricity.

The intensity of his gaze was worse.

She fought the urge to squirm. "You're joking, right?"

"How so?" He flashed that crooked smile again.

"Oh . . . only that I'm sure you know that you just have to breathe to draw attention."

His eyes crinkled with pleasure. "I'm glad you think so." He lifted her hand, kissing the tips of her fingers. "But I didn't come here to impress you. No' just at the moment, anyhow."

Mindy blinked, disappointed. "Oh, I thought—"

"That I'm here to make *trouble* for you?" He released her hand, but leaned close to give her a hard, swift kiss on the cheek. "I told you, sweetness, when I set about making your toes curl, there'll be no mistaking my purpose."

"So what is your purpose?" Mindy glanced at the hotel entrance, not wanting the proprietress to return and catch her talking to thin air.

Thankfully, no one else seemed aware of her.

She turned back to Bran, her heart flipping to see that his smile had gone from crooked to smoldering.

"Must you do that?" She shot another look at the door, nervous.

"Do what?"

"Smile at me like—"

"Like I'm ready to eat you?" His grin turned wicked hot. "Och, lassie, did you no' hear me? This isn't the time or place for—"

"Then why are you here?" She wasn't about to let him finish such a loaded sentence.

He put his hands on his hips. "I'm here because this is Barra. My Barra, and"—pride rang in his voice—"I want to thank you for returning my stones. I know the tower was gone and now—"

"They should never have been taken away." The words came from somewhere deep inside Mindy.

It was a thought that had never before crossed her mind.

But it was there now.

And—she wouldn't have believed it—some of Bran's love for his home started welling in her breast. An unexpected and unaccustomed feeling, it was an odd, fluttering kind of awareness that made her suddenly very glad she was doing what she was, even if she'd started on this venture for very different reasons.

She almost said so, but just then she felt a paw prod her thigh. *Gibbie*. The dog had pushed to his feet and lumbered over to her, paw prods and wet-nosed nudges letting her know he didn't want to be excluded.

He tilted his head at her, his dark eyes expectant.

"I don't have anything for him." Mindy looked down at the dog, then back at Bran.

But he, too, was watching the dog. "A few ear scratches will please him." The look on his face and the softening of his voice as he spoke about his dog melted her. "That's all he's asking of you."

"Well, then . . ." Mindy stretched out a hand, let her fingers touch Gibbie's shoulders. His coat was coarse and shaggy, but she could feel his warmth through the fur. Encouraged, she rubbed him a bit and then—greatly daring—even fondled his ears.

Gibbie's tail went into overdrive.

Mindy's heart split wide.

"How can he be so real?" She curled her fingers into the dog's thick fur. "I mean, both of you are not—" She broke off, embarrassed.

Bran of Barra didn't appear at all offended. "No' as you'd expect ghosts to look?"

"I meant—"

"I know fine what you meant." Smiling, he took her hand again, bending low to kiss the air above her knuckles. "I assure you we are real. We only dwell in a different place." He shrugged. "We're among you always, just behind the veil that divides us.

"Some, like me, cross back and forth as the mood strikes us. We all have the ability." Releasing her, he clicked his fingers to produce an oatcake, which he gave to Gibbie. "Others ne'er make use of such magic.

"Myself, I enjoy my ghostdom." He stepped back, dusting his hands, as Gibbie crunched his treat.

"But you're both solid."

"Aye."

"I always thought ghosts were thin and wispy." Mindy looked down, nudging the tartan-patterned carpet. "You know—insubstantial. *See-through.*"

Bran of Barra reached to cup her chin, lifting her face. "Tell me, lass." His blue gaze held hers, piercing.

"Do I look like the kind o' man who'd enjoy floating about like a waft o' mist?"

Mindy flushed. "No, but—"

He laughed. "There you have it! I enjoyed life too much to spend my afterlife drifting on a cloud."

"And now . . ." Mindy couldn't finish. It bothered her to think about his *now*. And it disturbed her even more that it bothered her!

It really shouldn't.

Especially not in a crowded hotel reception area, where, sooner or later, someone would notice her and see that she was having a conversation with a ghost, regardless of how solid he might or might not be.

She started to say so, but just then a tall, heavyset man in a kilt came out of the sitting room. His tweed Argyll jacket was slung over one shoulder and he wore a white, open-necked ghillie shirt. The shirt's old-fashioned Jacobite styling and his fur-covered, three-tasseled sporran made excellent foils for his brisk, confident stride.

Only his paunch and somewhat thinning red hair detracted from the image of Highland magnificence.

And—Mindy noted—perhaps, the glint of arrogance in his small, piggy eyes.

"Bluidy windbag." Beside her, Bran of Barra drew his sword, holding it menacingly.

Mindy blinked.

She was sure he hadn't been wearing it a moment before. His clothes were, and still appeared, totally modern. Except, and her heart began to race, for the low-slung sword belt now circling his hips and the great, gleaming length of steel he held in his hand.

"Who is that?" She watched a crowd gather around the newcomer, some people oohing and aahing, as the man drew to a halt.

He put back his shoulders, nodding regally as people fawned over him. Then someone moved and light from a wall sconce shone fully on his face and Mindy gasped, recognition hitting her like a bucket of ice water.

The pseudo Jacobite was the author.

Wee Hughie MacSporran.

And if the sound—almost a furious growl—coming from deep inside Bran's chest was any indication, her brawny Hebridean chieftain didn't think much of the man who styled himself the Highland Storyweaver.

"You don't like him, do you?" She glanced at Bran, only to find herself staring into the dark eyes of a big, bulky man with a shock of curly black hair and a weather-beaten, seaman's kind of face.

Bran of Barra—and his dog—had vanished yet again.

Mindy swallowed her gasp, not wanting the fisherman to think she was nuts. She hitched the shoulder strap of her bag again and then smoothed her hair, trying to look normal.

"Thon windbag?" The man jerked his dark head in the author's direction, his use of Bran of Barra's title for the writer making him instantly sympathetic.

"Nae, I don't like him." The man looked as if he'd spit on the carpet—were they standing anywhere but in the finely decorated reception of the Hebridean House.

"He's no' come here to put people in books." He hooked his thumbs in his belt, keeping his gaze pinned on Wee Hughie. "It's all show, I say you."

"Show?" Mindy's attention, too, was fixed on the writer.

It was clear that he was a performer.

"Aye, that's what he's about, that one." The fisherman's tone was cynical. "He's here hoping he'll find the

Barra sword, he is. That's what he'd put in his book! After"—he glanced at Mindy, still looking so ready to spit that she almost jumped backward—"he's made a fool out of all these good, trusting people.

"Then he'll sell the sword to some museum down London way and have a fine laugh at us all."

"Sorry; I'm not following you." Mindy didn't want to be rude, but she couldn't stop looking past the man, hoping to see Bran and Gibbie reappear.

And she didn't understand what he meant about a sword.

Until . . .

She went hot and cold, grabbing the fisherman's arm when he started to move away. "What's this about a Barra sword? I just got here and haven't heard anything about—"

"That's because there hasn't been a sword here for centuries." The man turned, but his gaze kept flashing to the writer. "No one except a historian or archaeologist would know it was ever said to exist.

"If it even did," he added, lowering his voice. "The sword belonged to the old Barra MacNeils and was half-mythic. Had strange powers, it did.

"Sword done went and vanished in the mists o' time, like so much from the auld days. But"—his eyes glinted—"there's some who believe it might be hidden in with all the stones some rich American has brought back to Barra."

Mindy looked at him. "And you think Wee Hughie MacSporran is hoping to find it?"

She shot another glance at the author.

He looked arrogant, true.

But she doubted he was a sword thief.

The fisherman shrugged, the inborn reticence of the

Highlands settling over him, closing his expression. He was clearly sorry he'd said as much as he had.

"Aye, well." He couldn't quite hide a trace of indignation. "If that's his plan, we'll be hearing soon enough if he finds the sword."

"But you're hoping he won't?"

"That I am." The man nodded solemnly. "There's some things shouldn't be disturbed."

The words spoken, he cut across the crowd, exiting through the hotel door to the dark night beyond.

Mindy started after him, sure that the sword he meant was Bran of Barra's. But before she made it halfway to the reception desk, the blue-cardiganed proprietress sailed up to her, the woman's beaming face heralding success.

"You're in luck!" The woman halted before Mindy. "I've just run down Jock and he's agreed that you can let the Anchor. In fact, he's heading there now to put on fresh linens and lay a fire for you."

Mindy blinked. "That's wonderful."

She hoped it was!

She'd forgotten all about the Hebridean House not having a room for her.

The Anchor hadn't sounded very inviting.

But beggars couldn't be choosers.

And if the little cottage wasn't exactly luxurious, she'd at least have a roof over her head. Better yet, according to the proprietress's earlier description, the Anchor also boasted its own bath.

She'd have privacy.

Much-needed alone time to relax and—her heart skittered—to think about Bran and the mysterious Barra sword, an ancient MacNeil heirloom.

Mindy's pulse skittered.

She was certain the two were connected.

When she stepped outside the Hebridean House and saw that the night had cleared, any doubts that might have remained left her. She'd never seen so many stars, and even from here, high up on a hill above the village, the lights along the waterfront twinkled brightly, reflecting in water that looked as still and glassy as a black mirror.

It was a beautiful night.

And with a surge of buoyancy that would have astounded Margo and the others at Ye Olde Pagan Times, she almost believed that the disappearance of the pea-soup fog was a sign.

A good portent.

And one that meant she was supposed to be here.

So she pulled her jacket tighter against the cold and started down the road toward her car, happier than she'd been in a very long time.

She inhaled deeply as she walked, filling her lungs with the chill night air. She relished how it smelled not just after-rain fresh, but also of the sea. And, she was sure, a trace of heather and woodsmoke. Enchanted, she tilted back her head and smiled up at the glittering heavens, hoping that a certain burly and too-full-of-life-to-hold-with-cloud-floating ghost would soon pay her another call.

Mindy grinned as she reached her car, surprised to find herself almost eager to left-drive down to the Anchor. The tiny village suddenly struck her as cozy. And with the rain stopped and everything so peaceful, she couldn't help but recall the noise and hecticness of the Newark airport that had been her last glimpse of America—plus the auto-fumed stink of the taxi stand and the crush of passengers and airport personnel in the always-crowded check-in area. Security had been a nightmare she refused to relive, even as a memory.

As for the concourses and boarding gates . . .

She shuddered.

Then she looked around, feeling the quiet like a living, breathing presence. It felt like heaven, she decided, fumbling in her bag for the car keys. Her hand actually shook when her fingers closed on them. And it wasn't because she was upset. She was feeling quite good, almost deliriously so.

Margo would say it was Highland magic.

And until this moment, Mindy would have scoffed at the very idea.

But now . . .

One night in the Hebrides and she was a changed woman.

Who would have thought it?

Chapter 10

Mindy's elation began to evaporate as she drove through the village. Although the lights still twinkled, many reflecting prettily in the night-blackened water, there wasn't a sign of life anywhere. The entire waterfront and harbor stretched full of emptiness. Across the bay, she caught the flash of white breakers on the rocks edging Bran's islet. She also saw the great piles of stone from the Folly, the sight making her breath catch.

The stones—now better termed *ruins*, she supposed— were everywhere. And although some even appeared to be stacked in wall-like formations, it was obvious that anything presently standing on the tiny isle was silent and roofless.

Even so, she slowed the car to a crawl. It was hard to look away from the sharp outlines beginning to take form on Bran's isle. But she couldn't stare out across the water as she drove, so she scanned the village instead, each turn of the wheel making her feel farther from civilization. No shadows stirred behind the drawn curtains of the whitewashed cottages along the road. Even the chimneys looked cold, without a trace of smoke rising above them.

A tiny, combined general store and post office was closed at this hour. And the pub, called the Islesman's Pride, appeared equally battened down for the night.

Only the fish-and-chip shop blazed, but as she drove past the shop's large, plate glass window, it was easy to see that the counters were bare and there wasn't anyone standing behind the till.

No one moved on the docks, either.

And if the fishing boats bobbing everywhere were any darker, they'd be invisible.

Mindy drove on, refusing to be daunted.

She did lift her chin, trying to recapture the wonder that had swept her on leaving Hebridean House. It was the same night, after all. So she leaned forward, peering briefly through the windshield, relief flooding her to see the heavens still brilliant with stars.

When she looked back at the road, she was rewarded by the sudden appearance of a small sandy beach. It curved along beside the harbor wall, shining beautifully in the silvery glow of the moon.

Feeling better, she passed the deserted Village Hall without even a twinge of ill ease. Her practical mind told her that all the locals were at Hebridean House, no doubt vying for Wee Hughie's attention. And—if she was of a whimsical mind, like Margo—she'd have to admit that the stillness, together with the lovely night, lent the village an entrancing, almost ethereal quality.

It was sort of like slipping inside one of those incredibly atmospheric, too-beautiful-to-be-true, cozy cottages-and-landscape paintings one saw in so many mall gift shops in the States.

She couldn't think of the artist's name, but his colorful, luminous work was right in front of her.

Come to life in Barra.

Something told her that she, too, would come into her own here.

That brooding gray skies, wild, cold rain, and starry nights like this one would soon have her believing she'd found something she didn't know she'd been seeking.

But before she let her mind wander down such a fanciful path, she needed to find the Anchor.

When a sloping, broken-stoned jetty at the far end of the beach appeared in her headlights, she knew the self-catering cottage had to be near. Especially as the road seemed to dead-end against a fast-approaching cliffside that reared up just ahead, its sheer, wet-gleaming heights effectively signaling that she could go no farther.

Sure enough, when she pulled over beside the jetty, she immediately spotted a small, thick-walled cottage across the road. A handmade sign propped in a window assured her in large, carefully printed black letters that the one-story dollhouse, with its corrugated iron roof and blue painted door, was indeed the Anchor.

She climbed out of the car, sure she'd never seen anything sweeter.

Her pulse quickened as she gathered her bags and crossed the road. But when she let herself inside—just as the woman at Hebridean House had said, the door wasn't locked—she found the cottage cold and smelling of damp. She shivered, but doubted the chill would last long. Someone, likely Jock, the owner, had lit a fire and even turned on a tiny heating unit that stood in a corner.

Better yet, a kitchen niche opened off the main room and she could see the makings for tea set out on the counter. A very modern electric kettle promised she wouldn't have to wait long for boiled water. And packets of Scottish Breakfast Tea and Earl Grey Cream gave her a choice, while a generously sized box of locally made shortbread reminded her of how long it'd been since she'd eaten.

There was also a large jar of hot chocolate, its thoughtful inclusion going a long way in impressing her.

In all her years of flying and sleeping in different hotel rooms every night, she couldn't recall ever finding a jar of finest hot chocolate waiting to tempt her.

Digital alarms she couldn't figure out, too-thin walls, and televisions that seemed to show only hotel information or pay movies without going fuzzy, yes.

Elevator noise, rattling air conditioners that could flash-freeze you within seconds, and—her personal favorite— the madness of landing too close to an ice machine.

But chocolate?

Never.

The Anchor was also spotlessly clean.

It might not have been aired for a while, but it was charming. The well-scrubbed stone floor reminded her of the cozy, old-fashioned kitchen in the farmhouse where her grandmother had grown up in White Horse, Pennsylvania. And the hearth fireplace at one end of the small, all-in-one lounge and dining area, though tiny, made her feel snug as the proverbial bug in a rug.

Not to mention what a treat it was to smell actual woodsmoke at the same time she could stare out the deep-set windows at the bay, even hear the slapping of surf against the jetty by the road.

The effect was magical.

Mindy sank onto a tiny sofa, beginning to understand why her sister and others like her went all moony-eyed at the first flash of plaid or glimpse of purple heather splashed across a hillside.

Scotland *was* special.

And there was something about the Anchor that made her heart pound. Skepticism insisted the strange sense of peace and rightness had to do with the cottage's lack of a television and phone. It followed that, in today's crazy world, a place without what Margo called *modern inconveniences* would hold a certain attraction.

Even so . . .

She glanced about, trying to pinpoint why the neat but humble cottage made her pulse race and even left her feeling rather breathless.

She couldn't see anything out of the ordinary.

Across from her, a door opened onto a shadowy bedroom. She could make out an old-timey wardrobe and a double bed, spread with the same red tartan as the sofa and an armchair by the fireplace.

Only when she returned her attention to the kitchen, drawn, perhaps, by the promise of a cup of hot chocolate to sip as she stared into the fire, did she see why she'd been swept by such tingly awareness.

It wasn't the Anchor.

It was Bran of Barra.

He stood watching her from the kitchen, his hands clasped behind his back and Gibbie at his side. Still wearing his modern-day outfit of worn cords and an Aran sweater, he was the personification of everything irresistible to women who loved rugged, manly men.

And as always, his blue gaze scorched her. When he started forward, his long strides bringing him straight toward her, his lips quirking in that oh-so-sexy smile, Mindy leapt to her feet, her heart flipping.

"Aggggh . . . !" she spluttered like one possessed. "It's you!"

"Aye." He kept coming. "I am myself, last I looked, anyway."

Mindy clapped a hand to her breast. She was sure the floor was dipping beneath her. She knew that his appearance, just the sight of him, made the rest of the world go away. There was only him, the thundering of her heart, and her inability to focus on anything else.

He affected her that badly.

The slow burn in his eyes said he knew it.

"We were interrupted." His burr was soft and rich, deeper than usual, and—she swallowed—so damned sexy that it made his three simple words sound like a declaration of undying love and devotion.

"You don't need to kiss me again." Mindy scooted behind the couch. If he so much as touched her, she'd be lost.

"Kiss you?" His broad shoulders blocked out the kitchen doorway. The pure-sin smile playing about his lips disproved the note of astonishment in his voice.

He wasn't surprised at all.

He was amused.

"Mindy-lass . . ." He lifted his hands, palms outward. "I'll no' kiss you unless you desire it, but"—he glanced at the plaid-covered sofa, his eyes twinkling—"dinnae tell me you've forgotten that a mere bit o' wood and stuffing willnae keep me from you if I wish to be at your side?"

Mindy gulped.

She had forgotten.

But she remembered very well when she found him towering but a handbreadth away from her. Gibbie had moved like lightning, too. The dog now lay sprawled across the sofa, his shaggy gray bulk taking up every inch and looking as if he meant to stay put for a good long while.

The beast's master looped his arms around Mindy's hips.

She stiffened, heated tingles racing through her. "You said you weren't going to kiss me!" She glared at him, seeing at once that he knew he made her absolutely feverish with *desire*, as he called it.

Why was she thinking like that?

. . . Unless she did desire him?

She drew in a tight breath. He made her feel as if they were acting out a scene from a romance novel. She was the resisting but soon-to-be-ravished-and-loving-it heroine and he was the dashing, impossibly sexy hero about to ride off into the sunset with her. Or, in his case, toss her over his shoulder and carry her up the winding, turnpike stair to the great four-poster bed in his castle turret.

And, heaven help her, she almost wished he would!

Instead, she lifted her chin. "About this kissing business, you said—"

"Nothing about no' touching you." He tightened his arms around her, grinning. "I said I'd no' kiss you. A kiss isn't touching."

"Touching leads to kisses!" Mindy tried to break free.

He laughed. "I could touch you into deepest pleasure. Were I of a mind to do so."

"O-o-oh!" His arrogance gave her the strength to pull away.

She dashed to the hearth, just managing to bite back a curse when she nearly tripped over the colorful scatter rug on the slick stone floor.

She whirled to face him. "You are insufferable! A great, swellheaded, domineering—"

"I am Barra." He folded his arms, looking more amused than ever. "And as such, I'll no' be arguing the *great* part. As for the rest—"

"Why *are* you here?"

"I was telling you before you told me no' to kiss you."

"Then tell me now."

To her surprise, his face turned serious and he went to stand at the window, looking out at the bay and—she knew—his own little islet and the stones that had once been the very substance of his home.

His life.

That it was so, that his tiny spit of rock in the bay and the jumble of stones she'd returned meant everything to him, stood etched on every inch of his powerful, brawny body. It was there in the proud set of his shoulders as he stared into the darkness.

She saw it in the way he clenched his hands at his sides. How his knuckles whitened and even the air around him seemed to take note.

He cleared his throat, fisted his hands even tighter.

"I came here for the same reason I went to Hebridean House. I want to thank you for returning my tower's stones." He glanced at her and she could see the passion thrumming inside him. "For truth, lass, I am"—his beautiful voice caught, the sound squeezing her heart—"a bit at a loss to put words to my gratitude.

"A friend has been out there"—he flashed another look at the bay—"and he tells me the stones haven't just been brought back, but that you're having my home restored. Building it anew as if it'd ne'er been torn down?"

Mindy nodded, unable to speak.

She did swallow hard.

She hadn't expected him to thank her. And—her head was beginning to throb—he had it wrong. She didn't deserve his gratitude. She wasn't the one responsible for the restoration of his tower.

She was only the instrument.

The three ghosties from the Folly and their fellow ancestrals were behind it all. They were the ones who should be thanked.

Not her.

"I had nothing to do with it." She blurted the truth before shame made it impossible to speak.

And it did pain her that, until very recently, she'd burned to sell the castle to the highest bidder and never see a stone of the place again. Not a single stick of furniture or even a whirling dust mote.

Now . . .

She felt like a callous, shallow fool.

And as much as the truth seared her, she felt compelled to make sure Bran of Barra understood. Only then could she look in the mirror again. And, at the end of the day, despite her years in a very modern profession, she still remained an old-fashioned girl at heart.

To her, honor was everything.

Bran of Barra defined honor.

She wouldn't have believed there were such men left in the world and—her heart clenched on the admission—she suspected there weren't. Leastways, not in the modern-day world she called her own.

She swallowed a sudden lump in her throat and glanced aside, certain that when she flew home, she could look far and wide and not find a man like him.

She steeled herself and looked the sexy Hebridean ghost in the eye. "Your castle stones are out there"— she, too, shot a quick glance at the bay—"because three ghostly cousins of yours threatened that they'd haunt me forever if I didn't return them."

Bran of Barra blinked. *"Three ghostly cousins?"*

Mindy nodded. "Cousins, kin, or whatever you wish

to call them. Fact is, they're Barra MacNeil chieftains who—I don't know how else to say this—lived several centuries after your time."

"I see."

"You do?" Mindy placed her hands on the back of the sofa, glad for its support.

Bran of Barra started pacing, his sword—he was still wearing it—clacking softly against his hip as he strode back and forth in the Anchor's tiny lounge.

"I believe I know the three chieftains you mean." He glanced at her as he passed the fireplace. "They visited my home some while ago. Their arrival was unexpected and startled a guest because, rather than coming to enjoy the revelries of my hall as most are wont to do, they were seen stomping about in an abovestairs passageway, fussing amongst themselves."

Mindy smiled. "That sounds like them. They do like to grumble. But"—her heart caught again—"I think they're happy now. I saw them just as my ferry approached Barra. They were in a medieval-looking galley and racing back and forth near the opening to the bay, making a ruckus and—"

"Aye, they will be Barra MacNeils!" Bran sounded himself again. "'Tis a flourish they were giving you." He beamed, pride glowing in his eyes. "Like as not, they were welcoming you to our bonny isle!"

"That's what I thought." The idea warmed Mindy.

She would never have believed it, but she'd slowly grown fond of the Long Gallery Threesome.

"There is something I don't understand." Bran halted suddenly, stood rubbing his beard. "Where was my tower? And why did my chiefly cousins press you to return it?"

Mindy hesitated. Not because she wasn't willing to

answer those two questions, but she knew they'd lead to more. And she wasn't keen on telling Bran about Hunter.

So she resorted to her airline training and posed a question of her own. "You said that the three other ghosts were at your hall. How can that be if"—the implication made her uncomfortable—"at the time, your tower wasn't standing?"

"No' standing?" His brows lifted. "Sweet lass, my tower has always stood as e'er. Nary a stone is changed nor a blade o' grass—"

"But how—"

"Because"—his crooked smile flashed—"I will it so."

"You mean in your ghostly realm."

"Aye, just." He nodded, looking pleased.

Apparently tired of pacing, he dropped onto the sofa next to Gibbie, slinging an arm around the beast's shoulders. "Now that you know, I'm for hearing where my home has been in your world. That it hasn't been where it should be, I already know. So speak true. I'll know if you're trying to cozen me."

Mindy's first instinct was to do just that. Instead, she took a deep breath. "Your tower was in Bucks County, Pennsylvania. Near a town called New Hope. Wealthy MacNeils of a past century—"

"Penn-*seal*-landia?" He jumped to his feet, his eyes round. "Sakes! 'Tis worse than I thought."

Gibbie barked, sharing his distress.

Bran of Barra shoved a hand through his hair, looking almost wild-eyed. "So I was right! I'd suspected you hailed from that wicked place. But I ne'er dreamed my tower would be—"

"In Pennsylvania?" Mindy didn't understand his concern. "It's a very beautiful place. Bucks County, where

I'm from, is especially nice. Not the same as here, but lovely. It's sort of like the kind of rolling countryside you see in England—"

"England?" He looked even more horrified.

Mindy could have kicked herself.

Not being a big fan of *Braveheart*, she'd forgotten that Scots of Bran of Barra's day wouldn't be too enamored of the English.

Her gaffe was making the back of her neck hot.

He looked so upset.

"I'm sorry." She took several calming breaths. "I fully agree with you that your home should never have been dismantled and—"

"So my tower was taken apart?" Bran's eyes narrowed. "And done deliberately?"

Mindy nodded. "Some of your descendants went to America and settled in New Hope. They did very well. One of them"—she took another deep breath, wishing she could skip this part—"made a fortune in steel and railroads.

"It's believed that he never forgot his Scottish roots, and so when he became rich, he traveled here. He went to Barra and ordered your castle taken apart and transported to Pennsylvania, where he had it rebuilt, stone for stone."

"God o' mercy!" Bran of Barra scrubbed his hands over his face. "How could a man of my own blood commit such a travesty?" He lowered his hands, shaking his head. "If he loved this isle, our good and bonny Scotland, why didn't he just come back here himself?"

Mindy looked down and plucked at a loose thread on her sleeve.

No way was she going to tell him that his New Hope descendant, however savvy in business, had been driven by pomp and greed. His head turned by the luxuries and conveniences of the New World. And, Mindy suspected, the oohs and aahs he hoped to hear when people saw his Scottish castle on a Bucks County hill.

Some people craved grandeur and attention.

Mindy shuddered, distaste and memories of Hunter making her stomach clench.

Bran crossed the little room and grabbed her arms, peering down at her intently. "Why are you so pale? Were you— I mean, are you of this man's line?"

She blinked.

It took her a moment to grasp what he was asking. She couldn't think when he stood so close, his big, strong hands holding her tight.

"No, I don't have a drop of MacNeil blood." She was so glad she didn't.

"That's good, then." He let go of her and stepped back, ran a hand through his hair again. "But I'd still hear how you're associated with us.

"Why"—he was eyeing her closely—"my three *cousins* put it to you to sort this for us."

"They . . . Their names are Silvanus, Roderick, and Geordie," she began, hedging. "They—"

"Good old Scots names." Bran nodded sagely. "They'll be fine men, then."

"I know they mean well." Mindy tried not to squirm. "As for why they chose me, I suppose they knew I had the money to see the deed done." She forced herself to hold his gaze. "They figured I disliked MacNeils enough to do whatever they wanted. They knew I wouldn't want them haunting me for the rest of my life."

"Pah!" Bran of Barra shook his head. "That can't be. There's never been a female born who isn't fond of MacNeils, especially Barra MacNeils."

"Exactly." Mindy gave him her brightest smile. The reminder of the wicked appeal of MacNeil men brought her back to her senses.

"You've hit on the very reason I had problems with them." She set her hands on her hips. "Too many women are crazy about the men of your clan and—"

"By the rood!" Bran slapped his forehead. "I've been a newt-brained gowk. But now I understand!" He looked at her, his eyes flashing. "A skirt-chasing MacNeil caught your fancy and then the lout stomped on your heart.

"Och, lassie." He hooked his thumbs in his sword belt and rocked back on his heels. "It grieves me to say so, but all clans have their scoundrels, even MacNe—"

"Can we please not talk about it?" Mindy glanced aside, not wanting to see the fire in his eye. Although hearing him refer to Hunter as a lout and a scoundrel was sweet balm to her soul.

His indignation on her behalf was dangerous.

She'd already pegged him as the kind of man a woman could depend on. A man of deep integrity, full of love for his land, his heritage, and those he cared about. He'd always have a ready shoulder and would glare daggers at anyone who looked cross-eyed at his lady. He'd use his sword if need be and—she was breathless to think it—he'd kiss a woman until her toes curled.

What he'd do naked, his woman caught up in those powerfully muscled arms, didn't bear imagining.

She gulped, her pulse running riot.

It'd be so easy to go to him, slide her arms around his very real-feeling, masculine girth, and lean into him, telling him that, yes, she *did* desire him.

Yes, she wanted—no, craved—his kisses.

Fortunately, she had enough wits to know that giving in to such a passion would scald her in a worse way than

Hunter could have done in a thousand years. In fact, she couldn't even remember what the bastard looked like.

But she'd never forget Bran.

Not even wanting to think about what that meant in terms of consequence and logistics, she pressed a hand to the small of her back—it ached suddenly, hurting almost as much as the throbbing at her temples—and tried to think of a way to banish Bran before he crossed the room again and reached for her.

That he might was certain.

She saw it in his eyes. She felt the passion building inside him. Any moment he'd come for her. And if she let him, life as she'd known it until now would end.

She could fall in love.

And that would lead to madness.

Blessedly, her good sense rode to the rescue, and she suddenly knew just how to steer him in a very different direction.

"What's with you and the author at Hebridean House?" She spoke quickly. "Wee Hughie MacSporran. I saw your face when he came out of the sitting room, heard you call him a—"

"A bluidy windbag?"

"I think that was it, yes."

"You remember rightly." Bran glanced at her, his eyes startlingly blue. "The bastard has more hot air in him than a peasant forced to exist on a diet o' beans."

Mindy laughed.

But she caught herself at once. She couldn't recall the last time a man had made her laugh. And she knew instinctively that Bran of Barra, if they were a pair, would fill their days, not just with blinding, white-hot passion and meaning, but with humor and fun the likes of which she knew would delight her all her days.

"I'll tell you this." His voice hardened. "The man thinks too highly of himself. He—"

"He did seem a bit arrogant."

"Arrogant?" His brows shot upward. "He's a preening peacock!"

"Is that why you drew your sword?" Mindy's heart hammered. This was about so much more than medieval weapons. "I'm curious. Did men in your day punish conceit with a swift swing of cold, hard steel?"

He jutted his chin. "I meant only to give him a fright."

"But why?"

"Because."

Mindy frowned. "That's not an answer."

"I know that fine." A muscle ticked in his jaw. "If you'd hear the truth, the puff-chested ox simply annoys me. He's irritating like a pebble in my shoe."

He folded his arms, his mouth set in a firm, hard line.

Under different circumstances, Mindy would have laughed. Bran of Barra wasn't exactly a modest man himself. As if he'd read her mind, he suddenly took a step forward, wagging a finger at her.

"Hear this, Mindy-lass." He kept up the finger wagging. "When I walk through Edinburgh, Glasgow, or where'er, men stand aside, clearing the way. They do so because I am Barra, no' because I waved them away or because someone blasted a fanfare on a trumpet, warning folk to leap out of my path.

"MacSporran is a trumpet blaster." The finger wagging stopped. "Such braggarts go against everything a Highlander believes. If you've ne'er heard the saying"— he grinned—"'tis the shallowest burn that makes the most noise.

"We, the true men of Barra, live by that!"

Looking pleased, he dusted his hands. "Next time I

see the Highland Storyweaver, I might just jab him in the belly! Rid him of some excess wind."

He winked.

Mindy found herself laughing.

She couldn't help it. Mercy, but she could lose her heart to this man.

"For now," he was saying, still looking righteous, "I'm thinking you need to learn the measure of a true Barrach." His voice turned all deep and Scottishy again, the smooth, rich tones chasing the laughter right out of her.

She started backing away.

He grinned and angled his head, the heat in his eyes making her short of breath.

"We're no' all like the blackguard who treated you poorly, Mindy-lass."

"I didn't say that." She scooted into the kitchen, wishing it were larger than two square feet, tops.

Bran of Barra stayed where he was, but he was looking at her with incredible intensity.

"You don't have to say the words. They're writ all o'er you, plain as day.

"When they're gone, or at least a bit faded, I'll show you that I'm different. Till then"—he glanced at his dog and clicked his fingers, nodding once when Gibbie sprang down off the sofa and trotted over to him—"we'll leave you to your night's rest."

"No, wait. . . ." Mindy started forward, expecting them both to vanish in a blink.

But this time, Bran of Barra simply turned and walked to the door, letting himself and his dog out into the cold, damp night just as a real, flesh-and-blood man would do.

And he'd looked so real as he went about it that her heart broke.

Wishing he *were* real, she ran to the window, hoping to see him standing on the road, waiting for her to come out and invite him back in.

Perhaps—if there was such a thing as Highland magic—he'd be out there, just as she imagined.

But when she looked, he was gone.

The narrow road was empty.

And the broken jetty across from the Anchor sloped down into the dark water. In the moonlight, she could see that its stones were crusted with limpet shells and glistening seaweed. But of a big, brawny man and his dog, there was no sign.

Damn it anyway.

What Mindy didn't see was the tiny black-garbed woman standing near the deserted Village Hall just a short way down the road from the Anchor.

Unaccustomed to modern trappings, the old woman adjusted her heavy jacket against the biting wind and then stooped to retie one of the red plaid laces on her sturdy black walking boots.

When she straightened, she rubbed her knotty hands together and crossed the road to better peer across the bay at the dark little islet that had seen such a stir of activity in recent days.

Seeing the piles of stone there made her cackle with glee.

It was good to see folk undoing some of the ills that the Highlands had suffered now and then.

Her own beloved Hebrides were most especially deserving!

As was the young American lassie, she knew.

She was fond of Bran of Barra, too.

He might bluster a bit, and, despite his claims, there

wasn't a modest bone in his great, hulking body. His heart was in the right place, though, and that was something she honored above all else.

But helping them just might prove beyond even her powerful magic.

Hoping it wouldn't be so, the old woman patted her frizzled white hair and glanced again at the red tartan laces on her boots.

The laces were a fine touch, if she did say so herself.

Even a crone like her enjoyed a bit o' spiff.

Pleased, she lifted her chin to the wind and returned her gaze to the little island in the bay. Soon there'd be more than just stout castle walls and cobbled baileys gracing the isle's long-empty shores.

It was time love and happiness reigned there, as well.

If she had any say in the matter, her magic would help it happen.

Chapter 11

Mindy was in Hawaii.

She could hear the pounding of the surf and the rattling of palm fronds in a tropical breeze. The sun's toasty rays were a caress, warming her from head to toe, and her supersized hibiscus-print beach towel was the softest, most comfortable she'd ever lain on. Best of all, she could smell fresh-roasted Kona coffee, the delicious aroma wafting on the air, tempting her....

Calling her from the sweetest of dreams.

But she wasn't yet ready to waken.

Sleep was good.

And early-morning z's were her idea of heaven. Whoever prided himself on being a lark had never tasted the pleasures of life as an owl.

So she flipped onto her stomach, content to enjoy the sun-drenched splendor of Kauai's Poipu Beach just a few minutes longer.

Too bad the soothing rattle of the palm fronds was beginning to sound like the patter of rain. And although she remained nice and warm, the sun's baking heat was starting to feel suspiciously like too many layers of wool blankets and an extremely thick duvet.

Mindy frowned.

She was sure she was sweating.

She cracked an eye to peer at her hibiscus beach towel and see if she'd somehow become tangled in its oversized length, but instead of tropical red flowers, she was treated to a glimpse of red plaid.

Mindy woke with a start. She sat bolt upright in her bed in the Anchor's tiny bedroom, seeing immediately that she'd swathed herself in a cocoon of red-tartaned bedding. And although there was a pleasing trace of roasted *something* wafting about and making her nose twitch, it wasn't the aroma of her much-loved Kona coffee.

It was the lingering scent of wood ash on the chill morning air.

And now that she'd thrown off the covers, it *was* cold.

More than that, the little room was subzero, frost-a-witch's-bottom freezing.

It was all she could do to keep her teeth from chattering. The still-dark morning outside her window looked wet and chilly and—she angled her ear at the ceiling—the sound of rattling palm fronds really had been the pitter-patter of rain on the Anchor's iron corrugated roof.

She groaned and considered rewrapping herself in the red plaid bedcovers.

But . . .

She could also hear the wild roar of the sea—that sound, at least, having been real—and as always, the crashing thunder of surf exhilarated her.

Even so, the warm comfort of her bed had her pulling the covers back up to her chin. Unfortunately, just as she rolled onto her side and lifted a hand to punch the pillows into shape, she heard a noise that wasn't at all pleasing.

Someone was knocking on the door.

Mindy's eyes snapped open. A quick glance at her travel alarm said it wasn't even eight a.m. She sat up again, hoping the clock was wrong.

But the frightful hour wasn't a mistake.

Nor had she imagined the rapping on the cottage's front door.

She could hear it still, loud and persistent.

"Oh, man." She stumbled from the bed and glanced around for her clothes, scowling. Who would have expected company—this early in the morning—in a teeny, end-of-the-road cottage in an equally tiny village by the sea?

Not her, for sure.

She considered not answering. After all, no one knew she was here. And even if somebody did, she didn't know anyone who'd wish to speak to her. The only person she'd like seeing wouldn't stand in the rain banging on her door.

He'd appear out of thin air, hands on his hips, and dazzling her with a smile.

So it wasn't Bran.

It could be the village constable. Given the wild tossing of the sea—she could just see a wedge of it from the bedroom window—and the rain, it wouldn't surprise her if the tide had risen and swept away her car.

She'd left it practically standing in the road, beside the tumbledown jetty.

Concerned, she dashed about, quickly pulling on her discarded clothes, albeit a bit haphazardly. Bending, she jammed her feet into her woolly slipper-socks, not wanting to take time to retrieve her hill-walking boots from the bath. Nor was she awake enough to fuss with lacing them.

She ignored her hair except to run her fingers through the tangles.

As for makeup, whoever disturbed her before ten a.m. deserved to see her as nature intended, naked faced and without mascara, though she did pop into the icy bathroom to gurgle a capful of mouthwash.

Thus prepared, she sprinted through the lounge and flung open the door.

It wasn't the village bobby standing there.

It was the big, barrel-chested fisherman from the Hebridean House Hotel. The one with the shock of curly black hair who'd spoken to her in the hotel lobby, claiming that Wee Hughie MacSporran had come to Barra to search for the MacNeils' mythic sword.

"Jock MacGugan." He bobbed his dark head. "I hope I'm not waking you?"

Mindy blinked. The way he was scrunching the cap he held respectfully in his hands said he knew very well that he'd caught her still in bed.

"Ehhh . . ." She blinked again. She was so not a morning person and sometimes—like now—her voice just wouldn't work right at such ungodly hours.

She secretly suspected that her vocal cords enjoyed their sleep even more than she did and that, wise as they were, they refused to perform until they'd had due rest.

"I mean, no—er, ah . . . yes, I was sleeping," she finally managed, seeing no point in denying what he could plainly see by looking at her. "What can I do for you?"

"This is my cottage." He thrust out his right hand, then, realizing he clutched his cap, switched it to his left hand and gripped hers in a firm shake. "I thought to make sure you felt at home. . . ."

"I do." Mindy glanced behind her at the darkened lounge.

Even now, the little cottage had an air of coziness that charmed her.

Scotland's pull, as Margo would call it, was indeed a force to be reckoned with.

Go figure.

Jock shuffled his feet. "I know the cottage is small—"

"It's perfect." She smiled, meaning it. "Would you like to come in?"

She made to step aside, but the fisherman—Jock—moved first, reaching to fetch a large, waterproof satchel he'd set beside the door stoop.

Unzipping it, he produced a box of groceries, which he handed her. "There wasn't time to stock the kitchen for you last night, so the wife sent along some eggs and streaky bacon, mushrooms, and tomatoes. There's also Irish butter, a bottle of milk, and"—he patted a cloth-wrapped packet—"some of her homemade breakfast scones, with bramble jam."

He looked up at her. "The scones are still warm."

Mindy felt her jaw slip. When he'd bent down, cold, gusty wind had caught her in the face and she'd needed only that quick glimpse of the road to see that the morning was even more damp and dark than she'd thought.

Yet now—given his kindness and the delicious smell of his wife's fresh-baked scones—the day seemed brighter and more welcoming.

"This is so kind of you." She put the food box on a little table just inside the door. "I don't know what to say. Please tell your wife how much I appreciate—"

"Ach, there's no need to be thanking us." He made a jerky gesture with his hand. "The grocer's doesn't open until ten and I'm thinking you didn't know that, as tenant of the Anchor, you're welcome to a full Scottish breakfast up at Hebridean House, or"—he glanced down the road, back toward the center of the village—"you can also eat at the Islesman's Pride.

"They open early for breakfast, serving us at the fishing, mostly. Though"—he turned back to her, frowning—"sometimes the good folk at the Islesman forget we have an arrangement for our Anchor guests. So if you go there one morning, don't let the rascals be for charging you."

Mindy started to smile, but caught herself. "I won't. Thanks for letting me know. And—"

She broke off, glancing over her shoulder to where her purse sat on the floor beside the sofa. "No one told me what I owe you for staying here. I can pay you now, if you like, or—"

"Ach, there'll be none of that, nae." The fisherman shook his head, looking embarrassed. "I should have known last night that you were the American lassie come bringing back the stones of our tower. You'll not be finding a soul on Barra who'd charge you a night's stay here. However long you remain with us. See you, we—"

"But that's not right—"

"It was the taking away of our tower that wasn't right." He turned to stare out across the bay and Mindy saw that raindrops clung to his black curls and netted the shoulders of his oiled jacket. The droplets glistened in the dim morning light, somehow looking so right and fitting.

As if he were as one with the blustery morning, a part of it in a way few others could be.

Except, perhaps, true Barrachs.

The thought pinched something inside her, and for a moment, she felt as if she'd come very close to understanding the magic of Barra.

To her horror, a lump started forming in her throat and she inhaled deeply, hoping to dislodge it.

"What they did, those years ago, carrying away the castle, tore the heart out of this community." Jock turned back to her, speaking as if it had happened yesterday. "We're all right grateful to you. If you be needing anything, anything at all"—his deep voice went gruff—"my mobile number is on a notepad in the kitchen drawer.

"Or just ask after Jock." He smiled, swiped a work-reddened hand across his cheek. "There's only one Jock on this island and that's me. I fish the herring, and just now I'm heading up work on thon castle restoration, so folk know where to find me."

"You're working on the tower?" Mindy was confused. "Are you with the Glasgow firm I hired? MacFadyen and Sons? The Building Gaels?"

She'd been assured they were the best and fastest.

And they weren't local.

She knew that for a fact. It shamed her now to admit, but she'd specifically sought a restoration and building company that wouldn't have any ties to Barra and the MacNeils.

She looked up at the fisherman. "I'm sorry. . . . I don't understand. I—"

"Could be the men of Barra hold that we of these isles have enough Gaels what are skilled with a hammer and trowel." Jock the fisherman-cum-landlord-cum–castle restorer straightened. Already a large man, his thick wool sweater and heavy, rain-misted jacket made him seem gargantuan.

The spark of pride in his snapping blue eyes—did all

Scotsmen have blue ones?—made him the most beautiful man Mindy had ever seen.

With the exception of Bran of Barra, of course.

When she found her voice again, it hitched. "I know the MacFadyens were here. I wired them money so they could get started. And"—she glanced across the water to Bran's islet, where in the dim morning light, in addition to piles of stone and some walls, she could also see some structures covered in tarpaulins and scaffolding—"it's obvious they've been busy. You can see—"

"I see the work my men have been doing." The fisherman followed her gaze. "All good Barrachs, every one," he said, his back fiercely straight. "We'll do as fine a job, working as steady and good, if not better than the Glasgow men. Sandy Budge, our joiner, who also looks after our banking for us, has the money you paid the Building Gaels. They returned it to the pence before they headed back to Glasgow."

"I don't understand."

"You will once you've been here a while." Jock the fisherman set his woolly cap back on his head, pulling it down around his ears. "It's right and fitting that we of Barra rebuild our tower. With Barra hands and no other."

He gallantly pretended not to see Mindy's astonishment. "When you're ready to visit the site, let me know. I'm also the one who runs the boat out to the islet and back."

Mindy hardly heard the part about the boat. "You mean you sent away the builders?" She had to know. "And they just left, like that?"

"Aye, well . . ." Jock scuffed his boot on the wet pavement. "They left, is all what matters."

"But—"

The fisherman touched his cap and nodded. "I'll be on my way, then."

And before Mindy could blink, he'd turned and he was striding up the road. She frowned and set off after him, slipper-socks be damned—they were already soaked through, anyway—but before she'd gone three paces, a deep chuckle behind her halted her in her tracks.

"He's a good man, Jock is," Silvanus's voice boomed at her shoulder. She'd recognize his baritone anywhere. "But dinnae think 'twas his efforts alone what rid us o' the Weedgies."

Mindy spun around, not surprised to find nothing but the Anchor's empty door stoop.

"Weedgies are folk from Glasgow," Silvanus intoned all the same. "And"—Mindy could just imagine him setting his hands on his hips and taking a deep, gloating breath—"if you dinnae ken, a *flourish* such as we gave you can also be used to scare the beards off some buggers what aren't expecting to see a ghost galley come flying out o' the mist at 'em!"

"You did that?" Mindy spoke to the cold air, not caring how silly it seemed.

"We did!" The proud gusto of Silvanus's answer rewarded her.

Then he appeared before her, just long enough to sketch a jaunty bow and vanish again.

Mindy stared at the spot where he'd been, then looked again down the road to where she could still see Jock the fisherman walking away.

Then she leaned back against the wall of the Anchor, cold and wet though its stones were, and clutched a hand to her cheek. She could feel the flutter of her heart and—again, she shouldn't be surprised—the hot, thick lump of emotion swelling once more in her throat.

She'd always heard that Scotland was a land of heroes.

Now she knew it was true.

Mindy felt her nerves quiver the instant she stepped over the Anchor's threshold. Her cheeks warmed and tingles danced over her skin. She knew why when she saw that Jock's box of groceries was no longer on the little wooden table beside the cottage door.

The table was empty.

And in the soft gray light of morning, she saw at once just where the breakfast goods had gone. They were lined neatly on the kitchen counter, the box sitting innocently on the cold stone flags of the floor.

Too bad she had a good idea how the foodstuffs made the move.

They'd had help of a supernatural nature.

And she highly doubted Silvanus had done the deed. He'd been too busy boasting about how he and his ancestral friends had used their *flourishing* skills to frighten the Building Gaels, chasing the MacFadyen work crew from Barra, straight back to their native Glasgow.

Nor could she see Roderick or Geordie sneaking into the cottage to carry her groceries.

Only a ghost wanting to get on her good side would do such a thing.

And that meant Bran.

She expected to see him leaning against the counter, with a wicked grin and twinkling eyes to let her know how pleased he was with his efforts to impress. But since she didn't see him in the cottage, perhaps he was more intent on teasing her and remaining invisible. Or—it was possible—he could be allowing her time to get decent before he put in an appearance.

She *did* look a fright.

Embarrassed, she swiped a hand over her rain-dampened hair, tugged off her sodden slipper-socks, then hurried into the bedroom to dress properly.

Unfortunately, the little room was even chillier than before. Somehow the window had come open and now the air wasn't just cold, but wet and smelling of the sea. She could almost taste the tang of kelp and brine. And—she could hardly believe it—their raw, invigorating bite made her pulse jump.

She'd never liked the cold.

And *wet* cold—like the gray curtains of rain beginning to blow past her window—was the worst transgressor of chill, dark, and dreariness.

Scotland had a patent on such days.

Everyone knew it.

Yet now . . .

The place was suddenly full of heroes and a wet day in Barra looked inviting.

Mindy shivered and rubbed her arms.

Amazing, but looking out the window at the wild, blustery day almost had her agreeing with the anonymous soul who'd said that anyone who thought sunshine brought happiness had never danced in the rain.

Barra was making a rain dancer out of her.

If she added how badly she wished to see a ghost—a certain big, brawny ghost with a crooked nose and a smile like sin—she was sure she was on her way to the loony bin.

Something was seriously wrong with her.

But she'd worry about it after breakfast.

Anything but a stick-figure girl, she had a healthy appetite, and as her mother always said, the world looks rosier on a full stomach.

So she marched straight into the kitchen and tore immediately into Jock MacGugan's wife's cloth-wrapped packet of fresh-baked scones. To her delight, she discovered they weren't just scones.

They were *scones*.

Huge, oven-warm, and light as air, they came in two kinds: cheesy scones, the likes of which she'd seen only once before, and apple cinnamon. Both smelled scrumptious, and, smeared thick with creamy Irish butter and homemade bramble jam, they tasted even better.

Mindy ate them all.

She was just licking the crumbs from her fingers when the air behind her stirred and she felt a soft kiss on the bared skin of her nape. She jumped, shocking pleasure ripping through her as the light brush of a beard tickled her neck. Then two large, strong hands gripped her arms, pulling her back against a well-muscled chest.

Bran of Barra's deep voice teased her ear. "Hungry, were you?"

Without seeing his face, Mindy knew he was smiling. She did feel his plaid rub against her. Its heavy wool was warm and rough, smelling faintly of woodsmoke.

Her senses ran riot.

He chuckled and slid an arm around her waist, holding her close as he nipped gently down her neck. "I'm pleased to see you enjoying yourself, Mindy-lass."

His amusement dashed cold water on the hot tingles racing through her.

"You said you wouldn't kiss me!" She jerked free, spinning around to face him.

It was a mistake.

Full-bodied, real-looking, and sexy as ever, he had heat in his eyes that almost singed her. She tugged at her sweater, backing away until she bumped into the minuscule refrigerator.

"Och, lassie, you wound me." He stayed where he was and clapped a hand to his chest, managing to look both guilty and devastatingly appealing. "Would you believe me if I told you that I just cannae help myself?

"Besides"—he reached out and grabbed her wrist, pulling her to him again—"I meant true kisses. Little nips along your neck don't count."

"Oh, yes, they do!"

He laughed. "You won't say that after I've really kissed you."

Mindy looked up at him, sure she couldn't breathe. "As we've decided there won't be any such kisses, that's a moot point, isn't it?"

She jutted her chin, knew she'd never looked haughtier.

Bran of Barra tweaked her nose. "I like a maid with spirit, so dinnae think you're dissuading me."

"I'm not a maid! I—" Mindy clamped her mouth shut, realizing too late how that sounded.

Sure enough, the blaze in his eyes turned to a slow, dangerous smolder. "That I know, sweetness," he purred, his rich burr watering her knees. "But you may as well be—as you've ne'er been loved by a true Barra man!"

"Never been—" The scald on Mindy's cheeks kept her from finishing.

He grinned.

"So it is, Mindy-lass." He curled his hand around her neck, let his fingers toy with her hair. "There's no point in no' stating what's true."

"Ahhh . . ." Her objection trailed into nothingness when he tightened his fingers around her wrist and looked at her with such intensity that she could feel all the manliness and power inside him.

His strength—and the desire she could almost see beating through him—rocked her to the core, making her light-headed and dizzy.

She moistened her lips, her heart galloping.

"The truth, sweetness, is that neither one of us wants this. Yet"—he put a hand beneath her chin, lifting her face so that she was forced to look at him—"here we are."

Mindy felt her jaw set. The blaze inside her was making her desperate. "Here we are what? Aren't you always here? This is your Barra, isn't it?"

"Mine, aye, though . . ." He paused, something indefinable flaring in his eyes. "No chief worthy of the title would deny that our holdings never belong to just one man. Why do you think thon fisherman and his friends willnae allow anyone but Barrachs to rebuild my tower?

"They won't because it's theirs, too." His words, the passion in his voice, made Mindy's breath catch. "That's the way it was in my day and"—he paused, his pride almost a presence in the room—"I'm right pleased to see that hasn't changed! We chieftains ensure that all is well, looking after our own and seeing to the right o' things. But the land, Mindy-lass, the land belongs to us all.

"And you're right. I am always here. But"—he smoothed his thumb over her jaw and she trembled beneath the caress—"I'm here, with my friends, in my own place and time. It isn't my wont to visit Barra of the moderns."

"But you're here now."

"Aye, that I am."

"You seem to be here every time I turn around."

"That, too." He sounded very serious. "I'll no' be denying it."

"Why are you, then?" Mindy knew she sounded breathless. The intensity of his gaze and the way his thumb kept circling over her cheek made normal speech impossible.

The man needed a license to wield such behavior!

And she was going to self-combust if he didn't stop looking so deeply into her eyes.

"Ach, lass." He shook his head slowly. "Surely you know I'm here because of you."

"Me?" Mindy blinked, her heart stalling. "Not because of the tower?"

"The tower does interest me." He grinned. "I willnae lie. But I could watch the work better from my islet than inside this wee bit cottage."

Mindy glanced aside. "It really isn't a good idea for you to be here."

"To be sure."

"Some would say it's mad."

"No doubt." He slid his arms around her.

She found herself gripping his plaid. "Really crazy," she argued, although the tingles racing through her said otherwise. She wanted him—hoped he'd at least kiss her—and the desire she felt building inside her was so against everything she believed in and had expected.

She'd had it with men—especially *Scots*men—and she certainly didn't need to be dallying with a kilt-wearing, sword-carrying Highlander who didn't even bother to deny he was seven hundred years young.

A ghost!

Yet, there she was, trembling with anticipation, burning with a need she'd never felt for any man.

He was just looking at her, his arms holding her tight,

and already she understood the cheesy phrase found so often in Scottish romance novels: that the hero's love-making set the heather ablaze.

Or was it the hills?

Either way, she was on fire.

And Bran of Barra knew it.

Triumph flared in his eyes and he even looked about ready to whoop. When he tightened his arms around her and grinned, she could almost see the word *conquest* flashing in the air between them.

He lifted a hand to stroke her face in a rough, claiming gesture. "So you're finally ready?"

Mindy swallowed.

Her mouth felt like sawdust.

"You needn't tell me." His voice deepened, his burr doing wicked things to her. "I can see it all o'er you. But I'll keep my word that until you admit—"

"Admit what?"

"That you want this." He took her chin in his hand and lowered his head to lightly flick her mouth with the tip of his tongue. "My kisses."

"I don't!" Mindy lied.

"I say you do," he challenged her, looking down pointedly at how she'd splayed her hands across his plaid, even plunging the fingers of one hand inside his shirt.

She followed his gaze and flushed.

But she didn't remove her hand.

She couldn't. The warm strength of his powerfully muscled chest felt so good beneath her fingers, and the light scattering of crisp, ginger-colored hairs she'd discovered there positively intoxicated her. She kept running her fingers over them, unable to stop.

He had a warrior's body.

Everything about him thrilled and excited her.

And—she could tell—he burned with wanting her.

She gulped. She was keenly aware of the thick, hard ridge of heat pressing against her hip. And it wasn't the hilt of his sword. She'd glanced discreetly down to make sure. It was all him.

Pure Highland man, eager and ready.

"I . . . uh . . ." She bit her lip, knew she was lost.

Bran of Barra's eyes gleamed in a way that should have sent her dashing out the door. Not that he'd have let her go. His arm was like an iron band around her, crushing her to him so tightly, she could hardly breathe.

She tried to focus. "This isn't the place—"

"Nae." He pulled back to look at her. "No' for what you're thinking. Only the grandeur of my own tower chamber would suit for that. But"—he tightened his arms around her again and she was sure their bodies would soon catch fire—"a mere kiss can be anywhere."

She almost choked. "I doubt there's anything even remotely *mere* about your kisses."

"Aye, that's true!" He laughed, his eyes twinkling with pleasure.

Mindy trembled, sure she was melting.

She *was* damp, God help her!

In fact, that part of her had never tingled with such abandon. The sensations were overwhelming, almost unbearable, but deliciously so. Could be, she'd been frigid until now, at this moment and with this man, and she hadn't even known it. She did know that she was close to climaxing just from being in his brawny, Scottish arms.

As if he knew, he lowered his head again and began nibbling on her ear. Then, as quickly, he feathered kisses along her jaw and down her neck. His hands were doing wicked things to her back, totally turning her on.

Who knew a touch to the back could be so sexy?

"Just say aye, sweetness." His tone made her feel hot and cold—the little kitchen was spinning away. . . . "One simple word and—"

"Yes!" Mindy clutched at him, clinging hard.

"Lass!" His hands swept upward, biting hard into her shoulders. He pressed his lips to her hair, rubbing his cheek against her. For one crazy-mad moment, she was sure he was trying to drink in the scent of her, branding her on him in a savage, primordial way that excited her so much, her knees nearly buckled.

She *was* shaking.

"Gods, but you're sweet." His voice was husky, the words soft against her temple. "Tell me you need my kisses, Mindy. I'd hear you say it. Now—"

"Yes, now!" She thrust her hands into his hair, tangling her fingers in the thick, cool strands. "Kiss me, Bran, kiss me, please—"

He gave a ragged groan, cutting her off as he slanted his mouth over hers, kissing her deeply. She twined her fingers more tightly in his hair, pulling him close and opening her mouth wide beneath his, welcoming his tongue when he plunged it between her lips to slide and twirl against her own.

He kissed and kissed her, ravishing her mouth in a way that could only be called that: *ravishing*. Or, perhaps, it was more like plundering. Whatever it was, nothing had ever felt more perfect and right.

She couldn't get enough of him, ached to have his entire hard, solid body naked against her, skin to skin, and without a sliver of air between them. Need surged within her and she returned his kisses with a passion wilder than she'd have ever believed possible.

The feel, scent, and taste of him electrified her—his savage, all-slaking kisses were almost a torture to bear, so exquisite was every touch, each dizzying, breath-sharing tangle of tongues. Every rasp of his beard was an erotic ecstasy that sent her spiraling, tumbling into an exultant whirl of hot, shivering need.

She was unraveling, coming undone. He slid his hands over her breasts, cupping and plumping them, then spreading his fingers over her, squeezing her fullness, before he began rubbing her nipples with his thumbs.

"Bran . . ." She swayed against him, felt the world's most thunderous orgasm cresting when he nudged her legs apart and slid his rock-hard thigh between. He thrust his hips against her, encouraging her to—

She didn't need coaxing.

"I can't stand it. . . . Ooh!" She pressed into him, grinding herself on his leg, not caring about anything but the sizzling heat flaming between them.

The world exploded, the kitchen's stone floor tilting crazily. From somewhere, the phrase *wild monkey sex* shot through her mind—but he hadn't even touched her there!—and then everything shuddered and went black. . . .

"Ahhh . . ." She gripped him tight, holding on for dear life.

His tongue plunged into her mouth, swirled hotly over hers, then withdrew, only to thrust even deeper on its return. The intimacy of his kiss made her gasp and writhe, the feel of his thigh rubbing into her softest, most tingly place drawing out the best climax—

"Odin's balls!" He leapt backward, bending almost double as he clutched his side. "Agggh . . ."

Mindy sagged against the counter, panting. She nearly slid to the floor—she'd gone that limp and weak-kneed—but the fiery blue sparks shooting from the pommel stone of his sword stopped her.

Passion sluiced, she stared, aghast.

She'd seen his sword glow before, but always from a distance. She'd even talked herself into thinking she'd imagined it. Now, up close and personal, the blaze was daunting. Like Fourth of July sparklers, the glittery blue flashes fizzed and crackled and—Mindy's eyes rounded—they almost smelled like burnt sulfur!

The smell hung in the air, as did a tinge of smoky blue haze.

"Oh, God!" She pointed before she could stop herself. "What *is* that?"

Bran groaned. He bent lower, bracing one hand on his thigh and grabbing his sword hilt with the other. Breathing hard, he closed his fingers over the spark-shooting pommel.

"It's the devil-damned reason I shouldn't be here!" He glanced up at her, his face a mask of agony.

Gibbie appeared in the kitchen doorway then and slunk over to him, whining. Mindy started forward, her own fear forgotten on seeing the dog's distress.

If Gibbie was worried, then something was seriously wrong.

But Bran straightened and staggered backward, warding her off with an outstretched hand. "It's no good, sweetness. You'll only make it worse if you come to me."

"But—" Mindy kept going anyway.

"I mean it, lass." He shook his head, holding out both arms now.

His sword hilt had stopped sparking.

"It'll ne'er work." Sweat stood on his brow and he lowered his hands, clenching them. "I thought I had the strength to ignore it. To kiss you, satisfy the need blazing between us, and then . . ."

He shoved a hand through his hair, shook his head. "I see now that—"

"Is that sword evil?" Mindy glanced at it, remembering Jock's words at the Hebridean House. "Did it warn you not to touch me? Is that why—"

"Och, nae, the Heartbreaker isn't evil." To her surprise, he laughed. "And it *wants* me to touch you. That's why it sparked. And why"—he clicked his fingers at his dog, nodding once when Gibbie leaned into him—"the damned thing sent tongues of fire slicing into my side."

Mindy could feel her jaw slipping. "I don't understand—"

"It's quite simple." He looked right at her. "The sword's telling me we're destined to be mated."

"Mated?" The old-fashioned word sent a thrill jolting through her.

"Aye, mated." He sounded anything but pleased. "And"—he looked ready to curse again—"considering I'm a ghost, my honor won't let me agree."

"But why me?"

He rubbed his brow. "Aside from the obvious"—his gaze went hot again, flicking her length—"considering the sword's power, I suspect it feels we're well suited. I'm no easy man, see you." A reluctant smile tugged at his lips. "My pride in Barra is great. Seven hundred years strong, and with each century, my love for this wee bit isle hasn't let much room in my heart for a woman."

"Then why is there—"

"Room for you?" He looked at her, awareness crackling between them. "Some might say there's never been a woman able to share my love for Barra. The women here"—he glanced at the little window, the misty gray sky, so brooding even at this early hour—"love the land as I do, but they know nothing else.

"You do." He strode forward then and grabbed her wrist, pulling her to him. "You, above all others, can best appreciate why to call these wild, rugged isles home means no' just to dwell here but to *live*."

He lifted her hand and pressed a kiss to her palm. "That, Mindy-lass, will be why the Heartbreaker knows you are the one for me."

On the words, he vanished, taking his blue-sparking sword and his dog with him. And leaving behind a horrible, aching void worse than anything Mindy had ever known.

But it was an emptiness she wasn't going to accept.

Not now that he'd kissed her so passionately. And taught her the meaning of crazy-mad, earth-shattering sex without even touching a finger to her! And especially not after the things he'd just said to her.

Mindy's heart began a slow, hard thumping and the most wondrous warmth spread through her, making her feel almost as if she were glowing inside.

She agreed with his sword. They were destined to be together. And—she was sure—if such a thing was even halfway possible, Scotland was the place where it could happen. She needed only to figure out the logistics.

And she would.

It was just a matter of time.

Chapter 12

Bran of Barra spun and tumbled through the thick gray mist of the Twilight World of the Great Beyond, sifting himself as fast as he could back to his beloved tower. Unfortunately, his fury slowed his passage through the dark place, which took severe umbrage to any souls daring to taint the fog-shrouded quiet with bursts of agitation.

Catching himself now, he set his jaw, trying to blank his expression. But it was too late. Already the whirling mists were darkening and jagged bolts of lightning ripped past him, bent on punishment. Some came so close he was sure they'd scorch his plaid or singe his beard.

Everywhere thunder boomed. Each deafening clap rolled over him like an angry, sulfurous wave, hurting his ears and echoing deep into the roiling black mist he couldn't sift through fast enough.

He should have known better.

Others had complained—and warned—about the like. Telling tales of how the vast and empty resting place for the damned switched in an instant from an innocuous swirl of billowy gray mist to a hellish nightmare of icy, angriest black, each dark cloud shot through with punishing jolts of lightning and earsplitting thunder.

"Lucifer's knees!" He clenched his fists, the infernal din rattling his teeth.

Just barely, he dodged a particularly wicked jolt of lightning, aimed—he shuddered—at a most sensitive part of his body.

Some of his dearest friends had been speared by such bolts, though, they insisted bravely, the pain was swift and vanished as quickly. Namely, once the victim released whatever foul mood or un-good thought had sullied his mind.

The Twilight World of the Great Beyond didn't tolerate annoyance.

A *quirk* that had never before concerned Bran because he'd always sifted through in high fettle.

This passage was different.

He wasn't in good spirits.

And at the moment, he deserved his foul humor.

But just when he was about to treat himself to an almighty scowl—jabbing, sulfur-stinking lightning bolts and thunder cracks, be damned—he landed with a great *whoosh* at his desired destination: his own opulent, well-appointed bedchamber on his precious Isle of Barra.

Regrettably, the room appeared occupied.

"I didn't think you'd ever return." Serafina stretched voluptuously in his bed, her dark, heavily kohled eyes a touch resentful.

Bran knuckled his own eyes, sure he was imagining her.

But the Saracen beauty *was* there.

Sitting up against the four-poster's lavish bolsters, she toyed with the edge of a richly embroidered sheet drawn coyly to her breasts.

It was clear that those breasts, like the woman herself, waited naked beneath the bedcovers.

"Serafina!" There'd been a time Bran would've flashed a grin and tossed off his plaid. Now he glowered. "What are you doing here?"

She ignored his glare and licked a finger, trailing its wet tip slowly down her throat.

"I've been lonely." Her voice was a smoky purr, as seductive and languorous as the way she stretched her arms over her head, letting the bedsheet slip down to reveal the ripe swells of her bosom.

A sensuous smile curved one corner of her mouth as she arched her back in a deliberate move to best display her lush, well-rounded breasts. Her large, dark-tipped nipples were drawn tight and thrusting in Bran's direction.

He stared, blood roaring in his ears.

But it was fury, not passion, that set his pulse racing.

"Since when do you have time to be lonely?" He crossed his arms, staying where he was. "There are scores of men in the hall below, each one surely eager to—"

"They're all fussing and stalking about." She threw back the sheets and slipped from the bed, standing before him in all her bare-skinned glory. Her shining black hair fell in a glossy skein to her hips and, Bran noted with annoyance, she'd adorned her navel with a ruby.

"Your friends in the great hall have forgotten I exist," she complained, pouting prettily. "I could dance naked on the high table and they wouldn't notice."

"I doubt that." Bran strode across the bedchamber and opened the door, indicating she should leave. "I suggest you perform again. They're sure to be appreciative."

"They've turned into eunuchs!" She tossed back her hair, sending a waft of her musky perfume beneath his nose. But she made no move to go. "I could offer them the pleasure of the gods and they'd still not quicken with interest. They've all got their backs up about the noise and—"

"What noise?"

"If you'd been here, you might have noticed." She cast him a sulky look, her red lips clamping tight.

"Aye, well, I haven't been here, so tell me." Bran snatched a plaid off a peg on the wall and swirled it around her nakedness.

Her eyes flashed hotly, but she hitched the plaid in place, knotting it deftly at one shoulder. "Everyone says it's the moderns. They're—"

"*Moderns?*" Bran felt the floor dip under his feet. "There aren't any such folk in my tower."

"Perhaps not before you took yourself off, but they're here now." She looked pleased to impart such information. "There are scores and scores of them, stomping about the islet and making a racket all the living day. Hammering, sawing, digging, and"—she put back her shoulders, spite in her eye—"if some are to be believed, even tromping through your hall!"

"That cannae be." Bran shook his head.

"Oh, no?" Serafina put a hand on her shapely hip. "I do not lie."

"But . . ." Bran puzzled, squeezed the bridge of his nose.

A sick feeling spread through his gut. There *were* moderns running all over his islet. Like as not, they were also fussing about in the present-day equivalent of his tower. Leastways, he imagined they would be once it stood again. That was their purpose, after all. And last he'd looked, they were making excellent progress.

He'd been quite thrilled.

He'd just never dreamed their goings-on would disturb his own.

"You can ask Saor if you don't believe me." Serafina swept past him out the door. "He's been up on the battlements these last days, watching it all unfold."

The words spoken, she flashed him another look of pique and then flounced away, disappearing into the shadows of the stair tower.

Bran charged across the room the instant she vanished, unlatching and throwing back the shutters of the tall, arch-topped window beside his bed. He leaned out, bracing himself for whatever he'd see, but all that greeted him was a gust of cold, damp air and the sound of the waves crashing onto the rocks below his tower. The tides were running fast and a sickle moon edged the horizon with silver.

It'd stopped raining and a wash of brilliant stars lit the heavens.

Bran felt a fool.

The night sea, he knew, looked the same in all centuries.

And if a certain American he never should have kissed hadn't turned his wits to mush, he'd have remembered that the windows of his bedchamber looked out onto open water.

Up on the battlements, with Saor, was where he needed to be.

His friend could fill him in on what had happened in his absence. Although he doubted even Saor would have satisfying answers. He, too, was a ghost, after all. And, like Bran, Saor enjoyed their raucous existence. Neither one of them had ever bothered to think too strenuously on the ins and outs of ghostdom.

They just enjoyed existing.

As did every one of Bran's friends who were now, according to Serafina, prowling about the great hall, their usual nightly merrymaking disrupted and disturbed because Mindy Menlove was restoring MacNeil's Tower.

Eager to get to the bottom of it, Bran hurried from his room and raced up the stairs to the battlements, taking the steps two at a time. He flung open the parapet door, bursting out onto the wall walk in the same moment Saor was ducking his head to step into the stair tower.

"Damnation!" Bran leapt aside, just avoiding a collision.

Saor jumped back, laughing. "Welcome back, you scoundrel!" He set his hands on his hips, flicking Bran up and down with an amused gaze. "You don't look any worse for the wear, having succumbed to an American's charms!"

"I haven't succumbed to anyone," Bran lied, hoping the bright starlight didn't show his flush.

"But you *did* seduce her?" Saor's smile flashed white.

"I—" Bran shoved a hand through his hair, stopping just before agitation had him roar that not only had he kissed Mindy; she'd enjoyed an earthshaking release while grinding herself on his thigh.

There were some things a man kept to himself.

Her passion had branded him.

And the memory was his alone.

So he assumed his most chiefly stance and fixed his friend with a stern eye. "How I appear and what I've done is my own concern and no one else's. I'd rather hear why you don't look as if the end of the world has come to our fine, fourteenth-century Barra? A certain Saracen beauty claimed as much when I found her in my bedchamber!"

"Ah, well . . ." Saor went to stand by the parapet wall, bracing his hands on the stone. "There has been quite a stir; 'tis true."

"The moderns and their restoration work?" Bran raised one eyebrow, waiting.

But before Saor could reply, the clatter of claws on stone interrupted them and Gibbie appeared in the tower doorway. Head down and tail wagging, he trotted over to join them. He sniffed along the base of the walling and then dropped onto his haunches beside Bran.

"So you've seen them?" Saor spoke as soon as Gibbie settled.

"To be sure, I've seen them." Bran flicked his wrist to produce a meaty bone for his dog, and after giving it to him, he shot Saor an annoyed look.

"A man named Jock MacGugan, a fisher by trade, has rallied the men of Barra." Bran glanced at Saor, but when he only nodded, Bran went on. "They must have been working for a good while or at incredible speed. Last I saw, the seaward walls and the tower stood to a goodly height.

"Indeed, there was no sign of the deep, dark pit you described and although there were quite a few piles of stone, each time I looked, they'd decreased in number.

"And as they did"—Bran adjusted his plaid against the wind, his stare fixed on the horizon—"new structures rose to replace them. I believe to have recognized the watchtower and the chapel. 'Twas a wonder the likes of which I ne'er thought to see, I say you."

"But we aren't here to dash our wits about the rebuilding of this keep in a time that isn't ours, are we?" Saor spoke like a wizened sage, his tone irritating.

Bran glanced at him. "So it's true?"

Saor shrugged. "No doubt Serafina exaggerated for you to say our world is nearing its end. What is true"— he drew his plaid more closely about his shoulders, as if the admission chilled him—"is that we're being disturbed by the building noise."

"That cannae be."

"So I would have said, too."

"But you no longer do?" Bran was sure he didn't want the answer.

Saor gave it anyway. "Nae." He shook his head. "Not after trying to eat my evening meat in peace and no' being able to take a single sip o' ale without having my ears filled with hammering, bangs, and the garble of voices when no one was there. I'd hear speaking around me, but without me being able to see anyone or understand a word of what they were saying."

"Perhaps you were ale-taken?" It was a small chance, but worth suggesting.

"Humph! You're no' listening. The chaos was too great for me to take the merest swig." Saor placed a hand over his heart. "Some men have even caught glimpses of the moderns. Those that have done say they move amongst us as if they were the ghosts and us the living."

Bran stared at his friend, disbelieving.

But it was clear that Saor was speaking the truth.

"How can that be?" Bran couldn't wrap his mind around such an absurdity.

This was his world and it should be impossible for a modern to enter it.

"Dinnae ask me." Saor shrugged again. "I can only tell you the men are complaining. Some have even been heard to talk of leaving."

Bran's heart sank on the words.

But he didn't doubt it.

His hall was a place where high-spirited men came to enjoy openhanded hospitality with free-flowing ale, excellent victuals, and as much revel as they desired— or not. Clean pallets or warm beds were provided for all, fires kept going, and never a question was asked or an eyebrow raised, tolerance and congeniality being the measure of the day.

Guests could come and go as they pleased. No one was ever turned away.

And as much as it swelled Bran's heart to know his tower would soon stand fully restored in Barra of the present day, it pierced him as greatly to think that the building mayhem might send his friends fleeing.

"That's just the half of it." Saor's tone was earnest.

Bran looked at him sharply. "There's more?"

Saor nodded. "You'll recall our three chiefly visitors who put Serafina in such a dither?"

Bran started to say that not only did he remember them, but he now knew their names, when Saor turned quickly back to the sea. He glanced about as if he expected the three ghostly chieftains to climb up over the curtain wall.

"They've been seen about, too." Saor kept his voice low. "But they haven't returned to the keep. It's out yonder they've been sighted." He made a sweeping gesture that took in the choppy, whitecapped water. "They appear in a galley, flashing back and forth across the bay, sending up clouds of spume and whooping like madmen.

"Some say they're the reason the moderns are working so fast and furious on the tower. That the three chieftains have threatened the workers and—"

"They're *MacNeils*." Bran found himself defending

them. "They'll no' be making trouble for Barra men. They—"

"Oho! You speak as if you know them." Saor's eyes sharpened.

"I ken all MacNeils. I—"

"That's not what I meant and you know it."

Bran tipped back his head and glared up at the heavens. "If there's a God up there, I'm asking him to tell me why I e'er chose a nosy bugger like you for a friend!"

"So you do know them?" Saor grinned.

Bran stifled the urge to punch him in the nose. "Nae, I don't know them. I know *of* them. Their names are Silvanus, Geordie, and Roderick. Serafina had the right of it when she judged them to be MacNeil chiefs of the fifteenth and sixteenth centuries."

"How do you know their names?" Saor's dark brows drew together in suspicion. "Seeing as you haven't met them, that is."

A muscle began to tick in Bran's jaw. "Mindy told me."

"*Mindy?*"

"So I said, just!"

"That's a lassie's name if e'er I heard one." Saor poked Bran's arm. "An American lassie, I'm thinking!"

Bran ignored the arm poke and focused on summoning his most fierce scowl. "Aye, that she is."

"Ho!" This time Saor slapped his thigh. "The maid from Ravenscraig Castle, belike?"

Bran nodded curtly.

He didn't bother glancing at Saor. He knew without looking that the lout would be smirking.

Saor's chuckle proved it anyway. "I'll wager my sword she's from that *Penn-seal* place."

"She hails from Bucks County." Bran almost choked on the words. "Bit place called New Hope."

"Right! But"—Saor leaned close, waggling his brows—"where in America is this Bucks County?"

Bran clamped his mouth in a hard, tight line.

Saor flashed a triumphant grin. "So she is from *Penn-seal-landia*. Sakes, man! Your time is nigh—"

"My time was *nigh* centuries ago, I'd mind you." Bran glared at him. "That being so, you can hoot and jig all you wish. It willnae be changing a thing."

Bran folded his arms, signaling an end to their discussion.

"What does your lady have to do with the three MacNeil ghosties?" Saor proved he was a master at persistence.

Or a fool.

Not caring which, Bran grabbed the loon's arm, gripping hard. "She isn't my *lady*. But I did learn from her why the three chieftains are here."

He released Saor as quickly as he'd seized him and then waited until he brushed his sleeve into place before continuing. "They're the reason for restoration," he announced, taking some small satisfaction in seeing Saor's black-bearded chin drop. "It would seem that some foul aberration of a latter-centuried MacNeil had my tower dismantled and carted off to America, to New Hope in *Penn-seal*-where'er. Thon three ghosties—and, like as not, all else that were here at the time—went along with the stones!

"You ken, I've e'er kept my own counsel, preferring to use ghostly skills to preserve Barra as I knew and loved it in my day. So—"

"You missed the greatest disaster in MacNeil history!" Saor was rubbing his neck, looking stunned for once.

Bran shrugged. "So it would seem!"

"And the three chiefs—Silvanus, Roderick, and Geordie, was it?" Saor recovered quickly. "What of them?"

"I just told you!" Bran started pacing. "They accompanied the stones. But"—he whipped around and jabbed a finger at Saor—"they weren't happy about it. And so they pressed Mindy to have the tower returned to its rightful home, here on Barra.

"That'll be why they're beating up and down the bay, causing a ruckus." Bran glanced out at the sea. "They'll be celebrating."

The notion made his heart squeeze and he vowed, silently, to lavish his best wines and feast goods on them if ever their paths crossed.

He owed them much.

Even if the restoration din was presenting difficulties. The troubles would pass, he was certain. One didn't live seven hundred years and not know that. Problems that loomed tall as mountains one day often proved to be less than a spit in the ocean, the next.

As for Mindy . . .

He refused to think about her.

He put back his shoulders and cleared his throat. "Those three chiefs will be glad to be back home where they belong, and our tower with them. I say they can make as many flourishes through the bay as they wish!"

At his side again, Gibbie barked agreement.

Bran reached down to rub the dog's ears. "Tell our friends to be patient with the building racket. The saints know why we can even hear it, much less catch glimpses of the goings-on, as you say, but I'm sure the disruptions willnae last forever.

"And"—he knew this was important—"reassure them all that I'll no' be going anywhere. My hall will remain as e'er. I'm no' a man for change!"

Saor nodded and made for the tower door. But before he ducked inside the torchlit stairwell, he glanced back over his shoulder. "I have your word?" He sounded skeptical. "You'll no' be going the way of our old friends Alex, Hardwick, and others? Following some fetching American lassie into her own time?"

Bran looked down at Gibbie, curling his fingers in the dog's coarse fur. When he glanced up again, he didn't hesitate. "Nae, I willnae."

"I'm glad to hear it." Saor gave another swift nod, and then thumped down the stairs.

But as soon as the sound of his footsteps faded, a cold nose bumped Bran's hand and he looked down again at Gibbie. He saw at once that his old friend knew what Saor did not. It was the same truth that, even now, was still making his side hurt as if a thousand red-hot fire needles were jabbing into his most tender places.

He *would* go to Mindy in her brash, characterless modern-day world.

"Eh, Gibbie?" He stroked the dog's head. "We'd get by somehow, wouldn't we?"

Gibbie's tongue lolled out the side of his mouth and his tail thumped.

Bran's chest tightened.

He'd even follow Mindy to Bucks County if she desired, though he couldn't stop the shudder that ripped through him on that particular possibility.

Not that it mattered.

He dropped to one knee and slung an arm around Gibbie, needing the dog's warm, familiar bulk against him. Gibbie licked his hand, understanding.

All Bran's ghostly skills—and there were many—couldn't do the one thing necessary if the Heartbreaker's blue sparks and pain jabs were to be believed.

He might be able to uphold his world, making it seem real, and to be sure, he could pop in and out of Mindy's day, easy as a breeze.

But he couldn't meld the two times into one.

That was a magic far outwith his ken.

And, he now regretted, he wasn't a ghost like his old friends who'd found happiness and love with Americans. No curse or spell hovered over him, waiting to be broken so he could be a mortal man again.

He was simply a ghost.

And—until now—he'd been glad to be one.

What a pity that had changed.

Unbeknownst to Bran, or anyone else for that matter, a tiny black-garbed woman who did possess great magic presently sat on the old stone bollard once used by Bran and his friends to moor their galleys.

Dutifully replaced in the same spot it'd once held for centuries, the bollard made a pleasing—if cold and damp—perch as the crone waited for Jock MacGugan to return with his boat and ferry the last of his workmen back to Barra's Castlebay village on the mainland.

Now that their day of labor was done, the men stood clustered in the lee of a seaward wall, sheltering from the elements and drinking strong black tea from a large thermos they passed between them.

Not a one paid her any heed.

But then, she did dwell in her own little niche in the great scheme of things, as it were. Even so, it was more than probable that one or two of them might see her if they chanced to glance her way.

All Gaels had such talent.

Sadly, many had grown unaccustomed to watching for those such as her. Even fewer believed in the wonders her like could employ. To those who did notice her, she'd be just what she appeared: a crone.

These men, in particular, had been too busy at their work to care about one bent old woman hobbling among them as they hammered and sawed.

Besides that, it'd poured since morning. Not that the stormy day had deterred them. Being good, stout-hearted Hebrideans, they'd toiled tirelessly. They'd ignored the cold wind and sideways-blowing rain as they'd gone about their tasks. Not a single one had complained or cast longing glances across the bay to where the lights of their cottages gleamed through the mist.

Such were Barrachs.

And though she hailed from Doon, she was no less a Hebridean.

She'd prove her mettle, too. But she'd have to wait until the men were gone from the islet, leaving her alone. Her task wasn't for others to see.

Not because it wasn't important.

It was.

But Barra men weren't just strong, brave, and dedicated. They were also proud. And the last thing she wanted to do was offend any of them if they saw her and guessed her reason for being there.

So she stayed on the little bollard, sitting as erect as her ancient bones allowed. She kept her knotty hands folded in her lap, and passed the time by watching the churning sea. And, every so often, looking down to admire her boots' fancy red-plaid laces.

Then, at last, Jock MacGugan returned.

The remaining men surged down to his bobbing boat, making haste to leap aboard. The crone cackled, happy for them. They were surely keen to be rid of their wet clothes and warm themselves before their hearth fires.

And when they came back on the morrow, they'd once again be astonished at just how much work they'd accomplished the day before.

Watching them go, the crone pushed to her feet, eager to get to her own business. She was, after all, part of the reason the tower's restoration was moving along so swiftly.

Delighted that it was so—this was one of the most important causes she'd ever taken on—she made her slow way to the seaward wall where the men had gathered. She didn't worry about being seen now. If any of the men looked back, she'd blend into the shadows.

When she reached the wall, she paused to push her frizzled white hair back off her face and then took a deep, grounding breath.

She also held out her hands and wriggled her fingers a time or two.

Then she reached into her cloak for a small leather pouch and a tiny silver vial. In the pouch were grains of sand from Barra's magnificent cockleshell strand, the Traigh Mhor. But there was also some rich dark earth she'd gleaned from the pit that'd been dug as the keep's new foundation. A pinch of dried herbs and other spelling goods, brought from her own Isle of Doon, lent additional power.

The vial held seawater from Barra's bay.

With great reverence, she set the vial on a stone. The water's magic must wait. First she untied the little pouch and began carefully scattering its contents along the base of the newly laid wall.

She chanted as she hobbled the wall's length. "Oh, Ancient Ones, hear me. By the powers in you, let this ground be disturbed no more. Accept this offering"— she lifted her cupped hand to her lips and puffed some of the earth-and-sand mixture onto the wall—"and keep these stones as stout and mighty as e'er they were.

"Guard and watch o'er those who dwell here, keeping them proud, safe, and honorable as e'er they were born to be."

Her spelling pouch now empty, the crone carefully tucked it back within the depths of her cloak and stooped to retrieve her vial.

This she opened with the same solemnity as she'd done with the pouch, though now she moved to the very center of the little isle. Slowly, for her knees pained her, she knelt and used one gnarled finger to scratch a small hole in the earth. She knew—for her wisdom was vast—that she was now directly over the islet's heart, the ancient broch that slept beneath the MacNeils' tower, gladly sharing its strength as the center and backbone of the keep.

Such places were holy. And for that reason, she tipped the seawater from her vial into the hole with her steadiest hand and deepest respect.

As the water seeped into the earth, she raised her voice once more. "Oh, Ancient Ones, I call upon you. See how I've returned this water to the place it's e'er loved and surrounded. Grant that no ripple or tide touching this isle will e'er again carry away what belongs here, at rest.

"And you, Powers of the Air"—she turned her face into the wind—"and you, Powers of Fire"—this time she peered across the bay at the twinkling cottage lights—"be one with the Auld Gods, join together, and . . ."

She let the words trail off and took a deep breath, readying herself for her last, somewhat unusual request.

"Help these men raise this tower with all speed!" She

spoke the plea quickly, half expecting a lightning bolt to wing down and fry her.

But as with each night she'd performed this spell, nothing stirred to damn her. No demons rose to seize her for her cheekiness.

So, as always, she pressed a hand to her thin breast and called out the final words. "Honor to the Auld Gods! My thanks and blessed be!"

Once more, she glanced around hastily, scarce daring to breathe. The Ancient Ones were all-powerful and lightning jabs were only one way they could show their wrath against servants who vexed them.

But the night remained still.

Nothing moved except the whitecaps on the bay and the ever-present wind, just now tearing at the crone's cloak and reminding her it was time to seek the warmth and cheer of her own merry hearth.

But before she left, she carefully picked her way back to the new seaward wall, just to see if her efforts had done any good.

She wasn't disappointed.

The wall stood a good three feet taller than it had moments before.

"Eeeeeie—!" She broke off her gleeful cry, quickly summoning a humble smile. She also bobbed her head in one more demonstrative show of thanks.

Just in case the Ancient Ones were watching.

Then she turned and hobbled into the mist, vanishing before she cackled again.

It was enough reward that, come morning, the men of Barra would see the wall and congratulate themselves on a job well-done.

They deserved the glory.

Chapter 13

Nearly a week later, Mindy stood outside the Anchor, hardly believing she'd survived so long in such complete, if glorious, isolation. It also surprised her that the charm of drearily wet days hadn't yet faded. Barra's cold, blustery clime continued to invigorate her. Even more amazing, she wasn't missing the noise and hectic pace of her usual life. Not that New Hope, Pennsylvania, was exactly a metropolis.

But compared with Barra—a truly edge-of-the-world place—everywhere else bustled.

Of course, the Hebridean House was still bursting at the seams. But the people crowding Barra's largest and best hotel weren't movers and shakers and walk-fast, look-no-one-in-the-eye city dwellers. They were just Scots hoping to be immortalized in a book.

Not that she'd seen any of them since her arrival.

Preferring not to brave the bay crossing in Jock MacGugan's surprisingly tiny boat—at least, as long as the weather remained fierce and she'd seen firsthand how the wind buffeted his boat and how the teensy vessel plunged and rose on the bay's huge, turbulent waves—she'd spent her time driving around Barra, exploring the island's many beauty spots and archaeological sites.

The island *was* lovely.

And with everyone and their proverbial uncle on Wee Hughie MacSporran's coattails and so many Barra men working on Bran's tower, the village stayed pretty much empty.

So she'd remained alone.

And considering she'd needed days to recover from her mind-blowing orgasm-on-a-kilted-ghost's-thigh encounter with Bran of Barra, the Anchor's remoteness suited her fine.

She wasn't comfortable admitting it, but Bran was one reason she'd been glad for the high wind and tossing, plunging seas. The stormy weather gave her a valid excuse to decline Jock's repeated offers to ferry her out to the islet.

Bran would be there, she knew.

The excellent progress of the restoration would draw him. Jock and his men were clearly more skilled than they admitted. In a relatively short time, the curtain walls already stood solid and the keep itself could now be seen rising above them. The work was galloping along at an incredible pace.

But it wasn't really the tower that concerned Mindy, not anymore.

It was Bran.

She missed him badly, ached to be in his arms again, burned for more of his kisses—and that terrified her. Just the thought of him filled her with both trepidation and excitement. Most of all, thinking of him sent ripples of longing all through her. She lifted a hand to her cheek, not surprised to find her skin hot.

Bran of Barra could make a stone blush.

She still couldn't believe she'd had the best climax of her life against his leg. Nor had she forgotten what he'd said about the grandeur of his bedchamber. What he'd implied he—or, better said, they—would do there prickled her nerves and made her shiver.

She rubbed a hand across her forehead, feeling faint.

The man was lethal. And she definitely wasn't ready to see him again.

But she couldn't avoid him forever.

The bad-weather gods had turned their back on her and although the seemingly ever-present mist hung everywhere, it wasn't raining. And the bay looked much less abysmal than it had all week. Not quite calm, but not threatening, either, the water slapping over the jetty stones was glassy black and the waves were nowhere near as high as they'd been.

It was, in fact, quite a fine day.

From across the bay came the sound of hammering and the steady buzz of saws, but the waterfront itself was quiet. The air smelled of woodsmoke and the sea. Colorful fishing boats, already returned with their early-morning catches, filled the harbor, bobbing peacefully at their moorings. She'd also seen a few seals rolling in the waves or clambering on the rocks that edged the quay.

Barra was showing its bonniest face.

And soon, she knew, Jock would come knocking on her door, wondering if today was the day she'd finally wish to see the islet.

Too bad he didn't know *seeing the islet* would also take her straight into Bran of Barra's arms. She was sure of that.

She was also starving.

A condition driven home by the cooking smells wafting to her on the wind. It was midday, after all, and she'd learned quickly that Barrachs supped at noon. And if she went by the tempting aroma of frying fish and sizzling bacon drifting her way from the whitewashed cottages lining the village road, every kitchen was a busy place just now.

Mindy's mouth watered. Her stomach rumbled.

She bit her lip, glancing between the Anchor and the heart of the village, where she was sure she could grab a tasty pub lunch at the Islesman's Pride.

She started walking down the road, not needing to consider long.

Food was an excellent alternative to making a fool of herself over a man—a ghost!—who, although he'd kissed her socks off and probably ruined her for life, had made it plain he viewed their kiss as a grievous mistake that shouldn't have happened.

His Fourth of July sparkler sword proved it.

Destined to mate, he'd said.

It made Mindy's heart ache to remember how he'd looked so deeply into her eyes when he'd explained why he believed his sword recognized her as his one true love. A shiver slid through her, and her pulse quickened. She could still feel his lips on her palm as he'd kissed her hand just before he'd vanished, leaving her alone and longing.

She shouldn't think about it, but he'd done more than drop a kiss to her palm. He'd nipped the sensitive inside of her wrist with his teeth and then flicked the edge of her thumb with his tongue.

He'd made her tremble, her insides melt.

And now . . .

She blinked, refusing to let emotion sting and burn her eyes. Then she started to see that she'd already reached the pub. The tempting smell of food was even stronger here, but she was sure the Islesman's Pride would be full of Jock's workmen friends. So she straightened her back and took a deep breath before she opened the door and went inside the crowded pub.

The interior was low, narrow, and dark, and the heavy black beams running the length of the ceiling signaled that the pub was very old. From what she could tell through the haze of smoke and shadows, framed photographs of fishing boats covered the walls, along with a motley assortment of what appeared to be centuries-old fishing and crofting paraphernalia.

There were also a few hand-painted wooden signs in Gaelic that she couldn't read and didn't even want to try to pronounce.

Margo would say the pub reeked atmosphere and she would have to agree. But it was also jammed. Even more full than she'd imagined.

But she'd been noticed.

She could feel people staring at her. And the last thing she wanted to do was offend the locals by popping into their pub and walking out a second later.

She especially didn't want to appear rude in front of Jock's friends.

But as soon as her eyes adjusted to the dimness, she saw that the Islesman's Pride wasn't filled with fishermen. The people sitting at tables and along the bar that looked like a sawed-in-half boat were people she recognized from the CalMac ferry.

She also knew the kilted man holding court at a table near the rear. If she had any doubts, the teetering pile of books at his elbow identified him.

He was Wee Hughie MacSporran.

And she'd walked into a book signing.

Mindy could've groaned.

The author looked right at her, gave a lofty nod. He clearly thought she'd come to tell him a tale for his next book. Or, worse, assumed she was there to buy a copy of the current one and get his autograph.

Mindy stood rooted to the spot, unable to move. Before she'd stepped inside the pub, she'd done her best to summon an open, friendly expression. And now she could feel her face freezing.

Could be she'd have to walk through life wearing an insipid smile.

At the thought, her sense of the ridiculous kicked in, and a laugh started bubbling up inside her. She pressed a hand to her chest and began inching backward to the door, her legs finally cooperating again. But before she could reach behind her and grasp the door latch, the author loomed in front of her, a book tucked beneath his arm.

"I'm the Highland Storyweaver," he announced, waiting a beat for her reaction. "In addition to writing, I run Heritage Tours, guiding small groups on their own ancestral journeys through Scotland. I also specialize in individualized clan or Scottish historical research.

"Robert the Bruce was my great-great-grandfather, eighteen generations removed."

Mindy's eyes rounded. Her tongue seemed stuck to the roof of her mouth. It certainly refused to move. After all, what did you say to a man who claimed Scotland's hero king was his granddaddy?

Equally annoying, she was getting a crick in her neck looking up at him.

He *was* quite tall.

And he seemed to swell his chest as he peered down at her. When she didn't respond to his spiel, he cleared his throat. He somehow managed to make the noise sound affected, and when she heard it, Bran's opinion of him flashed across her mind.

The bastard has more hot air in him than a peasant forced to exist on a diet o' beans.

Mindy drew a tight breath and touched a finger to her lips, trying to hold back another burst of laughter. But as she looked up, it wasn't easy.

The man really was preening.

As she stared, he smoothed the front of his tweed Argyll jacket. This time he wore the jacket, rather than slinging it artfully over one shoulder. He held out a copy of his book to her.

Hearthside Tales: A Highlander's Look at Scottish Myth and Legend.

Mindy didn't take it.

But good manners made her say, "Hi. Mindy Menlove."

"Ahhh, the American." He continued to proffer the book. "You're quite the local hero. I was wondering when you'd come to a signing."

"I'm here for lunch, actually." Mindy glanced about, pretending to look for a seat.

What she wanted to do was get the blazes away from him.

"I heard they have really good food here." She craned her neck to peer past him. "I'm thinking of fish-and-chips or maybe a steak and ale pie. Something rib-sticking, you know?"

Wee Hughie went on as if she hadn't spoken. "I have copies of my other books back on the table if you've already read this one. They were"—he cleared his throat again—"all best sellers. The National Trust for Scotland carries them in their gift shops. Culloden can't keep them in stock."

"I'm not a reader." Mindy loved books.

She also spotted an empty table against the wall and made to scoot past him. But before she did, she recalled Jock's suspicions about the author being on Barra because of the MacNeils' half-mythic sword.

It was a sword she now believed was Bran's.

And that changed everything.

This time it was Mindy who cleared her throat. "Ehhh . . ." Her tongue played hooky again. She so hated doing this. Pompous people really grated on her nerves. But the lesser evil sometimes brought great rewards.

And Bran of Barra was worth the pain.

She'd been kidding herself to think she could ignore what was between them. She meant to go after him.

And if the Highland Storyweaver could help her . . .

So be it.

She looked up at the author, wishing he were a few inches shorter. "Can we talk?"

He took her elbow, gently moving her aside as a family with four children surged through the door. They headed straight for the back table where his books were stacked, waiting to be signed.

Mindy recognized the family from the Oban ferry.

Wee Hughie nodded a greeting to them, and then turned back to her. "As you're not a reader, it doesn't seem likely, but if you're wanting to ask me how to get published, I do run online writing courses from my Web site.

"Here, I'll give you my card." He looked down, reaching to unclasp his sporran. "My rates are very reasonable. I only charge—"

"No." Mindy shook her head. "I'm not a writer, either, and don't want to be. I . . ." She took a deep breath, then exhaled slowly. "I want to talk to you about the Barra sword. The Heartbreaker—"

"You've heard of it?" His brows arced. "Not many people know the sword's true name."

Mindy's heart almost stopped on his words.

They were confirmation that Bran's sword was the fabled one.

But she didn't want the Highland Storyweaver to know that, so she pretended her heart wasn't beating as fast as it was, and lied. "Well," she began, "I did live in the Folly, you know. That's what the tower was called, back in the States. The name Heartbreaker was bandied about now and then, but no one really knew the legend of the sword.

"I was hoping you"—man, she hated this—"might be able to tell me?"

She wouldn't believe it possible, but Wee Hughie's chest puffed even more. "I've written a chapter about the sword for my next book, *More Hearthside Tales: A Highlander's Look at Clan Legend and Lore*. If you'll wait until after the last of my fans leave, I'll tell you all I know."

"That'd be wonderful. Thank you." Mindy smiled, feeling like such a hypocrite.

She did want to hear the legend, but Wee Hughie was so oily, she feared she'd float like a duck after speaking with him.

So when he left her to return to his signing table, she did the only thing a girl in distress could do. She went straight to the bar and ordered the Hungry Islesman's Steak and Ale Pie along with—she was so bad—a double side of the pub's supposedly famous hand-cut chips.

French fries to Americans.

And a favorite comfort food to her.

Thus fortified, she knew she'd be able to stomach the author's peacocking. And, she hoped, learn as much from him as possible.

She already knew the Heartbreaker was important.

Something told her it might be even more crucial than she realized.

Possibly even her ticket to Bran.

"The truth of the sword?"

Just saying the words sent a chill down Mindy's spine. It was hours later—she couldn't believe how many people had wanted a signed copy of Wee Hughie's book—and she sat at a quiet corner table with the author, listening to him regale her with his knowledge of the Heartbreaker's legend.

She was also trying not to feel so stuffed, having eaten every bite of her delicious Hungry Islesman's Steak and Ale Pie and also the two sides of the specialty hand-cut chips.

For a potato zealot like her, it hadn't been a breach of food etiquette to eat fries with a meat pie that was served with a mashed-potato crust.

It'd been a decadent indulgence.

The aroma of her meal still hung in the air above the table, especially the smell of the somewhat-greasy but scrumptious chips.

They'd been *good greasy,* and if she weren't so reluctant to embarrass herself, she'd order a third portion. The lingering smell was making her mouth water again.

But she resisted and took another sip of her Hen's Tooth ale. A stronger version of the highly rated Speckled Hen ale that the Highland Storyweaver was drinking, it was incredibly potent.

She'd opted for the double-barreled brew, thinking she might need its extra bang.

Now, having heard Wee Hughie's account of the fabled MacNeil blade, she was glad she'd chosen so wisely. Unfortunately, the Hen's Tooth ale was making it a tad difficult to concentrate on the author's ramblings.

And for all his apparent wisdom, he *was* long-winded.

She blinked when a huge dog crawled out from beneath a nearby table and shook himself, before dutifully following his departing owners to the door. For a moment, she'd thought the beast was Gibbie.

Seeing that he wasn't, she felt a pang of disappointment.

"So-o-o . . ." She set down her pint glass a bit too hastily and looked at the author. "You're saying the shimmering blue light that comes out of the sword hilt's crystal pommel stone is called the *truth of the sword*?"

Wee Hughie nodded. "That's what my research indicates, aye." He took a healthy pull of his own Speckled Hen ale. "The title does correspond with everything we know about the legendary blade and"—he leaned across the table, lowering his voice—"might even support popular belief about the origin of the sword's powers."

Mindy blinked. "I'm sorry. What did you say those powers were again?"

To her best recollection, he hadn't yet said anything about mating.

And that was what she was most eager to hear.

Wee Hughie straightened, taking on an almost regal bearing. "Legend claims the sword has many powers. Sadly, only a few of the stories have been passed down through the centuries. Those we know of, we have thanks to Highland oral tradition. Among the most interesting tales is that the sword chose its master. Whenever the blade changed hands, the switch occurred because the Heartbreaker is said to have magically appeared in the new owner's hand.

"Always"—he smiled—"at a most propitious moment, of course."

"Of course." Mindy eyed her half-full glass of Hen's Tooth, but resisted.

She didn't have any qualms about prodding Wee Hughie. "Didn't you say something about women and the sword?"

"There's quite a bit of lore concerning women and the Heartbreaker." Wee Hughie sat back. He inhaled deeply and then released a gusty breath. "Some historians have claimed that, at times, a woman's distress could unleash the pommel crystal's magic.

"It's believed these were women of MacNeil blood. Or they were females who were somehow bound to a MacNeil man, most often a chieftain."

He looked at Mindy as if expecting some response, so she nodded.

Apparently appeased, he continued. "Whoever the woman might be, the pommel stone's blue light—*the truth of the sword*—always sought and revealed the MacNeil male destined to champion her."

"Was he also destined to mate with her?" Mindy couldn't resist.

The Highland Storyweaver didn't miss a beat. "Who knows? In olden times, men who championed a particular maid often did wed her."

"I meant, were they fated to be together?" She was so pathetic.

Wee Hughie didn't appear at all put out. "I'd think so. Certainly the myth and lore surrounding the sword are indicative of such unions. Any pairing born of the blade might as well have been carved in stone."

Mindy tucked her hair behind one ear. Her heart was beginning to skitter. "Is that what you meant when you said the title *the truth of the sword* supports the stories about the source of the sword's powers?

"Because"—she sought the right words—"the sword brings together men and women destined for each other?"

"Not exactly." He dashed her hopes. "Though you could certainly put it that way."

Mindy brightened.

He fell silent for a moment as the kitchen door opened near them and a man hastened past, carrying a huge tray filled with steaming plates of fish-and-chips. Mindy looked after him, half afraid her stomach would rumble again.

Everything smelled so delicious.

Wee Hughie gripped the table edge and leaned forward, reclaiming her attention. "What I meant"—he sounded self-important—"was what no one but myself has yet managed to put together, the significance behind the sword's various monikers and the true origin of its power."

"I'm all ears." Mindy was.

Wee Hughie slid a glance at the neighboring tables. "Remember I told you that the sword's crystal pommel stone was believed to be enchanted?" He looked pleased when she nodded. "Well"—he drew a breath—"as I said, legend holds that the gemstone was formed by the tears of a MacNeil ancestress who lost her love in an ancient battle."

He paused, waiting as the proprietor hurried past

their table again, this time returning to the kitchen with an empty tray.

As soon as the door swung shut behind him, Wee Hughie pinned her with his blue gaze. "The wording *truth of the sword* doesn't just refer to the blade's magical blue light. I believe the term was chosen because Veleda, the storied ancestress, was one of the Vala."

"The Vala?"

"They were a race of half-mythic Norse prophetesses. Sometimes called Norns, their gift of divination was incredibly powerful. They were highly revered, their foretelling never doubted."

Mindy could feel her eyes rounding. "Are you saying the MacNeils are descended from Norse gods?"

Wee Hughie flicked a bead of condensation off his pint glass. "They could well be." He looked up. "After all, the Norse did rule the Hebrides for four hundred years. I'm only stating the history as I've researched it.

"No one today can say for sure if Veleda was one of the Vala. But she *was* Viking. And she did lose her Mac-Neil husband in a ferocious sea battle."

He smiled and flattened his hands on the table. "Those are the facts, indisputable. If Veleda was a Vala, then the powers ascribed to the Heartbreaker would have been formidable. I'd even say that those known to us are just the tip of the proverbial iceberg."

"Wow." Mindy couldn't help herself.

"Exactly." The Highland Storyweaver sounded pleased.

Mindy couldn't fault him. He'd told quite a tale.

"Do you think the sword is around here somewhere?" She had to ask.

Wee Hughie reached for his pint glass, draining it. "If

it is, someone would surely have found it by now. Such artifacts can bring a generous finder's fee, not to mention fame if, as with the Heartbreaker, such a treasure is legendary.

"Then there are those who sell such relics on the black market." The distaste in his voice negated any remaining suspicion that he might be a sword thief. "They turn an even greater profit.

"So, nae, I don't believe the sword is here. Though"—he considered—"it could well be somewhere in the stones you brought over from the States. If it is, I hope it's never found."

Mindy lifted a brow, curious. "I would have thought you'd like to see it."

"Ah, well . . ." He leaned back, his gingery hair glinting in the light of a wall lantern. "Of course, I'd be keen to have a look. But the risk of having the sword exploited wouldn't be worth it. I enjoy writing about such treasures and their history. I'd hate to see the Heartbreaker paraded about like a circus piece."

"I doubt there's any danger of that." Mindy broke down and took a small sip of her Hen's Tooth ale. "If it's not here anywhere, I'm sure it wasn't at the Folly. The American MacNeils would have displayed it if it was."

She was positive of that.

She didn't mention that the sword was depicted on the two portraits of Bran that had hung in the castle. She couldn't recall any of the other portrait ancestrals wearing the Heartbreaker, but that didn't mean it hadn't been in their possession.

Wee Hughie waved his empty pint glass at her. "Another ale?"

"No." Mindy hadn't been able to finish the first.

She glanced toward the front of the pub, to the one

window, which revealed that the afternoon outside was beginning to look seriously cold and gray again. "I should be getting on my way soon."

"One question first, if you don't mind?" The author sat forward. "Have you thought about what you'll do with the MacNeil Tower when the work is finished?" He, too, cast a glance at the pub window. "They're making amazing progress. Those in the know on Barra are betting it'll be habitable very soon, perhaps within days."

"Could be." Mindy wouldn't be surprised.

She'd never seen a building go up so fast, much less a medieval castle.

"But . . ." She tapped her chin, thinking about his question.

The answer came quickly.

"I'll have it turned into a Gaelic heritage center." She glanced at one of the hand-painted Gaelic signs on the wall. "Jock MacGugan and his men refused payment for their work, so that money remains untouched. There's more than enough to fund such a—"

Loud whoops and foot stomping from the front of the pub interrupted her.

Wee Hughie didn't seem to notice.

Mindy's heart hit her ribs.

Almost afraid to look, she peered again through the shadows, toward the pub entrance. Sure enough, the Long Gallery Threesome occupied the table beside the door. Grinning like fools, they were staring right at her, brimming ale mugs raised in the air as they cheered.

"Heigh-ho!" Geordie leapt up and swung his walking stick in a fast circle around his head.

Silvanus glared at him and grabbed Geordie's kilt, pulling him back into his seat. But when he released Geordie and looked back at Mindy, he was beaming again. He dragged his sleeve over his whiskery cheek, the brightness in his eyes making her breath catch.

The ghost had tears in his eyes!

"Oh, God!" Mindy's own eyes blurred.

"Are you okay?" Wee Hughie reached across the table, grabbing her arm. "Can I fetch you some water?"

Mindy blinked. "No, I'm fine. I just—" She looked again at the table by the door, but the family with four children that she'd seen before sat there now.

The three ghosties were gone.

Mindy's heart squeezed all the same. "I swallowed wrong," she lied, picking up a napkin to dash at her eyes.

"You're sure?" The author looked concerned.

"Yes, but I need to get going now." She stood, collecting her jacket and bag. "Thank you so much for sharing your tales with me."

She meant that.

Wee Hughie unfolded his tall form from his chair. "It was my pleasure. And I think you're doing a wonderful thing, turning the castle into a Gaelic cultural center." He spoke as if he were the prince of the Gaels, his usual loftiness slipping back over him.

"Too many of our young people no longer speak the Gaelic and have even forgotten our traditions." His chest started swelling again. "As Robert the Bruce's grandson, I see it as a personal responsibility to ensure that our culture is upheld."

He reached to help her with her coat. "But tell me, what will you be doing with yourself? Are you intending to return to the States? Or are you thinking of staying on here?"

She'd give anything to stay!

The words screamed in her head, so loud and strong she almost feared she'd spoken aloud.

"I'll be going back to my work. The airlines." She hitched her bag onto her shoulder, speaking the inevitable.

Never had flying seemed less appealing. The thought of returning to her onetime dream job weighed down on her like a ton of bricks. She didn't even want to think about faceless buildings of glass and steel or expressways crowded with rush-hour traffic.

Her chest tightened and she suddenly found it very difficult to swallow.

She *had* fallen in love with Scotland.

But she wasn't about to stay on without Bran.

She couldn't bear it now.

Chapter 14

Mindy let herself out of the Islesman's Pride only to step straight into a blast of cold air. The afternoon had turned chillier, and thick mist hovered over the bay and rolled silently down the village road. Cottage lights glimmered, but did little to break the darkness. She started on her way, realizing it was much later than she'd thought.

She'd spent hours in the pub.

But it'd been worth every minute to learn so much about the sword that—she was sure—belonged to the man who, with neck nuzzles and wicked, smoldering smiles, had thawed all the ice that had been inside her and already taught her so much about passion and need.

She wouldn't think of specifics.

The *thigh incident* was too fresh a wound to jab.

It was enough—and surely more than many people ever experience—that they'd enjoyed a few moments of incredible bliss. The kind of total, take-your-breath-away, sensual exhilaration she never would have believed existed outside romance novels.

Bran of Barra had shown her the truth.

She knew she loved him.

She loved his home, too. His wasn't a steely, impersonal world of glass and concrete. Teeming cities with people who looked like their faces would crack if they smiled. Or suburbs filled with cookie-cutter sixties bungalows, each one the same and all without character.

Bran's world was a place where the past walked hand in hand with the present, and tradition mattered. Showing her the wonder of Barra and the whole magnificent sweep of his Hebrides—opening her eyes so she could truly see—was just one more gift he'd given her.

And she wanted to give him so much more.

The Gaelic heritage center was just the beginning. She knew it would please him to see his home used in such a good way, benefiting the community. Owned and run by the people of Barra instead of a large national organization like the National Trust for Scotland.

Even worse would have been her original plans—to see the castle turned into a hotel or youth hostel.

Margo's suggestion, to open a parapsychology study center, would have been a complete disaster. Though she knew her sister would have pleaded otherwise if she'd been able to fly over as planned.

Mindy's heart squeezed. She did miss her sister and truly had hoped to see her.

Sadly, Margo's boss, Patience Peasgood, had slipped while jumping on her grandchildren's trampoline, injuring her knee so badly that she'd required surgery. Her absence left Ye Olde Pagan Times firmly in Margo's hands.

Mindy walked faster.

She did wish that Margo could have seen the tower's restoration. And she'd hoped, loving Scotland as Margo did, that she'd come around and agree that the Gaelic heritage center was the best solution. Bran's tower would belong to Barra. And she'd make sure that would never change. Ideas were coming fast and furiously now. Jock MacGugan would be keen to help run such a center. And if not, he surely knew someone equally qualified. His friend Sandy Budge, who took care of the island finances, could set up the trust. It would all be wonderful. And she wanted to tell Bran, see the pride and pleasure light his eyes when he heard the news.

Not that she could, not now.

The kitchen encounter had been good-bye.

And she didn't think so because she hadn't seen him since then. Or even because of the things he'd said before he'd disappeared. She knew it with a sudden, fierce pain that ripped her heart and made her ache so badly she was surprised she was still upright, walking down the road.

She felt like she was breaking.

"Damn!" She kicked a pebble and reached to turn up her jacket collar.

It *was* glacial.

Icy wind shrieked down from the hills that rose behind the village, the strong gusts howling round the eaves of the cottages and echoing across the water. The sound was lonely and keening, and made her shiver.

"Yeah, right." She hunched her shoulders against the cold and kept marching home to the Anchor. She didn't fool herself for a moment.

She was shaking because of Bran.

Not the weird howl of the wind.

It was Bran, all about him. She missed the warm intimacy of his embrace. The thrill of feeling his powerful arms tighten around her, drawing her close. How one intense look or just breathing in his scent could melt her. Or what it did to her when she felt the soft brush of his beard. Even the lightest touch of his lips against hers sent her spiraling into ecstasy. No one had ever excited her more.

Not like he did.

And that was only a fraction of it.

She ached for the taste and feel of him. The pulse-pounding excitement that swept her each time he appeared. She yearned to see his twinkling blue eyes take on a gleam and hear him say *Mindy-lass*. Let his rich laughter wash over her, and catch how it rumbled deep in his chest. She wanted all of that. Especially to relive how just being near him could make the air around them thicken with crackling desire and—she had to say it—a sense of rightness.

As if they were indeed destined to mate.

"Oh, Bran . . ." She whispered his name, ignoring how her voice hitched as she kicked another pebble.

Speaking to Wee Hughie about the Heartbreaker had set her spirits soaring. Something had told her the sword was the key to it all. Yet when she'd left the Islesman's Pride, the road had stretched empty.

It'd been a void that hit her harder than the cold.

She bit her lip and drew her jacket closer about her. She wished she'd dressed in layers, or worn thermal underwear. But in her heart, she doubted such measures would have made a difference.

If Bran continued to stay away from her—and she feared he would—she'd never be truly warm again.

Determined to wrench herself into a better mind-set, she glanced at the bay, trying to imagine the tower as a Gaelic heritage center. She couldn't see the castle—too much billowing mist stretched between the shore and the islet—but she did spot Jock's boat tied to a bollard.

It was empty, the fisherman nowhere in sight.

But a movement on the water caught her eye and she thought she saw the square sail of the Long Gallery Threesome's galley speeding across the waves. Yet when she blinked and looked again, it was only a patch of low, fast-moving clouds, blown by the wind.

Even so, her heart raced.

She was sure someone was watching her.

Whipping around, she peered through the mist, looking back the way she'd come. She half expected—no, she hoped—to see Bran striding toward her, his face lit with a smile and his arms opened wide.

But, of course, he wasn't there.

Nothing was, except the fog and encroaching darkness.

Even so, when she started on her way again, the sense of being observed intensified with each step. It prickled her nape and sent chills tripping along her skin. She resisted the urge to toss another glance over her shoulder.

She did quicken her pace. And it was then, as she neared the Village Hall, that she realized where the odd feeling was coming from.

Someone *was* staring at her.

It was the dog from the pub.

It was Gibbie. She'd known it was him!

Now he was sitting in the shelter of the glass doors of the closed community center, waiting for her. And—she had to knuckle her eyes, swipe the dampness from her cheeks—she hadn't heard the keening of the wind.

The pitiful noise had been the old dog's howls.

As if to prove it, he tipped back his head and gave a long, piercing *yeeowwwl*. It was a sound to split eardrums, attract attention, and break the heart of anyone who loved dogs.

SOME LIKE IT KILTED

Mindy did.

And she was especially fond of this dog.

"Gibbie!" She started toward him. But he leapt up and bolted away, charging past her to dash down the road in the direction of the harbor. Her breath caught and she began to shake all over again.

Dogs ran like that only when they were making for their masters.

"Oh, God!" Mindy's heart stilled.

She spun around just in time to see Gibbie disappear into the darkness. When happy barks and a man's—*Bran's*—deep, rich laugh came from inside the swirling, impenetrable mist, she could have whooped louder than the Long Gallery Threesome had done at the pub.

"Bran!" She shouted his name, not caring who heard her.

Then she ran, tearing down the road so fast that a stitch jabbed her side. But she kept on, nearly falling when she slipped on the slick pavement and her feet almost went flying out from under her.

"Mindy-lass." Bran caught her, sweeping her up into his arms and pulling her hard against him. "I'd sworn no' to come, but"—he pressed his lips to her hair, raining kisses from her temple to her ear, nuzzling and nibbling her neck—"I couldn't stay away."

Beside them, Gibbie barked. He was running circles around them, tail wagging.

Mindy thought her heart would burst. "I saw Gibbie in the pub. Then again at the Village Hall."

Bran leaned back to grin at her. "And who do you think sent him?"

"Oh, Bran." She twined her arms around his neck, her heart thumping wildly.

"I've been mad with missing you." She clung to him,

rubbing her face against his plaid. Its wool was rough against her skin and she'd never felt anything more wonderful. Her entire body was shaking, inside and out, but she didn't care. He smelled of woodsmoke and the cold, frosty night.

She wanted to drink him in.

Bran looked ready to toss her over his shoulder and carry her off to his turret.

She wished he would!

"I didn't think I'd see you again." She couldn't believe he was here. "I thought—"

"You thought wrong." He smoothed her cheek with his warm, calloused hand. "I *knew* I'd see you. Nothing could have kept me away."

His eyes blazed hotly. "I've got to kiss you now. Afterwards ..." His voice was low and deep. The last word hung in the air, throbbing with promise. He pulled her closer against him and slanted his mouth over hers, plunging his tongue between her lips to kiss her ravenously.

The world dipped and spun.

Castlebay and its cottages and harbor vanished, leaving only the fiery heat between them. The hot and urgent kiss Mindy didn't want to ever end.

"O-o-oh!" She reeled, her sigh lost in the blended breath of their kiss. She opened her mouth wide beneath his, needing the raging intimacy, the excitement of his tongue swirling and tangling with hers.

Nothing existed except the feel of his lips moving over hers, the racing of her heart, and her mad wish that he'd never stop kissing her.

She gripped his neck, digging her fingers in his hair. The strands felt cool and thick, smooth to the touch. She thrust her other hand inside his plaid, needing to feel his skin, the rock-hard muscles and crisp triangle of chest hair that had been the stuff of her dreams. Fantasies about stroking his chest hair had kept her awake at night, making her tingle and burn, aching to touch and explore him.

Then, without her even realizing they'd moved, he was setting her down on the edge of the quay, very near Jock's little boat. Except that she saw now that it wasn't Jock's boat at all, but an even smaller one.

It was a rowboat.

But it resembled a cockleshell with oars. She stared at it, suddenly comprehending. It was medieval. She'd read somewhere—or maybe seen on a TV documentary— that such a teacup on water was called a coracle. And she could think of only one reason for it to be here.

Mindy swallowed.

Bran grinned, looking delighted.

"You can't mean for us to get in that." All the pleasure that had been sizzling inside Mindy congealed into a cold, tight ball of dread.

Bran gripped her arms with his big, strong hands. "I needed days to summon the energy to sift the boat here. Now that it's bobbing in the water before us, do you think I'd let it sink beneath you?"

Gibbie hopped into the tiny boat, proving his own faith.

Mindy wasn't reassured.

"Ahhh . . ." She looked from the dog to Bran, then at the bay. The water that only minutes before appeared mildly choppy now looked like heaving, plunging seas.

"Sweet lass, I want to show you my home." Bran swept an arm around her, pulling her close. "The grandeur of my tower—"

"Your tower bedchamber," Mindy finished for him, not missing the implication.

He wanted to make love to her.

No, he'd just *told* her he was going to. And that fine difference sent a whirl of flutters through her stomach and places lower.

But the cold, hard knot of fear of his coracle wouldn't be budged.

"Aye, my bedchamber—and you know why I wish to take you there." Bran spoke as if she couldn't possibly have any objections. He released her to make a broad, expansive gesture, taking in the bay and his islet with its tower and curtain walls. "I also wish you to see my home before it becomes a Gaelic heritage center."

His grin said how pleased he was about her plans.

"How did you know?" Mindy stared at him, the cockleshell forgotten. She flashed a glance at Gibbie. "Surely he couldn't have—"

"Told me of your talk with a certain preening peacock scribe?" Bran planted his hands on his hips and shook his head. "Gibbie is a fine beast—the best—but the powers of speech are no' one of his talents."

He laughed. "It was thon three chieftain friends of yours who told me." He glanced at the water where, just beyond the opening of the bay, a tiny yellow light and a large square sail could be made out, if one squinted and peered deeply into the night.

Mindy stared. "You met them?"

Bran followed her gaze. "This is my Barra, lass. No one comes here without my knowledge. No' even other chiefs of my own proud race!

"To be sure, I spoke with them." He leaned down to kiss her brow. "It's in their interest, as it is my own, that this ends well. Though, just now, I happen to know they're off to visit friends they haven't seen in centuries."

He slid an arm around her, squeezing her close as the

galley sped across the dark water of the open sea. "Perhaps someday we'll see them again. There truly is magic in Scotland, you know!"

He looked down at her, winking. The sword at his hip gleamed blue. "The scribe told you of my Heartbreaker, didn't he?"

Mindy nodded. She could feel warmth streaming off the sword's enchanted hilt. "I understand now why—"

He pressed a finger to her lips, silencing her. "Wee Hughie MacSporran isn't as all-knowing as he'd like to think. Just so there aren't any doubts in your mind"—he replaced his finger with his lips, giving her a hard, swift kiss—"the Heartbreaker only lets MacNeil men know where the woman of our heart is waiting for us.

"The sword's magic doesn't choose that woman. Our own hearts do that."

"Oh, Bran!" Mindy blinked hard. She swallowed against the hot thickness in her throat. "I love you so. I—"

"I know that well!" He grinned again. "And you're about to see firsthand how a Barra chieftain shows his woman how much he loves her."

On the words, he swept her up in his arms again, depositing her into the coracle with Gibbie. Then he was in the boat beside her, taking the oars and rowing them swiftly out to his islet, where, she saw now, lights—looking like the flames from medieval torches—flickered in the square keep's narrow slit windows.

Another torch appeared to hang on an iron bracket on the seaward wall near a small, sloping jetty, complete with stone steps and even a rail.

The light from that torch—the one at the jetty—shimmered brightly on the water.

And then they were there.

Gibbie sprang out of the coracle first. Bran followed as quickly and then turned to lift Mindy ashore. The tower—and it no longer even resembled the Folly she knew from Bucks County—loomed dark and solid before them. A magnificent place that, she knew, was not of her century.

She looked up at Bran, awe and wonder taking her breath.

"This is your Barra, isn't it?"

"You know it is."

"But how—"

The hot glance he shot her quelled her question. He grabbed her hand, was already leading her up the short and steep path to a massive, iron-studded door set deep into the curtain wall.

"Come, lass, it is time." He pushed open the door and pulled her with him into the night-darkened bailey.

But it wasn't really dark.

Here, torches blazed in archways and from high above them, on what she knew had to be the parapets along the seaward walling. The light was soft and luminous, shining in golden pools on the damp cobbles of the bailey.

Bran flashed a look at her. "Much finer than the cold lights of your day, eh?"

"Oh, my, yes." Mindy meant it.

There *was* a difference. And it was to the disadvantage of her time.

But she didn't have long to admire the bailey's medieval ambience. Bran was leading her to his hall, where—her heart stalled, then galloped madly—she could hear loud pipe and fiddle music, raucous laughter and song. The sounds of many men enjoying themselves and, she thought, a few snatches of female laughter, as well.

They were nearing the hall now and she glanced at him, suddenly unsure.

Here—in his world, only steps away from the entrance to his keep—he looked even larger, more irresistibly rugged and proud than she'd ever seen him.

Yet she . . .

She looked down at her black pants and waxed jacket, her clunky hill-walking boots.

"Wait!" She dug in her heels, glancing round. Glad that they hadn't yet encountered anyone else.

A medieval.

Dear God! She ran a hand over her hair, tugged at her jacket. "Bran—wait!"

He was already reaching for the door latch. "Aye?"

She swallowed, her mouth suddenly ash dry. "What if someone sees us? Sees me?"

"The whole of my hall shall see you, Mindy-lass. And"—he flashed that wicked smile—"I shall be damned proud when they do!"

"But my clothes—"

"Think you any friends of mine willnae ken you're a modern?" He spoke as if that settled everything.

He reached for the door, but it swung wide before he could close his fingers on the huge, black iron handle.

"So you're returned, at last!" An incredibly handsome man, with dark hair and laughing eyes, swept out an arm, welcoming them inside.

"Saor MacSwain, my lady."

He bent a gallant knee, his charm almost physical. "'Tis long that we have waited for you!"

"Mindy Menlove." Mindy felt like she'd stepped onto the stage of a costumed opera.

But the man's flashing-eyed smile—and the firm grip of Bran's hand—put her at ease.

"MacSwain, I know you're eager! But you'll have to wait longer still to properly meet my lady." Bran started forward, pulling her with him across the crowded hall. "We've personal business to attend first."

He tossed the words over his shoulder, looking straight ahead as he practically dragged her to a shadowy archway that, she saw at once, could only be the entrance to a torchlit stair tower.

Though, leading to the castle's oldest tower, the archway had been walled up at the Folly.

Before she could digest that, Bran stopped. He flicked his wrist, producing a large beef rib, which he tossed to Gibbie. The dog had been trotting beside them. Now he leapt to catch the bone in midair, before loping off with the treat clamped in his jaw.

Bran turned back to Mindy. "I don't want poor Gibbie blushing once I have you to myself." He leaned down to kiss her quickly and—she gasped—swept a hand down her hip to squeeze her buttocks!

"Come, now." He grabbed her hand again, tugging her along even faster than before. "I cannae wait much longer—"

"Ho, Bran!" Saor MacSwain rushed up to them just as they reached the bottom stair.

This time a woman hovered at his side. Her stare gave Mindy frostbite. Worse, she was the most beautiful female Mindy had ever seen. She had shining masses of sleek, raven black hair that tumbled to her hips, creamy golden skin, and incredible cleavage.

Mindy felt herself blanch.

The woman smiled cattily.

She was clearly some kind of exotic courtesan, judging from her almost-transparent clothes and the nearly overpowering musk perfume swirling around her like a cloud. She also had unnaturally red lips and heavily kohled eyes.

They were eyes that glared daggers at Mindy.

And Mindy saw now that Saor hadn't chased them across the hall. The woman had. Bran's friend had clearly hastened after her, a fact displayed by the way he held the woman's arm in a fierce grip.

"Serafina prepared your chamber as you requested." Saor spoke to Bran.

Serafina kept her feline gaze on Mindy. "I've readied everything," she purred, her voice just as smoky and seductive as Mindy knew it would be. "Though"—she narrowed her dark eyes, taking in Mindy's clothes—"I am sure you will not be in need of such accoutrements for long. Indeed, I wonder why you even wished me to take such trouble?"

Bran stepped between her and Mindy. His voice hardened. "If you do not treat my lady with respect, you will regret the next task I put before you. It would involve"—he slid a meaningful glance across the hall—"walking through yon door and never again—"

"I am sorry." The woman simpered. She leaned into Saor, linking an arm through his and pressing her breasts into his side. "Lady"—she glanced at Mindy—"I wish you well here."

Mindy nodded, not believing a word.

Serafina reminded her of everything she disliked—most especially women who were described as being catlike. Unfortunately, she also felt unbearably hot, and not in a good way.

Nor did it have anything to do with the general heat of the hall from the massive fireplace piled with logs that burned with a crackling roar.

She was flushing because the Serafina woman had

made her feel like a great, galumphing amazon. Gads, even the she-wolf's shoes looked like wisps of spun silk. The slippers were even beaded. *With jewels!* Mindy thought of her own sturdy, thick-soled boots again and wanted to die.

That was why the tops of her ears burned like flame. And why, she was sure, she'd run tomato red.

But before she could catch her breath and count to ten, Bran gathered her into his arms again and was carrying her up the winding tower stairs.

When he paused on the second landing and looked down at her, treating her to the full force of his most devastating smile, she forgot all about Serafina-the-Seductress.

"Forget her," Bran said, as if he'd read her mind. "She is here for the entertainment of my friends. They are good men who, in life, weren't always treated kindly and now deserve a spot of pleasure and fun.

"She means nothing to me." As if to prove it, he lowered his head and kissed her, his tongue once again sweeping deep into her mouth, its mastery making her forget everything except that they were here, together.

And that they'd soon be naked on his bed . . .

It was going to happen fast, she knew, because they'd reached the top of the stairs and he was practically sprinting with her along a short corridor. He stopped before a door, shouldering it open. He set her down and stepped back, letting her take in the room's astounding opulence.

"Wow." Mindy's jaw slipped.

Bran nodded, pleased.

No Hollywood films or even highly respected research books on the medieval period and castles could match the glory of his bedchamber.

The furnishings of the Folly were nothing like comparable.

Richly embroidered tapestries in dazzling colors hung from bright, limewashed walls, and candles blazed everywhere, surely dozens and dozens of them. The room was a flickering wonderland of golden light.

A log fire blazed in the hearth. And—she'd never believed this was truly done, but she couldn't doubt it now—the floor rushes had been strewn with sweet-smelling herbs and rose petals. The result was a feast for the senses.

A table near one of the tall, arch-topped windows held a different kind of feast. Jewel-rimmed wine and ale glasses had been set out next to large ewers, obviously filled with the finest libations. A tray of superbly roasted capons, still warm, smelled heavenly. There were also platters of cheese and fresh-baked pastries, and several small dishes of dates and sugared almonds.

Nothing looked less than sumptuous.

There were even water-filled finger bowls and carefully folded linen napkins.

Bran of Barra knew how to live.

But it was the bed that really took Mindy's breath.

It was huge.

And so high there were steps to climb into it. Four-postered and with its dark-gleaming wood intricately carved, the bed boasted thick, heavily embroidered curtaining and covers. A welter of equally fine bolsters and pillows rounded out the bed's glory, while neatly folded furred bed rugs at the foot waited to spend extra warmth if desired.

It was a bed of dreams, straight out of a fairy tale.

Mindy's heart thumped.

"Did you know . . ." The splendor made her sharply aware of the *ordinariness* of her twenty-first century. ". . . there was a time of greatness here, at your Barra, though later than your day, when the MacNeil chief would order his trumpeters to stand on the battlements at night and blast a fanfare? Their duty was to announce that now that he had dined, the rest of the world could eat their own supper."

Bran's eyes rounded. Then he grinned. "Come, sweet—"

"It's true!" Mindy waved a hand. "You can read about it in any history book.

"I believe the words were, *'Hear, O ye people, and listen, O ye nations. The great MacNeil of Barra having finished his meal, the princes of the earth may dine!'*

"Now"—she looked about the lavish bedchamber—"I understand why they were so proud. Now—"

"Mindy-lass!" Bran put his hands on her shoulders and looked at her very intently. "I am torn between throwing back my head and laughing and turning you over my knee! To be sure, we are a proud race and I'll no' deny any such boast.

"Like as no' "—his lips twitched—"such a fanfare was started by your own Silvanus and his friends. But I promise you, the greatest magnificence I see in this room is you.

"Nor"—he slid his hands down her sides, locking his arms around her hips—"did I bring you here to be taught a history lesson. You forget—I am history!"

"That's not why I told you." Mindy glanced aside. "It's just that—"

"It's about us, sweetness. *This.*" His gaze not leaving her, he ripped away the large Celtic brooch at his shoulder, then threw off his plaid. "Nothing else matters. This night, we make our own history."

Mindy stared at him, her heart pounding.

He grinned and pulled his shirt over his head. Then he kicked off his shoes.

He was wearing nothing else.

His naked skin gleamed in the candle glow, the dusting of cinnamon-colored hair covering his broad, powerfully muscled chest glistening like gold. He stood proud, totally unself-conscious when her gaze dipped low, seeing at once how much he wanted her.

Mindy gasped and bit her lip. She should've been prepared, but she wasn't. She swallowed, her entire body flushing. "Dear God, you're so—"

He grinned. "It's the fine, brisk air o' Barra, what does it!"

Raising his arms above his head, he cracked his knuckles, clearly enjoying her perusal. And there was a great deal of him to see.

Mindy tore her gaze away, sure she'd catch fire if she kept looking.

"Now you." He reached for her jacket, whipping it off her with incredible speed. He plucked at her shirt's buttons and her pants zipper, then dropped to his knees and used his teeth, as well, tearing her clothes away, bit by bit, until she stood before him, equally unclothed.

"Mother of God, you're lovely." His gaze raked her, making her tingle everywhere. He ran his hands up and down the backs of her legs, holding her before him as he rubbed his face against her naked thighs and the damp curls between them.

She held on to his shoulders, breathless as he kissed

his way across her stomach. Then he looked up at her, holding her gaze as he slowly licked his way lower and lower until, flashing a wicked grin, he eased her legs apart and swept his tongue along the wet, heated length of her.

"Och, lass." He breathed the words against her skin in a husky whisper. "I could taste you forever."

"Ahhhh ..." Mindy dug her fingers into his shoulders when he licked her again. White-hot bolts of pleasure shot through her.

She swayed against him, every inch of her catching flame as she opened her legs wider to give him better access.

"You're so sweet, Mindy-lass." He turned his head, gently nipping the inside of her thigh before once again letting his tongue probe and swirl, each curling sweep flooding her with sensation.

No man had ever done this to her.

And when he paused to look up at her, the tip of his tongue poised to flick across her most sensitive spot, she thrust her fingers into his hair, holding fast.

She *was* about to shatter.

"No-o-o," she cried when his tongue touched her there, circling lightly. "Not this way ... yet. I want—"

"And I want to pleasure you." His eyes darkened and he suckled that spot. "*This* way and all ways, Mindy-lass. I've burned to taste you and—"

"But I'm going to—" She couldn't finish, only gasped and arched against him, trembling, trying so hard not to give in to the pleasure about to sweep her.

"Please, Bran, wait...."

"Ach, as you wish ..." He lifted his head, turning his attention to her breasts. He spread his hands over their swells, squeezing and plumping, circling her nipples with his thumbs, before leaning close to lick and suckle, each swirl of his tongue making her ache for more.

The climax she'd just managed to stave off threatened to break again as waves of electrifying sensation streaked through her, making her deepest female places clench with hot, tingly need.

"Bran . . ." She was trembling. "Please . . ."

He stood and plunged his hands into her hair, holding her fast, as he kissed her roughly, plundering her mouth. Then—she'd waited so long—he scooped her up and carried her across the room, lowering her to the bed.

Stretching out beside her, he pulled her close so that they were flush against each other, naked skin to naked skin. She loved the feel of his hard, warm length beside her as he stroked and caressed her everywhere. His touch turned her skin to flame and made her quiver with longing such as she'd never known. She started rocking her hips against him, this time wanting more than a thigh climax.

As if he knew, he pushed up on his elbows to look down at her, his eyes dark and smoldering with heat. "The whole of me, Mindy-lass." Not taking his gaze from her, he reached between them, sliding his hand between her legs to probe and caress her.

Mindy almost shattered then.

Bran grinned, knowing. He nudged her thighs apart, tracing the hot, slick center of her, circling his thumb across her most sensitive place. His fingers worked magic, making her melt and burn.

When she jerked and cried out, lifting her hips off the bed, pushing against his hand, he slid over her. He kissed her deeply as he plunged inside her, making her his at last.

He began moving, heated tingles sweeping her as he kissed her again and again, using his tongue to match the rhythm of his hips. He kept one hand between them, his questing fingers teasing and stroking, driving her closer and closer to a glittery, mind-blowing climax.

As it broke, her body tightened and she cried out. Hot, shimmering waves of sensation rolled through her, carrying her into a tingly whirl of spinning, endless pleasure.

It seemed to go on and on and she clung to him, almost dizzy, near blinded by the glory of it. How good it felt to have him inside her. Then, even through the languorous haze, she could tell that he'd withdrawn. He wasn't kissing her anymore, either, but he *was* lying hot and heavy on top of her. His wonderful beard tickled her chin, and his weight was starting to bear down on her, almost suffocating....

Bran of Barra was a big man.

Mindy let her arms slide away from his back, but he didn't roll off her. She tried to ease out from under him without disturbing him—she could tell he'd fallen asleep—but it was making her so hot to lie beneath him.

She twisted her head to the side, just to catch her breath. But when she opened her eyes, she screamed. The richly embroidered bedcovering of Bran's bedchamber was gone. She was eyeball-to-weave with the tangled mess of her overly thick red-tartaned duvet at the Anchor.

It was the heavy duvet piled on top of her that was taking her breath and making her sweat.

Mindy shoved it aside, leaping off the bed.

Horror washed over her.

She wasn't in Bran's splendiferous bedchamber out

on the islet, having just been ravished and made love to by the man she knew she couldn't live without.

She was in the tiny bedroom at the Anchor.

It couldn't be, but it was.

Yet, she was sure she'd been with Bran. She could smell the sharp musk of sex in the air and—she had to do it—when she slipped a finger between her legs to check, it came back wet and glistening with evidence they had been together.

She was also naked, her breasts still flushed with excitement and—this really ripped her—she could see the red imprints of large hands on her hips, just where Bran had gripped her.

"Oh, God!" She sank to her knees, pressed her forehead against the edge of the bed, and cried.

She *had* been with Bran.

And she'd been there with him in his time and it'd all been so real. She could still remember her terror at crossing the bay in the teensy medieval coracle. The horrid creature called Serafina and Bran's friend, the dark-haired, laughing-eyed man, Saor MacSwain.

Dear, sweet Gibbie and his meaty bones. They'd all been there, plain as day and all around her.

Most of all, Bran had been real.

Their lovemaking the best she'd ever had.

Now . . .

Something had gone terribly wrong. She knew it with a worse certainty than ever before. This time Bran really was gone from her.

And a dreadful chill Margo and the good folk at Ye Olde Pagan Times would call her sixth sense told her that this disaster was one that even Bran, with his ghostly magic, wouldn't be able to breach.

Their lovemaking must have violated some unwritten code of behavior between ghosts and nonghosts.

And now they were both being punished. Mindy would never see him again.

It was over.

Chapter 15

Bran of Barra was going to kill someone.

He hoped it wasn't Serafina.

He'd never in all his days laid a hand to a woman in anger. Not in seven hundred years of living. Or *un*living, as some folk would surely insist. But if the sultry Saracen beauty had anything to do with Mindy's disappearance, he might be persuaded to adjust his thinking.

A raging ache already blazed between his eyes.

His skull was splitting.

And—the very worst of it—he hadn't imbibed a drop. An ale-clouded, wine-befuddled head wasn't the reason for his misery. The libations and delicacies that he'd ordered to his room, hoping to seduce and delight Mindy's appetites, remained untouched.

Neither he nor Mindy had indulged.

Save that he'd carried her to his bed and made love to her.

"Odin's balls!" Scowling, he tore away the bedsheets. He dropped to his knees and peered beneath his great four-poster, half hoping, but not really expecting, to find her beneath, sleeping on the floor rushes.

She wasn't there.

Just as he'd known she wouldn't be.

"Nae!" He threw back his head and roared the denial.

Then he ran to the windows, dashing from one to the other and opening the shutters. Cold morning wind rushed in, chill and bracing, but not a single damning gust gave a hint as to where Mindy had gone.

Yet he knew he'd brought her to his world—the ghostly place he held together with the sheer strength of his will.

It wasn't as if they'd coupled in her world, a place where she could have brushed off their mating and gone about her business as if nothing but a wink and a smile had passed between them.

He'd brought her here, summoning all the power he had to whisk her into his own fourteenth century. And, may the Great Ones scald and flay him, but she'd seemed impressed.

Oohing and aahing as she'd noted the fineries of his Barra. And, he was sure, deeming each wonder grander than what she had in her own day of the moderns, where, he hoped, she wasn't whiling just now.

He'd used so much of his strength to bring her here.

It could take days—maybe even weeks—before he could summon enough power to set things right if she was indeed gone from him.

He'd left her only to visit the jakes.

To think such a simple need, sought in the middle of the night, might have cost him so much.

It was beyond bearing.

"Skirt of the Valkyries!" He snatched his clothes off the rush-strewn floor, still fragrant with meadowsweet and petals of roses. Cursing, he pulled on his shirt, threw his plaid around his shoulders.

Mindy couldn't have returned to her world.

Not without him sending her there.

His long years of ghostdom had taught him that.

He'd brought her here and she'd come willingly. That being the way of it, she couldn't have left without him granting her leave to do so. And—he could have laughed if the truth didn't pain him—he certainly hadn't sent her away.

He burned for her!

His head was breaking in two.

Scowling, he scrubbed a hand over his face, doing his best to ignore the pain. Though he did grind his teeth and clench his fists as he glared again around his bedchamber, searching for clues.

A reason she'd left him.

He found none.

Only red-hot memories of the night they'd shared. Each one crashed over him, stealing his breath and haunting him. He could taste the scent of her on the back of his tongue. His hands were branded with the feel of her, every curve and dip of her sleek, smooth skin a forever imprint he knew would never leave him. Their love had been poignant and sweet, blessed by the Heartbreaker. And, he knew, desired by the Auld Ones. They shared a love that had been divined before either of them had ever drawn their first breath.

Even so, their love hadn't been a mere whim of the gods.

As was the way of such things, they'd had the choice to seek and acknowledge their bond.

Now that they had, he knew he couldn't exist without her.

There could be no reason for her to have vanished without even saying good-bye. Unless someone in his household had confronted her, filling her with nonsense and lies. Sending her on her way before he'd wakened. He wouldn't have believed it. Not even of Serafina. But he could think of nothing else that would explain why his bed loomed empty.

He'd expected to greet the morn with Mindy in his arms.

Instead, he stood alone in the cold gray of morning, frowning at his mussed bed. Temper rising, he balled his right hand and then pulled back his fist, slamming it into his left palm.

The pain was sharp and blinding.

He was, after all, a strong, hot-blooded man.

If need be, he'd punch holes in the fine, lime-washed walls of his silent bedchamber. He'd haul each member of his household, kinsman or friend, into his thinking room and question everyone until they broke with the truth.

In the worst case, he'd sift himself to Barra of the moderns and fetch her. And—the possibility gutted him—if she'd already hied herself back to Bucks County, he'd take himself there.

He would do anything to get her back.

They'd slept together so sweetly. They'd *lain* together in ways he'd never shared with another woman. After their loving, he'd held her, pulling her into his arms, knowing they could sort the complications of their differing times on the morrow, after the rising of the sun.

He'd never dreamed the new day would bring him sorrow.

He paced around his bedchamber, his brow creasing more deeply with every step. Gray light was beginning to seep into the room. Below his tower, he could hear the waves washing over the rocks, the morning wind beginning to rise.

And, he noted with annoyance, the embers of the night's fire no longer even glowed. The messy pile of wood ash on the hearthstone didn't even glimmer. Like Mindy herself, their night together was turning into a fast-fading memory.

Only he didn't want it to!

"What can I do?" He growled the words to no one.

His gut twisted and he wheeled around to glare again at his empty bed. Scene of such happiness and wonder just a short time before, not that it mattered now. Soon, he would have to go belowstairs and confront his men. One of them would know something.

But, for now, he wasn't ready to face anyone.

The shock and pain were still too great.

"Serafina had naught to do with it."

Saor's deep voice came from the door. Bran could have flown at him and strangled the lout. Instead, he pulled in a tight breath, trying for control. He didn't want to glower at a man who surely meant well.

Even if hearing Serafina's name grated on his last nerve.

"You'll have good reason to defend her?" Bran eyed his friend across the room.

He wasn't surprised when Saor's face colored. "You know I am fond of her." He came forward, hands spread. "She was with me the night through, Bran. I swear to you, whatever you might think of her, she did your American no harm."

"Then where is she?" Bran knew Saor would understand whom he meant.

Truth was, Mindy's name—her presence—hung in the

air, tangible and vibrant, as if she had only just slipped from the room and would return any moment.

Bran knew she wouldn't.

He leaned against the window arch, welcoming the chill air pouring in through the open shutters. He needed the fresh, brisk air to think.

But no answers came to him.

Even Saor was silent, his most-times snapping, laughing eyes more solemn than Bran had ever seen them. "At least, the infernal building din has lessened," Saor observed, crossing the room to pour a measure of morning ale.

"For a while"—he lifted the cup to his lips, draining it—"I was sure that everyone with ears, or even desirous of a good night's sleep, would show us their back.

"It truly has been intolerable." Saor set down the cup, wiping his mouth. "Let us be glad that chaos seems to be behind us."

"I hadn't noticed." Bran folded his arms.

He wasn't in the mood to be good-spirited about anything.

Not even the cessation of the restoration havoc.

"Och, come." Saor strode over to him, gripping his elbow. "You cannae hide yourself up here all morning. Folk are talking in the hall, wondering what ails you. Your American isn't lost." He gave Bran's arm a shake. "I say she's just slipped away to tend urgent business—"

"Humph." Bran glared at him.

"And"—Saor ignored both glare and snort—"she'll be all the more glad to run into your arms when you sift yourself back to her."

"Think you it's that simple?" Bran went to stand at a window, staring out at the cold, gray morning.

He clamped his mouth shut, refusing to say more. If

the gods were kind, they'd take heart and encourage
Saor to leave him be.

"I think . . ." Saor let the words trail off and—praise
the saints—left him alone.

When his departing footsteps faded away, Bran lifted
a hand to rub his shoulder. A terrible, crushing weight
sat there and all Saor's good words and encouragement
hadn't done a thing to help rid him of its burden.

His friend meant well, but he didn't understand.

It'd taken Bran days and fiercest concentration to
hold his world together tightly enough that Mindy could
join him here, albeit quite briefly.

Even so, he'd done the best ghost magic he'd ever
managed in all his centuries, and—his heart dropped like
a stone to admit such a scalding truth—Mindy should
have been able to stay with him much longer.

At least until his honor told him it was time to return
her.

Unless she left by choice.

Either way, he knew that he wouldn't be able to go
to her now. And that knowledge gutted him. Hadn't he
told her that nothing would keep him from her?

He'd said the words with a grin and so much
swagger.

His heart had swelled and he'd been so proud. He'd
been able to speak such words because they'd been
true.

Yet now . . .

Something wasn't right.

He could feel the difference in the air, though he
didn't know what it was.

Bran slumped against the side of the window arch.
He did know that the rocks below his tower and the
whitecapped waves were looking more blurry by the

moment. Even the sharp, gray edge of the horizon was no longer distinguishable. He couldn't tell where the sea ended and the sky began.

And when he turned away from the fool window, he found that he couldn't see his room very well, either.

His eyes stung too badly.

"Damn it all!" A painful tightness squeezed his chest, pulsing and burning until he could hardly breathe. When a tear rolled down his cheek, he balled his fist and almost slammed it into the wall.

Instead, he sank to his knees and buried his face in his hands.

But when familiar footsteps announced a certain long-nosed, flat-footed gowk's return, Bran leapt to his feet and brushed at his plaid.

Broken or no', he *was* Barra. And no one, not even his best friend, was going to see him in such a state. So he grabbed a linen napkin off the table, then blew his nose as discreetly as possible. He was standing at his window again, hands clasped casually behind his back, when Saor strode into the bedchamber.

"I spoke with everyone in the hall." Saor joined him at the window. "No one has seen the lass. Nor does anyone have an idea as to where—"

"Word does spread like a fire in the heather, what?" Bran shot him a glare.

"I thought you'd want me to question them?"

"What I want—" Bran couldn't finish.

If he'd blurted how much he loved Mindy and needed her, *ached* for her, Saor's face would have filled with pity. And he didn't want to suffer his friend's sympathy.

He wanted Mindy.

"Is there naught I can do for you?" Saor was looking at him oddly.

Bran set his jaw, trying to appear resolute rather than crumbled. "Nae. I require nothing."

"As you wish." Saor eyed him a few moments longer than necessary, then walked from the room.

Suddenly, Bran desired to be elsewhere, too. His bed-chamber held lingering traces of Mindy's scent. And although he'd pulled the bed-curtains to hide the mussed and tangled sheets, he knew they were there.

He'd probably never sleep in his bed again.

Could be, he'd avoid the room entirely.

And just now he needed air. A brisk turn about the bailey, or two or three, followed by an hour or so of vigorous sword practice should help banish the god-awful ache in his chest.

He hoped so, anyway.

If need be, he'd go down into the keep's vaulted basement and spend the day shoving heavy wine barrels from one end of the storage rooms to the other.

He'd do whatever it took until he could at least walk again without feeling like an auld done man.

A pity he couldn't address the sorrow in his heart as easily. Wishing he could, he started for the door.

"Come, Gibbie." He glanced at his dog, clicking his fingers.

Gibbie was sprawled, snoring quite loudly, on his tartan-covered bed before the fire. But now he cracked one eye and peered at his master.

"Come, laddie." Bran waited on the threshold. "I'm for the bailey, I am."

Understanding *bailey*, Gibbie found it worth his while to abandon the comfort of his bed. Leaping up, he bounded across the room, making for his favorite exit from the bed-chamber. It was a small section of wall near the door that, unlike the other walls, wasn't covered by a tapestry.

But instead of flitting through the wall, Gibbie stopped before it, barking.

Bran stepped into the corridor, waiting.

When Gibbie didn't join him, he folded his arms. He should have known even his most faithful friend would make this morn difficult for him.

"Gibbie, come!" Bran was growing impatient.

Gibbie started to whine.

"Odin's balls!" Bran strode back into the room.

Then he stared, puzzled. His jaw slipped.

His great beast of a dog stood trembling in front of the wall. Bran rubbed his beard, not knowing what to do. Gibbie wasn't a shivery, whimpering lapdog.

Yet . . .

There the dog was, cowering.

Bran frowned and went to the table across the room. It still held the remains of last night's victuals. He snatched a bit of cheese.

He tossed the cheese at the dog's spot in the wall, knowing Gibbie would chase after it. Then they could be on their way to the bailey.

But the cheese didn't pass through the wall.

It bounced off and dropped to the floor.

Gibbie barked like mad. He didn't even touch the cheese.

Bran stared, disbelieving.

Then, like his dog, he began to shake.

There could be only one reason the cheese didn't go through the bedchamber wall.

The wall was solid.

But that couldn't be. Not in Bran's own ghostly realm, where, thanks to his strength of will and experience, everything appeared real yet, in truth, was as insubstantial as Highland mist.

Bran felt a sickening dread in his stomach. He crossed the room and dropped to one knee beside Gibbie. Then, still trembling as badly as his dog, he reached to press the flat of his hand against the wall.

His hand didn't go through.

His palm and fingers remained splayed against cold, hard stone.

"Dear God in heaven!" Bran stared at his hand, tears blurring his vision. His entire body shook and blood roared in his ears.

Gibbie was suddenly beside him, licking his face. Bran scarce noticed, though he did sling an arm around the dog and draw him close.

He needed his old friend's support.

The unfathomable had happened. Something that he would never have dreamed possible—or even desired— had changed his world, taking him and everything in it straight back to, well, his world. They were no longer ghosts.

There could be no other explanation.

Bran looked at Gibbie. He saw at once that the dog knew. His excited eyes and wagging tail said as much. As did the sudden silence that had descended upon the tower so eerily, heralding—they'd all believed—a stop to the noisy restoration work.

Under different circumstances, Bran would have bent double with laughter.

It would seem the cessation of building noise was due to his tower no longer being in the day of the moderns.

Only now—he could still scarce believe it—the fourteenth-century world around him was real.

Just as he was real again.

And Gibbie.

And everyone else in his unsuspecting household.

Somehow the return of his tower's stones to their rightful setting had also thrust them back into their own time. It was an unexpected miracle that would have delighted him had it happened sooner.

Before he'd fallen so desperately in love with Mindy.

A woman whom, he now knew with surety, he would never see again.

Ghostly magic made anything possible, but the divide between the true fourteenth century and her day was a barrier he couldn't cross.

For the first time in seven centuries, Bran of Barra felt cursed.

He didn't think he could bear it.

Weeks later, Mindy stood alone in the bailey of Bran's tower, taking the most difficult farewell she'd ever had to make in her life. Completely restored to its former strength and glory, the tower with all its outbuildings and curtain walls truly appeared as if it'd never been anywhere else except here, on this tiny spit-of-a-rock island where it was first built so many long centuries ago.

Jock MacGugan and his men had done beautiful work.

And, she knew, the whole of the Hebrides stood in awe of the speed with which he'd done the next-to-impossible.

MacNeil's Tower was magnificent.

And only Mindy knew how much more grand it'd really been *then*.

With each passing day, it became more difficult to believe that she'd really been there. That Bran had taken her across the bay in a medieval coracle, leading her up the same tiny stone jetty where Jock MacGugan had dropped her off an hour ago, reluctantly accepting her wish to spend the afternoon alone on the islet.

She needed to make her good-byes in private.

And—for what was surely the thousandth time since she'd entered the tower—she fished around in her jacket pocket, retrieved her damp cotton handkerchief, and dabbed the tears from her cheeks.

This was why she'd wanted to be alone.

She didn't want anyone else, not even a man as kindly as Jock, to see her break apart.

And she *was* breaking.

Everywhere she looked, she saw Bran. She saw him standing in the shadows of the door arches. Or she'd see him striding across the cobbled courtyard. He was up on the battlements, too. She saw him there as she knew and loved him: a big, brawny man, looking out to sea, surveying his world. But then he'd turn and see her and his face would light with his wicked smile and he'd tear down the stone steps and run at her, his arms held wide. He'd grab her by the waist, lifting her in the air and twirling around and around until they fell, laughing and dizzy, to the ground.

And then he'd reach for her again, this time bracketing her face with his strong, calloused hands as he kissed her and kissed her.

And she'd throw her arms around him and kiss him back.

So fiercely!

She'd hold him as tightly as she could and never stop kissing him, because she absolutely couldn't bear to let go of him.

How sad that when it came to it, the choice hadn't been hers.

Or his, she was sure.

She knew he loved her with the same fierceness. And knowing that he did just made everything hurt even worse.

"Oh, Bran . . ." She drew a ragged breath, pain sweeping her. The agony of losing him felt like being pierced by hundreds of scorching, razor-sharp knife blades.

She. Just. Couldn't. Stand. It.

Needing to sit, she dropped onto a stone bollard near the newly restored chapel. She closed her eyes and tipped back her head, taking long, deep breaths and releasing them slowly. Finally, when the sharpest edge of the pain eased, she reached down to touch the bollard.

Worn smooth and shiny by the lines that had held countless MacNeil galleys, or so she'd been told, the bollard dated to Bran's time. Sitting on it made her feel somehow closer to him. It was, after all, something he would have passed, and seen, every day.

Much of the castle belonged to later centuries. As so often with such places, each generation of chieftains had added his own embellishments. So she'd decided to spend her time seeking out all the special spots that, she knew for certain, hailed from Bran's day.

Such as the little stone bollard.

She was making memories.

Not *history* as Bran had assured her they'd do on their fateful last night together. She was touching, seeing, and absorbing images—memories—she could cherish later, when she returned home.

"Damn!" She reached for her crumpled handkerchief again, wishing she'd brought more than just one.

Who would have thought she'd come to think of Barra as home?

But she had.

And it was going to crush her to leave in the morning.

Her last tie to Bran . . . gone.

Not wanting to think about it—not *able* to—she turned her face into the wind. She wasn't surprised that her last day on Barra was also the most beautiful. A fine brisk day, full of sun and with only a light chop on the bay, it seemed like the final indignity.

She'd come to love gray, wet days of mist and rain.

This day dazzled.

She would have preferred wild and blustery.

Mindy sighed. Somewhere a dog barked. The sound was faint, so it must have been a dog on the shore. Much closer, she could hear the waves hurling themselves against the rocks that edged the base of Bran's curtain walls. And just above her, several seabirds wheeled and dipped, their shrill, lonely cries almost seeming as if they'd come to say good-bye.

Too bad she hated to go.

At least Margo would offer her a sympathetic shoulder. Sisters were good for that and hers was the best. She had missed Margo and would be glad to see her. Perhaps someday they could return to Scotland together and—if she could bear it—she would even bring Margo here, to Barra.

She knew Margo would be ecstatic to visit the Hebrides.

But just now . . .

Mindy swallowed the heat in her throat. It was too painful to think about returning to Barra when she knew in her heart Bran wouldn't be here. "Damn!" she cried again, this time not bothering with her hankie.

No one could see her tears.

Or that she was clenching her fists so tightly that her nails were digging into her palms.

Nor could anyone guess that she was taking great

gulps of air, not just to calm herself, but because she hoped that when she was stateside again—and so many of her breaths would taste of traffic fumes and city smells—she could then remember sitting here on a stone bollard at Barra, drinking in clean, cold air that smelled of the sea.

"Gaaaah!" She pressed a fist to her mouth, not wanting to sob.

This was killing her.

No, she'd died the morning she'd wakened without Bran at the Anchor.

She might not look dead, but she was. Her soul had bled out and she'd never be the same again. Not after having met and fallen so madly, wondrously in love with the man she *knew* was meant to be hers.

How horrible that their centuries hadn't matched.

And how annoying that Jock had forgotten his promise not to ferry anyone else out to the islet until she'd said her farewells and was gone.

An old woman was poking about inside the chapel.

Not that Mindy had planned to go inside the little stone building. Even though she knew very well that the chapel was of Bran's time. For that very reason, she'd decided not to enter it.

The chapel would have been where Bran would have married her if she had been able to stay with him in his time.

So-o-o . . .

Mindy swiped a hand across her cheek again. She knew what was good for her and what wasn't.

The little chapel was out of bounds.

But it still annoyed her that someone was there.

She'd so wanted—no, she'd *needed*—to spend this time here alone.

So she sat a bit straighter on the bollard, folded her hands in her lap, and stared down at the cobbles, pretending she hadn't seen the woman.

But when a shadow fell across her and—oh, no!—she found herself looking at two very small black boots with red plaid laces, she couldn't ignore the woman any longer.

It was the Hansel-and-Gretel crone from the Oban ferry.

The tiny, black-garbed old woman who'd vanished from the ferry deck. And whom the waiflike red-haired girl had called the Goodwife of Doon.

As she remembered, a shiver raced down Mindy's spine.

She jumped off the bollard, staring at the woman. "I know you."

"So many folk say." The woman smiled, her blue eyes twinkling. "That be a fine bollard, eh?" She hobbled over to it, taking Mindy's seat. "I enjoy a good sit-down here myself, I do."

"Then please don't let me bother you." Mindy clutched her jacket tighter. The day felt suddenly colder.

The old woman gave her the willies.

"You needn't fear me, you know, lassie." She gave a little cackle. "I'm on your side."

"My side?" Mindy's eyes rounded.

"So I said, just." The old woman lifted a gnarled hand and clutched a fist, meaningfully.

For some strange reason, Mindy's heart started to pound. As if the old woman knew, her wizened face wreathed in another smile.

It was a rather cheeky smile that lifted the fine hairs on Mindy's nape.

"I'm afraid I don't understand." Mindy's mouth was

going dry, too. Something weird was definitely going on. "I'm just here to say my fare—"

"Och! I know fine why you're here." The old woman placed her hands on her knees. "And what you're looking for."

"I'm not looking for anything. I—" Mindy's heart slammed against her ribs. She blinked, her eyes suddenly brimming again. There was something about the old woman's words that electrified her.

She set her hands on her hips. "Since you seem to know so much, why don't you just tell me—"

"There be no need. You'll see soon enough."

"You're not making any sense."

"Nae?" The old woman cackled again. "Then perhaps you should visit yon chapel. . . ." She turned her head, glancing at the ancient stone building.

"The chapel?" Mindy didn't think so.

The crone nodded once.

Then she pushed slowly to her feet and hobbled away in the direction of the jetty. Mindy wasn't sure, but she thought the woman was chuckling to herself as she went.

As soon as she disappeared around a corner, Mindy hurried straight to the chapel. She'd so wanted to avoid going in there. Small, damp, and musty, and reeking of *age*, it was exactly as she'd imagined it would be. Right down to the strange dreamlike atmosphere that seemed to hang in the air, almost a soft, bluish haze.

It was freezing in the chapel, too.

Mindy turned up her jacket collar and wished she'd brought gloves. In fact, it was too cold—and dark—to stay in the little building any longer.

She'd come. She'd seen. And she hadn't found anything earthshaking as the old woman had implied she would. So she shrugged deeper into her jacket and turned to leave. But the floor was an uneven mix of broken stone and earth and she tripped as she neared the low-linteled door.

"Owwww!" She slammed hard onto one knee, sure she'd cracked her kneecap on a rock. But when she pushed to her feet and looked down to brush at her pants, she saw that it hadn't been a stone that had jabbed into her so painfully.

It was the corroded black hilt of a rusted sword.

Half-buried in damp, hard-packed earth and half-hidden by slabs of cracked, mossy stone, the sword was clearly hundreds of years old and in terrible condition.

Mindy dropped to her knees in the dirt, this time carefully.

She stared at the sword.

It looked as though it would crumble if she even touched it with a finger.

No way was it the Heartbreaker.

But there was something about it. And it did have a rounded pommel. Biting her lip, Mindy pulled out her cotton handkerchief and tried to smooth away the worst mud and grime from the hilt. When her efforts revealed a crystal gemstone, she clutched a hand to her breast, almost afraid to breathe.

It *could* be the Heartbreaker.

When the crystal suddenly turned brilliant, luminously blue, she knew that it was.

And from the near-blinding light pulsing inside the gemstone, she knew that this Heartbreaker—the real one—possessed even more power than the ghostly sword Bran wore at his hip.

"Oh, God!" She began to shake, pressed trembling fingers to her mouth. "Oh, God, oh, God . . ."

She started digging, scraping away the earth and

pulling at the stone slabs. But her hands were shaking too badly to get much accomplished and her eyes were streaming now. She couldn't recall ever having cried so hard. She shed hot, fast rivers of tears that poured down her cheeks, spilling onto her jacket and her hands, dripping onto the rusted sword.

She blinked hard, not understanding how or why the sword was here. Perhaps it'd been buried in the chapel ground all these centuries and the rebuilding work loosened the earth around it? Or maybe it'd been lodged deep in the recess in a stone or underground crevice. Perhaps now through some magic she couldn't understand, it was showing itself to her?

Whatever the reason, she worked harder and harder to dig the sword from the cold, hard-packed earth.

Finally, she lifted it free, taking it carefully from the ground. It didn't crumble as she'd feared, but it felt so light and brittle and *old* that holding it was agony.

Could this piece of thin, rusted nothingness really have been the gleaming steel at Bran's side?

That the blue crystal remained relatively intact, and still so valiant and loyal to its mission despite the years and damage, tore her soul.

Holding the sword against her heart, she folded her hands around the gritty, age-roughened hilt. She let her fingers close over the crystal, as she'd seen Bran do. Only she knew he'd done so in desperation, at first, anyway, hoping to resist the sword's magic.

Mindy held the blade reverently.

"Oh, Bran . . ." She squeezed shut her eyes, pain wracking her.

From a great distance, his words flashed through her mind:

"Just so there aren't any doubts in your mind, the Heart-breaker only lets MacNeil men know where the woman of our heart is waiting for us."

She tightened her fingers over the crystal, her heart splitting. She hadn't only heard the words. She'd also heard Bran's voice saying them. His buttery rich burr, so deep and seductive.

A voice she'd never hear again, unless the Heart-breaker's magic could work in reverse. Not leading a MacNeil man to his woman, but taking her to her Mac-Neil man.

It was worth a try.

But before she could think of a prayer, some chant, or whatever, the sword started slipping from her hands.

"Agggh!" She grappled with it, losing her balance and nearly toppling over. She couldn't let it fall. But it was so heavy, the hilt so smooth. It was slippery as an eel, suddenly felt almost alive, and was already sliding out of her grasp again.

"Oh, no, you don't!" She held the sword with both hands, gripping the pommel gemstone as tightly as she dared. It felt hot now, almost blazing, but she kept her fingers clenched around it anyway. Until—she gasped— she realized she was holding nothing.

The sword was gone.

But the soft blue haze in the little chapel was everywhere.

Thick, swirling, and full of brilliant sparkles, it nearly blinded her. As did the bright gleam of the sword that winked at her from the hip of a tall, broad-shouldered man limned in the chapel's open doorway.

The sword was the Heartbreaker.

And the man was Bran of Barra.

But it was neither the sword's glint nor the whirling blaze of the blue mist that was blinding her now. It was Bran of Barra's dazzling wicked smile and the hot tears stinging her eyes.

"Dear God!" Mindy shot to her feet, running to him. "It's you! You, you, you! You're here and—"

"Nae, Mindy-lass, 'tis *you* who are here!" He caught her to him, crushing her against his big, kilted body as if he wanted to squeeze the breath from her. "You're here, with me, on Barra, in my time, and I say you welcome! Praise all the saints and whatever magic brought you back to me!

"I've near lost my mind, without you." He grabbed her face between his hands and kissed her hotly. "I love you so much I couldn't breathe without you. Dinnae you e'er leave me again. The world will become a very dangerous place if you do, so be warned!"

"I am!" Mindy wrapped her arms around him, holding on for dear life. "And, trust me, I'm not going anywhere. Never. I promise. I'll be like flypaper—"

"Flypaper?" He raised his brow.

"Never mind." Mindy shook her head, laughing. "Just kiss me, you great big handsome Scot!"

Bran grinned, then laughed with her. "Saints, but I've missed you!"

At his side, Gibbie barked, letting her know he'd missed her, too. Leaping forward, he jumped at her, nearly knocking her down in his enthusiasm.

Laughing, Mindy dropped to her knees to hug him, accepting his welcome. And rubbing his ears heartily enough so he'd know the affection was mutual.

"Enough!" Bran clicked his fingers, calling off Gibbie. "He can welcome you back later. Just now, you are mine. I'm ne'er letting you go!"

And then, much as Mindy had fantasized on the bollard, he seized her by the waist, carrying her with him from the chapel and out into the bailey, where he hoisted her high in the air and twirled in a circle, laughing and kissing her again and again as they spun around.

Except, when they stopped, Bran of Barra being, well, *Bran of Barra*, he didn't look even slightly dizzy.

He did toss a glance and a wave to his friends who were lining the parapet walk cheering and jabbing their swords in the air. Even Serafina was there, hanging on Saor MacSwain's arm and waving a silk veil above her head. And—Mindy was amazed—the courtesan's expression was soft, her eyes a bit misty. And the woman's eyes weren't the only ones that looked damp.

Bran's Barrachs truly were giving her a grand homecoming.

Mindy swallowed and stared at them all, once again feeling a need for her handkerchief.

Especially when she spotted a *walking stick* being thrust high in the air, right along with all the swords. She also heard a very distinctive *whoop* that could be only Silvanus's.

"It can't be. . . ." She flashed a look at Bran, but he only grinned and shrugged.

"I told you I had a feeling we'd see them again. They're still ghosties and pop in now and then. You'll understand"—he winked at her—"none of my men mind their visits. There's no one here afraid of ghosts!

"As what can and cannae be . . ." He planted his hands on his hips and laughed heartily. "I can see I'll be needing to teach you about Highland magic. Scotland is a place full of wonder. And Barra . . ."

His chest swelled proudly. "Barra is Barra! There's no

finer place in all the land, as I'll soon be showing you
when I take you round to see the other isles.

"But first"—his grin turned wicked again—"come
here, you, and let me kiss you properly."

And he did.

Again and again and again—until her toes curled.

Epilogue

"Keep your eyes closed." Madame Zelda's soothing voice echoed through the quiet of the New Age shop's darkened back room. Each softly spoken word settled onto Margo's consciousness like one more gently weighted urge that should, but didn't, send her spiraling into a relaxed state where she hoped to establish contact with her sister.

"Focus on your breathing." The fortune-teller was leaning over her. Margo could smell the other woman's lemony perfume, the slight trace of onions from the hoagie she knew Madame Zelda had eaten for lunch. "Inhale deeply, then breathe out slowly, releasing all the tension and worry that's troubling you.

"Feel peace and serenity surrounding you." Madame Zelda had moved away—her voice was growing fainter. "Relax and let your mind drift. Imagine soothing hands stroking your forehead and your face, feel gentle fingers—"

"It's not working." Margo sat upright on the therapy couch, frowning.

She believed as firmly as anyone in the power of soul ties and that no one is ever truly separated from those they love dearly.

A connection was *always* there.

At least, she was sure, through the unbreakable bonds of energy. The karmic threads that kept our many lives so tightly entwined with those destined to share our journey.

Even now, so long since Mindy's inexplicable disappearance, Margo knew her sister was well.

She'd feel it if something bad had happened.

Instead, each time she thought of Mindy, she felt only a strong sense of joy and peace.

Her sister was alive and happy.

Certain of it, Margo couldn't quite suppress a yawn. She considered lying back down. Madame Zelda had sworn she could reach Mindy, and Margo was willing to try anything to know the truth.

But the pungent scent from eucalyptus aromatherapy oil was making her nose twitch. And no matter how hard she'd tried to *breathe* herself into a state to discover her sister's true whereabouts, her every attempt at going under proved an abysmal failure.

"You weren't visualizing." Madame Zelda smoothed her voluminous purple caftan. "You need to imagine a bright white light at the top of your head and then feel its warmth descending, slipping down through your body to—"

"I can't be hypnotized." Margo tucked her hair behind an ear, wishing she had the strength to jump to her feet and exit the room.

But she was so tired.

Her legs felt much too leaden to swing off the sofa. And even if she managed to stand, she doubted she could do so without swaying. Not that her exhaustion had anything to do with Madame Zelda's attempts at trying to help her probe the cosmos for signs of Mindy.

She was just worn-out from having to run Ye Olde Pagan Times these last few months, during Patience Peasgood's unavoidable absence as she recovered from knee surgery.

Overtime hours and no sleep took a toll on everyone.

She deserved a rest.

So she allowed herself to flop back onto the sofa, secretly closing her ears to Madame Zelda's soft, calming voice. She'd sleep just ten minutes and then she'd waken, refreshed and free of the aching tightness that seemed to sit fast between her shoulders in recent weeks.

Sleep was good.

Though her much-deserved rest would be more restorative if she didn't sense Madame Zelda looming, leaning close and peering at her.

Irritated, Margo opened her eyes to say so, but the sight before her stole her speech.

Madame Zelda had grown a beard.

In fact, the face staring at her wasn't the Puerto Rican woman's at all.

It belonged to an aged, magnificently kilted Scotsman who now leapt back and made her a graciously formal bow. "I greet you, my lady." His voice boomed as he straightened, the huge Celtic brooch pinning a swath of plaid to his shoulder glinting brightly. "You may call me Silvanus."

"Sil—?" Margo blinked.

He had a beard that would put every shopping-mall

Santa to shame. The great sword strapped to his hip could be only a museum piece. And although he didn't appear poised to draw the dangerous-looking blade, he *was* regarding her with a steely, determined gaze.

Margo pushed up on her elbows, sure she was dreaming.

"Where's Marta—I mean, Madame Zelda?" she asked anyway, glancing about.

The fortune-teller was nowhere to be seen.

Silvanus—whoever he was—ignored her question and, with a grand flourish, plucked a small leather pouch from the air.

Margo stared, suspicious. "How did you do that?"

"Many years of practice!" He smiled, his eyes twinkling as if from a private joke.

Margo didn't share his amusement. There was something odd about him.

And if she wasn't sleeping, she needed to slip off the therapy couch and press the emergency alarm button hidden under a shelf near the door.

"I brought this from your sister." The man's words froze her just as she'd been about to push to her feet.

"Mindy?" Margo's heart began to race.

"Herself, and no other." The man held out the packet, an old-fashioned sack made of oiled sheepskin, Margo saw as she took it from him. "Though"—he cleared his throat—"I do think she'd meant for you to find this on your own. Someday, as it were."

"Where is she?" This time Margo did jump up.

"Is she—" Her jaw slipped and the leather pouch almost dropped from her hands.

She was talking to air.

The kilted man was gone.

But she still held the oiled packet. Her entire body

trembling, she sank onto the couch and began untying the brittle red ribbon that held the sheepskin together. She hadn't noticed how fragile the ribbon was until she began plucking at it, causing it to crumble.

Dear God ...

The leather was disintegrating, too.

Not oiled at all, but cracked and dry, it was splitting apart in her hands. As was the folded piece of thick, yellowed parchment the pouch had held. But it wasn't disappearing so quickly that she didn't see her own name scrawled across the note in Mindy's distinctive, looping handwriting.

"Oh, God!" Margo couldn't breathe.

The world slammed to a halt and then started spinning madly, the dark little room whirling around her so fast, she grew dizzy.

Her hands shook as she unfolded the parchment and her vision blurred, hot tears making it difficult to read the words swimming before her eyes.

Dearest Margo,

You were right—Scotland is magical. And if you are reading these lines, you'll know that I am well and happier than I ever dreamed possible. You might remember the grand portrait of Bran of Barra, the fourteenth-century MacNeil chieftain who built the tower? If you do, you'll know I was always drawn to his painting and now, thanks to a wonder I can't begin to explain, I am with him in his time. We've wed and ...

The note turned to dust, sifting through her fingers to the floor, before she could finish reading. Within the blink of an eye, her hands were empty. The parchment, the leather pouch, and its red drawstring ribbon—all vanished as if she'd only dreamed them.

But she knew she hadn't—it would just have been so nice to have had something to keep with her. Something that would prove such a miracle was really true.

"Good God, what happened to Patience's EMF meter?"

Madame Zelda stood in the doorway, her eyes round as she stared at Margo's feet. "It looks like it's been buried in a sewer!"

"Hah!" A second voice, deep and with a thick Scottish burr, came from outside the window. But when Margo flashed a glance that way, she didn't see anyone.

She did look down at the carpet, her heart racing again when she recognized Patience Peasgood's all-the-bells-and-whistles super-duper ghost-detecting device.

It was the very one she'd lent to Mindy for her trip to Barra.

It must've fallen from the leather pouch when she'd untied the drawstring, the note distracting her. She reached for it, relief sweeping her as she closed her fingers around its solid mass and—thank God—didn't feel it begin to break apart in her hands.

But it *was* corroded.

Blackened with age, not muck as Madame Zelda erroneously guessed.

And Margo had never seen anything more beautiful.

A certain kilted Scotsman peering in through the window found her tremulous smile a very fine sight.

"I told you two loons she'd be wanting thon contraption!" His chest swelled as he turned to his friends. "We all knew the rest wouldn't last long in her time. But that wee black box, now, it belongs in her day and—"

"I knew that, too, you great lump!" Geordie poked him with his walking stick. "Why, it was me what suggested we bring it along. As I recall—"

"You're both addled." Roderick snorted. "The idea was mine and no one else's."

"Yours?" Silvanus's brows shot up. "I needed all my powers o' persuasion to get you to even come along."

"And with good reason, I'm thinking." Roderick flipped back his plaid and glanced round, shuddering. "Or have you forgotten how many centuries we spent in this place?"

"Hear, hear!" Geordie agreed heartily.

"It was a matter of honor." Silvanus held his ground. "You saw how much the packet meant to the lassie."

"Well, she has it now, so I'm for leaving." Roderick folded his arms.

"And you?" Silvanus turned to Geordie.

The other ghost examined the end of his walking stick, not meeting Silvanus's eyes. "I am rather homesick, aye."

"Then let us be away." Silvanus clapped a hand on both their shoulders, knowing they'd instantly sift themselves back to Barra.

And they did, much to his relief.

He didn't want them to see him take one last peek through the shop window. He'd once made a vow that he'd do a good turn for Mindy and now that he had, he wanted to make sure he hadn't failed.

So he took a deep breath, put back his shoulders, and strode to the window. He looked just in time to see Mindy's sister reverently wrapping the little black box in a soft blue cloth.

She was still smiling.

And when she pressed the cloth-wrapped box to her

breast and sighed, looking most content, Silvanus knew that he, too, could go home.

But first he gave a little leap in the air.

It'd been a long time since he'd made a fetching lassie so happy. And it felt good.

Very good, indeed.

Read on for a preview of Allie Mackay's
next exciting Scottish paranormal
romance,

Must Love Kilts

Available from Signet Eclipse
in January 2011

Ye Olde Pagan Times
New Hope, Pennsylvania

Margo Menlove lived, breathed, and dreamed in plaid. At the age of sixteen she'd single-handedly convinced nearly all the girls in her high school—and even a few of the female teachers—that there was no man sexier than a Highlander. In those heady days, she'd even founded the now-defunct Bucks County Kilt Appreciation Society.

Now, more than ten years later, locals in her hometown of New Hope, Pennsylvania, considered her an authority on all things Scottish.

And although she was officially employed as a "luna harmonist" at the town's premier New Age shop, advising clients according to the natural cycle and rhythm of the moon, many customers sought her assistance when they wished to plan a trip to Scotland. Sometimes when one of those Glasgow-bound travelers consulted her, she'd surprise even herself with how well she knew the land of her dreams—she really was an expert.

She knew each clan's history and could recognize their tartans at a hundred paces. She prided herself on being able to recite all the must-see hot spots in the Highlands in a single breath. Her heart squeezed each time she heard bagpipes. She could dance a mean Highland fling before she'd learned to walk. Unlike most non-Scots, she even loved haggis. And although she didn't wish to test her theory, she was pretty sure that if someone cut her, she'd bleed tartan.

Her only problem was that she'd never set foot on Scottish soil.

And just now—she tried not to glare—a problem of a very different sort was breezing through the door of Ye Olde Pagan Times.

Dina Greed.

Margo's greatest rival in all things Scottish. So petite that Margo secretly thought of her as Minnie Mouse, she was dressed—as she nearly always was—in a tartan miniskirt and incredibly high-heeled black boots that added a few inches to her diminutive but shapely form. The deeply cut V neckline of her clinging blue cashmere top drew attention to her annoyingly full breasts. And her cloud of dark curly hair shone bright in the late-autumn sunlight that slanted in through the shop windows. She was also wearing a very smug smile and that could only mean trouble.

Margo shifted on her stool behind her Luna Harmony station and reached to rearrange the little blue and silver jars of organic beauty products that the shop's owner, Patience Peasgood, urged her to sell to those seeking celestial answers. With names like Foaming Sea Bath Crystals and Sea of Serenity Night Cream, all inspired by lunar seas, the cosmetics made people smile—even if most Ye Olde Pagan Times regulars found the prices too steep. Margo secretly agreed. No one loved a bargain more than her.

But just now she was grateful that so many Lunarian Organic products cluttered her counter. If she appeared busy, fussing with the display, Dina Greed might not sail over to needle her.

At the moment, the pint-sized brunette—who never failed to make Margo feel like a clunky blond amazon— was browsing the aisles, her chin tilted as she peered at sparkling glass bowls filled with pink and colorless quartz crystals. She then drifted to study the large selection of herbal teas. Margo eyed her progress from beneath her lashes, willing her to leave the shop.

Instead she stopped before a display of white pillar candles arranged in trays of small, river-polished pebbles, then moved on to the bookshelves set against the shop's back wall, where she stood watching Patience carefully unpack a box of newly delivered books on medieval magic and Celtic and Norse mythology.

Neither woman looked in Margo's direction.

Yet the fine hairs that lifted on her nape made her certain someone was watching her.

Margo shivered. The whole atmosphere of the shop suddenly felt a shade darker. She wondered whether it was Dina—the woman did ride her last nerve—or whether a shadow had passed over the sun.

Either way, it was a creepy, unsettling kind of dark.

"She's going to Scotland, you know."

"Gah!" Margo knocked over a bottle of Sea of Nectar Body Lotion. Whipping around on her stool, she came face-to-face with Marta Lopez, the Puerto Rican fortune-teller who became Madame Zelda of Bulgaria each morning when she stepped through the shop door.

"Jeesh." Margo pressed a hand to her breast as she

stared at her friend. "Didn't anyone ever tell you it's no nice to sneak up on people?"

Instead of backing away, Marta stepped closer, low ering her voice. "I thought you'd want to know befor she ruins your day. That's why she's here." She flashe a narrow-eyed glance at Dina Greed's back. "She wan to make you jealous."

She is. The words screamed through Margo's Scotland loving soul, turning her heart pea green and making he pulse race with annoyance.

"How do you know?" Margo tucked her chin-lengt hair behind an ear, hoping Marta wouldn't notice th flush she could feel flaming up her neck. "Are you sure Or"—she could only hope—"is it just gossip?"

Dina Greed had been making noise about going Scotland forever. So far she'd never gotten any clos than watching *Braveheart*.

But the way Marta was shaking her head told Marg that this time her rival's plans were real.

"You should know I only speak the truth." Mar smoothed the shimmering purple and gold folds of h caftan. "One of my cousins"—she straightened, assur ing an air of importance—"works at First-Class Lugga and Travel Shoppe. She told me Dina was in there tw days ago, buying up a storm and bragging that she w about to leave on a three-week trip to the Highlands.

"She even has a passport." Marta imparted this of info with authority. "My cousin saw it when Dina i sisted on making sure it fit easily into the tartan-cover passport holder she bought."

Margo's heart sank. "She bought a tartan-cover passport holder?"

"Not just that." Marta's eyes snapped. "She walk out with an entire set of matching tartan luggage. I a new line First-Class just started carrying. I think my cousin said it's called Highland Mist."

Highland mist.

The two words, usually the stuff of Margo's sweetest dreams, now just made her feel sick inside. As long as she could remember, Dina Greed had deliberately targeted and snatched every one of Margo's boyfriends.

Three years ago she'd also somehow sweet-talked the manager of a really lovely apartment complex—where Margo wanted to move—into giving her the last available apartment, even though Margo had already put down a deposit.

Now she was also going to see Scotland.

It was beyond bearing.

"So it is true." Margo looked at her friend, feeling miserable. She also felt the beginnings of a throbbing headache. "Minnie Mouse wins again."

Marta shot Dina a malice-laden glance. "Maybe she'll fall off a cliff or disappear into a peat bog."

"With her luck"—Margo knew this to be true—"some hunky Highlander would rescue her."

"Leave it to me." Marta winked. "I have lots of cousins and one of them practices voodoo. I'll just put a bug in her ear and have her—"

"Margo!" Dina Greed came up to the Luna Harmony station, her dark eyes sparkling. "I was hoping you'd be here today. I need your advice about—"

"Scotland?" Margo could've bit her tongue, but the word just slipped out.

"You've heard?" Dina's brows winged upward in her pretty, heart-shaped face. "It's true. I'm really going. In fact, I'm leaving"—she smiled sweetly—"in three days. But that's not why I'm here."

She set her tasseled sporran-cum-handbag on the

counter and unsnapped the clasp, withdrawing several sheets of paper. "This is my itinerary, if you'd like to see it. I'm doing a self-drive tour and will be concentrating on all the places connected to Robert the Bruce." Her eyes twinkled at Margo, as Dina was well aware that the medieval king was one of Margo's greatest heroes. "I've been planning this trip for years, as you know." She clutched the itinerary as if it were made of gold and diamonds. "I don't need your help with Scotland."

Margo forced a tight smile. "I didn't think so."

Out of the corner of her eye she saw Marta swishing away, making for the back room, where she did her tarot readings. Margo hoped she'd also use the privacy to call her voodoo expert cousin.

She looked back at her rival, wishing she had the nerve to throttle her.

"So, what can I do for you?" She hated having to be nice.

Dina held out a hand, wiggling her fingers. "I'm on my way to have these nails removed"—she glanced down at the diva-length red talons, clearly fake—"and someone mentioned you might have a tip for keeping my real nails from breaking. I'll be exploring so many castle ruins and whatnot, you know? I'd hate to damage them when I'm off in the wilds of nowhere."

"Oh, that's easy." Margo felt a spurt of triumph. "Just be sure you always file them on a Saturday," she lied, knowing that was the worst possible day for nail care. Friday after sunset was when the moon's magic worked on nails.

"My fingernails thank you." Dina tucked her itinerary into her furry sporran purse. "I really must go. I need to pack. I'll stop by when I'm back and tell you about my trip."

"I'm sure you will," Margo muttered when the shop bell jangled as Dina swept out the door.

Free at last, she released a long breath. It was good that her nemesis had left when she did. Margo could maintain her always-be-gracious-to-customers demeanor for only so long. Dina had pushed her close to her limits. A white-hot volcano of anger, envy, and frustration was seething inside her.

On the trail of Robert the Bruce.
Highland Mist luggage.

Margo frowned. She wouldn't be surprised if the other woman wore plaid underwear. She *had* left her mean-spirited residue in the usually tranquil shop. Sensitive to such things, Margo shivered and rubbed her arms. They were covered with gooseflesh. And the odd dimness she'd noticed earlier had returned. Only now, the little shop wasn't just full of shadows; it'd turned ice-cold.

Of course—she saw now—that rain was beginning to beat against the windows and the afternoon sky had gone ominously dark. In autumn the night drew in rather early in Bucks County.

Still . . . this wasn't that kind of chill.

Margo sat frozen on her stool. She wanted to call out to Patience or even to Marta, but her tongue felt glued to the roof of her mouth. She felt her palms and her brow dampening.

And her ill ease only increased when the door jangled again and she caught the backs of Patience and Marta as they dashed out into the rain. The door swung shut behind them, leaving her alone.

She'd forgotten it was Marta's half day.

And Patience had told her that morning that she'd be leaving early to join friends for high tea at the Cabbage

Rose Gift Emporium and Tea Room. Margo had agreed to close the shop on her own.

It was an unavoidable situation, but she regretted it all the same.

Especially when—*oh, no!*—she saw the shadow by the bookshelves.

Tall, blacker than black, and definitely sinister, the darkness hovered near where Patience had stood earlier. And—Margo sensed as she stared, her stomach clenching—whatever it was, it oozed an ancient malevolence.

It wasn't a ghost.

This was more a portent of doom.

Then there was a loud rumbling noise outside and, as a quick glance at the windows revealed, a large cement mixer that had been stopped in front of the shop lumbered noisily down the road, allowing the gray afternoon light to pour back into the shop.

The shadow vanished at once.

And Margo had never felt more foolish.

She wiped the back of her hand across her brow and took a few deep, calming breaths. She shouldn't have allowed Dina Greed and her upcoming trip to get to her so much that she mistook a shadow cast by a construction truck for a gloom-bearing hell demon.

She didn't even believe in demons. Ghosts, you bet. She'd even seen a few of them and had no doubts whatsoever.

But demons belonged in the same pot as vampires and werewolves. They just weren't her cuppa. And she was very happy to keep it that way.

She was also in dire need of tea.

Knowing that a good steaming cup of Earl Grey Cream would soothe her nerves, she pushed to her feet and started for Marta's tarot-reading room, a corner of which served as the shop's makeshift kitchen.

She was almost there when she heard a *thump* near the bookshelves.

"Oh, God!" She jerked to a halt, her hand still reaching for the back room door. The floor tilted crazily, and she was sure she could feel a thousand hidden eyes glaring at her from behind the bundles of dried herbs and glass witch balls that hung from the ceiling.

Very slowly, she turned. She half expected to see the shadow again.

There was nothing.

But a book had fallen, and it lay open and facedown on the polished hardwood floor. Margo went to retrieve it, glad to know the source of the noise and intending to return the book to its shelf. It was from Patience's new shipment, and the title jumped out at her.

Myths and Legends of the Viking Age.

For some inexplicable reason, just seeing the words— red and gold lettering on a brownish background—sent a jolt through her. It was so strong and forbidding that she almost walked away and left the book where it was on the floor.

Stubbornness made her snatch it up; the painful shock that sped through her fingers and up her arm as soon as she touched the book underscored why she should have heeded her instincts.

But she'd had enough—enough of everything—and wasn't going to let a book get the better of her. So she ignored the burning tingles racing along her skin and peered down. She immediately wished she hadn't, for it'd opened to a two-page color illustration of a Viking warship off the coast of Scotland.

She could have groaned.

She didn't care about the fierce-looking Norse dragon ship.

But the oh-so-romantic landscape was a kick to the shins.

Beautiful as a master painting, the illustration showed a rocky shoreline with steep, jagged cliffs soaring up around a crescent-shaped cove. The sky above boiled with dark clouds and looked as wild and turbulent as the churning sea. Margo's heart responded, beating hard and slow. It was such places that called to her soul. In fact, she often dreamt of just such a Highland coast.

She brought the book nearer to her face and strained her eyes to see because the light in the shop seemed to be fading again.

Now, looking more closely, she saw a man on the golden-sanded strand. He stood at the water's edge, his long dark hair tossed by the wind. Clearly a Highland warrior, he could've been ripped from her hottest fantasies. Big, strapping, and with a plaid slung boldly over one shoulder, he'd been depicted to raise a sword high over his head and yell. He was staring out to sea, glaring at the departing Vikings, and his outrage was so well drawn and palpable that she could almost hear his shouts.

Margo shivered, feeling chilled again.

She glanced at the windows, but this time there weren't any big trucks blocking the afternoon light.

Everything was at it should have been.

Except when she looked back at the illustration, the man had moved and was now actually in the water, with the foamy surf splashing about his legs.

"What?" Her eyes rounded. Waves of disbelief shot through her entire body. Worse, she could hear the rush of the wind and the crash of the sea. She also felt the scorching heat of flames all around her; the air even smelled of burnt ash and terrible things.

Somehow, in the space of an eyeblink, the illustration had come alive.